Ghost in the Stables

Moss Croft

Copyright © Moss Croft 2023

This edition: Copyright © Moss Croft 2025

The moral right of Moss Croft to be identified as the author of this work has been asserted by him in accordance with the Copyright, Designs and Patents Act of 1988.

All rights reserved. No part of this publication may be reproduced, transmitted or stored in a retrieval system, in any form or by any means, without permission in writing from Moss Croft, nor be otherwise circulated in any form of binding or cover other than that in which it is published and without a similar condition being imposed on the subsequent purchaser.

ISBN: 9798386904654

The Novels of Moss Croft

Ghost in the Stables
(Love story with a Cumbrian-sized dollop of hate)

Raspberry Jam
(The great social work novel)

The Flophouse Years
(Party like the spaceship's coming to collect us)

Stickerhand
(Also known as "Brains Turn to Mush")

God Help the Connipians
(Meet our most edifying cousins)

Crack Up or Play It Cool
(Skeletons in the family crypt)

Boscombe
(A Christian-Atheist romance, ha-ha!)

Rucksack Jumper
(Algeria, 1980: the double odyssey)

About the Author

Moss Croft is a pen name. If you know a guy called that, it's not him.

Contents

Chapter One:
Honoria, My Take   Page   7

Chapter Two:
A Mere Waitress   Page   117

Chapter Three:
Unbridled Joy   Page   203

Chapter Four:
Stuck-Up Little Runt   Page   265

Chapter Five:
Our Stairs at Night   Page   353

Disclaimer

This is a work of fiction and any resemblance to real persons is, likely as not, their fault.

Dedication

For Regine

Chapter One

Honoria, My Take

1.

She's good. That's my opinion and I've seen a few. I don't believe a word but the way she does it is quality. Convincing a dumber me as inwardly I laugh at the whole show. That's as much as I can look for in a séance. Fool me for a second or two while I gather my true thoughts.

This one, the medium, Sandra, sounded histrionic when she arrived. 'No!' she shrieked at my wife. And she, Corrie—without whom I'd be doing none of this—was only trying to say a thing or two about her mother. Sandra didn't want to know.

Lady Casandra, she calls herself now. It's like a stage name. Sandra by day, and now that she's in role, made us dim the lights like a Victorian melodrama, she becomes Lady Casandra. The name is improbable, she's as common as me. It suits her funny clothes, I suppose. A frumpy old dress: they have curtain drapes like it inside Bramall Hall. Floral and florid, more shades of green than I knew there to be. And she talks to the dead using an upside-down glass. Runs it between letters. We've seen this jiggery-pokery—spelling out words on a Ouija board—a couple of times before. When the glass first started moving, Sandra—drawing on the mental strength of Corrie and I, and Morty, our fourteen-year-old son, maybe Honoria too if we take the old fraud at face value—briefly became a class act. Startling even.

Not many of them will come to your house. We reckon most

mediums want you in their homes because they've rigged up some contraption or other. Squirreled away devices that prompt the swishing of curtains, the scraping of an empty chair. Let you think it's ghouls and poltergeists when they might be doing it with a foot pump, or something daft like that. I am no fool and Corrie is smarter than me. Sandra, the latest medium she is trying, says house calls are better. Our dead, the late relative with whom we seek communication, almost certainly never went to her house, and very likely came to ours. That is Sandra's reasoning. Lady Casandra's too, I presume. Fair play to her, there's logic in it. With regards to Honoria Dalton, the medium is wrong. She never made it to our house here in Marple. She never visited Cordelia, her daughter, in the modest link detached we have made our own for the last fifteen years, or to the rented flat—off Hillgate—in which we lived when first we came down here. Nor the little two-up and two-down, our first proper house, in Lower Bredbury. Not in any of the homes which Corrie and I made our own, far away from the family farmhouse of her childhood. Low Fell, Cumbria. I find that indescribably sad. Honoria came very, very close. She died here in Stockport.

It's gone a bit downhill; the overdressed charlatan is spelling out the word S-O-R-R-Y with her supposedly self-propelled glass. Letter to letter it goes, only she and Morty, our son, are currently touching it. Only lightly touching, and still it moves rapidly. My boy screws up his face as if he's sucked a lemon. Mortimer is far more enthusiastic in his pursuit of contact from beyond the grave than I am, although I will do anything for Corrie. For example, I do this: evenings in the company of mediums. Good ones or crummy ones, I do it only for her. The disbelief on Morty's face is brief. We are not a family to explicitly offend a ghost hunter. There is no point: they are impervious. There can be no other way to practice their profession.

At the start, when Sandra asked Cordelia—Corrie, as family and friends call her—to be silent, it was after my wife had

Honoria, My Take

already told her that the relationship with her mother was a difficult one. I did not see or hear any incidental clue which might have prompted Sandra to spell out the word H-O-R-S-E and declare it to be a communication from Honoria to her daughter. Contact after many years of silent death. It surprised me, astonished me, an unlikely and credible first utterance from her late mother. Believe it, I do not, but the glasses arrival at that word did give me pause to think her good at whatever scam this really is. Even Mortimer sees that the second word, S-O-R-R-Y, is obvious, unimaginative, given Corrie's initial burst of unnecessary honesty. What worries me, maybe Morty too, is that his mother might be lapping it up. There is a glistening in her eye. It has been fourteen years since her mother passed away. Corrie would like to speak to her again. I can't see it happening by this route. Not with Lady Casandra. Not with any of them.

I don't know what I will do if my wife believes it has taken place: communication across the realms. Should I tell her she is being deceived? If she believes her quest complete, we may lay the matter to rest. I can't imagine holding my tongue if I think she has let herself be taken in. Cordelia Tripp is not a gullible person.

* * *

Sandra is sweating, shrieking. Her dress flaps as she sways, swings her head like a blind jazz singer. It is this emotional drama which Morty and I like best. We must be very careful how we share such a thought with Corrie, with his mum. The glass left the table and hit the kitchen floor. Didn't break and it's not one of ours. Even the peripatetic ones bring their own paraphernalia.

'Daddy,' says Lady Casandra, in a voice quite unlike any she used on entering our home. If it is an impersonation of Honoria, I think it a poor one. 'It was under duress,' she says, and that is a complicated phrase for so infantile a voice. 'Daddy made me. I love you, Cordelia.'

My wife bows her head. We have arranged no such signals

between us but I believe she means, enough! To me, her posture suggests disbelief. This could be that old fox, wishful thinking, playing with my mind. I'll not know until the over-perfumed one is gone from our house. Until Corrie and I debrief each other.

'I didn't think you would stay away so long,' shouts the frantic medium. Random words, by and large, although this phrase is the closest that she has come to a credible sign since the Ouija board spelled out the word horse. 'Can I speak to Victor?' Her baby-voice sounds a little calmer as she says it. Not shrieked: a tad lower.

'I think she means Vincent,' says Corrie. Vincent is her brother, once her brother in arms.

'Vincent,' says Lady Casandra. 'Can I speak to Vincent.'

'He's not here,' my wife states. Vincent still lives in Cumbria. Hasn't been down to see us in Marple for a couple of years.

'Well, he certainly isn't here,' says the hoaxer. Clever, she's right about this. Vinny is not on the other side, not dead with Honoria, which is who this Sandra-woman is pretending to be channelling. I don't know how she fathomed that one, Morty looks more pleased about it than it merits. Beaming at me and his mum.

She started by calling him Victor. Not close in my book.

2.

I have been married for the same number of years as my eldest son has lived, plus nine weeks. You can figure out what that means, although you will only be guessing. There are many possibilities.

My son, Leo—whose temporary residence inside Corrie's womb precipitated a marriage I was more than happy to embark upon—is eighteen. The century is just a few weeks away from turning. Big numbers: we will enter a new millennium. There is someone missing in my wife's life. It is a state which I can do nothing to rectify.

Honoria, My Take

As I have already stated, Honoria, my mother-in-law, was taken from us many, many years ago. I think Corrie—christened Cordelia but that's a mouthful—will not fully acknowledge the truth I willingly confess. Ironic given that she is the Roman Catholic which I am not. I stand by this assertion, it is honest and objective whatever light it may cast upon us: when Honoria passed away, neither Corrie nor I cared for her much. I expect there were moments of love between mother and daughter. Moments which predated me, came before I was a fixture in her daughter's life. I met Honoria Dalton only twice. Oh, and another half dozen times if there is anything in these posthumous encounters. I shan't be including them in any tally I relate. I have no inclination to believe even the most impressive of them. The spooky horse reference tonight, for example. In the succession of mediums Corrie has consulted over the last year, we have seen the full spectrum. From entertainers to grief-counsellors. Who knows which approach is more likely to bring the dead back into the room. The showier the better in my view. I think this primarily because a little entertainment is the best outcome I can foresee. Dialogues with the dead do not take place. That is the cat I keep in the sack, although I am near certain Corrie knows it is what I think. I rather hope tonight's brouhaha is the last; I suspect it won't be. Quite what my wife makes of the different mediums, their theatrical or downright insincere displays, troubles me more than it probably should. We may laugh about Lady Casandra later this evening, I cannot yet read the runes. Whether we laugh or not, Corrie will also shed tears for her mother. For Honoria Dalton. In crying she will evidence greater sympathy than the woman ever showed to her daughter. That's my opinion more than it is Corrie's, not that she would wholly contradict it. I think she wants to meet her mother once more simply to check if that lukewarm bond is really all there was. See if living in the hereafter has found Honoria more attuned, less beholden to her husband, Corrie's father, the one we shall never forgive. Sometimes she claims it has happened already, that the tide had turned by the time of Honoria's death. It is plausible, we simply have no way to be sure. Corrie will say that she enjoyed their relationship in her childhood, that her mother's love offset sharing a house with her swine of a father. Compensated for all the crap. I love Cordelia, I hate make-believe history: it can be awkward. The wrong expression on my face can start a row. Not a major falling out, we never do that. A misunderstanding. She might feel I am dismissing what she thinks and believes, and I do not. I simply trust my recall of our first year together. All she told me. Our marriage was never like this until Honoria returned from the grave. Or failed to return. Whichever it is that she has done.

The Dalton family were always a challenge to me, although I like two of her siblings, Thomasina and Vincent, well enough. For Corrie the family remains a life sentence, and this after I thought I'd sprung her from its jailhouse. Jeremy, her father, and Killian, her other brother, are both bastards. We are of a like mind on that score. Where Honoria fits in—when she was living or now that she is dead—is far beyond my reckoning.

Cordelia grew up at Low Fell, one of the largest sheep and beef farms in South Cumbria. Jeremy, her father—three-six-five in his wellington boots—was still running the place at the time of his wife's untimely death. Killian lives in the farmhouse now. He is the older of the two sons. Just he and his wife to rattle around the old place. Jeremy Dalton has a cottage within a quarter of a mile. It used to be a labourer's cottage when my wife was young. He lives alone, with a daily coming in to do the housework. He turned seventy-three earlier this year. Corrie may have sent him a card. Probably not.

Corrie tells me that she misses her mother more than her sister does, or either brother. More even than the clapped-out old fume now living in that isolated cottage who spent thirty-six years married to her. I don't disagree but it is a complicated equation. By my calculation Corrie spent more of their living years letting her dislike show than any of her siblings did. I also note that, by dint of being the youngest and leaving home at

Honoria, My Take

sixteen, she spent less time living in the same house as their mother than any other sibling. Killian never left. Still up there with the sheep and the mist. Low Fell: I think it is the largest holding on magnificent Ulpha Fell; hell under a slate roof.

They were getting on a little better before she died. Phone calls. Not sure they agreed about the past, simply didn't let it silence them. Now—with a mother somewhere beyond the grave—Corrie believes Honoria has come to see the sense in her decision to leave home when still a child. To do so with me, without notice. The great bunking off. I thought Honoria a bit slow on the uptake when she was living and cannot imagine death has quickened it. That seems most improbable. Cordelia is keen to contact her mother, to find out. Cement their improved relationship.

We have two sons. Mortimer who never knew his grandmother. Technically they met, recall it he cannot possibly. Leo, our eldest, was also too young when the poor lady died to now reach out for simple memories. In contrast to Morty, he thinks we are crazy to consult mediums. Lumps me beside his ghost-seeking mother because I attend the séances with her. He is a student of chemistry, an eighteen-year-old would-be scientist. He can't understand why I don't reject the sorcery. I tread a careful path. My participation is simply how a good husband treats a wife he loves. I would walk over hot coals for Corrie. I have already reinvented myself—once a meagre farm-hand—to become a successful businessman. For her: I did it only for Corrie. Morty, on the other hand, comes for the excitement. He's fourteen, loves ghosts: they scare the bejesus out of him.

Doubtful as I am, Corrie's quest has taught me that the dead never really leave us. They are always there, carrying on being dead. It is what they know.

3.

Leo is home from Leeds. We see him every other weekend, give or take. His mother has done all his washing in his first term at university and we give him generous grocery boxes when we go up. He complains, says that we are 'clingy'. Never refuses the boxes: clever student.

He arrived home last night, Friday, and interrogated us relentlessly about Thursday's séance. Corrie told him that Sandra was 'trying her best'.

'To relieve you of your hard-earned cash,' he quick-fired, and I inadvertently smiled.

Corrie, who at almost forty is more beautiful than ever, looked crossly at me. I should have been supporting her against the rationalist's onslaught. There is a little grey in my wife's chestnut hair, not so much as to deflect from her still-youthful face. She says she will dye it when two come off on the comb at once. I tell her there is no need on my part. I have enjoyed looking at her for more than half a lifetime. I always will.

The hard-earned cash which Leo thinks we must preserve is a joke. We are the lucky ones. No mucking out cowsheds or bashing down fencing posts for us. Corrie gives piano lessons, puts a lot of thought into it but primarily it is a passion. I suspect she would do it for nothing. I think she has fourteen students at present. She's phenomenal, deserves her hefty hourly rate. Her students win prizes, not that she pushes them. She helps them to feel the music, to find expression. I manage—manage and own—a small car hire company. I expect one of my larger competitors to swallow me up one day. Currently it is money for old rope and, with best play, I'll cash in handsomely when it is time for that swallowing.

'And you encourage them? Join in?' Now he has turned his sceptic's ire on poor Morty. The young lad is a less argumentative child than Leo and correspondingly more at sea in their debates.

'It moves though. If she was pushing the glass deliberately, I would know.'

'Watch proper magicians, dumbbell. You've seen those Americans on the tele, right? The little one who doesn't talk and the loudmouth. They set fire to each other; the big one drives over the little one in an articulated lorry. Those guys have the decency to show you how it's done afterwards. Let you see what a clever illusion is. I don't think they'd even bother if all they'd done was make a glass—which their own fingers were touching—spell out, miss you.'

Mortimer looks to Corrie and I, his Mum and Dad. Wants our support in this argument. My wife agrees with me that we are not trying to turn either son into a believer in the supernatural. We're good with Leo's reverence of science, it will take him places. Corrie's unfinished business propels her to visit the likes of Lady Casandra; she is not superstitious or of an airy-fairy mindset, not in normal times. And Morty only comes along for the ride.

'Sweetie,' says mother to eldest son, putting an arm around his waist, a mismatch now that Leo is five or six inches taller than little Corrie. 'Humour me: I know it could all prove to be in vain. The lady this week was well meaning. Believed in her own performance, I expect. It's hard to tell. Honestly, she sweated half a bucket, this channelling seems to be quite a workout. She picked up the wrong scent though. By the end I thought she was probably phoney...'

'And they'll all be phoney, Mum...' There is a quaking in Leo's voice when he interrupts. '...every last one of them. It's tragic you can't just pick up the phone but if we could we'd all call Julius Caesar or those Kennedys Dad rabbits on about. No one has heard from any of them. The dead guys. Not really heard, not if you see through the crap.'

She puts her other hand on Morty's shoulder, the son who has yet to outgrow her. 'I just need to talk. If my mother can listen that would be a bonus, it's just something I'm trying to finish...'

'Why not go to church? Pray? It's a bit dumb but not as out-there as all this ghoulishness.'

'I did, you know, Leo. I went to church for weeks and weeks. Not when she died, a couple of years later. I thought that had sorted me out. Put everything in its proper place. Now the feelings are back.'

This is completely true. I accompanied her once or twice. Moral support but it was impractical. Cordelia was raised a strict Catholic and I a fervent nothing. I was happy to sit beside her in a pew if the liturgy, prayer and all the rest of it was doing something for her. I didn't believe a word. Scarcely moved my lips through a hymn, never nibbled on a eucharist. I supported Corrie, not God. We also had two small children to look after, so she went solo more often than I accompanied her. Corrie laughed when she stopped. Said I was probably right: religion might all be make-believe.

I think she's been missing her mother since long before the lady died, from the time before Corrie and I left Cumbria, came down to Stockport. She was a woman one might miss when she was in the room. Truly. We talk and talk. Her stories convince me that Honoria was a crummier posh mum than my thick one. I think her mother's limited impact on Corrie's childhood has created a hole in her soul: the absence of the richer mother-daughter memories she envies others for having.

* * *

It has taken me until now to see what has long been staring straight at me. Leo has always earned higher marks than Mortimer in school—A grades to his younger brother's B's—but he doesn't have Morty's sensitivity. His emotional intelligence, whatever that really is. Fathoming other people's feelings: the stuff you learn from life, not from school or books. I can't do it and I'm not even keen on having it done to me. I can usually tell what sort of car a punter would like to hire. That's my limit.

'Tell me about her, Mum?' asks Morty at tea-time. The four of us are munching on slices of pizza, salad bowls to our sides, all sprawled in front of the television. The dining table in our lounge-diner piled high with fresh-washed laundry. It is Leo's primarily, bound for his case and tomorrow evening's train to Leeds. The programme is rubbish, a formulaic dating show.

Honoria, My Take

Leo has muted the sound, talked over it. 'If you were my pet guinea pig, how would you show me that you deserved to be taken out of the hutch?' Then, changing voice, he quipped: 'Oh, Dorothy, I'd spell out, I love you, in my tiny poo pellets.'

Mortimer laughed at this and he'd been the only one watching the proper show. But then the next thing he says, he directs at his mum. 'Tell me about her?' We haven't talked about Honoria since this morning. Like I said, the dead never leave.

'Okay then,' says Corrie. Leo looks slightly peeved. He'd turned the sound off so that he could star in the show. Now his mother—or his dead grandmother—has the floor. Plans in our family have always been flexible and Leo is a caring boy. He's simply second fiddle to Morty in that department. He turns the set off, dismisses the moving pictures as comprehensively as he already has the incessant verbiage that accompanied them.

'If I tell you that she was a wonderful mother, you'll know I am lying. You've both heard stuff down the years.' I like watching my wife's face when she talks. Her brown eyes share every feeling that courses through her. Fun when the mood takes her, although discussing the Dalton family is seldom that. I make the beans but she is the beating heart of the Tripps. The boys love her every bit as much as I do. 'Funny that I am so small, my mother was truly statuesque. Auntie Tommie is the nearest likeness in the family…' The children's aunt, twelve years Corrie's senior, Thomasina Stapley, née Dalton, is the eldest of Honoria's four. The only other to leave Cumbria, make a life not watched over by Jeremy Dalton. '…and they might be more alike than just looks, not that I wish to burden Tommie with such psychological baggage…'

I found out long ago that my wife—who can move one's emotions within the first few bars of a piano recital, so tender is her touch—will often talk for a good ten minutes before approaching the point of what she has to say. She's wired that way. Or possibly she has adopted it as a strategy, a way of gauging her audience before determining how much to reveal.

Quite endearing. It can be a struggle not to drift off into my own thoughts.

'...my mother was ambivalent to my move into a private school. I hated the thought, wished to retain my friends...'

This could be a long night. At least Morty is listening, the emotionally attuned one.

4.

The first time I met Honoria my eldest son was a little shy of two years old. It felt to me as though he, our little Leo, might be a bargaining chip, and that was not a role in life I wished to bestow upon him. My only son—as he was at that time—could walk a bit and talk a bit, proficient at neither. I remember thinking the bargaining-chip thought as I drove the Morris Marina slowly down the farm entryway, seeking to avoid, or gently descend and ascend into and out of, the many tractor-made divots which punctuated the soft track from the lane to Low Fell. Probably just as ill-laid to this day. I have only been there twice—no, it is actually three times—in my life. The first preceded this visit and I did not make it over the threshold. I hoped that Corrie, Leo and I would receive a better welcome than I had on that first occasion. Thomasina had told us it was assured, Honoria overjoyed to have Corrie return to the family home, where I, her husband, would also be warmly received. 'Let's chance it,' were Corrie's more circumspect words.

She and Honoria had spoken on the phone a few times in advance of the visit, she and Killian once or twice but the latter were the briefest of calls when Honoria happened to be out of the house. After six years without speaking to him, I was still unsure if she would or would not talk to Jeremy, her father. I put the question directly to her the evening before we drove up there.

'We'll see,' she said, clearing up nothing whatsoever.

A lady stepped out of the front door, walked confidently towards our car, I knew exactly who she was and I did not recognise her at all. This was a surprise to me on both counts. I had never met Honoria before, nor her me, but I did once spy her across a church carpark. I think I even watched the back of her head throughout a church service. I lie: it was Corrie whom my eyes sought, her mother just happened to be sitting at her side. She made no mental imprint, I must have imagined one in its place. I noted immediately—maybe remembered it from that darkened church—that Honoria was tall, the opposite of my Corrie. And I saw how white-haired she was, that was the surprise. Glossy white, she might have dyed it; Corrie would be able to put me straight on that. It was certainly not the colour I had seen six years earlier across the carpark of the Catholic church in Coniston or when I watched her inside the place although I recall the church being too gloomy to take in more than their presence. Honoria and Corrie. On the December day of our first true meeting, she was wrapped in a warm brown coat. Sensible, this was Cumbria in winter. It was my calculation then that she was very thin beneath the coat. Her face was angular in a way that Corrie's is not. For the whole journey, my wife had been sitting in the back with Leo beside her in his booster seat. The lady went straight to her daughter and they exchanged a greeting while Corrie unstrapped our boy from his hundred miles of bondage. Her mother said, 'May I?' reaching out hands to take the child.

'Careful,' said Corrie.

To be fair, she said that stuff to me back then. It was a reflex, not a lack of trust at all. We believed our boy a rare thing, produce of a marriage of love.

The tall woman lifted Leo from his seat, turned her head to me, now that I was out of the car. 'Father,' she said, 'I am so pleased to meet you at last.'

It took me a moment to comprehend. I am not a priest and nor was I this woman's progenitor, I am father to Leo, the child she was holding, I realised. Addressing me through him: strange but not unpleasant.

'Mrs Dalton.' I stretched out a hand to shake. She could not, hers were holding my boy.

'Honoria,' she said, leaning a cheek towards me, a cheek which I duly kissed. This was an odd ritual for a Cumbrian housewife. I should know, I once lived a few miles from there. A farm hand for eighteen months. And my formative years were spent on a much smaller farm in North Yorkshire. Kissing on cheeks is a French thing to do, unless you intend to take it a little further. That is the agricultural perspective and Low Fell a working farm.

Corrie asked if Vincent was already here.

'Tomorrow,' said her mother.

'And Tommie?'

'They're in the house. Her little ones have been running up and down the stairs all morning. I'm sure she has more than two.' Honoria put a finger upon the smile line on Leo's fat cheek, it made the boy giggle. 'You see more of Thomasina than we do, Cordelia. Come. Come inside, Simon.'

On the steps of Low Fell, I was pleased to be unburdened of the title, father. Another man attracted the appellation here. Corrie and I had one or two other choice names for him, for Jeremy F. Dalton. Still do.

The welcoming party of one puzzled me. Perhaps her husband was working, Killian also. Just by driving up here, I felt to be participating in a betrayal, offering my family to the devil for nil return. No immortality, no eternal youth. A Christmas dinner at best and a miserable one was a possibility worth putting a fiver on. We had left a fridge full of food back in Bredbury, Stockport, on the off chance that we decided to do a runner. Get away from the gathering of the clan. Disappearing act number two they might call it; Corrie had only to say the word.

I went to the back of the car, began to unload.

'John can assist you with all that later,' said Honoria.

I closed the boot and instantly regretted it. I did as she asked simply because of the clarity of her diction. If the Queen was a northerner, she would talk like Honoria. I could have carried

Honoria, My Take

up a couple of cases. Corrie would help, she's not a spoilt girl. The piano was an obsession, a glorious labour; she oftentimes groomed her own horse. Jeremy Dalton never the sort to spoil his children. Nor spare the rod.

As we entered, I glanced around, saw that taking off of shoes was not required. The kitchen we walked into was not cold while looking like it might be. A grey flagstone floor and bare white walls, pale marble sides busy with cookery. As I stepped closer, I could feel the intense heat emanating from the aga, making the difference. There was a smell of baking, of fresh bread, something acidic too. A sauce of the type I never let spoil my meat back then. I could not place all the odours that flourished. Herbs, I supposed. I was in a wealthy household and it felt daunting to me. A cauliflower, some uncooked red meat, cloves of peeled garlic strewn across the kitchen sides. Three, maybe four, different bottles of alcohol were there too. Involved in the cookery extravaganza taking place. Corrie looked relaxed, smiling at her mother. I felt its opposite. I realised this house held no surprises for her. Not so far.

A man came into the doorway. Filled it. A chequered cap on his head, an affectation worn while broiling in the kitchen's warmth. I recognised him as he might have done me. Couldn't read his face at all.

'Hello, Killian,' I said, voice calm, heartbeat up a notch.

'Young Simon, protector of our Corrie. Good to see you. Good to see you.' He pumped my hand, slapped the other against my shoulder like I'd just scored a try. I will always be the protector of his sister. From him and the likes of him. From Jeremy Dalton more so.

Initially I said nothing. I was expecting the other one to follow him through the doorway, the father who Corrie had told me she thinks she should forgive. I am no Catholic, not religious at all, but I would have thought it was for God to work out a schedule of forgiveness, set a mighty high penance before contemplating so generous a step for that man. Or to conclude, fuck him. Fuck Jeremy Dalton, sayeth the Lord. Rotting in hell must be the outcome of choice, after a balanced weighing up of a life's worth, for a small number of miscreants. For the likes of Corrie's father. I think she was hoping to stumble across a happier ending but, as the saying goes, wishes are not horses.

'It's been a long time,' I finally came up with for the son, the imitator. Jeremy not on his heels it seemed. And I envisaged Corrie's forgiveness of her father to be an entirely hypothetical state. Could not imagine it happening in real time. Not in this life; everything was far too raw.

Honoria made cups of tea. The Stapleys—Corrie's sister and her husband, their two youngsters—swarmed upon us. I knew them well, their house just a dozen miles from our own. The children both tugged at Corrie and I, they were more circumspect with Killian. With Honoria also.

John Stapley was always the one amongst us with the least personal baggage by my calculation. He started to jabber away about our journey. 'Newby Bridge is always a bottleneck.' Corrie concurred with his view although I was driving and it really wasn't a problem. I'm not sure if Killian had ever been that far from the farm. He dressed like a country squire, thirty at that point in his life, unmarried. One near miss; Corrie and I had laughed about it once or twice. She thought the girl a dunce but far too good for Killian. He already did the bulk of the farm work back then. Nineteen eighty-two. Did it at his father's direction, we were sure. They had a couple of labourers; paid them the pittance I was given a few years earlier. I didn't work on the Daltons' farm though. Not on Low Fell, never ever. Jeremy owned thousands of sheep, a beef herd too. Killian is not meek, not before anyone except his father, yet still he would inherit the Earth. Inherit Low Fell when his father tired of it all. The eldest son in this most traditional of families.

Our tot, Leo, liked his cousin Terence, worshipped him back then. For six months or so he had showered his older cousin with hugs and kisses at every arrival or departure. Terence was seven, still soft and playful enough to enjoy the adoration. It amused him. Today's hug was their first in over a month. I

Honoria, My Take

watched Honoria. She was grandmother to them but saw Tommie's children only infrequently. They had the same hundred miles to travel up as us.

Her second son, Vincent, was by this time managing a dairy herd several miles away. He lived in Ulverston, having moved out of, and back into, the family home about three times since Corrie and I left the county. Killian, the stay-at-home, loyal-to-a-fault eldest son, remained firmly in the nest. Neither son had wives nor children. There was a wedding announcement concerning Killian a couple of years before and we had still to learn who called it off. Vinny had a girlfriend but I was unsure if we would or would not meet her on this visit. I expect that Honoria felt she was missing out: three grandchildren all a hundred miles south of the farmhouse. I rather hoped she was, not that it was a feeling I wanted to dwell upon at that first meeting. I knew I should try to get to know her with an open mind. Corrie had taken to saying how much she liked her mother but, honestly, it fluctuated. A different view six months previous.

Cleverly, Honoria said, 'Terence, let me show you where young Leo will be sleeping.' My boy gazed up at the lady who had spoken his name. 'Do you want to see too?' she asked. 'See your bed?'

'Yem,' said Leo. It was one of about twenty words he could expel at that time.

'You'd best come too, Corrie, Simon,' she added. Corrie had already advised me that Leo would be sleeping in our room. Might have insisted on it.

As we went up the narrow staircase—Low Fell is a large, not a grand, house—I wondered how it felt for Honoria. When we—her daughter and I married in Stockport Registry Office, Vincent and Thomasina were present, John and the children too. Killian, Jeremy and Honoria not. These things have always mattered in such a household. Home to generations of churchgoers. How births, marriages and deaths are marked weighs heavily into the collective future of any

23

family, may determine whether the future is a shared venture at all. Corrie spoke to her mother by telephone the night before our wedding. It was Jeremy we strictly did not invite. I never detected my wife's shift from an adamant never-visitor to Low Fell into this relaxed give-it-a-go daughter. In fact, I think she was just trying it on for size.

When, over a month earlier, Thomasina suggested we might visit the farm that Christmas, Corrie turned to me and said, 'Will you go this year, Si?' I don't believe I had been the obstacle in previous years. I supported Corrie distancing herself from her father. Visiting or not, it would be her choice although I thought remaining in Stockport very wise. The increased warmth within mother-daughter phone calls was responsible for her conversion. I could foresee Farmer Dalton's behaviour proving the wildcard. I thought, while going up those stairs, that Honoria might be contemplating the very same pitfalls as I. Wished to see as much of Leo as she could as quickly as possible. Our plan was to stay for four nights but we both knew there might be a knockout long before the final bell.

* * *

'It's his way of letting us know how busy he is,' said Corrie when I questioned the meaning of her father's absence thus far. We'd arrived two hours earlier and it was, by this time, dark outside. Honoria told us that Jeremy planned to work all day tomorrow too, only on the twenty-fifth would he stop. Christmas Day alone does he do the bare minimum. A blind man on a galloping horse could have spotted that the jobs which occupied him were not pressing. He or Killian will have fed the sheep at the start of the day, the only essential. The constant attention to boundaries, fences and hedging, the clearing of ditches—work Killian said he was engaged in until early that afternoon—would have waited until January if Low Fell were a normal farm. I was a farmhand before I ever entered the motor-trade, my father a smallholder, I knew very well how it worked. My own holiday getaway required a bit of preparation, a few early deliveries. I passed a Christmas Eve vehicle collection on to the garage owner. May have lost a little favour in doing it although, broadly, I kept myself in Pete Conway's good books throughout my time with Chapel Motors. I was annoyed that Jeremy delayed the reunion with Corrie. Didn't appreciate the trouble we'd gone to. I expected that Corrie's stomach was churning. Glass in a washing machine. She was never one to let that stuff show. Seeing her mother after six eventful years, seeing her for the first time since she turned seventeen, had gone well. Neither hugged or squealed, spat or punched. You might have thought she'd been away a week.

We put Leo down for a nap. He didn't sleep in the car coming here which was unusual for our boy. He may have sensed something was up. Not Christmas excitement, that nonsense had yet to infect him. He can have had no recollection of the previous year and was still to be born the Christmas before that. Within Corrie, known but not by gender. Visible only to the most discerning eye. Now he was good and chubby, a presence. Smiled all day long except for the odd grumpy mood. Me and him, both. The journey up was the little boy's longest ever, and even when his mother sang to him, she seemed distracted, sang like an ordinary mother which she is not. Her voice is velvet when she tries. Tots know when odd stuff is going through their parents' brains, they can read the signs. At least, I thought they did back then. Haven't really changed my view, not that I've heard if it's been proven yet.

We had a baby monitor, wouldn't have left him alone in a strange house without one. I stayed in the bedroom while Corrie went to plug in the downstairs component, complete the circuit. When she had been gone thirty seconds I started saying, 'Testing, testing,' intermittently. Saying it quietly and directly into the device in the room, mindful not to wake Leo. After about the fiftieth time—feeling mildly foolish—the lightest of raps came upon the bedroom door. 'Simon.' It was Thomasina's voice.

I stepped out into the corridor. 'Hi. Is it working?'

'Fine. Corrie is talking with Killie. She got caught up.'

I nodded, unclear if she meant that they were catching up on lost time, a regular brother-and-sister chat, or if she had become tangled in a web. I descended the staircase with Tommie. I like her but she is a little peculiar. Tall, even better spoken than Corrie; I guess she's has always been embarrassed that half her family are nutters.

As I entered the dining room, where the brother and sister sat—John and the two Stapley children also in there—Corrie said to me, 'Killian and Sarah are back together. She'll be coming over for Christmas luncheon.'

I looked back at her, my eyes slightly narrowed. Unsure how I was meant to react to this turn of events.

'Great news, isn't it?'

'Yes,' I said, fixing on a little smile now that I knew.

Killian looked relaxed. He wore a hand-knitted sweater, navy-blue. His eyes are the same deep brown as Corrie's, cheeks far ruddier. They certainly were then: he virtually lived outdoors. 'Sit,' he said, and there was invite in his command. 'Tell me about life in Stockport.'

I slid into the chair beside Corrie. 'Town life…' I took his eye, he seemed in good humour, friendly. '…isn't like living up here. Everything's on the doorstep except the scenic views.'

'And I don't think I could stand that,' said Killian. 'I go up Ulpha Fell every day. Walk, Land Rover or tractor. Feed the sheep, check on them, all that. In the depth of winter—no sheep on the fell, we bring the blighters down to where the snow isn't so deep—I still go up once a day. I look at God's country. I think…' He scrutinised me a little more suspiciously, cocked his head to one side, left eye half closed. '…He created this and only man created Stockport. You might think I'm talking hooey; you're not bothered about all that, I understand. But just think about it for a moment. The grandeur of the valleys, the wash of the heather. They're a sight more spectacular than right-angled buildings, they really are. A richer order than any urban sprawl. That tedious town planning.'

Honoria, My Take

'I don't have a god, Killian, but I almost agree. We drove out to the Peak District, walked across it before little Leo came, just to be there. See it, smell it. I miss the freshness of the air, its clarity, the sight of rolling hills. Life's good in Stockport but it's an ugly town. We have eyes in our heads.'

Corrie laughed, she and I said similar all the time. How looks can be deceiving. To this day Corrie dreams of Ulpha Fell; the Yorkshire Dales have always infected mine. We neither had even a fleeting wish to live back. Stockport suited us nicely—still does—but we would never hang pictures of its dilapidated mills or its functional shopping precincts upon the walls of our home. 'You can't grow up on Ulpha Fell and not miss the sight of it, Killie,' she said. 'The other side of the coin is that it traps you, as Stockport does not. Deprives you of choices, defines your life.' She spread her hands upon the dining table as if it were a piano, turned from Killian to me. 'We're happy in ugly town...' And back to her brother, a silent beat in her commentary. '...as I hope you and Sarah will be here.'

The way she said it made me think his marriage must have been back on the table. Quite a turn around. I didn't know Sarah Pollard, hadn't met her once back then, not even when I lived a dozen miles from the Daltons, worked on a different farm. Corrie told me she likes her, said one or two less complimentary things about her too. I think there are two sides to everyone. Why the girl should choose to marry Killian, big stiff uptight square that he was, formed the puzzling question. The size of the farm he would inherit, its lonely answer.

Honoria entered the room. 'Supper in ten,' she said.

I glanced at Corrie.

'Is Daddy eating?' she asked.

'Showering. Down for supper.'

'Let me help serving up,' said Thomasina.

She and Honoria left the room; I glanced across at John, Tommie's husband.

'The food's always top notch up here,' his solemn words.

* * *

'He'll be down,' she said, serving parsnip soup from a large tureen. I assessed Honoria's mood to be one of expectation with a dollop of foreboding tugging at its edge. The mirror image of my own.

Killian was telling us all about the closure of the Grey Mare, the only pub in Corney. I didn't know the village. Never went when I lived close by. John Stapley said that the little hamlet sounded too small to sustain a pub, its obsolescence as inevitable as that of the scythe.

'Rural folk need a drink,' argued Killian. 'We don't want them driving all over just to sup ale. Vincent's done enough of that.' I winced at the put down of his yet-to-arrive brother. Vinny had told Corrie, in their most recent phone call, that his pleading—were he to lose his license, his job would likely go with it—won sympathy with the magistrate. A fine and some points. He seemed to be in the last chance saloon with court and family, both.

'I like those little pubs. We come across one or two in Hayfield and places. The countryside near us,' I said. A conciliatory, not a contradictory, comment.

'We all like them,' said John, the farmer's son who has turned financier. 'Liking the odd pint isn't enough if they don't get the footfall.'

'I was in it—in the Grey Mare—on the night the Argies surrendered.' Killian was determined to outpoint his brother-in-law on this topic. 'No shortage of custom that night. We were shoulder to shoulder. A lovely little packed-out pub. God Save the Queen, we were singing. Beer flowed. The taxi companies made good money too.'

Thomasina spoke before John, to deliver the same message, I'm sure. 'If the country won a war every day of the week, the pubs would never shut, Killie. As it is…' She left him to work out the irrelevance of his observation.

The door from the hallway opened. He walked in. Grey-haired, no longer carrying the head of thick brown which I remembered from the doorstep six years earlier. The glint in his eye was unchanged. He looked neat and tidy, wore a woven tie, green and black, tucked inside a light brown jersey. His shirt was a dark shade of grey, thick flannel. He was in his church clothes, I guessed. Nothing special but smarter than many a Cumbrian farmer.

'Cordelia,' he said by way of acknowledgement.

'Nice to see you, Daddy.'

No one voiced a thought as his chair scraped the flagstone floor and he pulled himself up to the table. Honoria immediately ladled soup into his bowl. I do not know if it was an unspoken demand or her own form of distraction.

'Introduce me then,' he said.

Corrie let escape a short little laugh, barely audible. 'Simon, this is Daddy.'

'Jeremy Dalton,' he said, lifting himself far enough above his seat to stretch a hand across the table.

I mirrored his action and we each gripped the other firmly. 'Simon Tripp.'

'Aye, Tripp. You've to take care of Mrs Tripp, you know? She's flown the nest so it's up to you now.'

My mouth moved with the intention of stating that I would do exactly that. Corrie spoke over me. 'I can take care of myself, Daddy.'

There was another silence, short, before he said, 'Happen. Happen you can.'

Below the table Corrie squeezed my left hand with her right. I think that acknowledgement was a victory of sorts. It was not my family; I could have been misreading every silent second.

'You're a farmer's lad, our Vincent tells me.'

I explained to him about the sixty acres, some of it is poor land, barely tamed hillside, thirty dairy cattle. My father's adventures with turnips.

'No,' he said sagely, speaking on home soil, 'it's not enough these days. Not the way things are going. No wonder you got out, lad.'

I had long ago told Vincent that I'd no wish to inherit Penton

Farm, North Yorkshire. My sister would get half when our father was done with the place. Break it up. Neighbouring farmers could buy plots; the house was run down, ageing badly like its owner. Worth only a little. Vinny must have told Jeremy my musings on the matter. 'I grew up tinkering with old Massey Fergusons, cars are the same beneath the shine.'

'It's a mechanic you are, is it?'

I glanced aside at Corrie. She was supping soup from a spoon; I had no idea what she was thinking. I long ago resolved not to get along with this man, however, this was only gruff farmer talk. He had offended me no times thus far. 'I did that briefly. Now I run the hiring operation for Chapel Motors. Keeping them ship-shape. The cars are mostly new, not much to fix. At two years we move them on.'

'What's the chapel, lad? Simon, I should say. You go to chapel?'

'We don't go to any church, Daddy,' said Corrie. 'Simon works at a garage in Heaton Chapel. It's a place name, sits between Stockport and Manchester.' He was giving her a puzzled look, as if she was not making sense. 'A suburb,' she added.

'I'm sorry to hear you've lapsed, Cordelia.'

My wife shrugged. I think staying away from church was, on balance, a relief to her. The Heavenly Father who roams the pages of the bible and her own Earthly one became intertwined in her mind. Steering clear of both kept her in calmer waters.

'It pays better than farming,' I said, thinking myself vulgar on completion of the phrase.

'Happen it depends on the particular farm, young Simon,' replied Jeremy.

Killian laughed at his jibe. Then Honoria spoke for the first time since his arrival at table. 'I'm glad it's keeping the wolf from the door.'

John Stapley asked me questions about the ownership of the fleet of cars which Chapel Motors hired out. He and I had—around three months earlier—talked about exactly this, and I

Honoria, My Take

think I was pretty clear then. The company had a good deal with Vauxhall who we bought the cars from, all done with borrowed money, interest to pay back. Cars always depreciate in value, so we had to make a greater return than the slide each car made from its price point. I saw to that: got them hired out for a strong percentage of the time. Keeping them in good nick helped. And it was Chapel Motors which sold them on when their hiring days were up. I presumed John asked me this again simply to demonstrate to his father-in-law—mine too but Corrie and I have always called him by cruder terms—that I was a long way removed from a mechanic. 'You are very business savvy,' said John by way of conclusion.

'Sounds a rum way to make money, son, although I can be wrong on these matters. I know I can.' I appreciated Farmer Dalton's humility. I was not his son.

* * *

John Stapley's earlier assertion was bang on the nail: the food at Low Fell was excellent. After soup we enjoyed roast beef, a cut of meat which bore the name Alicia. Only farmers and their offspring are so devoid of sentiment that they can enjoy recalling the face of the animal which they eat. I am one of them. It does not lessen its flavour, it assures. I think Corrie had strayed even further from this belief than from her church-led religion. Honoria poached her an egg. Chicken was the only meat she ate by then, and that quite infrequently. Never touches it now. She was less fussy when we first began living together, and she certainly ate beef throughout her Low Fell childhood. Corrie has her reasons for everything she does.

During the meal, father and daughter exchanged the odd pleasantry. Nothing heartfelt on either side to my tin ear. He also muttered, 'I see our food isn't good enough for you,' while nodding at the poached egg. Corrie didn't engage with that. After the main course the patriarch pushed back his chair. 'There's a cow as may calve,' he told the room.

'I can go, Daddy,' offered Killian.

A hand gesture indicated he needn't stir.

'Sponge pudding, Jeremy?' suggested Honoria.

'I'm sweet enough.'

We all caught him lying, as he left the room. Off to watch a cow in discomfort.

* * *

During the evening Honoria invited Cordelia to play the piano. We were all assembled except Jeremy. She told us he would be with us, 'as soon as he's finished the books.'

Corrie suggested Thomasina might play a duet but she declined. 'Lost touch with piano playing,' she told us. Honoria excused herself similarly although John Stapley shook his head, implied she knows a tune or two. As they spoke, my wife was deftly lifting the lid of the grand piano. Fixing it in place like I do a car bonnet. Then she slid onto the stool, said the single word, 'Schubert,' dipped her head and music filled the room. The sound she made was beautiful, delicate and pompous; she has long mastered the contraption. And she was playing more in Stockport by then. Considerably more until our little one's birth. Leo sat on my lap and listened. A tot who already loved that kind of harmonious soundscape, attended the drama within. Corrie was in another place, her head swaying with the music. Her eyes scarcely glanced at the keys she caressed. As the extended Dalton family sat and listened, I was pleased to contemplate that we had acquired a piano of our own. An unwanted one from my manager, Peter Conway. Corrie called it an orphaned piano. Pete confessed to me that he'd had it valued only to learn that it had none. He and I moved it with a Chapel Motors van. Corrie knew of a tuner, learnt of him from a colleague at Stockport College, where she was then working. He was blind; brought himself to our house on the bus, took himself home again. No dog. It was not as soulful a piano as she played up there at Low Fell, but it enabled her to practise. A pub piano, she called it. Leo used to bash on the keys while seated on her knee; it was too early to say, back then, if he was destined to be me or Mozart.

She was about ten minutes into the piece—letting the chords

Honoria, My Take

ring, the feeling of each successive harmony, even the haunting sound of little dissonances, burrowing down within each of us—when I realised Jeremy was in the room. He looked becalmed. I adjudged his bookkeeping to have been no more urgent than the ditch-digging which kept him in the fields all day. He watched his daughter, her side profile. She paid him no mind, may have been unaware that he was in the room such was the fugue in which her hands drew out this carefully ornamented sound. I would have guessed he liked to listen to patriotic songs in the now-closed Grey Mare. Or maybe that was just Killian's fare, the son not a chip off his begetter's block but a parody of him. When I looked around a minute or so later, I saw he had closed his eyes, taken a hold of Honoria's hand.

Upon completion Tommie and John applauded as though we were in a Stockport pub. Their children copied them. It was already a couple of years since Corrie's last performance in one of those, and she would never have let a classical piece of that length make the playlist. 'You've a talent still, I'm pleased to say,' said her father when the room had quietened. Corrie looked at him, mouthed a thank you, and then the man turned to me. 'Have you bought her a Bechstein, Simon? Or something like it.'

I looked at Corrie. I could guess what the question meant but also feared showing my ignorance.

'Our piano is Italian, Daddy, very old. Passed from house to house. It's worth tuppence.'

'Ha,' he emitted with a backward nod of the head.

I started to see him for what he was. A simmering man, that was Jeremy Dalton back then. And to this day, one might imagine. It was an odd thing that he should laugh, that he placed a heady expectation upon me with his question, then laughed at my failure. Or perhaps it was just Corrie's way with words that amused him. I resolved not to take offence; I was only there for my wife. She had tolerated him so far and I would too. Toleration not warmth, that much was clear to me. And there could have been some disdain in there; she was holding a lot back.

'Play something by Debussy,' said Honoria. I saw her husband nodding agreement with the request.

Corrie touched the keys so gently that they moved in a slower timeframe than the one we all live in. The sound of summer clouds emerged. I never listened to this stuff in my regular life, heard her play it only on our rough-and-ready piano. I knew that she was good; the sound that night was mesmeric. Even the children were stilled. It transported me far beyond the overwrought farmhouse to a place without tension. It must have done the same for us all.

Her father came across, stood beside her. As she finished— Stapleys all applauding again, uncoordinated little Leo trying to do the same from my lap—I saw him dip down to speak softly into my wife's ear. Corrie looked bemused. Not a disagreement, I thought, but not quite in accord. She turned to the room. 'By popular request.' It is a phrase she used in the Adswood Hotel, the White Hart, back when she made a few pounds tapping the keys, getting the old ones singing in those Stockport pubs. It meant she had no time for it.

The introduction was brief. Initially she sang alone. Jeremy mouthed the words that Corrie relayed to the room. Didn't try to compete.

> ***What Child is this***
> ***Who laid to rest***
> ***On Mary's la-ap is slee-eping?***

Her voice was rich. The best. Others joined in. I could not. The words were unknown to me, I paid no attention in school assemblies. John Stapley surprised me; he sang beautifully. He met Thomasina at church. They attend but not religiously.

> ***So bring Him incense, gold and Myrrh***
> ***Come Peasant King to o-wn Him***

Honoria sang at a higher register than Corrie. Fifths perhaps, I've learnt something from her. Jeremy and Killian were singing by this time. Their voices rough, holding the tune

Honoria, My Take

in an agricultural manner. Songs around a piano were never in my childhood, not in the range of possibilities in the Tripp household. Not even when my mother lived. We gathered hay as a family, sat down together for liver and onions. That was it.

This, this is Christ the King
Whom shepherds guard and Angels sing

The swelling sound roused everyone in the room. If they felt the Holy Spirit, then good luck to them. It was only something more earthy which could ever register in my gut. This was once a family. The Daltons hit the mark and Jeremy pushed it a country mile over the line while they were at it. My lot, the Tripps, were never at the races. Shared a roof plus nothing.

When Corrie moved on to the shepherds-watching-their-flock song, I sang a little. The poorest voice in the room, excepting the young children. The words I recalled from Swale Valley Comprehensive included a few dirty ones. I did the goldfish mouth when those came up.

* * *

Corrie and I were whispering across the short divide between our twin beds. I had lifted Leo from the pre-war cot that Honoria placed in our room, nestled him in the arms of his mother at her request. It would not be the first time he slept the night beside her. Not even that month. She loved the feel of his flesh against her own. I'd have been jealous had I not wished him the same comfort I aspired to for myself.

'Are you going to ask him about the horse? Find out what happened to it?'

'He told me what he did years ago, Si. I'm not letting him humiliate me again. Not on that score; I couldn't bear it.'

I let it go. The story of her horse was both a sadness and a mystery to Corrie. Before the birth of our son, she used to go over it with me every three or four months. I think she was searching for a meaning or a better ending than she ever learnt when she lived on the farm. Perhaps that is only how it seemed in Stockport, and on returning to Low Fell she experienced only the emptiness of loss. I knew better than to poke my nose in where it didn't belong, while also fearing that it was a small act of cowardice on my part. Corrie never had any expectation that I should confront her father, cause a scene. Might have hated it had I done so. She was on my side, would have remained on my side against the old fucker if I'd smacked him one for old time's sake. Held my coat, so to speak, but it was never the turn she was rooting for. Nor would a fight have been a very edifying spectacle to sit alongside Leo's first family Christmas. I never saw the horse once, didn't so much as hear its hooves. It was easy for me to drop the subject.

I slept the night in Low Fell for the first time in my life. If it all felt too familiar to Corrie, she did not share the insight with me. I sensed then that she was retreating inside a shell. It crossed my mind that she could be hating the memories it invoked, or feeling remorse for all she had missed. She played the piano for an hour and a half after supper. A superior piano to any she had laid a finger on since she stopped wearing school clothing, one which reciprocated her loving touch.

5.

Leo and I were fooling around. He was a jockey clinging to my back for dear life; I played the horse, down on all fours, waddling across the lounge. Corrie—a white apron upon her as I had never before seen her wear—came into the room briefly, told her son I was a giant tortoise, not a horse at all. The creature whose motion I most resembled. Then she went back into the kitchen aiding her mother, preparing food. The Stapley children, Terence and Olivia, helped entertain my boy. Neither stooped to tortoise impressions. Their father, John, talked with us while reading the Dalton's copy of the Correspondent. Shared his observations about the state of the stock market, where the wise money was going: well-intended advice which I hadn't the means to follow. The brains either, I suspected.

The doorbell rang and, while John and I were looking at each

Honoria, My Take

other, Honoria had left her cooking pots and answered the door. She brought the guest straight into the lounge. Vincent had arrived.

She watched as her three grandchildren went to hug their uncle. It might have stung her a little. Leo had met Uncle Vinny three times before that day and he came to our wedding. Leo and I had never met Honoria until we arrived the day before, Cordelia an absentee from the family home for six years. Left when she was a few weeks shy of seventeen. They say that you reap what you sow, I sometimes think Corrie's mother sowed nothing whatsoever. She lived her life in the shadow of a man who oiled up to priests while sustaining no worthwhile relationship with his grown children. And I include Killian in that grim appraisal: the grooming of a henchman is no achievement.

Young Olivia asked her grandmother to sit with her. Honoria hovered, watching. I wished I had suggested it myself.

'I shall,' she said, taking hold of little Olivia's hand. A broad smile from her for Leo and I. The boy was so cute at that age, we all smiled at him. I was still that Blackpool donkey, splayed across the floor, toddler clinging to my back. Perhaps the sight of it charmed her. I have heard no stories from Corrie of the hateful farmer playing likewise when she was little. A father indulging his small child, it could have been an education. And it was Olivia, talking calmly with her grandmother, telling her that Uncle Simon was being stupid only because it made Leo laugh, who seemed most senior in the room. A ten-year old with a little brother and a miniscule cousin.

'Tommie knows how to prepare salmon,' said Honoria, settling on to the settee.

John shot me a look. 'I've eaten hers and yours is better,' he told his mother-in-law. I really think he'd driven up to Low Fell for the gastronomy. Steering clear of the emotional rollercoaster: very clever.

'Has Hodgkinson given you a break?' I asked Vincent from my prone position. I learnt early in life that there is no respite for a dairy farmer. Bank holidays are for bankers; a bloated udder must be twice-daily milked.

'Hadge will do tonight and the morning, I'll do the late milking tomorrow. Christmas is over then,' said Vinny.

The farmer Vincent worked for sounded better than most. This brother—Corrie's favourite in the family, her kindred spirit through childhood—would stay on the family farm for twenty-four hours. Christmas Eve followed by Christmas dinner. More than enough.

'Do you have cars hired out over the Christmas period, Simon?' asked Honoria. I was surprised by her question. She had gazed upon me frequently; I imagined that she was seeking to divine what type of man her daughter had hitched her trap to by observation alone. This was her first enquiry about me or my work, my convoluted hunting and gathering.

'There are about nine out on loan. Not even a quarter of the fleet. In January it goes mad again. And I've a couple of new cars coming in.'

'You're a proper businessman then,' she said. 'Very well organised.'

This seemed to be a rehash of the conversation she didn't join in during the previous evening's meal. 'Do you know, I think I am. The first one out of Aysgarth, North Riding.'

She laughed at that. 'Surely not?'

'There may be others,' I conceded, 'but scratching a living from rock-strewn fields was the sum total of my upbringing. It's been exciting for me ever since we went to Stockport.' While saying it, I wondered if it might wound. I took her daughter, left under cover of darkness.

'I'm a farmer's son, Honoria,' said John Stapley, 'and a successful businessman, wouldn't you say?'

'You're not like Simon, here. You didn't start with nothing.' Initially I liked this comment, thought she was putting down the man who had inherited a farm, hit the jackpot when he turned it into stocks and shares and paper promises. In the immediate silence I started to think the reverse. Her daughter was without a Bechstein.

'Vinny,' squealed my wife as she came into the room from cookery, dashed four paces to give him the type of hug only he and I received from her. Leo too for closeness of contact, if not tautness of grip.

'Back in the fold, sis,' said Vincent. He was not a man who looked one straight in the eye, even let his long fringe exclude such possibility back then, but his right-hand brushed it aside. His eyes devoured the sister whom I know he missed as sorely as she did him. The two who relieved each other's testing childhoods.

Thomasina came to the door and flapped a tea-towel at her brother. A welcoming gesture, she held a spatula in her other hand, an apron around her waist.

'Hi, Tommie,' he said. They've been on good terms lifelong but it was always his little sister who held Vincent's delight. Honoria glanced over three of her four children. The three who did not live at Low Fell all got along famously.

Killian, Jeremy, they were still out working, making certain that the fences were secure, the animal feed sufficient. Looking for the lost sheep who had snuck into the farmhouse behind their very backs.

* * *

'I don't ride them,' I told him. 'Never have.'

'You can have a go, same license. You're a car man.'

I shook my head. No wish to venture out on Vincent's motorbike solo and I suspected he'd had a snifter or two, so I wouldn't be riding pillion with him either. I did that in the Peak District a few months before Leo was born. Fun, but he tore across the moors like he was fleeing the plague.

On the track outside Low Fell, he told me about his bike, how he helped it over a stalling problem. Got hold of the right oil. I used to hear that type of bluster for a living; all sorts get suckered in by the fuel adverts. There's nothing like stripping back and reassembling with that type of engine. Oil is oil, if it cured the stalling then he just got lucky.

Ghost in the Stables

'Are you still seeing that girl?'

Kat was the name of the girl in question, Katherine in old money. He met her in an Ulverston pub. Corrie and I had yet to meet any girlfriend of Vinny's and privately we were unconvinced by the suitability of the match. Last time we saw him, Kat infiltrated her way into much of his conversation, clearly smitten while leaving her back in Cumbria on his weekend away. 'We were both drunk, so we've that in common,' he proudly told us of their coming together. Love at first blurred sight.

'The chappies here don't know about Kat,' said Vincent. He wore a sheepish grin that went well with his unkempt hair, the light stubble on his chin.

I gave him a look, wanted more information.

He shrugged.

'I know. Corrie knows. If Leo could talk properly, he'd tell anyone and everyone.'

'I told Tommie, too. Silly of me. She can keep a secret though.'

'I thought it was serious, Vinny. I thought she was the one.'

'For me it's a maybe. For my father, best say nothing unless I…' Vincent looked over his shoulder at the slate-tiled farmhouse that has dominated too much of his life, although at this point in time he had a flat and a job twenty minutes away by motorbike, or maybe ten if he let rip the engine. '…hot-foot it to Stockport.' He grinned as he said it.

'What's with the maybe, Vincent?'

'Kat's a terrific girl but she drinks like a fish, you know?'

I couldn't help laughing. If she drank more than him, she must have been dead already. Vincent looked a little irked by my reaction. I couldn't stop laughing at his serious face. Eventually he cracked another sheepish smile. Saw that I had a point. 'Start it up,' I said. Corrie would talk to him later about the girl, find out more. No secrets kept from his adored sister.

Vincent kicked the engine into life. It didn't sound to me as if his oil change had done as much good as he boasted. I told him it was purring nicely and he nodded his head. I could more truthfully have said it sounded like a prolonged fart emitted after eating a stonking great portion of stale meat.

I signalled for him to cut it. 'We'll keep quiet on the girlfriend front if you bring her down to Stockport with you.'

He held out a flat palm, wobbled a maybe. I guessed she might be off the scene the next time we saw him while hoping to see my brother-in-law settled. He took a lot of flak off Corrie up in that isolated farmhouse years earlier. Owned up to stuff solo when a lesser lad would have dropped her in it.

* * *

Once more the man was the last to enter the dining room, the early evening meal. Different smart-for-a-farmer clothes upon him, the same woollen tie. 'Vincent,' he said, a nod of the head in his son's direction. 'Hadge doing the milking then?'

'Yessir,' said Vinny. Could have been ironic, probably not.

It was Christmas Eve. I suspect it was the special day which drew a grace to the dining table. We had managed perfectly well without the day before. First up, Honoria, Thomasina and my Cordelia scurried around the table with pots and dishes, jugs and a breadbasket. Vincent said a pronounced 'Thank you' for every spoonful scooped on to his oval plate. We were all given plenty. Plenty-plus, and I have never been one to complain about that.

When we were all finally sitting down, Jeremy bowed his head. 'Mother,' he said.

'Bless us oh Lord, and these, Thy gifts, which we are about to receive from Thy bounty,' she intoned. Her voice was the most fantastically projected hush I have ever heard. A whisper we could not fail to pay attention to. I don't believe in it but if there is a God hidden away somewhere, He must have heard what she asked of Him. 'We thank you, Lord, for the safe arrival in this place of Tommie, John, and dearest Olivia and Terence. We thank you, Lord, for bringing Cordelia home to Low Fell, finally bringing Simon to meet us, and lovely Leo.' She said it nicely but Corrie had been calling Stockport her home for years by this time. The little house she and I shared, not Low Fell of bitter memory. 'Thank you, Lord, for once more bringing Vincent safely to this house on his motorised death-trap. Please know, Lord, we are each grateful in our own way, truly grateful. Through Christ our Lord, Amen.'

As our heads came up, the family were smiling. I could see it: mothers dislike motorbikes. Vincent took the joke well, put a hand upon Honoria's. 'Not a drop when I'm riding.'

'Not any longer,' she replied.

I started to eat, following Terence's lead. Leo was sitting in a portable highchair we had fetched up from Bredbury, Corrie checking what was in his bowl.

'And I hope you are, in your own way?' said Jeremy. This odd formulation he directed exclusively at me.

I looked into his face. His cheeks had colour; several veins broken just below the surface. A wind-blown face; untrained eyebrows giving him a startling asymmetry. I think Honoria was noting that I never pray as a matter of course, not berating me for it. That was my assessment of her choice of words. 'I'm grateful for the life I've found. The home Corrie and I have made.'

'Daily food,' he said, 'do you take it for granted?'

I think he was angling for praise because he raised livestock. That was about as much sense as I could make of his pious question. 'I know what goes into it. God, I have no opinion about.' Then I mumbled, never met the man. Not said for the hearing of this infuriating intimidator.

'What's that?'

'Farmers are paid for their labour, one way or another. God I can't see, so I'm only grateful in the most general of ways.' I wanted to add, will that do? Elected not to but nor would I lie, congratulate him on digging his stupid ditches.

'Alright, lad, but I'll thank you to respect the beliefs of the house you're beholden to.'

I nodded. I wasn't looking for a fight; nor would he win one without a punch thrown back.

Honoria, My Take

Tommie told the table about the church she and John attended in Macclesfield. Her story was neither religious nor funny. It centred on the relative youth of the priest. He was assisted in his duties by four old ones. I think they were also priests but she used a funny word for them, acolytes. So old they could hardly bend down to tie their own shoelaces, while the leader of the faithful, she emphasised, 'has cheeks as smooth as any nun'.

Vincent winked at his older brother. 'We've met some rough nuns though, haven't we, Killie?'

I've no idea what he was referring to, there was recognition written across the older brother's face. Must have meant something. Jeremy coughed. 'Ladies present,' he said behind his hand.

'Don't change the topic on my part,' said Corrie, which made her red-faced father cough some more.

Thomasina took away the option. 'It's nice to see a young priest though. Dedicated, truly dedicated.'

I don't know how often she went to mass back then. Always happy to skip it if we were visiting. I'm sure she has long been a part-time Christian, probably with more faith in God than Corrie had retained. Not that religion ever left my wife completely, I don't think so. In fact, she might have believed it all back then while simultaneously disliking God. Even going to Low Fell seemed more like an obligation than an elective choice.

When Thomasina had made her point for long enough, talked of church life in Macclesfield, no one attending closely, no one interrupting—the Daltons are all very polite on one level or another—I turned to Honoria to congratulate her on the succulence of the salmon. She would take no compliment. 'Cordelia and Tommie did the real work,' she said.

I wanted to ask more. Ask why she hadn't boarded a train to see us in Stockport. Why she was only a peripheral figure in my wife's childhood. A shadow of what she needed. I could have said, why don't you leave the buggering bastard? I'm sure she'd

43

have figured out who was who. Instead, we engaged only in small talk, said nothing at all when the dust had settled. She asked again about the house Corrie and I share. Our house in Bredbury. When I used the phrase, two-up and two-down, she said in her sing-song voice, 'How delightful. You must have another child to fill it.' I hoped Corrie hadn't heard. I wasn't for putting her through more of that unless she wanted another child for herself. Wasn't giving Grandmama any say in it. Not then, not ever. The birth of Leo was difficult. Corrie talked me through it more times than I actually listened to. I was in the hospital of course, not needed in the delivery room. By the sound of it, I missed a horror show. I'd resolved to do the same next time, if there ever was a next time. Unless Corrie wanted me with her, of course. A mate of mine had stayed with his wife while she endured what they must. He might have been a help, fetched a pan of water or something. I'd probably have resorted to telling jokes between contractions and Corrie would have hated that.

Jeremy graced us with his presence for the duration of this meal. The pudding was not something I'd seen before. Pear in gelatine within a sponge base. The family all poured cream on it; I didn't like to make sponge go so flaccid, not unless it was custard wreaking the carnage. The old man tried to rib me. 'And you were a dairy man,' he said, raising his eyebrows as if milking a cow might make one crave the stuff.

I recall that looking into a tankful, a thousand pints of swirling white milk, chilling in a huge stainless-steel vat, would do quite the reverse. Could really give a body that sickly feeling.

'He likes cream, Daddy,' said Cordelia. 'Takes the top of the bottle for his morning cereal. He's not used to Low-Fell food, Mummy's delights. It is richer fare than he ate in his Yorkshire upbringing.'

She was spot-on with this assessment although I'd rather she hadn't said it. I felt like a peasant paraded. 'You're cooking is wonderful,' I said again to Honoria. She smiled back, accepted

Honoria, My Take

it this time. It would have been true to say I'd not eaten baked salmon before either but I enjoyed it. I was never a total stick in the mud, it's just that cream on sponge crossed a line. No point in trying to explain that to Farmer Dalton.

'I'm a dairy man,' said Vincent, pouring a copious amount of cream across his pear flan. Corrie laughed but I suspect he left precious little for those further round the table. I even wondered if he'd snuck in a drink or two.

* * *

I'd watched Corrie put the elegant crimson dress in her case back in Stockport. I really should have put two and two together. Now she had me in my work suit, the smartest thing I own. Having lifted the dress over her head, she asked me to zip her up. In my mind, it was time for bed, not this rigmarole. Of course I helped her, couldn't resist lingering a hand on her shoulder, a kiss behind the ear. Always beautiful, in or out of such finery.

'Leo might scream the place down. I could stay here with him,' I said.

She leant into me and kissed my lips. 'Simon, just follow the crowd. I miss this.'

Her observation unnerved me. I didn't think she had been inside a church for three or four years. I've never tried to influence, have no strong feelings about this stuff. It means nothing to me. Not then, not now. Up there in Cumbria, nineteen eighty-two, she had me headed for Midnight Mass. It would be underwhelming. How else could I possibly experience it? Preachy, sombre, straightlaced: the words which describe church ritual have never set my pulse racing. And I think it a bit rich to bang on about miracles unless you can do a few.

'And comb your hair,' she said. Her instruction came with a loving smile. She's never been one to nag about what doesn't matter when the world is turning normally. That night there were to be priests with candles and so, apparently, I had to make an effort.

Our lucky boy got to wear light-blue dungarees to church.

Ghost in the Stables

Better rules for little ones. He looked terrific, a tartan shirt beneath. God would forgive Leo if he screamed and cried. Corrie said that He understands it is boring for children. Why I wasn't being cut the same slack was beyond me. It was way past everybody's bed time and still I was going without complaint. Would not throw myself upon the cold stone floor of the church, kicking out my legs and yelling blue murder. I've opinions but I'm not a rebel. I resolved to do what had to be done. For Corrie and only for Corrie.

* * *

As we were leaving, I spotted that Vincent had shaved. Possibly combed his hair too. Midnight Mass was that important. He went with the Stapleys who took their own car; Killian ferried the rest of us in the Land Rover. There was no room for a child's seat, Corrie held Leo on her lap in the front. I found myself sitting between Honoria and Jeremy.

Corrie told her brother to drive slowly. There were no cars about but I could recall those narrow lanes from my time in Cumbria. The sharpness of the bends. Tractor and bicycle I took across them at the time of my first paying job. It felt like a lifetime ago and I'd only just turned twenty-four.

'He's been driving Ulpha Fell all his life, Cordelia,' observed her father.

'Slowly there, slowly home,' she said.

* * *

Leo was sleeping in my wife's arms. The rattle of the car didn't wake him, nor the grumpy engine noise as Killian crunched the gears reversing into a parking space. The protracted silence of the vehicle's occupants remained intact—my son's gentle snoring its mood music—I glanced at Honoria. She was beaming, enjoying the sound of her grandson sleeping as if it were spring birdsong.

As we emerged from the car, the Stapleys already standing close to the church entrance, the chatter finally began. A man came across, began a conversation with Jeremy. Seasonal

Honoria, My Take

greetings grunted between farmers. We drew closer to the waiting priest and an elderly lady and Honoria exchanged a quick word. 'Cordelia Dalton,' said the stranger in a firm voice.

My wife turned. 'Mrs Breslin, merry Christmas to you, Mrs Breslin.' Corrie managed to hold the sleeping boy in a single arm while clasping this lady's hand. Not a shake, an improvised touch and more personal for it. 'I'm Tripp now, Corrie Tripp. This is Simon...' She nodded in my direction.

'Pleased to meet you,' I said. She was very elderly, hair like snow. I'd not heard the name before but Corrie came to this church for many years. Sixteen of them.

'...and Leo.' He got more of the lady's attention than I. Quite right too, although he continued to sleep through it.

Tommie came over to talk to Mrs Breslin; another young mother stepped towards us and I recognised her pretty face immediately. It was a little fuller than when I saw her last. Her jet-black hair shining and glossy under the dim lights that punctuate the path to Our Lady of the Rosary Catholic Church. A young boy was holding her hand; I could not work out how old he was, guessed he was at school already. Struggled to recall the little lad's name.

Corrie passed Leo to me, our sleeping son. 'Millie, Millie, Millie,' she said and held out her arms. Her friend accepted the embrace. She was the only school friend of hers to come to Stockport and that happened so long ago it felt like a falling out. I hoped not. I liked Millicent Green a lot; she was once so good and helpful to us. Her parents too.

'Simon,' said a deep voice.

I turned to see Patrick Vulliamy, six years older than when we both attended the Young Farmers' evenings at The Boar in Broughton. A small paunch extended above his belt. A beer belly and Patrick no older than Vincent. 'Hello,' I said, giving him a handshake which he didn't seem to expect. The father of Millie's child. It made me recall that she was no longer a Green. Like Corrie and I, they wed after the seed was sown. I hoped they were as happy as us. He told me about work, shepherding nearby. Not his family's farm, his father was similarly in the employ of others. The Vulliamys were shepherds down the generations. He and Millie rented a small council house. Corrie had told me about it; they wrote to each other, spoke on the phone now and then. I asked after his in-laws. As I said, 'Are the Green's still in Hawkshead,' he winced, and I wondered if her parents were disappointed that a pharmacist's daughter should marry a shepherd. Nothing wrong with it in my book. I know Corrie could have done better than me if parental wealth was a measure worth squat.

'Here they are,' he said.

Millie's parents, Mr and Mrs Green, were coming up the path. Both gave me a wave. Or perhaps it was for Corrie. As he arrived alongside us, Michael Green clapped his hands together. 'Merry Christmas, Cordelia,' and then he shook my hand. 'Simon, Simon, you've married her, I hear.'

I nodded enthusiastically. Marrying trumps living together in church circles.

He continued with the small talk, asked our boy's name. 'Oh, I like that,' he said. 'Very classy.'

I thought Leo would sleep through Christmas.

Inside the church we sat in no order, fumbling our way through the shadowy interior candlelight, the indoor mist. Corrie kept looking round at Leo and I while sitting herself in front with Millie Green as was, now Millie Vulliamy, whose own son was on the other side of her. The pair were once best friends in a Roman Catholic girl's school. I left them to rekindle their bond. Millie's parents sat alongside their daughter and grandson. Patrick strayed to the pew across the aisle; I didn't see him exchange a word.

Vincent sat beside me, and Killian by him, then their parents, my in-laws. I couldn't have been better buffered. It was not a place I belonged: church. I looked upon the backs of the heads of Corrie and her friend. The midnight light was shadowy, Corrie's was the head I knew best in the world and still, on that Christmas Eve, she looked slightly mysterious, her friend too.

Honoria, My Take

Witches in a school play, casting a make-believe curse in the candlelight. Then a recollection fell into my mind: Patrick Vulliamy telling me over a pint of beer that gazing on Millie and Corrie was his principal reason for attending mass. I think they were still in school when he told me this. Must have been, it was so long ago. The prettiest of witches: nothing to be scared of. Patrick and I each got our quarry.

When everyone arose, sang, I tried my best for a minute or so. I could hear my wife's voice and she didn't even hold the hymnbook. Remembered the words after all this time. I knew she would remember the tunes: at the piano, she will pick out the melody of any song I care to name. If I go obscure, little known album tracks, Johnson Ronson or Templeton Ca., she'll find it if she's heard it. Doesn't much like the bands I go for, and yet she can recall the tunes more precisely than I ever will.

I discovered then that Christmas carols wake babies; my little boy was agog at the cavernous room in which he emerged from that other state. Perhaps he thought himself still dreaming. I kissed his cheek and he smiled back at me. A face that has always melted my heart when he shines that happily. Leo stretched his hands out towards his mother, who had turned around. I passed him across, had to lean into Vincent to make the transaction. Corrie continued singing while she took a firm hold of our son. Never wavered in a note. When he was a toddler, Leo loved music, wanted to cradle in the arms of its source, feel the vibration in her breast. The gurgling church organ sounded as pent up as Manchester traffic, only the singing softened it, made the overall sound pleasing.

Then we sat ourselves back down. I took in the size of the building, its yawning roof, the stained glass illuminated by strip lighting. The priest in his white smock began telling us of the glory to follow, the birth of Jesus. Inwardly, I wondered about all that: the complicated goodness of contingent faith; religious wars fought. We were not far shy of two thousand gatherings of the faithful to proclaim this annual event: the birth for which we should all be grateful. God gave us his only son. And if he hadn't, what difference would be afoot in the world? I looked aside at Vincent. He winked at me. I think his attention wavered before mine, probably went to the joys of laying with Kat while mine drifted to philosophy. I'm a car rental man—then and now—don't really have the grey matter to figure the whys and wherefores of Christianity. The bottom line, you're either in or you're out. I worried that Corrie and I had long ago called opposite sides in the coin toss, and we each continued to assume we had called it right. The penny lost in the long grass.

Next thing, we stood up again, praised Him for something or other. It's all praise in those places, no one checks to see if the numbers stack up. One bloke dies—killed, nailed to a cross, no less—a heck of a long time ago, and for that all sin will be forgiven. I couldn't even give it a maybe.

* * *

When the singing and praying, and listening with a contemplative smile upon one's face, were done, and I had learnt that a shake of the hand and self-introduction to congregants one does not know is the proper way to bring the curtain down upon a Midnight Mass, we went outside into the starlit night. It felt chillier than upon our arrival. Leo looked very puzzled. He might have thought the entire church to be a room in Low Fell having slept through the journey down there. It was to be a thirty-minute ride back and his wakeful state would require occupation. I took him on my knee in the back seat, Corrie at one side and Honoria the other. Again, my wife advised Killian to drive carefully. I've never warmed to him, still reckon he's a safer bet behind the wheel than tippling Vinny.

'You caught up with young Green, I see,' Jeremy stated. I thought it impolite to call a girl by her surname. And Millie married in his church; her name by then was Millie Vulliamy, as he surely knew.

'My best friend,' answered Corrie. 'My best friend when I was growing up.'

'I think it's infectious, this turn for getting with babies. That's how it looks to me.'

'Leo is four years younger, Daddy. There is no contagion.'

'Aye. Well, you'll know what I mean.'

Corrie will have known what her father meant although it passed me by completely. I've never learnt Greek, Latin or Dalton. None of the incomprehensibles.

6.

The little one sucked a thumb in the car coming back to Low Fell. Went to sleep without a fuss once we got into our room. Corrie woke me on Christmas morning by clambering into my bed; it was a couple of paces from her own. Instinctively, I reached for her skin, an arm around her on the narrow mattress. Just like old times. She grinned, pointed over the covers at our boy who was sitting on the floor between the two beds, waiting expectantly with a couple of sizeable parcels in front of him. Some smaller ones too. Teddy bears wearing pyjamas adorned the wrapping paper of the largest.

I smiled at him. Leo looked to be puzzled rather than excited. Everything must be bewildering first time around. Or second but he was scarcely six-months old at this time on the previous year.

When we lived on Hillgate—the first Christmas she and I spent together—Corrie explained how the Daltons always opened presents alone in their bedrooms. No gathering around a tree in Low Fell. Not for grubby materialism, only prayers and carol singing meriting shared time. Leo was just taking everything as it came. I wasn't sure if he even realised the wrapping paper foretold a gift inside it. When she was young, my wife would awaken to a pile of presents which she was free to open before coming down the stairs. I do not know the origin of her family ritual. Corrie said she thought her family was normal until she hit the age of eleven. It must be the realisation of children the world over although the Daltons left more clues to the contrary than most. She and I had placed presents in others' rooms, did so before setting off for Midnight Mass. There were some in our room for she and I. It was all as bizarre as Catholicism to me. Both practised by the Dalton's but otherwise unrelated, I understood.

Corrie left the warmth of my counterpane, deprived me of the feel of her legs against my own. She helped Leo to reveal a soft toy penguin to the world, followed this up with a play centre. This latter gift had bells and hooters on it, a noisy toy which could annoy any family—in this one it looked like child's play—of course, Corrie might have been able to get Oh Come All Ye Faithful out of it.

I told her so and she looked away. 'Stop adoring me, Si. I had piano lessons, that's all.' I really don't believe she wished for me to stop adoring her. That would be disconcerting to the pair of us.

I opened a smallish packet, thin, light to lift. Laughed when I took out the present. 'It's the old bugger's tie,' I said softly to Corrie.

'From Killian though. There's a store in Kendal.'

I wondered if she was right, if the shops she recalled from her school days were still supplying all the same merchandise as they did back then. Stockport was changing underneath our feet: a pedestrianised shopping precinct. This was up in Cumbria and, like Honoria's pantry, everything had been preserved.

Corrie unwrapped a silk scarf, her face lit up only when she read the accompanying tag, saying that it was from Vincent.

More presents were revealed to us. I thought it a shame this family uncovered their gifts alone, required substantial preparation time before conveying the simplest thank you to each other. Had first to wash away any contrary emotion that might be sticking to the sentiment.

* * *

We left our room to be greeted on the landing by a floury aroma. Corrie went down to its source, ahead of Leo and I.

'You've baked bread!' she declared, in the direction of the kitchen. I wondered if Honoria had slept at all since church.

Before entering the dining room, I took Leo into the front hallway, showed him the Christmas tree which had not been there the night before. Close to, the smell of pine needles overpowered the flour. I wondered if Farmer Dalton cut it down only yesterday, or the day before, recalled Corrie telling me years ago that spruce grow on a couple of different patches of Dalton land. It was very large, plain yellow lights illuminated it in the gloom of the December morning. The ends of about a quarter of the branches had been adorned with small strips of tartan ribbon. It was too big a tree for even Low Fell's large hallway—it hid the coat rack—a plastic angel sitting on the very top was scrunched up against the ceiling, trumpet in hand. Somebody put this up in the night. There had been no sign of Christmas before their beloved Midnight Mass, and none after save this bit of misplaced forest. Back in Bredbury, I'd put up a cheap plasticky tree from Woolworths in the corner of the living room, put a lot more sparkle on it than the Daltons got to the pound.

Leo found it funny, a proper tree inside a house. I started telling him that this was where Santa left the presents, stopped myself mid-sentence. I knew I might try again the following year while thinking it sounded as crazy as the born-to-a-virgin guff that the priest tried to peddle the night before. Laughing at one while soft selling the other isn't my way.

We went into the dining room. Corrie was already sitting at the large table, her father in his place, eyeing us coming in. In front of him there was a pork pie the size of a footstool. I thanked him for his gift, a wallet.

'You're to see it's full yourself, lad. It's made of leather, always leather.'

I turned to thank Killian for the tie. He was standing with a piece of bread in his hand.

'Just popping out,' he told us.

'Fetching his young lady,' said Honoria, more mouthing than

speaking.

The breakfast was a grand affair. We each had plates big enough to serve two. Coffee and tea in individual pots, cold meats and cheeses, pickles and beetroot. Jeremy held a knife in his hand, nodded at the large pie. His gesture enquired if I would like some.

I was reluctant to accede to this man's hospitality but made an exception for pork pie. The piece he gave me was large; he pushed a pickle jar at me too. I couldn't eat something that sour for breakfast. Back home I usually had instant porridge. Corrie would sometimes make the real thing on the hob with oats—which I ate and praised—but I liked the powdery variety best: no flakes between the teeth. This celebratory breakfast was like nothing I'd ever eaten at that time of day. Not before and probably not since; good in a wicked way. Very tasty, rich and fatty. I ate far more than I should have, required a lot of coffee to wash it down. I told Honoria that the bread was marvellous, said it truthfully. When I asked how she made it, she told me it was simple, and then went into the method and lost me altogether. 'Killian kneaded the dough yesterday afternoon,' she added, as he was leaving. Daddy's boy was a mummy's boy too.

Leo ate his regular breakfast cereal. Jeremy cut another slice of pie, tried to push it on our tiny boy. Corrie put her foot down.

* * *

We were one big gaggle of Dalton's and hangers-on leaving the farmhouse. A Christmas morning walk up Ulpha Fell. I had been looking forward to this, the Lake District views are the best. Honoria, Tommie and Corrie stayed behind to cook dinner. The paths were muddy; it was that time of year. I wore an old pair of Killian's boots. Sarah Pollard, his lady-friend, was a nervous girl, seemed more pleasant than he deserved. She would be eating with us and the morning walk came with the package. The girl was not a Dalton—not yet—and this excused her from kitchen duties.

As we set out, I was in step with John Stapley. He had the

Honoria, My Take

two children snapping at his heels, so excited were they by Christmas. They chattered about a roomful of presents, a little early morning chocolate inside them both. Leo was back in the farmhouse, Corrie keeping an eye out while she cooked. Perhaps his grandmama would even find a moment for him.

'You're getting along, I see,' said John. He nodded at Jeremy Dalton, up ahead, as he spoke.

I had not swung a punch at the man, John's assertion was broadly correct. 'He's a reptile,' I replied quietly.

John shrugged. 'The dinosaurs were all reptiles, weren't they? I think he'd admit to being one of them. My old man was much the same. Died last year. Rather wish I missed him more than I do. It's just the way it is up here. These old-time farmers think their anger is God-given.'

I was surprised by his comment. I'd long thought Dalton to be one on his own, although my own inept father might have been a bully if he'd had the know-how. 'I think it's tough for Corrie,' I said. 'She misses the farm but not the farmer.'

'She's his favourite, not sure if she wants to know it,' said John.

'She is not. Killian is that. Corrie might scrape above Vincent.' I said this in a hush; her favourite brother holding Terence by the hand just a couple of steps in front of us.

John was the most casual of fell walkers. Hands in pockets, so unfit I could hear him emit frequent tiny gasps. His talk was calm despite the breathlessness, very measured. A thoughtful man who doesn't waste his energy on emotion. 'Jeremy trusts Killian, that is very different from liking him. Cordelia's got a mind of her own. And she can make grown men weep when she plays the piano. Marvellous. Killie's skills only range from pitchfork to tractor. He's not allowed to touch the precious Bechstein these days.'

This was true. The Dalton siblings all had music lessons when young; Corrie said Killie couldn't get a tune out of a record player.

'Really Simon, come and go three or four times a year and

you and Cordelia could swing the inheritance from Killian. We'd be rooting for you.'

I'd never imagined such a thing. Killian was to inherit the farm, take up the reins whenever Jeremy retired. A Dalton farm, and Jeremy adamant that it must remain whole to ensure its profitability. There could be but a single inheritor, that was his firm opinion.

'I'm done with farming…'

'Really? You were good at it, unlike me.'

'…and grovelling isn't my style.'

'I don't think Jeremy likes grovelling either. I think he admires Corrie's independence. She's made her way, made no demands upon him.' In a whisper he added, 'Vincent's barely flown the nest.'

I knew I would talk to Corrie about this, John's notion that we could inherit a thousand acres. Glorious Ulpha Fell. That morning it was brown with dying bracken, stone cropped, as we rose on the path out of the tree-laden valley. We could see very little, the high ground shrouded in cloud. Yet the air was the freshest. Even the dampness that invaded our nostrils might have dripped off fruit. I liked living in Stockport but it stank by comparison. Olfactory comparison. There were a few sheep up there, wintering on the fell; not Dalton sheep. When we were setting out Jeremy railed about the stupidity of farmers who let their flock spend the coldest months on the highest ground. There are always sheep on every fell in Cumbria, year-round. It might be that old Dalton was the shrewdest farmer in the county but I more than doubted it. To my mind his bombast was only ever to goad others into disagreeing. He loved the row. Whatever he did he declared it the only sensible option. The leather wallet. There are many ways to farm any tract of land. His cast iron rules were average; the size of the farm was his good fortune, far above his method. I didn't even want it; I'd take whatever Cordelia chose, of course. The car rental was going well. I'd been doing some calculations on how I might set up on my own. I needed a little capital but surprisingly little. Any advice from my financially astute brother-in-law would be welcome. I thought I would bend his ear at some point over Christmas if I got the chance. Car rental firms rent their cars too, it's all sleight of hand. Being business-savvy, as John had called me two nights earlier, is mostly about holding your nerve.

Nor did I think John Stapley right about Jeremy liking Corrie. He liked to hear her play the piano. Would have liked her back in the fold, me out of the way. That was never going to happen: she'd been the love of my life since first I caught sight of her. And her horse certainly wasn't coming back.

* * *

It was all change on the way back down the hillside. I fell in with Killian and Sarah. We'd all said a 'Hello' when she arrived. She climbed the hill with Jeremy at her side; looked neither more nor less nervous for the experience. A rabbit with a gun in its face, that was her all morning long.

'Is your father a farmer?' I probably should have known the answer already but the off-again-on-again nature of Killian's relationship had mislaid the details.

'Yes,' she replied.

'He works for Collins,' added Killian. I didn't know any Collins, nor where his farm was, but it all started coming back to me. Her father was a shepherd, a farmhand, on a farm a dozen miles from here. And she was not a Catholic. That's as I remembered it. She and I shared a lack of religion, not sure where it left either of us with Jeremy. The old sod hadn't really given me a murmur of approval; and keeping on his wrong side felt like a badge of honour. No religion or being of the wrong one might have been behind their off-on relationship. And there were other possibilities. Killian was a good catch financially, on the other side of the balance sheet lay a charmless twat.

I asked her if she recalled Cordelia; my wife had spoken kindly of Sarah. Not always kindly but it was in there. 'She's younger than me, she was a couple of years behind me at primary school. I liked her but we never played together.'

57

Ghost in the Stables

I wondered if they went to the same secondary too, before Corrie was moved to the private school in Ulverston, the Catholic girl's school. I didn't ask: we were long out of those childhoods. I could have queried how she met Killian but the answer was guessable. All farmers knew each other back then; the Pollards most probably lived in a cottage tied to whatever land the Collins's had around there. And there was always the Young Farmers' club.

'You've left the Lakes,' said Sarah.

'Yes, Stockport. That's Manchester, give or take.'

'It must be nice.'

I saw Killian looking puzzled by this observation, it contradicted his opinion. 'It's okay,' I said. 'A lot more jobs, more types of jobs.'

'I didn't think there were many jobs anywhere,' said Sarah. 'Nothing I could find.'

I glanced at Killian. Unemployment was a sensitive topic to talk about back then. Some old friends from our Hillgate days used to get really screwed up about it. Froth at the mouth about the government destroying this industry or that. 'What type of work are you looking for?'

'I can cook. I did that at a café in Gosforth in the summer. And the summer before. Winter's the worst.' As she was speaking, Killian strode on ahead, caught up with Vincent and started talking to him. I could have felt snubbed when relief described it better. Listening to his girlfriend, Sarah, tell of her trial with unemployment was the spur, I am sure. His motivation for leaving the conversation. Twat, as I have said.

'Do you live in the wilds?'

Sarah sniggered at that phrase. Turned her face properly towards me for the first time. Her hair hung straight and the knitted hat she wore did not flatter. Her eyes looked rather faint, pale; there was no movement to them, appeared as if she was holding her breath although she could not be. Not while walking in the cold.

'No wilder than Low Fell. Do you know Beckfoot? The farm.'

Honoria, My Take

I shook my head. Everyone knew all the farms for twenty miles around, all lived here for ever. I spent fewer than eighteen months and that was at the far side of Broughton-in-Furness. 'I come from Yorkshire,' I told her. 'I met Corrie soon after I started working here.'

'You ran away together,' she whispered. I heard envy in her voice, maybe just for the romance of it. I wondered if she'd figured who we were running from.

'Ask Killian to whisk you off, he could marry you in Gretna.'

I don't think I should have said this. She looked away, before turning back, not to look at me, keeping her eyes straight ahead.

'He's for the fancy wedding. You'd think he was the girl, the way he talks about it.'

I could see that this might be a problem. A shepherd's money could never stretch beyond the back room of a pub. Corrie and I managed on less. She married in denim, said wearing white would be hypocrisy.

'How do you spend the time? Is it a lonely place to be out of work?' I reckoned this sensitive subject was easier for me than the other. The finer qualities of Killian Dalton.

'Crotchet.' That was all she said. Nothing more on the subject of hobbies, of how she passed her unemployed days. Grilled me about Greater Manchester. 'Have you done the Granada studios tour?' she asked. 'Are there Christmas lights on every street?'

This girl crocheted winterlong, she lived in a cottage beside a pretty lake and dirty Stockport sounded like heaven to her.

* * *

It seemed to be only me who saw the stupidity of it, a kind of disrespect. We had all pulled crackers, read out the inane jokes, patted the paper hats onto our heads. Honoria had even ladled soup into bowls although that is not a frivolous task at all. Then after this forced hilarity, Jeremy had us bow our heads and ask for the grace of God to bless our meal. Vincent's hat fell in his soup. Corrie grinned at that. I winked at Sarah. Not suggestively, solidarity between non-believers. I hope she got that. I wasn't trying to come between her and Killian. He could keep her. She was a cracker joke next to Corrie.

I found myself sitting between Honoria and Vincent. Little Leo's highchair was at a separate table, with only Terence and Olivia for company. He was happy with that. Corrie went to and fro. The fro of it had her sitting next to her father. Neither looked comfortable with it. I heard no easy chat between reunion long.

Honoria bobbed about like she was playing a party game. It is what she did: service to the wider family. I'd barely started my soup, and she was spooning vegetables on to plates.

Jeremy Dalton laid into the turkey. Carved, left hand holding a two-pronged fork, keeping the dead bird from sliding off the plate.

As we ate, I noticed that Sarah Pollard was utterly silent. Looked at neither of the Dalton parents, an occasional glance at Killian, unreturned or possibly unseen by him. He and Jeremy discussed the highlights of the year past. Their own hay crop and the Falklands War seemed to be vying for first place.

'Italy were pretty spectacular,' I suggested. 'How they knocked Brazil out of the World Cup. Went on to win it.'

The conversation simply reverted to the war—Killian even talked up Geoffrey Howe's budget—not footie fans, I assumed.

Honoria asked me if I had visited Italy. I thought it a curious question. The games were all on television, and watching the box is not the grand tour. In fact, the pictures were beamed from Spain, Italy the winners not the hosts. I don't think she had a clue how watching sport worked. 'No,' I told her. 'Corrie would love to hear an opera in Verona.' I dredged this polite conversation up from memory, something she'd told me in passing a year or two earlier. 'I don't listen to that music myself.'

'Oh, you must, Simon. It's delightful. I cried when I first heard Verdi.'

This was news: Honoria Dalton displaying emotion. 'You

Honoria, My Take

go?' I asked, sensing that mother and daughter must have had a common interest. I know that Corrie listened to it only on vinyl and Radio Three. 'To the opera in London?'

'Not since I was a schoolgirl.' She glanced up the table, at Jeremy, as she said it.

'Operas come to Manchester,' I said. 'I must take Corrie to the next decent one that's on.'

'You must, Simon. Lend yourself to it. Such a rich experience, one's first opera.'

The meal we were eating was a carefully crafted one. Home-made cranberry sauce, home-made everything. Corrie cooked well enough but we never did any of this. And I'd no need for it, fancy food. I wonder why this lady had not enjoyed a ticket to the opera in her married life. Money was clearly not the obstacle. I looked across at Farmer Dalton, the same woven tie not even nearly throttling him. He mouthed on about the service last Easter in a neighbouring church. Telling the table that a priest in that parish was fearful of the war. Not his favoured Benedict of Coniston but another guy up at Whitehaven. 'We prayed for victory,' he said proudly, having related how, in that lesser church up the coast, they prayed only for an end to hostilities, the safe return of the Falklands Taskforce. Killian, even Vincent, were hanging on to the old curmudgeon's every word. Corrie was at the children's table with Leo. She stood and turned, getting back to her own meal, rolled her eyes at me. I looked at Honoria. She smiled back at her cynical daughter.

* * *

Only when the meal was over—Christmas pudding, the whole stomach full—and we had all decamped to the lounge, which Jeremy pompously called the withdrawing room, did a bottle of alcohol emerge. Sweet sherry. Thomasina passed tiny glasses around. Vincent was on his feet, pouring Harvey's Bristol Cream. The sommelier. He filled his father's glass first; I thought it should have been his mother's.

'You'll not have had this before,' said Jeremy.

Ghost in the Stables

'I have drunk sherry a time or two, Daddy,' said Corrie. She wore a bemused smile on her face. I wondered if he imagined time to have stood still for her since she was last in this farmhouse on the side of the hill. Nothing of note happening in Stockport save the birth of a grandson he had barely looked at.

'Not with family, you haven't.'

As I put it to my lips, Tommie, with whom I shared a sofa, put her foot on mine, a caution. I lowered the drink, recognising that she wished me to wait. Killian was by the television, switched it on. This had not occurred so far this visit; I thought the Daltons were above such diversions. I held my sherry at the ready as we all listened to something two notches short of a hymn coming out of the TV. I recognised the voice, Phil Deacon, the ageing pop singer. A good voice but I was never a fan. All a bit too schmaltzy. As the song ended and the camera cut away, I saw that we were watching Top of the Pops, the song must have been his Christmas hit. I'd never have guessed this show to be on Jeremy's radar.

While I was studying the faces around me—all clippers standing to attention—the continuity announcer told us that the Queen was to address the nation. Now I got it: sherry with Liz. We watched in silence as she, the nation's favourite monarch, gave a short history lesson about her own castle; praised the Commonwealth Games; reminded us that she has a yacht. Then she mentioned the Falklands War, did it in passing. It seemed to have ranked lower in the royal family's list of highlights than it did up at Low Fell. Then she praised the Commonwealth a bit more—well, it's her farm, isn't it?—and finally she quoted a poet: "No man is an island." Well, I knew someone who was but chose to let it go, it was Christmas, after all. When she had said her piece, Vincent raised his glass, caught his father's eye. The man was finally smiling, put his own drink up to his lower lip and began to angle the stem. We all followed his lead, sherries met mouths. Tipped back, a small swig for the Queen.

I thought it was quaint, patriotic, another stupid ritual her

Honoria, My Take

father enjoyed. We'd not be adopting it in the Tripp household.

* * *

Once Queenie had fired the starting gun, Low Fell's status as a previously dry house fell away completely. Beers and wines and ciders flowed. By six o'clock Honoria was on her feet, signalling to Tommie, even to Corrie who was rolling a giggling Leo around on the rug in front of an open fire, that they should prepare turkey sandwiches.

'No, Mummy, we're stuffed up to our eyeballs,' said Killian. He had a glazed look on his face. A glass of beer unsteadily wavering within the large hand with which he gestured.

The Stapley children were not in the room. The custom of opening presents in bedrooms had driven them back there. No flashy parading of new acquisitions in this family, save the odd woollen tie.

'It's tea-time. We must eat something,' repeated Honoria.

For once I was one with Killian: replete of food. And I had gone more lightly on the beer than the Dalton brothers. Vincent drank four in quick succession before leaving for that other farm where he must, by this time, have been milking cows. Then he would return to his flat and, I presumed, the Kat who infatuated him. A short family Christmas for Vinny. I don't think his mother saw him crack the last couple of bottles, his father handing them to him. Didn't share her concern about the motorbike.

Corrie was on the cider; her glass full each time she came back from the kitchen. I like it when she lets her hair down, my reservations were only about the company she was doing it within.

'What will you have, Simon?' asked Honoria.

I had to refuse. Food because I was stuffed, alcohol because I was feeling agitated. 'Maybe later. Christmas cake for supper.'

Jeremy intervened, called rank. 'Cordelia,' he said, 'carols now and eat later. What do you say?'

She signalled for me to keep an eye on Leo. I knew that would be an easy task, that he might dance. She sat herself once more at their superior piano. When the singing recommenced even the missing children came back into the toyless room.

This was how the Dalton family functioned. There were very few cryptic comments to interpret while they belted out Come All Ye Faithful. Corrie slipped in Jingle Bells for the little ones. I guessed that Honoria had played piano for the last six years. Or even Vincent. The deference to the youngest daughter—only Corrie touched the Bechstein in our few days under the roof—told me what I already knew. Once a prodigy, a truly exceptional talent. Left her family back in the grade books.

* * *

I went for a second bottle of beer, after all. Corrie had already drunk about half a keg more than me. It didn't affect her piano playing, not to my ear. The old bastard told her to 'go easy on the vino,' as if he had a hold over her. She downed her glass and went straight into Flour Power, the song from the West End Musical, Making Do. She used to sing it in the pub in Stockport. Cockney-accented singing, just like in the film version. I used to think it sentimental and it embarrassed me ever so slightly back in the pub. Hearing her sing about her love for a man who had no money.

> *My fella buys me flour*
> *So that I can bake us bread*
> *Although we've 'ardly got enough to go around*
> *He wants to buy me diamonds*
> *Says 'e would do if 'e could*
> *But cha don't get many diamonds to the pound*

She never played this stuff at home. Called it music hall nonsense. It's good fun, I guess. Witty. Tommie's children were lapping it up. When she'd finished the song, Tommie and John laughed and clapped. Sarah joined in and just as quickly stopped. Must have spotted that the man beside her was doing no such thing. 'What a star!' said Corrie's brother-in-law. The brother, meanwhile, Killjoy—a man who praised whatever singing they got up to in his beloved country pub when the

Honoria, My Take

Union Jack was flying over Port Stanley once more—stared at his talented sister with eyes that might have been set in a rock face. Honoria had picked up a magazine and Jeremy was looking elsewhere, disengaged. I haven't a clue what code she had broken: the urban accent; warm acceptance of poverty; her common touch. They must all have been in there. Jeremy thought himself gentry, Low Fell a manor house. He fooled no one with an ounce of sense in their head. I reckoned he was the obstacle to Honoria attending the opera. Corrie had long ago told me of the bedlam that sporadically blighted her childhood. The man was a fucking horse murderer. She only sang it to raise a smile and he hadn't the good grace to sit up and listen.

* * *

As I was putting Leo to bed, I found him a wide-eyed kind of exhausted. He didn't quite know it yet. Wriggled like a kitten in my hands. I got his pyjamas on him; he wasn't actively against it, simply not cooperating. Corrie was sliding her legs out of her blue jeans, so unsteady at first that she had to sit on the bed, lean back and push them down that way. I usually thought her funny when she got tiddly. Feared she could cry this time.

I pulled Ted out from under Leo's bed. He would clutch that bit of sponge across his chest, helped him get off to sleep at that age. As I looked back at Corrie, she had the jeans off, stood up looking into the open suitcase by her bed. She put her bum in the air just for me. Her knickers were flimsy things. We'd not done this with Leo so close at hand, it felt good and wrong. I said 'Sleep' to my boy, wishing myself the powers of a hypnotist. He was happy with his bear. I touched my wife's leg gently. 'You got a few jars down you.'

'I wasn't allowed to touch it when I lived here. Daddy always had some before he beat me or Vinny.'

I put an arm around her, had not realised that these were the memories the evening had brought up. 'Corrie,' I whispered in her ear, 'let it go.'

She was not tearful, I realised, as she sat beside me on the bed undoing the polka-dot blouse that has spent the day beneath her denim jacket.

'He wasn't the kind of father who got drunk and trashed everything, you know? It was very infrequent and then very calculated. I would think something I'd done had sparked it but I've worked out since that he was days in the planning. His drinking was just fortification.'

As she described those times, she removed her blouse and bra. I handed her the pyjama top she had worn the past two nights. Much as I liked to gaze upon them, her breasts and that conversation were completely incompatible.

'The only difference was when he heard I was seeing you. He had no inkling of who you were, Simon. Said it was all because you weren't church. Not a Catholic. That doesn't follow, not with his acceptance of sweet dumb Sarah. He didn't want me making my own life, that was the long and the short of it.'

'Corrie,' I said, 'John thinks it's all a bit different to that. Jeremy uses Killian. He respects you the more because you're independent. He even thinks…' Before I completed my phrase, I tried to help my inebriated wife button up her top, the reverse of many a drunken evening's fun and games. '…you could inherit Low Fell if you patched things up with…'

Corrie pushed away my helping hands. An angry push, an indignant splutter from her mouth. Her unbuttoned pyjama top flapped open. 'John isn't family,' she hissed. 'Nice guy: knows shit all.' She arose from the bed she was sitting on, hands on hips at the top of her knickers. 'My father hates me ten times as much as he loves himself. Uses me like a fucking organ grinder's monkey. I wish we'd never come.'

'Sorry, love, I didn't mean I wanted the farm…'

She was finally crying. I'd thought the tears were in there right from the start. 'You can live here without me if you want it that much. The place is a fucking hell hole.'

I comforted her as best I could. A little whimper from Leo; I lifted him onto her bed and Corrie snuggled with him as she couldn't with me at that moment. I knew I'd be forgiven; we had long been soulmates. I can't think what possessed me to raise John Stapley's half-baked theory when she was so on edge. I was a thick farm boy before I met Corrie. It doesn't go away. Lived through a bit of shit myself but Corrie endured trailerloads, I've always known that.

7.

Before I had even left the bedroom, I could hear a flurry of activity below. I dressed quickly and slipped down for breakfast while Corrie and Leo remained in the world of sleep. She has always been one for lying in after drinking too much. Infrequent but pleasing, excluding that Christmas eve. Leo didn't touch a drop. Corrie had played piano throughout the previous evening; Honoria sang two songs in German to her resonant accompaniment. I decided that when the car-rental business I was planning turned a profit, I would definitely buy her a Bechstein.

As I arrived in the dining room—not a 'Good morning' said by any—Tommie asked me brusquely, 'Toast?'

I shrugged a yes. The pork pie was absent although there must have been a hefty bit leftover.

'Where's Cordelia?' asked her mother.

'Sleeping.'

She looked up to the ceiling.

'Is she coming?' asked her father. 'And you? You can handle a horse, I trust?'

'I don't ride. Corrie will be down when she's ready.'

'We've barely twenty minutes,' said Jeremy.

Killian laughed at my vacant face. 'You've forgotten, haven't you?'

'I suppose so,' I said. I would have a better idea of the accuracy of my reply when I learnt what he thought me ignorant of.

'The hunt stops by Low Fell. Always has. You're welcome to ride, member or not.'

Ghost in the Stables

'I'm the member,' said Jeremy. His status brought a glow to his ruddy cheeks, chest expanded the half inch.

'I don't ride,' I repeated. Glugged down a coffee from the lukewarm pot, nibbled on a piece of toast with butter. 'Back in a moment,' I said, heading up the stairs.

In our room Corrie was stirring, Leo not. 'Boxing Day hunt,' I told her.

'Shit. Haven't they been and gone yet?'

'Here soon. Your father wants you to ride.'

'The buggering bastard can want away.' I hadn't heard her call him that in a while. Sensed a hardening within her. 'I told him last night that I wouldn't be going near the damned hunt. Tell them I've got a migraine.'

'Do you want something?' I asked. 'Aspirins? Or are they the wrong tablets for it?'

Corrie was out of bed now, thick pyjamas upon her. She stepped up close and embraced me. 'Si, Si, you live with me, dumbo, I don't get migraines, do I? I'm only asking you to tell Mummy that I have one. Mummy and Daddy. I've never been back to the stables since he did what he did…' She stepped back, held her temples in clenched hands. '…to my horse. I won't start now.'

I kissed her quickly on the lips, gave a small salute, an order understood. I put a hand on my sleeping son. He expelled air through mouth and nose simultaneously, in the tiniest bursts. 'Look! In his dreams he's a jazz trumpeter.'

'He won't remember a second of this,' said Corrie. She still had two hands clutched upon her head as though the migraine might be real. 'I envy him.' Then she shook her head, her chestnut hair falling loosely in front of her. I think she was trying to shed a few memories, to let them fade like the age-old Axminster carpet on which we were standing. What the stay felt like for each of us must have contrasted enormously. For me it was all awkwardness, for her it will have been far more visceral. A stick thrashed across the legs.

'Don't make out I'm so close to death's door they feel obliged to look in,' she said, picking up clothes from the floor, opening up the large suitcase with which we had brought a smattering of our belongings. The wealth we have accumulated since she left this place carrying only an old rucksack stuffed with clothing. Her hand and mine clasped together journey long.

* * *

That morning I learnt I'm far better at lying than it is wise to admit. Honoria asked me questions about tea and toast, whether she should take some up for her daughter. 'No,' I said, 'when she gets like this she just needs to lie down, keep the curtains drawn. Food makes her more nauseous.'

'I could look after Leo. She won't want him bothering her.'

'Sleeping,' I said. 'I'll listen out.'

'It's last night's wine that's done it,' said Farmer Dalton.

I nodded sagely. The old fool believed his every pontification and I had no reason to challenge this one. It completed his mistaken picture.

'Would she like me to stay back?' asked Honoria.

'No, no, I'll be here.'

I gave a hand with clearing away the dishes. Sarah Pollard and I took over kitchen duties. Everyone else had donned jodhpurs and britches and calf-covering boots. Hard black hats. She and I were still at the sink when the dull trill—the hunting horn's strangulated fart—announced the arrival of the toffs and hangers on whom we alone would not be joining.

Long ago, Corrie told me that the hunt passes across Low Fell each Boxing Day, an October and March hunt too. Jeremy always joined in. Killian became a regular while Corrie was still living up there. I've never spoken about it with Tommie but I knew she had ridden with them. Felt no surprise that she did so again that day. Vincent has hunted; missed Boxing Day eighty-two only because he was working dairy at Broughton Beck. My wife was the refusenik. Absolutely and resolutely. Even when she had a fine horse of her own, she would purposefully ride away half an hour before the hunt came. Go in the direction she was most confident they would not. No family member allowed to borrow her horse. Not to participate in the ripping of a fox to shreds.

Her horse aside, I think Corrie enjoyed very few aspects of farm life. She plays the piano with a subtlety, a beauty and a dedication to perfection which must be agriculture's opposite. I also believe she and Honoria were similar in half an outlook: they shared a love of, and a feel for, music that put my light-rock record-spinning to shame. Honoria told me she cried at the sound of opera; Cordelia touches the piano keys with a feeling I can never really find within me. Only by listening to her delicate playing can she chaperone me to its gate. Jeremy Dalton's wife permitted her husband's pernicious presence to reduce her artful side to dust. Corrie has been true to herself. Had to board the train with me, take flight—out of the hated man's reach—to maintain the integrity her mother lost years and years and years before.

Migraine indeed.

* * *

'What will I say?' Sarah Pollard picked up Leo's highchair as if to carry it to the car, then put it back on the hallway floor. We were going while the fox hunters were diverted, it agitated her like a nettle rash.

'Tell them you were having a lie down. I'll leave a note,' said my quickly revived wife.

'Can't you just wait until they're back?' she asked. This girl did not want a nugget of explaining to do although our actions were not hers.

'Work,' I said. 'Car hire never sleeps.' Lying was getting to be a habit. I wondered if we should be more expansive. I could have told Sarah that it was a mistake for us to come. This family had capsized Corrie a time or two when we were not even in contact. Visiting was bound to be an ordeal. It can cause Corrie psychological seasickness. All in the mind and stomach. Sarah Pollard needed to know what she was marrying into. Or maybe she never would. There was a date set in the nineteen-seventies which got away, had yet to be replaced.

'Killian will question me and question me,' she said.

'Fuck him,' said Corrie. It was a dismissal of the subject; she had no interest in what her brother thought on the matter. No wish to see any more of him. She could have said the same as relationship advice; it is how the unhappy couple might have fathomed their compatibility or otherwise. Sarah looked shocked, like she had never heard such language. She was brought up among farmers, I wasn't the only liar in the room.

I took the cases and all Leo's paraphernalia from house to car. When I returned, Corrie—holding our little one to her body, his legs splayed around her left hip like he was riding a horse—was engaged in a heart to heart with Sarah. The outsider touching Leo affectionately as they spoke.

'This is what I want,' I heard Sarah say.

'Of course. It's a terrific farm and he'll manage it well. I'm not sure that my mother has ever enjoyed living here, you know?' Sarah turned her head sharply at this, dropped Leo's hand from hers. He paddled his round and round, wanting it back. Enjoying her touch. 'Not the farm or the lifestyle. It's the marriage which is murder.'

'Hers, not mine,' said Sarah.

Corrie nodded while narrowing her lips. Implying, I guessed, that she should contemplate the similarities between father and son.

The two girls stood for a moment in silence. Sarah was wearing a small beige anorak over navy blue slacks. It looked as though she had dressed for riding before recalling she could do no such thing. 'He is a moody man but he loves me, Cordelia.'

I thought at the time that my wife was giving Sarah a harder time than was fair. She and I disliked Killian because of the past. The father-daughter rift seemed buried alive for the duration of this visit. Killian kowtowed to Jeremy, an easier life than arguing given he worked with him every day. I was in no position to judge how he treated Sarah, nor was Corrie beyond her knowledge of Killie of old. Never wise to interfere, that was my motto then and now.

Ghost in the Stables

'Good. Sorry we can't talk more,' said Corrie. She let Leo slip to the ground, carefully landing him on his feet, taking his hand in hers. Her free hand she placed upon Sarah. 'Take care of yourself.' She leant in and kissed the one who would stay, kissed her on the cheek. Then Corrie lifted Leo into the car, started to buckle up the boy.

I turned to Sarah. We were not really kissers, Corrie nor I. Not how-do-you-do and see-you-next-year kissers, her parting warmth surprised me. I offered Sarah a hand to shake. 'Don't forget to invite us,' I said. It might have been foolishness. Coming back here was a dreadful mistake, a misjudgement by both myself and my wife. I was certain of that.

* * *

At the motorway services near Preston, we stopped for a cup of tea. Leo asked for milk. A fine request, and his diction was the best I'd heard it. We bought it at the counter, a couple of scones too. There was little to choose from. I was quite surprised it was open, on a Boxing Day.

On the drive from Low Fell, Corrie talked and talked. She thought me gullible for shooting the breeze with Jeremy, Killian, Honoria. 'Bloody cold breeze,' I told her. She was missing the mark there. Punching would have been all wrong, so I had to chat. She was cross that Tommie and Vincent still went hunting. I pointed out that she was the only one against it, possibly in the whole of Cumbria. I've sided with Corrie on this since I've known her, must admit hunting and shooting never bothered me back in Aysgarth. My father killed badgers on the sly. Ours was by this time an urban perspective. To be fair to Corrie, she's been defending foxes since birth, so well done her.

'The carol singing and listening to Daddy's pontificating about the state of the country. Why do they do it?'

'Couldn't they ask the same about you?'

Corrie was sitting behind me when I asked that, it sounded as if she was spitting with anger when she replied, 'I was keeping the peace because Tommie said I should. I wish I'd never played the fucking piano.'

'You were a star, Corrie. Now they've had a dose of what they're missing, they can carry on regretting. No coming back. You said that was possible, all along.'

'And isn't she cold?' I knew she was referring to her mother. A woman with her own flagstone floor.

And by the time we reached the service station, having put many a mile between us and the farm, my wife started to relax. 'Sorry if I flipped out a bit back there,' she said, breaking off a piece of scone. Offering it to Leo. The little boy seemed unaware of the tensions of the yuletide past. I had come to think that eighteen months a glorious age: no one recalls a darned thing. He pointed at the blackcurrant jam. Corrie put a bit on the scone, just a little bit.

'Bad for your teeth,' she told him.

He grinned, showed us what he had. Tiny white pebbles poking through his pale pink gums.

8.

I park several houses down the road from the one we are to enter. It is bumper to bumper around here. No off-road parking, the kerbside lined with cars. It reminds me of Hillgate, or more specifically Charles Street, the road off Higher Hillgate where Corrie and I first shared a flat. Found ourselves a toehold in Stockport. Morty has come with us; Corrie and I are both fine with that. She advised him not to tell Leo. I think she is embarrassed by how rigidly opposed to all things séance our eldest son has become. She can take a little ribbing, doesn't enjoy hearing Leo criticise his younger brother. I suspect Morty and I are just enjoying the show, waiting for his mother to own up to the pretence of it all. Leo is not wrong, just a little narrow in his perspective. Honoria's death was a tragedy. And more tragic still, to my mind, is that it is not her but the idea of her, which my wife misses like a lost limb.

We are on Carrington Road, Hyde, and the sight reinforces

what I already know: psychics and clairvoyants belong in the ropier parts of town. Our first two addresses in Stockport were no better; I don't look down on people with nothing, wish them the luck I came across.

This side of Hyde comprises row upon row of two-up and two-down houses. Doorsteps out on to the pavement. Number sixteen looks to be in decent shape. Unlike the neighbouring house, its front door is undamaged. I don't see a bell, so knock lightly on the frosted glass. Mediums are meant to be perceptive, may sense an arrival before the caller has found the house. You'd think. Mortimer, who wears a black polo shirt that I last saw on Leo about three years ago, looks like a magician. He was sitting behind me in the car and it is only now that I see him properly—white gloves too—that I think he might be taking a little rise out of us. Dressed with his tongue in his cheek. I look at Corrie; she smiles straight back, gesturing our amusing son. She takes a lot of things in life seriously: music, vegetarianism, the past. I think she spotted months ago that doing so with ghost hunting would be a humourless turn too far. I like this about her. I know that she is losing sleep, running over and over those brief times she shared with her mother, sometimes as an eight-hour alternative. We've talked at two and three and four in the morning, my wife describing some occasion when—as a child—she feels she may have let her mother down. It's my take that Honoria did all the letting down. She may have had her reasons; even I have spotted that being a parent is a complicated job. Fulfilling those responsibilities with Jeremy Dalton breathing down your neck may be nigh on impossible. That is context, it doesn't alter the bottom line. If she had just explained all that to Corrie—told her that she wanted better for her, even if she couldn't make it happen—the pair might have found more common ground. Instead, my wife has been left confused by her childhood. She feels guilty for giving so little back to her mother, for leaving her to bear Jeremy alone before she turned seventeen. I say what goes around comes around.

Corrie is wearing a floral dress this evening, blue and red flowers on a white background, and a navy cardigan. I think it's a funny choice for winter. The best dressed person on Carrington Road by a country mile. I guess Honoria would have liked it, she was quite stylish herself. I can recall that about her if little else.

'The Tripps?' enquires the tall man who has opened the door.

I am quite taken aback, glance at Corrie. She says, 'We are the Tripps.' He's not six-foot-six, he's taller. That's what I reckon.

The medium invites us in, tells us he is called Percival. It's a name, I doubt whether it's his real one. If he's older than me it can't be by more than five years, and I've never met a Percival from my own generation before today. I suppose the name is weird enough to be Corrie's cousin, she may not spot the absurdity.

'Please go on through to the back,' he says.

Morty leads the way; it is six paces, eight tops, so small is this gigantic man's house. Between front and back room, a staircase rises up steeply, angled at ninety degrees between his two ground-floor rooms, like a priest-hole. I feel I am invading the man's privacy just by glancing up. In the back room, there is a small candelabra on the rectangular dining table. No electric light on, just a glow coming through the frosted-glass doors between here and the front room we have passed through.

'Be seated. Please be seated.'

As we sit, Corrie grasps my hand. 'It feels right,' she says. I've seen nothing to make me agree, not so far. I don't voice it. Have I said that I love her? My wife. Want whatever she wants, pretty much.

'There is no moon tonight,' says Percival, 'which is perfect for our purpose, you know?'

I think I've heard this said before, maybe read it in the magazine Corrie's been taking. "From Beyond:" it's not a bad read so long as you don't consult Leo on the detail.

'Thank you for seeing us,' says Corrie. 'Have you all the information you require.'

He sits down next to Morty. My son turns and his eyes are at the same level as this man's chest. Percy is head and shoulders taller, in a seated position. It's preposterous. Corrie and I sit opposite. The candle flames cast a wavering light over the two we look upon. Percival has a lined face. He is quite skinny but every bone is long, forehead and all. If heaven's above, he's closer than the rest of us.

'You are Cordelia Tripp,' he says in his dull Mancunian inflection. 'Born Cordelia Dalton, raised at Low Fell, a sheep farm in Cumbria…' Without pause for breath, he continues. '…your mother, Honoria Dalton, passed from this life in the year of our Lord nineteen hundred and eighty-five. Passed tragically and only a few miles from where we now sit, although she always made her home in Cumbria. You have not heard from her since that terrible tragedy and fear she has not heard the words with which you wish to comfort her. I am to rectify the situation if the good Lord should kindly grant me the opportunity.'

Mortimer's mouth is open like he's watching a strip show. I don't think mine is; could be, I suppose. Percival is an original, something of the ethereal about him.

Corrie says, 'Yes, Mr Townsend, that is us. You have understood our wishes.'

'Percival, please. There are only close friends in my parlour.'

Corrie nods, does so demonstratively in the dim of the room. It illuminates the vitality in her eyes, the black and brown of them shining in the candlelight.

'Drinks?' queries the tall man.

The tone could be offering us stiff ones but that is not the way of these affairs. Morty asks, 'What is there?' I see his mother look at him askance although it only sounded rude because we are in a poorer house than our own. Not dissimilar in size to the house Corrie and I shared when his older brother

Honoria, My Take

was born.

'I have a slew of contrasting beverages young man. From crème de menthe to raspberry cordial. I advise cocoa. It is a warming drink for the activity we are to embark upon; it will counter the chill we may feel upon entering where we must.'

Corrie nods along to this. 'Cocoa please, Mr Townsend.' He raps very gently on the table and Corrie coughs. 'I'm sorry. Percival,' she says.

'Thank you kindly, Cordelia, I'm not one to hector but it is friendly decorum which will entice the spirits.'

I ask for cocoa. I'm with Leo in presuming all these ghost conjurors are frauds while finding appreciation for this one. I didn't understand his knocking on wood, first off, but Corrie did so he's clearly on her wavelength. His antiquated language amuses me, compensates for his intimidating height.

'Cocoa's great,' says Morty.

'Now, Family Tripp, I advise that you await my return with the hot drinks, seated in silence, eyes closed. Holding hands and dwelling upon the missing boy. Not your mother, Cordelia. We shall usher her amongst us in good time. Leopold, is he called? The boy who has not come.'

'Leo,' I correct him. 'He's in Leeds. At university in Leeds.'

'Splendid. A scholar. I fear he would not be here even if he were in the family home tonight. And I ask you to think about him, the folly of his doubts. The avenues such scepticism closes.' I know my wife talked to Percival Townsend on the phone, agreeing time and purpose. I wonder what has not been said, so much does he seem to know about us.

We are a close family: holding hands, closing eyes, this is not difficult. Our host has risen from the table; I hear him rummaging in the small kitchen. Just an alcove off this room really. I try to do as he says, let my thoughts go where he has directed. Leo doesn't doubt that his mum is grieving the loss of her own mother. He knows the story; we have been honest with them from a young age. Honest about her death, its unfortunate timing and circumstance. They know that Corrie's childhood was difficult. A few details we have omitted. The ones which didn't carry the under-twelve certificate and we've not updated their insight. Never felt the need. I often wonder if Leo, Morty too, miss seeing Jeremy Dalton, Killian Dalton, family members from whom we are too estranged to meet. Not missing them personally, just feeling devoid of extended family. I guess a smart medium would just pick up the phone to those two. It is surely the closest Corrie will ever come to talking to the dead.

Unseen through my firmly closed eyes, I hear the gentle placement of mugs on the tablecloth. Then a dining chair's movement as it is lightly pulled across the carpet; it sounds like an army rising, so still is this room. It is easy to picture this distinctive man with my eyes closed, sitting across from Corrie where he began. I sense that he has joined hands with my son and wife. He is welcome within our family circle.

'We are prepared,' he says. 'Prepared as we can be for where we are going.'

Then my lovely wife and son release their grip upon my hands. I understand that Percival has signalled this. Probably dropped his own grip on theirs, brief as it was. I feel bereft. I liked being in communion with them. With Leo too. I felt his presence although I am astute enough to know it was all in my mind. I know and love my sons sufficiently to feel a closeness from here to Leeds. From here to Mars should they ever venture so far.

'Cocoa,' says Percival.

I open my eyes to ensure I take hold of the mug properly, don't spill it or scald my thumb. I am surprised to see Mortimer looking back at me like a rabbit. His face is his own but the impudence has left. I hope it comes back. I think he has dwelt upon his brother as sincerely as I have.

Corrie slides sideways on the chair, puts the hand that held mine around my waist. 'I love you, Simon,' she says. This is not news to me, not that I can recall the last time she said it in front of a near stranger. I push her hair back with my hand. She has

Honoria, My Take

the nicest eyes; I want to die in her gaze. Not tonight, obviously, but there can be no better place. No better view for me than to behold her face.

We all sup a little cocoa. Percy makes it well.

The light from the candle-trio is spooky. There is something of that in every medium's house. This one has a barer room than most. No oriental knick-knacks, no tarot cards. Thankfully, no Ouija board. The tall man has a kindly face. He will relieve us of a little money for this palaver, yet I am certain he cares. Wants Corrie to be at peace in the relationship she cannot exit. The look emanating from Mortimer scares me slightly. He might have seen a ghost, so serious is the expression upon his face. I take his eye, a slight smile from me to him.

'I love you, Dad,' he says.

This trumps Corrie's admission. We are close but he is fourteen, in a stranger's house, and ours is broadly the unspoken love of a dad who nags his son about his untidy room or the volume at which he plays the jarring grunge music which he likes and I do not. And he will tidy away, turn the sound down. We love each other certainly but with deeds more than words. That was the manifestation before this evening's visit to Hyde.

'Family Tripp, Family Tripp,' says Percival.

I wait, expecting a greater declaration to follow but it does not.

'We all love Leo, you know?' I say, to Percival. It is already known to the others. 'I love them all. Not something I say regularly, not to the boys.' I put an arm around Corrie again, let my fingers slide up to her far cheek, feel her hair fall across the back of my hand. I don't have a clue why I've said what I have. Nothing to prove on my part and if he's a real medium he should have known it already.

'Eyes closed,' says Percival.

I do as he asks, then hear hands clap loudly, once, twice, three times. I blink them open and closed again. He has extinguished

Ghost in the Stables

the candles. The aroma of wax, the flame's signature goodbye, drifts to and past me. The room is in darkness save the glow coming through the glass panel of the door to the front room. Just a wall light on through there, I reckon.

In a higher pitched voice than his usual deep timbre, our host says, 'Leo is here and he's not here. I am seated in the place he is not. Were he present, he might deride us for the speculative invitations with which we beckon forth his grandmama. I am in his place. I do not.'

He spoke the words quickly, like a riddle, I sensed little power in them. I warmed to the man before but he isn't Leo.

He claps again. In a very strange voice, a quavering falsetto, he says, 'Cordelia.'

I hear her make a whimpering noise. I keep my eyelids together but allow myself to see through the lashes. My wife is crying.

'Mummy,' says Morty, concerned for her. I am back in the dark of my fully closed eyes. My son's hands brush my own as we each reach out to comfort her.

'Mummy.' Now Corrie's voice has changed, up a register, gone as high as she ever sings. 'Mummy.'

'The words we should have said.' Percival Townsend says this as if it is the title of a poem he is to recite. Then he repeats his phrase, voice deepening. A pause between every syllable. 'The... words... we... should... have... said.'

We hold hands again, a circle around an extinguished candelabra. I think Morty's is very clammy, sweaty. I worry that he might be running a temperature. Don't think the sweat is my own.

'Mummy,' says Corrie once more, 'I do remember.' I flick my eyes open; her head is hanging down. I worry how upset she sounds. Her tone is squeaky, frightened, not really her. 'You took me to the stables before I could walk or talk. Showed them to me. Many proud horses. Told me all their names. You walked from stall to stall, holding me close, cradled in your arms. Every foal, colt, steed, a couple of old mares, occupying

80

the stables. You showed them all to me that day.'

Now I glance at Morty. He has opened his eyes, staring at his mother. It's a bit crazy. No one can remember being a baby. Corrie sounds convincing to me. Always will.

'There was a horse called Galley. I'm sure that was the name. A white horse that you liked more than...' She pauses, says nothing for fully a minute and nor does Percival. Then she continues, still the infancy within her voice that is never there in real life. '...Gallant was its name. Gallant was your horse. Not later, not when I was riding. The day you first showed me. A wonderful white horse called Gallant.'

As she is saying it, I feel momentarily relieved that Leo isn't here to see his mother in a trance, and then it hits me that he is. Eyes open, I look at Percival through the gloom. He looks nothing like my son, but his eyes, the way he watches Cordelia, that truly is Leo's look. This man did not carry that face earlier this evening. He's channelling the living. Unbelievable. I last saw that astonished look on Leo when his mother played him Shostakovich on the piano. She had never played anything by that composer before. He bought the music in a second-hand shop, said it was better than Debussy, the music Corrie likes most, plays the most. She told him she'd need to practice: 'Shosty is complicated stuff.' He was insistent she play it there and then. This was in the summer holidays a few months back. When she tried, put the music on the little shelf above the keys, started to play, he was mesmerised by how richly she interpreted the challenging piece. One she had never before attempted. I think he is exactly that astonished now. And this time it is in the guise of Percy Townsend and her performance is even stranger. Back in the summer, when she finished, stopped playing the Shostakovich, said, 'I could improve with practice,' he was all over her. 'Bloody hell! Why aren't you famous, Mum?' He had been hearing her faultless playing all his life. Leo's a scientist. Wouldn't believe the obvious until he'd set an experiment which he considered fool proof. Corrie cannot be found wanting in the musical realm. He should have known that from experience; he likes to point out that science sometimes yields counterintuitive results. Now I think he's learning something new about his mother's relationship with Honoria. Maybe even about ghosts and spirits and how memory can conjure the past back among us. Learning it from Leeds if Percival's channelling is a two-way street.

My doubts slip through my fingers to the floor. I feel lightheaded without them weighing me down. Mustn't forget to collect them on the way out.

9.

'Why are we doing this again?' I asked.

'I like her,' said Corrie.

'You hardly know her.'

'I like her. We're family.'

I wanted to laugh at that but not at Corrie. I had to drop a couple of jobs just to keep the weekend free. I was working a bit every Saturday by this time, Sundays too if needs must. What I was doing back then was only small scale; I couldn't afford to pay Sharon or Alan, my employees, for odd jobs. That's all it ever was over the weekend. I might have been foolish borrowing money to start a business, mortgaging up for a new house, all at the same time. Corrie was working hard too. She'd never had so many students.

That summer Saturday required quite an early start, a long drive ahead of us. We were finally going to meet Vinny's ladyfriend, so that would be a bonus. We'd not been to Cumbria since the Christmas before last. Obviously not.

'I wasn't really impressed.' As I said it, I wondered if it was a mistake, whether speaking ill of a bride on her wedding day might jinx the whole thing, and that was not my wish. I had even asked to be invited. My parting shot to Sarah the last time we were in the South Lakes. I supposed that this would make it doubly rude not to attend. Killian looked a shit catch, Low Fell a spectacular one. That was the entirety of my assessment.

Honoria, My Take

My wife was in jeans and the same denim jacket that came out of Cumbria with her years ago. She had a lovely dress for the wedding which she would be changing into when we were close to the church in Coniston. 'Simon, don't you think she's more than he deserves.'

I laughed at that. Agreed with my wife as ever. 'How will you put up with him, though?' I was referring to her father, Corrie knew that.

'I won't. Tommie says more than a hundred guests have been invited.'

I suspected that Corrie had told me this a few days ago. The arrangements. I feared it would be a disaster, like our only other visit up there: Low Fell. I knew that she felt excluded from family but she had also said she was never speaking to her father again. It could be a difficult day, the biggest family reunion since I had been a part of her life. And I worried I would be a hopeless support this time around, preoccupied as I was with the new business. 'And they'll all fit in the farmhouse?'

'A marquee. He's a prickly swine, you know. Won't be letting the masses into his farmhouse, his so-called withdrawing room. The crummy library.'

'I thought they threw dinner parties?'

'Very select. Father Benedict and the odd returning missionary.'

I had to sort a couple of things out with the Granada before we went. It was one of my hire cars so I needed to write down the mileage, check the spare was where it should be. I brought it home from the garage the night before, forgot to do the paperwork when I was at the car lot. Another trip to Coniston Catholic Church was in the offing. And I'd always thought it sickening the way Jeremy contrived to get himself on the right side of God's balance sheet. Not an all-seeing God, just the myopic one.

Corrie was dressing Leo for the big event, checking his holdall contained something for every eventuality. A teddy bear for the bed and breakfast. I wouldn't be speaking to her father either. Not if Corrie wasn't. Finger food and a disco: that sounded fine and dandy for me and my three-year old.

* * *

The drive up there took longer than I calculated. A jack-knifed lorry just before the Carnforth turn-off did for us. We didn't move for twenty minutes. I still thought we'd make the church before the bride, simply going to be tight. I turned up a side road, a quiet one, so that Corrie could change into her red dress. High Nibthwaite was on the signpost—I was working there when I first met Corrie—so small it's not even a hamlet. Working at Sark Farm. I wasn't for calling in, never kept up with the crosspatches who paid my wages. I doubted that they still lived there. Mr and Mrs Browning: a marriage like a prize-fight. Once Corrie had changed, I'd be turning the car around, get back on the through route to Coniston. Couldn't stop and do this on the main road: a pretty girl in a layby taking off her jeans, putting on a dress, might cause a terrible accident.

'Stand there, please,' said Corrie. She's never been the sort to undress out in the open. Only wore the jeans in the car from concern that the dress would become crumpled had it spent two or three hours scrunched beneath her. She left the passenger door open wide, I stood the other side of her so that I blocked one view and the door covered the other. 'Turn your back,' she said, and I replied, 'No way.' She smiled about that. I expect most men enjoy watching their wife undress. To this day, I love it: Corrie is the best. Weddings I could take or leave, this little preview might be what I came for. This and whatever we got up to in the B and B once the party was over. There were to be no more overnights in Low Fell, we were both agreed about that.

'It's not funny,' she said, hopping on one foot with her jeans more off than on. That set me off in hoots of laughter, her too. She was stripping for me on a Cumbrian hillside, sure to beat whatever nonsense was to go down in the church later. This would be the main feature in my remembered home movie of Killian's big day. Killian and Sarah.

Honoria, My Take

It wasn't even a layby which I'd parked in, just a slightly wider stretch of road. There was little or no traffic on those tiny country lanes, and any car that needed to pass was going to have to slow down just to get through safely. She had initially asked me to stop as we went through woodland, the road had been too narrow there. This was open countryside and my wife had no trousers on, sexy knickers and she was going for the blouse. An old open top tractor loomed into view. The farmer sat high up in his contraption; the screening of the open car door would hide nothing from his vantage point. I felt embarrassed on Corrie's behalf; an old fella in a navy-blue one piece was squinting at her as his tractor neared. He must have been cooking in it, so hot was the July sun. He was pulling an empty hay trailer. If the bumpkin scratched the Granada, I knew I'd go apeshit. My fleet were like a second family to me, those early days in business.

'Help me,' said Corrie. I guessed she was hoping to get the blouse off and the dress on before the bespectacled old fella could make out any detail. I pulled but something was stuck on the clasp of her bra. I turned her round and fiddled with it. Pulled it over her head just as she said, 'Stop.'

'Miss Dalton,' said the farmer.

Corrie was in bra and knickers, head forward and hair hanging across her face. It surprised me that anyone might recognise her. It was only her second visit to Cumbria since she turned seventeen and I didn't remember seeing this fella the first time around.

Looking up at the man on the tractor seat, her right arm protecting her exposed cleavage, Corrie answered. 'Thornton.'

'You've come back for the wedding.'

'I expected you to be there?'

'Reception, Miss Dalton. I don't go into your kind of church.'

'No.'

I thought the old man was just going to sit on his tractor and stare at my wife in her undies. Mrs Tripp, I should've told him. I tried to attract Corrie's attention but she was settling in for a chinwag with whoever the hell Thornton was.

'I was just changing for it,' she told him.

'Aye.'

'It's naturist themed, Thornton. Everyone's going to be nude. You'll have to take your boiler suit off if you want to get into the reception, you know.'

I handed Corrie the dress which she pulled over her head as the man laughed at her joke. Choke-laughed, enjoyed himself a good splutter. 'You look like a picture, Miss Dalton,' he said when the resplendent red dress was finally upon her.

'Now or before, you dirty old man?'

Thornton's choking laughter throttled back up. As did his antiquated tractor and he went on his way. Inside our car, little Leo had caught the Thornton disease. Giggling and writhing so much it caused a nasal discharge which I had to clean up. Mothers without clothes on are the funniest thing. We could all see that.

* * *

Inside it was gloomy, the faint light a disorienting contrast to the bright sun shining off bonnet and mirrors throughout the drive up. The usher signalled for us to sit on the right; the church was heaving. That astonished me: at least two hundred people in a church in sleepy Coniston. I wondered if tourists had wandered in, swelling the numbers. I could see the family at the front. And Killian standing beyond the pews—I assumed it was him—his back to us as we sought seats. John and Thomasina were with the Dalton parents, Honoria and the other one whom I was sworn to avoid. There were no spare places near them. We dipped in four rows behind. Only two seats but Leo was still small enough to sit on my knee. Corrie introduced me to her cousin, a young woman called Leah. She whispered back in a Scots accent. I didn't know where she fitted in. Surprised she talked to Corrie, I thought we were unclean. Banished to Stockport. Instead, the cousin kissed my cheek. Corrie said, 'I told you about her.' I'm not the sort of bloke who ignores what his wife says but I had no recollection of any such conversation.

The organ started rumbling soon after we were seated. An ugly sound. The famous tune soon followed. I think the man at the keyboard, the pedals, was initially checking all the stops worked. Gassing up. Everyone was peering around. I was trying to figure how many relatives I had through my marriage to Corrie. How many Leahs and how many Vincents. Just three came to our wedding, Vinny, Tommie and her husband John, their two little ones if tiny people counted as guests. I'd thought of inviting my sister, Rosie, but we're not close. And I didn't want my father there. It wasn't a point of principle—we speak now and then, visited two summers back—I thought having him present would stir the wrong emotions in Corrie. At that time, she had occasional phone contact with Honoria; not a word spoken to her father since nineteen seventy-six. Neither parent stood in her presence until fully eighteen months after our modest nuptials.

Leo seemed utterly enthralled by the music, by the great throng of people. I lifted him up so that he could look around. Sarah was coming down the aisle. The white dress, the gauze across the face.

Corrie told me that the poor girl did a crash course in Catholicism and endured a baptism, in order to be married in the Catholic church. I said it was diabolical—akin to all the worst cults—subjecting people to a brain washing before they could spend the night together. She called me a heathen and a bad influence. It was entirely light hearted; we never bothered with any of that bollocks before we took to sleeping with each other. Doing *it*, as we used to say. I think she influenced me at least as much as I did her, and it was the disapproval of her family that gave us no choice but to crack on like we were married when we were too young by far. When we did tie the knot, a council official took us through it, not a man in a frock spouting old-time religion. Leo was cooking in the oven too, quite close to being pricked with a fork. Maybe Corrie still felt this circus meant something, I have never thought so. When I look back, I know we were both kids when she and I fled Cumbria, committed our lives to each other without any hymns, hokum, presents or paperwork. I swear on my sons' lives it was the best bloody thing I've ever done.

'We are gathered together...'

The priest sounded highly animated. He must have said every word a hundred times before and yet he breathed a life into them as though this union was the most important of all possibilities to him and God. When it came time for the marrying couple to speak, to repeat their own names and those of their partner, I listened with interest. Killian Rupert spoke very confidently and strictly without emotion, that was my analysis. Sarah's voice cracked on every other word—nerves, you'd think—she was always a bit of a stay-at-home, never lived beyond a valley full of sheep. I thought there might be a few doubts too; we believed it was she who called it off first time around. Thomasina and Vincent were of that mind, and they met Killie as we never did. It was five years earlier, the near miss. Neither Sarah nor Killian moved on from it and so here they were, marrying for fear of worse. When the priest asked if anyone present had reason to object, I could have shouted out that I did. Told Sarah that she was marrying a hard-hearted cur who couldn't possibly resolve the nervousness and worry that her face told the world was within her, whether she owned up to it or not. Vincent—who had helped us move house a couple of months earlier—might've objected on the grounds that Killian is a homosexual. It was always his gripe, not mine. Vinny named a couple of lads he thought his brother went with back in the seventies, said that he's 'more careful now'. I wasn't going to raise the issue myself. His denigration of older brother sounded all bluster to me, a way of getting his own back: Killian battered Vinny as often as he liked in their miserable childhoods. She was certainly marrying a bully who wasn't a patch on the warm-blooded brother five years his junior. I hoped Sarah knew that much.

A crowd as large as that sing a nice hymn. They did the

Honoria, My Take

Holy-Holy-Holy one that I remembered from school. Chimed up loud for Leo. He had a go. His voice clear but he'd not heard it before. Corrie laughed at us while rendering it beautifully. I knew she would be his encouraging music teacher when our boy needed one.

The couple exited the main church to sign the register; there was some kind of anteroom for that. We drifted into the aisle and towards the exit, all moving slowly. Corrie wanted to talk to Millie Green, except that wasn't her name anymore. It took me a moment to remember. Of course, it was Vulliamy, although Green trips off the tongue better. I remembered her husband, Patrick, very well. We were friends when I lived up there. Attended the Young Farmers together. I spotted Vincent and went towards him, holding Leo's hand in mine. A carnation in the button hole of a rented suit was a good look on him, more uptown than cowshed, which might have been a first. The girl beside him, blond—natural hair, not bleached blond—was something else. Slim and wearing a red summer dress, a higher hem and a brighter shade than the one my wife had on.

'Kat, this is Simon,' he said, 'and my cutest nephew.' Vinny took Leo's hand from mine, lifted him off the ground. They had long been pals.

The pretty girl narrowed her eyes a fraction. 'Married to Cordelia, right?' I said, yes, and she embraced me. From within a tight clasp, Kat whispered in my ear. 'You and I must be the only normal ones here.' I hugged her back on account of the truth she spoke. As we leant back again and I looked into her face, she was smiling confidently. 'You stay away, right?' Vincent had clearly filled her in. It wasn't yet midday and her breath reeked of Bacardi.

When we had all spilled into the sunshine, the could-be happy couple followed us out and confetti was thrown. Sarah was finally smiling, looking very pleased with herself. Killian always had an entitled sneer. Like he was clenching a pound coin up his arse. I hung back with Leo and then saw that Corrie had wheeled herself to the front. She gave her brother a peck on the cheek, then a long embrace for the girl who was going to be putting up with him from here on in. Leo was pointing, wanted to join her. I noted that the old git we were avoiding was talking to someone near the churchyard hedge, so took Leo up to be with his mother.

'Congratulations Killian...' I stretched out a hand to shake, fixed a look on my face that may have masked the metaphorical bad smell I always sensed in that man's company. '...you've made an honest woman of her.'

'I've done no such thing,' he said, quite breezily but holding his expression a firm neutral. Corrie could interpret that for me later. If he was implying that they were both still virgins, I thought it a sorry state.

My wife had let go of Sarah after the longest time. I dipped in and pecked the bride on the cheek. 'A Mountie always gets his man,' I told her, then thought I might have said something inappropriate. Or hit the nail on the head. Maybe both.

'Thank you,' she said. She thrust her head towards mine and I only realised why when I turned my own. The returned kiss met my lips not my cheek.

'Sorry.'

'Don't be.'

Corrie lifted Leo and he greeted his new auntie. One I doubted he would be seeing much of. She ruffled his hair nicely; talked to him in simple kiddie words. Killian was waiting, my wife pricking his balloon of importance. He turned towards another man who had approached the couple. It was Mr Green, Millicent Vulliamy's father. Killian shook the proffered hand quickly, did the same with the hand of his wife, Teresa Green, who was next in line. No words passed between them. Not even eye contact. I deduced that these church congregants were closer long ago, before the Greens sided with Cordelia. Contrived to help us outwit her intolerable father.

Stepping from the line, I tried to speak with these old friends although it was Corrie who knew Millie's parents better, not I. They were polite, remembered me perfectly well. Perhaps they

Honoria, My Take

did not like it known how firmly they once supported Corrie and I. Our flight may have given them cause for regret, lowered their standing in this church in which Jeremy Dalton remained a respected figure. They were heroes in my eyes but too much time had passed to go back over why, to tell them how appreciated they really were.

My wife had found her mother and they were deep in conversation. She had telephone chats with her at that time, not many, no more than three in the preceding year. I asked once if her father knew that they talked and she replied, 'They're not joined at the hip.' Technically true but they seemed to me to be closer than most. I thought he had infected her, rendered Honoria incapable of independence. Corrie used to agree. I should have welcomed the new entente, found that it only confused me.

I went to seek out Millie and Patrick. In the church Corrie had whispered to me that the whole congregation had turned up for this wedding, so well-connected are the Dalton family. She did not expect the Greens at the reception, neither Millie nor her parents. Old rifts didn't heal back then. Not in that part of the country.

'How's he doing,' I said, gesturing towards their young son.

Millie turned to me. 'Michael's the best,' she said.

Her profile displayed what Corrie had not told me. Another Vulliamy was just a few short weeks away from entering this world. I tried to say something congratulatory, muffled over a 'Well done on...' and then let my words drift to nothing as I looked at Patrick, pointed at his wife's taut waistline. Foolish of me to congratulate a man on his minimal, and surely well-enjoyed, role in bringing forth the birth of a child. 'Where are you living now?' I managed, trying to cajole the couple from their silence.

'Still in Broughton,' said Millie. 'I want to buy the council house we're in, can't see us managing it on Pat's money.'

'In years to come,' he said.

'Are you still working for Lennox?' The name of his

employer from many years ago had jumped into my brain. Patrick and I were both farmhands in this district before Corrie and I struck out. He is three or four years my senior; his father still a shepherd on Cartmel Fell, assuming he was still going strong.

'Yes, for Lennox,' he replied. I felt an unspoken pity for him. The thought of treading the same fields year in year out, reassembling drystone walling once more toppled by a careless motorist, depressed me greatly. It was for Corrie, to get her away from her despicable father, that I left Cumbria. Giving agricultural life the slip was the bonus. Not that I saw it so clearly when we fled. Everything in focus by the time of Killian's wedding, seven years later.

'I run a small car hire business now. I need to grow the fleet but the returns are looking good.'

Patrick jerked his head back slightly, narrowed his eyes. Looked at me as though I'd confessed to a petty crime, declared myself a shoplifter or a vendor of knock-off watches. Millie was smarter, interested. She asked if Corrie worked with me. I told her that Corrie didn't drive yet. She was having lessons but she isn't really a car person. I added that Corrie teaches piano.

'She should play for the world to listen.'

I agreed with that, explained that Corrie had recently done a recital in a church hall. Millie was delighted to hear it, a greater enthusiasm than the one she mustered for my car hire outfit. I have often felt outshone by Corrie. She was miles cleverer than me when we met and nothing since ever changed that pecking order. She poured it into her love of music, her piano teaching. Her parenting too, if I'm honest. We've always been a good team but I'm the lucky one. I said none of this to Millie and Patrick.

'You should encourage her to play more,' said Millie.

'I'm not sure if she wants anything to change.'

'Bet you miss it,' said Patrick. He gestured the hills behind us. Every shade of green sitting beneficently beneath the unbroken blue sky; the long-necked church crouching, a short elevation up from the lakeside.

'Yes and no.' Mucking out cow shit was in my no-column. I'd put the six o'clock starts on winter mornings on the same side of the page.

'Millie thought Stockport was a bit dirty. Didn't you love?'

I was there when she came, the only time she visited. Hillgate was a bit that way, probably still is. But it was dirt we were rising above, me and Corrie, cracking on by ourselves.

'I think busy was the word I used.' Pregnant Millie was not owning the disparagement whatever she had said years before. 'Even Broughton is dirty,' she told Patrick. 'It was all the traffic I didn't like. All the noise.'

'We're in Marple now.' I realised as I said it that these two could have no way of knowing how different our new home is from the little flat Millie once visited. 'It's a village of sorts; miles quieter than where we were.'

'That's nice,' said Millie. Patrick had found someone else to talk to, stepped away. Her hair remained long, straight, the blackest sheen, just as I recalled from her teenage years. Face radiant with a richer tan than most in northern England ever acquire. Her husband was a lucky man, didn't appear to know it. For all that, she looked a little world weary, tired. Perhaps it was the pregnancy; Millie was the same age as Corrie, twenty-four years old back then.

'I hardly know anyone,' I said. 'It's odd coming here only once in a blue moon.'

She patted my hand. 'It must be.'

I think she caught me glancing again at her protruding stomach. I felt like a peeping Tom: is it rude to look intently upon a pregnant woman's waistline? I was puzzling over whether she and Patrick would make it, long term. In Stockport not, up there in Cumbria it was a maybe.

'This one had better be a girl,' said Millie.

'Yeah. Good luck with that old coin flip.'

'This world hardly needs another farmhand.'

I recalled that she was a clever one in the same private school as Corrie those seven or eight years ago. Patrick, on the other hand, was one of many rural Cumbrians who—brighter when younger—had gradually taken on the characteristics of the ewes which populated his beloved fells. I kissed Millie on the cheek. 'I hope it's a girl too.'

* * *

At Corrie's insistence, I pulled the car up on to the grass verge just outside the gate. Parked like a getaway driver. We weren't the last to leave the church, still there were countless vehicles up ahead of us, a little sign directing them through a gap in the trees and onto the parkland that fronts Low Fell. The farmhouse sits a long way from the road, down a track, and the marquee was behind it and to the right. It must have been the largest size possible, biggest tent since Barnum's heyday. Like a spaceship landed on Ulpha Fell. Corrie was re-tying Leo's tie; he pulled at it. Couldn't get it quite right, a simple skill she has never had reason to master.

'Let me do that.'

'No,' she said, 'I'm cracking the code.' The knot of a tie wasn't going to defeat Corrie. Nothing would. She'd been in the most buoyant mood since first light.

'You circulate and I'll eat,' I told her as we were heading down the drive, closing in on the throng. Honoria's food was the biggest pull for me. Cumbria means nothing, I'm Yorkshire really.

'I'm checking in on Sarah's family. I bet they don't know I'm a pariah,' said Corrie.

'You don't know them, do you?'

'I'm a Dalton. They know me.'

'You're not a Dalton now, love.'

'I am here; these fuckers don't count registry office jobbies, never heard of Stockport.'

I shushed her. My wife only ever swore when her family were on the horizon. I worried Leo might pick it up, tell the buggering bastard his proper name.

Walking up the drive she came across person after person

Honoria, My Take

who greeted her warmly. 'Look, it's Cordelia.' They said her name in full, time after time. She introduced me; it might be the first any knew of my existence. I heard my name—'Simon,'— echoed back as I introduced myself. I don't think it was going in though. They had no reason to remember me. The name Cordelia Dalton never left their lips. Farmer Dalton's youngest; used to sing solo in church; the piano prodigy. Slipped from the face of the Earth. They told her she looked wonderful and she really did. The red dress was pure class; above the knee by about an inch. No more than that. And she was slim back then, my Corrie. The slightest hourglass; rich brown hair too. They admired our son, her child. The youngest in the whole clan. Leo was bashful and that was the first time I'd seen him display that trait. Turned his face into his mother's pretty clothing.

As we got to the marquee there was a line: best man, two sets of parents, then Killian and Sarah. My wife picked up Leo. 'Meet the stars,' she told him, then turned to the line, shaking hands, a short hug for her mother. 'Yo, Daddy,' she said, play punching the old sod on the shoulder. He was too slow witted to do anything but smile and she passed him by.

As she was shaking Killian's hand for the second time that day, telling him he didn't deserve Sarah—a big grin hiding the sincerity of the pronouncement—her father tried to start up a conversation. 'Spare a thought for the man who raised you.'

She never turned, not to him, nor to the priest who was following behind us. In her clearest public-speaking voice she said, 'Raised a stick to me, I recall,' kissed Sarah and moved on.

I couldn't help myself from glancing back; I'd only stopped shaking his slippery hand the second before. The face was thunderous, every broken vein glowing redder. Killian's darkened in unison. 'Nonsense,' said Jeremy Dalton. Then his tone lightened instantly. 'Lovely service, Father. You've done my boy proud.'

* * *

The seating arrangements put us on separate tables. Corrie was a rule-breaker simply by being there. She ignored the plan, sat herself beside me. We belong together. Vinny and Tommie were not far away, nice as ever. They always appreciated us.

When we were first talking with the Stapley's, the old man from the lane, Thornton, walked right up to us grinning from ear to ear. 'Miss Thomasina,' he said, 'your sister tells me we've all meant to be naked at this wedding shebang. No clothes on at all. That's how she said you were doing it.'

'Oh dear, Tommie,' Corrie interrupted, 'Mr Thornton seems to have gone quite off the rails. Send for the men in white coats.'

Thornton grinned while looking simultaneously astonished. I wondered if he was beginning to doubt himself. 'She did,' he told Tommie. 'This morning. I see-ed her with no clothes on. That's what I saw.'

'Now you've been dreaming again, haven't you? Such a dirty old man.'

I was in stitches. Corrie could be very funny back home but this was a different order. Something had unhinged itself. A last blast through Cumbria.

Thornton was on the next table along with his old wife. She must have been feeling troubled by his assertion that he spied this young one wearing so little. No one believed him; he was an old fool and Corrie the bright young thing. She'd glugged down a glass of white while he was watching her, took a second off a girl with a tray. The food was still a promise. We sat with Leah and her boyfriend, Chris, plus a Great Aunt Monica and a pair of Sarah's schoolfriends. The family all seemed to be from Honoria's side. Leah was keen to talk to me. Must have been broadminded. She lived in Edinburgh, worked in town planning. Asked questions about my new business.

'Start-ups are the future,' she said.

'It's certainly mine.' I asked her how long she had been living in Edinburgh.

'My whole life.'

This surprised me. Honoria was a Cumbrian. Carlisle, I recalled. I'd no idea about her sister, Corrie's aunt. Never knew she'd moved to Scotland. Corrie talked about her wider family now and again but never joined up the dots. Assumed I knew them as she did although I'd never met a soul from outside of the Low Fell brood before that wedding.

When the girls came to serve the food, I was surprised by how plain it was. Honest Cumbrian fare, I suppose. Ham and new potatoes, cabbage, all covered in a creamy sauce. I must admit, it was exactly the stuff I liked. I talked to Leah and Chris as we ate. Leo kept me occupied too; Corrie made contributions. Only ate the vegetables and she drank a third and then a fourth glass of wine. She also talked to Sarah's old school buddies. They laughed a lot. Sarah Pollard moving up to Low Fell was a fantastic proposition in their eyes. Corrie put them straight. 'They're not getting their own place, not while the old man breathes. It's a couple of rooms in the farmhouse. Shared kitchen, shared bathroom.' The friends didn't buy her pessimism. A massive farm in a beautiful setting. 'The world's worst tombola prize,' said Corrie.

I had thought the Great Aunt to be in her own world, eating but not talking. Then she guffawed at the tombola comment, even started to choke but then guzzled down some water from her glass. 'There's many would like it but you're one on your own, Cordelia Dalton,' she said when her coughing was over.

The father of the bride, Sarah's dad, had risen to his feet. Speechmaking was to begin; a fuss Corrie and I were pleased to do without. We quietened down anyway. I hoped they would be good, witty. We were half way up Ulpha Fell where nothing more erudite than a sheep's bleat gets heard year in and year out.

* * *

'Attention.' The man was tapping his wine glass with a teaspoon, doing it with a vigour that could've smashed it. 'As father of the bride it's tradition that I say a piece. This is it.'

In the time it took for Mr Pollard to say those few words, the tent was transformed from a sustained din to an expectant still. The high-pitched voice of a child I did not know was silenced with a whispered scolding, and we were ready for the man. To hear out Sarah's dad.

'It makes me very proud to see my Sarah...' He turned to look at her. His daughter still wore white, the veil no longer obscuring her face. She'd eaten glazed ham. And a few glasses of wine may have deadened the look in her eyes; a contrast with Corrie's, shining brighter with every glass she knocked back. '...marrying into Low Fell. I don't know that we were born to it but here we are. You'll all know that she and Mr Killian Dalton have been seeing each other for a goodly few year now. I am so pleased he couldn't wait no more. No longer. He's got a good girl in Sarah and don't I know it. The knot's tied and I want you to have a sup on your drink, please. All raise...rise up...what's the blinking phrase? Raise your glasses! To the happy couple!'

'That was short and sweet,' I whispered to Corrie.

'I expect he worked on it for weeks,' she replied as we chinked our glasses together.

Then Mr Pollard chunnered on. 'Tradition has it that it's meant to be the groom as speaks next. Well, he'll get his turn.' Killian Rupert was nodding his head, fork in hand. Finishing every last shred of ham appeared to be his priority. 'I've only said a few words because I'm not much of a talker. Not really, even Dorothy says that.' It was an obvious truth: he had gone quite red in the face, flustered from standing before the amassed locals. 'Firstly, I'm going to hand over to Mr Jeremy Dalton here. He can say a few words about the couple better than what I can.' He looked sideways down the top table. 'The father of the groom.'

Leo looked backwards and forwards between his mother and I. By rights this was the part in the pantomime where we should have taught our child to boo and hiss. It might have been impolitic to do so, Corrie's mood lent me to think she might give it a go. She pulled the boy onto her lap so he could see better. Her own look turned steely. The smile she had worn all day was taking a break.

'What a fine turnout. Father Benedict, the Pollards, the Daltons, the sunshine. What a fine turnout. I need to thank Stephen…' Farmer Dalton gestured to Stephen Pollard, the man who ceded the floor to him. '…a fine fellow who I have known for so many years.' He scrutinised the audience; the tightly packed dining tables within the tent; the forced autumnal light, summer filtered through the beige tarpaulin of the marquee. 'Stephen and I go back to childhood. He was a young labourer here at Low Fell around the time I was matriculating. Weren't you, Stephen?'

The shy man nodded. A labourer, not a master. Farmhand, not farmer. Corrie gave me a short shrug. I believe even she did not know that link between Low Fell and the Pollards, so long before her birth did it occur.

'How long have you been at Beckfoot?' Jeremy asked Stephen, his projected voice including the entire wedding party in the conversation. I'd heard of Beckfoot some years ago, a farm as large as Low Fell, sheep grazing the shores of Wast Water.

'It's thirty-two year,' said Stephen.

'Loyalty, ladies and gentlemen. The finest of qualities, I'm sure you'll agree with me. Stephen Pollard has worked for more than thirty years with you, David.'

From a table near the rear of the tent another old farmer stood up, raised a beer glass. 'He has that, and I thank him for it every day.'

'Collins,' whispered Corrie. 'He's thick with Daddy.'

'Now when my son, Killian, began seeing Sarah, lovely Sarah here…' He gestured the newest Dalton, a little further along the top table. '…did I have misgivings? You know, I probably should have. Young Sarah was not a Roman Catholic back when they met. Strangely…' The smooth-talking tyrant was looking into the apex of the marquee, as if this was just another little chat with his best friend, God. '…this never bothered me. It could have if she were a different soul, you know? Sarah I'd met at many a function, spoken of with Stephen and Dorothy…'

His head turned to her overdressed mother, the only lady wearing a hat with fake fruit on its brim. '...they told me what a fine girl she is before I ever knew my Killian was sniffing around her. That right Killie?'

Killian Dalton, in three piece and button hole, mouthed, 'Yes, Daddy.'

Leo had rolled off Corrie's lap, taken himself to the Stapley's table, joined his cousins under the table where they'd set up camp.

'Sarah was behind Killian in school, a few years younger. I expect he noticed her there, pretty girl that she is. He couldn't meet in church, not like our Thomasina. She found a husband without no converting from this religion to that. Killian is a complex soul. He gets himself entangled with a girl from chapel. Lovely girl, like I'm saying. They met at a barn dance, that's as they told me. It's not true though, is it? We're country folk, everyone has always known everyone else, even when they don't know it.' Mr Dalton looked perplexed at the laughter which his idle digression provoked. It was probably wisdom to his thinking; I could even see a morsel of truth in it. 'We do though. Now I'll tell you a story. Old Bob Thornton there...' He pointed to one of the few faces I could've named without the prompt. '...he's been a-telling me how he saw our Cordelia this morning with not a stitch of clothing on. He knows her so well he can imagine himself that, although she's not been living round here of late.' A few of those on the near tables laughed although he seemed to be embarrassing Thornton for no clear purpose. Embarrassing Corrie more so. Jeremy must have impressed himself with this attempted banter—wore a smug face—never a comedian, his closest to it a country mile away. 'Is that right, Cordelia?' he shouted.

My wife rose up from her chair with a wine glass in hand, her other hand tucked behind it; she said nothing, just swung her pretty head slowly around one hundred and eighty degrees. Showed the tent her loveliest smile, beaming from table to table. Slowly she moved the glass to reveal a V-sign, a quiet fuck-off, which might have been for her father, for Blabbermouth Thornton or for the whole of Cumbria. Most people continued to laugh. I'm biased but I am sure she was the finest sight in the marquee, could've got away with anything that day. Farmer Dalton's frown clouded over his face once more. Corrie turned the gesture into a fluttering wave of her fingers, smiled more broadly, and quietly slid back down into her seat.

'That aside,' said the now-flustered father of the groom, 'it wunner long before myself and Honoria here could see they was a-serious. It's a big noise marrying an eldest son, you know. Many of you are aware, this man...' He placed a hand on Killian's shoulder. '...big boots to fill. My farm he's getting, sooner or later.' More laughter came which Dalton wasn't prepared for, rippling from one table to the next. 'It's true. And she's married a good farmer whatever else he is. My Killian here has understood the art and the science of it since way back before his voice broke.' He turned to his new daughter-in-law. 'I hope he's as good at all the other as he is at the farming,' he stated, lifting a wine glass as if to toast his innuendo. The laughter inside the tent increased, Honoria—sitting next to the speaker—leant forward and dropped her head into her hands.

He droned on, a confident and inane ramble now. Told us that Sarah Pollard, or Sarah Dalton as he corrected the name, could embroider better than his own wife. I think this tale enhanced neither's standing. He related a story of Killian and Vincent becoming lost in the snow, high up on the fell. It was from long ago, Killian in his early teens. The punchline, 'Whoever got them lost it was Killian who got them back down again,' sounded more like a put down of his younger son than a commendation of either. And Vincent was eight years old, only negligent parents would let him go up there with that viscous sod. Then Jeremy had us toasting the bride and groom again, and one for Honoria that made no sense to me. I dribbled a little wine into my mouth. I had only to drive to a bed and breakfast in Broughton-in-Furness when the lights went out on this bumbling parade.

* * *

Killian was up next. His face, mannerisms, all looked drawn and languid, speech delivered in a lifeless manner. Standing behind his chair, hands on the top rail, he told us that meeting Sarah changed his life without revealing any sense of how. He thanked his father for teaching him 'the craft of farming,' and his mother for 'making meals at all hours.' They had an aga, I recalled: she cooked meals only once, then simply left them within it. He said that he loves his new wife, I've sensed more excitement when a radio announcer intoned, "St Mirren nil, Stenhousemuir nil." Corrie whispered to me that he had no more passion than a badger, and it made me snort wine into my nasal passage. Summed him up to a tee. Poor hapless Sarah marrying into that plagued sett.

Killian then introduced his best man. He was to make the next speech, a man called Ned. I asked Corrie who he was. 'Edward Thorpe,' she told me, as if reminding me of our next-door neighbour's full name.

Ned sounded to me like the name of a horse and I was resolved to say nothing of those for the duration. 'Is he a close friend of Killie's?' I whispered.

She pointed a finger at her own raised eyebrow. 'There's no getting close to a hissing badger. His father and Daddy have talked at every mass since the year dot.'

I gave her a puzzled look but Corrie just took another drink of her wine. 'What do they talk about?'

She made a two-handed gesture, expansive, as if she was holding up the world. 'Another crack at the gunpowder plot, I suppose.' Sometimes I need a textbook to get to the bottom of Corrie's jokes.

Leo had come back to us, put himself in his original chair. It pleased me that he was so relaxed in that big tent, not feeling the oddity of our presence among those in the family we never saw.

I had to hand it to the guy, Ned, his public-speaking prowess stood out in a poor field. He started politely, then levered in some well-calibrated jokes about farming tradition, the inheritance. 'Vincent was in Sarah's class at school,' he said, 'but the girl saw the finer attractions of the older brother.' He went on to speak about Thomasina and even Cordelia. 'Farmer's daughters can be well provided for...' The man eyed the audience, came to focus upon John Stapley whose fortunate inheritance will have been known to most of the guests. '...if they have the good sense to marry the right farming boy.' Corrie took my hand for his follow-up line; she must have developed a heightened sense of awareness in the rarefied fell air. It could've been a car crash. 'Cordelia Dalton found a farmer's boy without a farm. Good for her, it's what she wanted. Still figuring the wherefores and the whys of it, Jeremy?'

Not too bad, I thought. My wife squeezed my fingers, then let them go. She stood up while the eyes of all those gathered in the marquee were still upon her. Clapped. Whooped. No one else followed suit; I think her father squirmed. 'I chose you,' she said in her well-projected voice, putting a hand upon each of my cheeks, holding me like a basketball as she bent down and kissed me demonstratively. Licking my lips with her tongue.

Her performance stirred the onlookers but not the smooth Ned Thorpe. 'Corrie Dalton,' he said simply. A hand in her direction as if signalling the winner of a boxing contest. It strained credulity to think she had not surprised him. She was never a public kisser or a V-signer back when she last lived up there, to my certain knowledge. Not stunts my ever-polite wife pulled in Stockport either.

Ned followed this up with stories from the kitchen across the yard, Low Fell. Honoria had prepared the food we were eating. Worked like a Trojan for the last week. Ned thanked her with more feeling than the old bastard could muster. We gave her another, more heartfelt, toast. She was aided by a Mrs Greening, by Thomasina also, and Ned had the good grace to thank and toast them too. Amid these accolades he advised Father Benedict—after praising his conduct of the service—

that he was to be first up on the disco floor. An amusing image: the spindly cassock-wearer suddenly looked as nervous as Sarah Pollard, as the bride. Ned Thorpe was pulling the would-be revellers out of their watchfulness, their scrutiny of the rich and awkward Daltons, into something akin to a celebration. 'In a few minutes,' he said, 'the lovely serving girls will be giving you all pudding.' These were schoolgirls, enlisted for a pound or two each; that was Corrie's estimate. She has long said her father is a miser—earned less than I imagined—richer by not spending money. I was unsure about her maths. Corrie spent three years in a fee-paying school, had many a piano lesson. To each Dalton a horse. My own father was a dirt farmer, didn't have any money to be miserly with. 'Eat it up, fill your glasses, let your hair down. Lucky old Killian is taking Sarah Dalton—that's her name everyone, Sarah Dalton—all the way to Paris.' Edward Thorpe looked at them both, squinted his eyes together as if making an important calculation. 'The beds are narrow in the sleeper carriage, Killie. Don't break anything falling out,' he concluded to laughter. 'If they can go to Paris, we can have a knees-up. Raise your glasses please.'

The tent was standing, Corrie had done likewise, whispered to me, 'What's my brother doing in Paris?' She made a very fair point. Killian Dalton had always been a philistine. And Sarah, like me, was as a peasant through and through.

'The bride and groom.'

We echoed it back. 'The bride and groom.' The couple up front even managed an inexpert kiss; Corrie's upon me would be the one to linger in memory. Mine and Thornton's at the very least.

* * *

Leo and a couple of country girls started the dancing; they were not much bigger than my little three-year old. I watched from the edge of the floor, making the occasional rhythmic move. Cordelia was having a field day. Drinking and talking, laughing and clapping them on the back. Knocking back the whites and the reds. Even a glass of cider, I noted. She had a word for everyone, a smile and a compliment. Everyone who was not called Jeremy Dalton.

Vincent stopped by for a chat. No Kat on his arm this time.

'How are you doing?' he asked.

'It's incredible,' I told him. 'Yourself?'

He tossed his head back. 'Killian married: it's mental.'

'They've been going out since forever,' I reminded him.

'After a fashion.'

I had no idea what he meant by that. I'm wary of speculation, it can miss the mark. 'She looks happy enough.'

'Don't they always. We never put a white dress and cake alongside unremitting misery but that's the ever after, often as not.'

I couldn't help smiling at his bleak appraisal. 'I did it, Vinny. Me and Corrie. You were there, mate. Stockport Registry Office. I don't think we've condemned ourselves to an ever after of weeping and wailing. We're good.'

'Oh, you're the best. You did it despite appearances, not because…'

I cut him off. 'You and Kat? Any plans?'

'I don't know if Cordelia is commending me to her or talking through all of my shortcomings.'

'Are they together?'

'Getting pie-eyed. The free booze is a bad idea.'

He was laughing as he said it, sending himself up, but it must have been Corrie's glugging it down which surprised him. I'm pretty certain it has always been Kat's way, his too.

I glanced at Leo dancing on the near empty floor. On the drive up here, Corrie had said that a little drunkenness might be in order. Help her to 'hop over the log.' I believe it was her own phrase. Couldn't see any logs and still she was necking the drinks just in case. 'It's the first time they've met,' I reminded Vinny.

'And my sister is in her bat-stuck-in-the-belfry mood. I'm only staying around to watch her bump into Daddy.'

I was hoping that would not happen. Her mood was striking,

a lightness to everything she said and did. She clearly wanted to leave an impression. She floored poor Bob Thornton after his chance encounter with her wearing nothing but skimpy underwear. Her subsequent ribbing left him stumped, unable to confirm if he chanced upon a lucky sight or was simply the slow-in-the-head pervert she implied. Corrie is against cruel sports: that Saturday was her day off.

We talked for a while and then watched as Vinny's blond girl and my wife, an arm draped across each other's shoulders, sidled onto the dance floor. Kat gave a thumbs up to the DJ, a teenager by the look of him. The music changed, thumped out a dramatic beat while a banshee-like keyboard wailed across it. I recognised the song: Crazy Maisie by the American rocker, Johnson Ronson. I had the vinyl; it's probably still up in the loft. Corrie was indifferent to it back then, never a Ronson fan. That afternoon, on a Cumbrian hillside, she and Kat were swinging their heads, electrified hair, moving like they were as terrifyingly crazy as the girl in the song. I'd seen her dance plenty of times; she has what it takes. A hard rocker she is not. Another exception made that evening.

> *A hurricane's coming, it was said on the news*
> *That it's all going to get a bit wild*
> *She's wearing bright red lipstick and high-heeled shoes*
> *Which all look so wrong on the child*
> *At the midnight hour, when her parents are sleeping*
> *She enters their room with a gun*
> *Does as she must, all the while weeping*
> *Orphans herself when she's done*

I don't know if Kat chose it or Corrie. She was peppering something around Low Fell but not gunfire. A performance. The little ones tried to dance like Kat and Corrie, to shake their hair in time. Only Corrie's was long enough to cause a stir. Others came on to the dancefloor, the younger generation. The

Honoria, My Take

old farmers were always going to sit it out until some soppy old-time music began playing. Home Is Where the Heart Is, that stuff. I asked Vinny to keep an eye on Leo and stepped up to the floor myself, tried to break up the all-girl dance and meet my partner's eye. I could see Vincent with my son in his arms coming to join Kat. The girls were laughing at us; they had no wish to stop. Dancing inside a marquee on the side of Ulpha Fell, quite exhilarating. There was no dancing here when Corrie was young. Jeremy Bellyache had attached himself to the furthest bit of tent canvas. Wouldn't be showing us his moves. Before Vinny had bobbed up and down more than twice, impeded by Leo clutching him around the neck, a new song was on the turntable. The beat was equally up-tempo but the sound smoother, disco replacing rock music. Not my bag.

Corrie and Kat were still rocking, shaking imaginary dandruff from their hair, when the bride and groom made it onto the dance floor. In deference to this, both girls stopped tossing their hair back and forth, it didn't suit the new song anyhow. They made a little space for the newlyweds. Sarah could dance okay, did a move or two, then put her hands on Killie's shoulders. So far, he had only stood still on the dance floor, no bobbing around in time to the music. Sarah encouraged him but nothing in Killian's demeanour suggested success with the project. He placed his hands briefly on her waist only to remove them immediately and turn away. He started shouting to Vincent, seeking to be heard above the song he should have been dancing to. Telling him of some job that needed doing while he was in Paris. The storage of silage beneath tarpaulin before the rains came.

'I'm not on the payroll,' said Vinny.

'I can hardly ask Daddy,' Killian shouted over the music.

Corrie must have heard the little spat; she took my hands in hers as if to share a dance and then she thrust her face in her eldest brother's direction. 'Fuck the farm,' she said. 'Dance with your wife.'

Sarah was standing alone, no longer making the effort.

'You don't understand me,' said Killian.
'There's nothing to it,' replied Corrie.

Killie didn't argue—not a chance of winning one with his sister that day—he simply walked off the dancefloor. Corrie let go of me, put a hand on the small of Sarah's back and gently danced with her, moved gracefully in time with the trite song. Her smile beckoned Sarah to do likewise. 'He's like that,' I heard her say.

The new bride shrugged.

* * *

Much later in the evening I sat alone with Leo asleep on my lap. Turned my head when I sensed company arriving in the seat beside me. It was Honoria. I noticed that the side of her finely coiffed hair had become misshapen; a brooch on her dress was a jewel-encrusted tractor. Funny. Funny-odd really, she was more cultured than gimmicky jewellery like that implied. Had taste, or did have the only other time I had met her. The brooch would have better suited Bonkers Bob Thornton.

'Simon, we've not talked properly.'

'Are you having a good day?' I asked her.

'Delightful. I am so pleased to know that Low Fell will not lack for feminine stewardship when Jeremy and I leave.'

'You'll be here for years,' I replied. 'What else could he do?' I glanced across the tent. Her husband and Killian sat together at the top table, in everyone's sight and nobody's earshot. They could have been talking farming or he might have been telling his son what it was he must later do on that his wedding night. I was never a lip reader.

'He could take me to Paris, for a start,' said Honoria.

I wanted to query this. Killian was taking Sarah there when the music stopped; I was sure it would never become his habit. He missed the farm when he was sitting in the marquee; talked silage when dancing was the better fit. 'Where did you honeymoon?' I asked her.

Honoria gave me a questioning look. Perhaps it was a very improper question to put to my mother-in-law, we hadn't

Honoria, My Take

spoken for two years and never once before that. She glanced around the tent before answering. 'Whitby. A proper hotel there.'

Corrie and I stayed in our new house, Lower Bredbury, Stockport; I had taken on the biggest mortgage the building society would allow. My wage back then just enough to get us the front door key. Corrie was pregnant, of course. No Paris for us and no Whitby either. 'I'm jealous,' I said.

'Corrie tells me you never managed a honeymoon.'

She was clearly thinking down the same track as I; if she was about to rub salt into our modest means it would only lower her in my estimation. Money is like oil, greases everything around it nicely enough, nothing special in its own right. And all the hardship was behind us: we'd moved out to Marple, a better house than the tiny terrace. The bank loved my business plan; I was always confident my little car hire firm would come good. 'Life's a honeymoon for me. Just being with Corrie, with your daughter.'

Honoria nodded her head. 'You've rather taken her away from me.'

I didn't feel this was a fair comment at all. She wasn't describing the true order of things. Corrie's mother did nothing to hang on to her fourth child. Never stood up to Jeremy. He was always a hateful father. She could not have been ignorant of the fact and nor did her good manners mask the truth. Not from me, Cordelia's soulmate. God alone knows how the congregants at Honoria's church saw it. Or blind God. Her schoolgirl daughter running away with a farm labourer, I could see it might have been a tricky time for Honoria. I only shook my head.

'I know it was nothing personal, Simon. Don't look so worried.'

I didn't think I was looking worried. Couldn't see myself, so it was hard to be certain. Honoria never worried me, not once. On balance, I liked it that Corrie phoned her now and then: it was a nugget of normality. 'I'm sorry if you miss her. Sorry for you. We'll not be living back in Cumbria though.' I knew Corrie agreed with me, whether saying it at the fag-end of a family wedding was wise or heartless.

'She's done well for herself. Picked out a good husband, Simon. You do look after her.' I looked quickly into Honoria's face. She held my eye, hers were light brown, not as rich a colour as Corrie's. I never expected such praise. 'If Jeremy asks, I said you're both wasting your lives so far from God's country.' She gave a little laugh as she said it; I only frowned at the cowed comment. 'Love you and leave you,' she parroted, rising from her seat. I saw tears forming in the corners of her eyes.

* * *

I managed to locate the bed and breakfast in the darkness; drove Corrie and Leo from Ulpha to Broughton-in-Furness where we had booked ourselves a room a month earlier. Pulling up, I realised that it was situated across the street from The Boar. The very pub in which Corrie and I met each other back in the nineteen seventies. Night-time after a long day, and she was still the live wire she'd been since the car first crossed into Cumbria. I managed the checking-in process; the lady in charge had only a small reading lamp on in the hallway by which I had to sign the visitors' book. Corrie carried our sleeping son in her arms. When I had put the pen down, passed the lady the money, Corrie transferred Leo to me, I was to carry him upstairs. Managed it without rousing him. She took the small suitcase.

The lady led the way up, showed us to the room. A good standard of service considering it was after midnight. A double bed, a single to its side, all we could possibly need. She left, nothing more to show, and we became our tight little family for the first time since mid-morning. Corrie let out an overdue laugh.

'Look at him,' I whispered, pointing at Leo. He was already sleeping before we put him in the car at Low Fell, never woke all journey. It was hot in the room. His tie was off, shoes too. Left them back in the car. Tonight, our boy would sleep in his best clothes. He looked contented, exhausted. Danced out.

My wife began to recount the day blow by blow. She kept her voice low, alcohol slurring the occasional word. Said it was fortuitous that I stopped the car where I did, so that she changed clothes exactly where Bob Thornton came poking his nose in. I wasn't sure about it, a little embarrassing, he saw nothing terrible. She kept her essentials on; he saw something pretty terrific, that's a fact. If he'd kept it a private memory, she wouldn't have made such an ass out of him.

I pushed the curtain back a short way, pointed out the pub sign opposite our window. Reminded Corrie that it was where we met. She kissed me quickly on the lips. We had not talked of it in a long time but I'm sure it meant the same to each of us. Corrie loves me; sentimental expression she gives a wider berth.

'Sarah Pollard is a fool,' she said.

I told her that this was no longer Sarah's name and Corrie said it only proved her point. 'You were nice to her when Killian wouldn't dance.'

'And I've gone while she's on a train to Paris with Stone Heart.'

I thought Corrie right on every count. The groom seemed a pale imitation of his father, and Sarah may have less fight in her than vapid Honoria. The thought prompted me to ask if she had caught up with her mother. Corrie started to remove her clothes as she answered.

'We talked. She means well. Misses me. Suffers from a hell of a lot of inertia does my mother.'

She pulled the dress over her head. I saw what Thornton saw. The crest of her breasts within a black lace bra; her stomach, smooth white skin that I know I would shortly be kissing. I ran the back of my hand across it. Her knickers were black too. I'd unbuttoned my shirt. Corrie kissed my lips once more and I slid my hands inside her underwear.

The wedding, the Dalton family, the assorted farmers and Catholics of south-west Cumbria, were long behind us. I told Corrie that the two fingers raised during her father's speech was a triumph. She pushed her hands into my trousers.

'Forget that nasty fucker,' she whispered. 'Fuck me.'

10.

Now he's gone back to Leeds I hope the family will settle down again. The two boys get along great, I think, despite the ribbing, arguing. They never fight, never have and that's an achievement raising two growing boys under one roof. Something has upset Morty though. I wonder if it has been the to-ing and fro-ing with mediums, particularly the last one. He got under the skin of each of us. I haven't raised this thought with Corrie and the boy seemed to love it at the time.

We stopped going after Hyde: the Percival experience. Corrie's choice all ways up. I didn't ask her about it until a fortnight later. I'd thought she might wish to go again and not to any medium. I expected it to be another chat with Percy Townsend—and those in his funny phonebook—but she said once was enough. It was the evening Leo got home from university. A Friday. I collected him from the train station; he went out in the evening, once we'd eaten, saw some old sixth-form friends. Morty was at Karen's. I don't think it's serious, he doesn't call her his girlfriend. Both too young, they just hang out. Morty was perfectly well back then, three or four weeks ago.

'Do you feel,' I asked Corrie, 'that contacting your mother has run its course?'

We had the television on when I said it. There's a nine o'clock comedy we both enjoy. I was finding that episode a bit daft though; it might have been the writing or could have been me. Not in the mood for it; thinking about my wife's childhood can do that. Corrie leant across and stroked my cheek. She clearly didn't mind the question. 'I told her what I had to say,' she answered.

I felt a little unnerved by her reply. Percival was a master of his craft. Even his height added to the sense that the

Honoria, My Take

extraordinary was probable. I never really knew Honoria. Her presence was hard to feel back in the eighties, back when she was truly in the room. Now she's dead there's no chance.

'You thought he brought you together?'

Corrie ran a hand up through her hair, glanced quickly at the TV screen. 'Did you?'

'I never tried speaking to her.' Corrie turned her head back to me—her brown eyes flecked with black—the warmest of stares drank me up. 'Only managed it once or twice all those years ago.'

'You missed out on my mother,' she said. 'Really. For me, Tommie and Vinny too I expect, Mummy was the antidote to Daddy. When we were small, she had time for us. Brought us little things—treats—even if the old git had us in the doghouse.'

'It was more than the doghouse,' I said.

'True. He leathered us sometimes.'

'And she couldn't stop it.'

I wish I hadn't said that. I saw tears forming in the corners of my wife's eyes. She wasn't cross with me. I know how she has contained these feelings. It's the past that upsets not the reminders of it.

'I hated her because she couldn't stop it. I think she died just when I was seeing a bit past that. I never got to share the view with her. She wasn't one for talking about feelings anyway. My mother baked.' As she said this bland truism, I gripped Cordelia's hand firmly in my own. Wanted her to feel my closeness, feel heard. A skill Percival Townsend must have in abundance. 'She baked as a panacea. We can't really stop the north wind, can we? Baking is as good a remedy as any. Nothing works. It was stupid of me to hate someone for not having magical powers, for baking as an alternative. I think not spotting that has been the folly of all the Dalton children, one way or another.'

'But she could have left him. Taken you somewhere safe…'

'Could have, should have. Does a rabbit in a hutch picture a space rocket, Simon?' She shook her head in answer, crying more freely as she held my eye. Tears of relief, I thought, not entirely unhappy. Something inside was coming away. 'I've made my peace. I don't hate anyone now.'

I watched her a moment, noses inches apart, my hands upon her shoulders. 'Nobody?'

'Not unless you count those two fuckers mooching around Low Fell,' she spluttered, gripping my hand more tightly than I ever had hers, an anger still there. Not towards me, never directed at me.

* * *

Our Christmases are always pretty good. We have seen a little of family over the years. Never the unmentionables, of course, not since Leo was tiny-tiny. This year it was just the four of us. One year back we had my sister, Rosie, and her husband, Keith, around on Christmas day. Their boy was in Thailand and daughter at her in-law's house. This year we were to go to the Stapleys for Boxing Day. It was after Christmas dinner that Mortimer first complained about stomach ache. I feel ashamed that we laughed about it for a little while. Only took it seriously once we understood. Corrie gave him something to settle it anyway, we're not heartless. It just sounded to be the result of overeating; I felt terrible when I realised it was more than that. Making light of life's problems has never stopped us from being a loving family.

I was up with Mortimer in the night. He pointed to where the pain came from, never cried. Wincing all the time, suffering. Corrie and I were both for getting the doctor out on Boxing Day, cancelling the visit to Tommie's.

The on-call was an old man. Old enough to be retired but this one worked Christmas. He isn't from our surgery, a Hazel Grove doctor, not Marple. He was thorough, examined Mortimer on his bed although he'd been up and about earlier in the day. In a lot of discomfort, up or down.

Then the doctor asked me questions. His principal line of enquiry seemed to be anxiety. What was different this

Honoria, My Take

Christmas? That was his angle.

Leo at home was the major change. Dr Corrigan asked about that. The sibling rivalry stuff. I didn't buy it. Said it couldn't be that. Leo always tries to prove he's the clever one but it's not a big deal. Long ago he gave Morty the nickname Farm Boy. We've all laughed, Leo's funny with it. I pointed out to both my sons that this put-down belongs to me. I'm not ashamed of it, proud my kids are flying higher.

I didn't mention the séance stuff, Morty didn't either and the doctor asked him plenty of questions. It just seems possible. There is no connection between him and Honoria beyond the coincidence of one's arrival and the others passing. I don't mean reincarnation: utter rubbish, I rule it out without consideration. It's the way the life and death conundrum might prey on a teenager's mind that worries me.

Dr Corrigan prescribed something stronger than the over-the-counter remedies we'd tried ourselves. I had to run down to Stockport to fetch it. Get to the only chemist open on the bank holiday.

It seemed to work quite well at first and we saw Dr Murray at our local surgery before the seven-day course was over. The pains hadn't stopped though, came back before he took the next tablet and our doctor just ran a blood test and gave Morty another seven days on the same stuff. Neither Corrie nor I were happy with that.

Morty's not gone back to school. I weighed him on the third and again today. He's lost four and a half pounds and he started skinny.

* * *

The three of us go in to see the specialist. She's very smartly dressed, red-rimmed glasses beneath jet black hair, skin of the same colour to my eye. She has not seen any of us before, I'm not sure what our doctor has told her. 'Mr and Mrs Mortimer.'

'Tripp,' says Morty. 'I'm Mortimer. We're all Tripp.'

The doctor looks quickly at her notes, then back up at us. 'What a lovely name, Mortimer. I'm so sorry I misread your

Ghost in the Stables

names, Mr and Mrs Tripp.'

Cordelia waves the apology away. 'It's all right, doctor,' she says. 'Can I start by letting you know something we never got around to telling Dr Murray? I've worried that I should have owned up to this much earlier, feared it would be labelled satanic abuse or something. Most of last year I was going around mediums, people who think they can talk to the dead. I was obsessed with my late mother. It was silly really. My grief, nothing to do with Morty here. He and Simon...' She gestures towards me, at her other side. '...they both came along, supported me. Do you think I might have upset him with this nonsense? She died at the same time he was born, you see...'

Dr Tetteh puts her hand up at this point. I'm surprised Corrie has said it, we never discussed the matter. Surprised and pleased. We need to get to the bottom of whatever's wrong with Morty.

'Mrs Tripp,' says the specialist, 'I do thank you for your candour. I think you are worrying yourself up a dark alley, as you might say. I have the results of tests which Dr Murray initiated. Your son is very poorly, we need to bring him into the hospital. Run more tests, I'm afraid. Look right inside him. I am sure this is a purely physical problem, nothing to do with those activities you undertook. Nothing at all; I hope that puts your mind at rest.'

Corrie puts a hand to her mouth. 'What's wrong with him then?'

'We don't know for certain, Mrs Tripp. It is very unusual in a child of his age, so we wish to do more diagnostics.' She looks levelly at us, glances quickly at my son. 'We believe he may have cancer of the stomach,' she says quietly.

Corrie dives in to hug her son, I can see from her shoulders that she is in tears. Morty looks over her into my face. His eyes are the exact same shade of brown as hers.

'We'll see you through this,' I tell him, my hand on his shoulder. I will do whatever it takes.

Chapter Two

A Mere Waitress

1.

Stockport: it is an extraordinary square to have landed on. Simon says it is anonymous. If her parents really are looking for her, it is to London they will think the couple to have fled. That's where runaways are supposed to go.

They spent their first night here in a bed and breakfast, a dirty room atop a pub, just down the slope from the market. Newbridge Lane, cobbles and all. She did not enjoy her only night in a double bed with Simon. Liked that she and he were together once her guilt had subsided. The circumstances of it—becoming a fugitive—she could not enjoy. She cried, couldn't explain her tears. Relief. Simon used that word and she nodded. Did not wish to burden him with her multiple worries. Fear trumps relief in her pounding heart. It always has.

She was frightened of being rumbled, found out as a fraud. She has a small birthstone ring, a gift given by her mother years back, on her thirteenth birthday. It sports a fiery little garnet stone. She never used to wear it, so worried was she that it would click on the piano keys. From here—with no piano in sight—that feels a silly concern to have ever given houseroom. On fleeing Cumbria with her boyfriend, she placed it on her left-hand ring finger. Pretended to be the wife which no one in their right mind could believe her to be. She wonders what she's playing at—what they're playing at—Simon wrote 'Mr and Mrs,' in the guestbook that first night. Mr and Mrs Thompson, he used. They both agreed that Tripp would leave a trail and

Smith sounded plain stupid. Simon scarcely looks eighteen either, although it was his birthday on the day they awoke in that double bed. He said that she was his present.

Corrie is a child, a schoolgirl, pulled out of sixth form by circumstance, by fate. By a blue-eyed boy. It is slowly dawning on her that not looking married isn't the issue in Stockport. The prospect here is different to any she has known before. Ulpha so small it's scarcely a village, and Our Lady of the Rosary, her church in Coniston, a very partial perspective. What her headmistress, Sister Carmel, would make of it, Corrie doesn't dare to think.

She finds her fake husband resourceful. She hoped it might be so, took the chance. Simon is definitely the more grown-up; that becomes more certain in her mind with each hour they pass together. One way or another, both are learning fast. He secured them permanent accommodation after just one night in the flea-ridden Weavers Arms, the room above the pub. He found employment on the same day. A clever birthday boy. She singled him out at Young Farmers. The first two times she went, Ben Jones kept pestering her and so she stopped. Only returned when Vincent said a new boy had joined the group. She liked the sound of him. 'He's a young Yorkshire lad,' said Vinny. 'Not as rough as the ones from round here.' Simon looks nice and he doesn't show off. Only now and then. She is growing to love him, believes it truly.

The job Simon has secured does not embarrass Corrie. He cleans and polishes in a car repair garage. Doing it will enable them to stay away from Cumbria. She is never going back to Low Fell. It is written on her forehead, on the inside. She says it to herself about a thousand times a day. Maybe five thousand. Having a lover is an unstoppable rebellion. Gone for good, whatever way she looks at it. Gone to Stockport and no one knows they are here.

The pay Simon earns doesn't match what he made at Sark Farm. Not if the free board he enjoyed up there is factored in. They may have to economise until Cordelia finds work too. She likes history and literature, won the Cumbrian all-schools piano prize. How this will translate into paid work she has yet to learn. 'Fuck school,' she told him, when Simon came up with the plan they have now implemented. And she is a girl who used to enjoy studying, had an aptitude for it. It is her home life which she has fled. Couldn't bring school along, didn't fit in the rucksack.

The flat—and this, the first of December, is only their third day in it—is an odd thing. The upper floor of a tiny terraced house on a side street off Higher Hillgate. The front door is theirs, leads straight up the stairs. The place was once a three bedroomed house, one with an outside toilet. Corrie has deduced this, no one said it. Their front room, previously the principal bedroom, is the main living space. A single window stares out at the red-bricks of similar properties across the narrow road. The middle comprises a small kitchen which one must step through to reach the bathroom. She thinks this pair of tiny rooms has been fashioned from what used to be the second bedroom. The third room is a box. They sleep there, huddled together in a single bed. Simon has put only his name on the tenancy. It is a flat for one, her presence a secret. Leave no trail, raise no suspicions. Simon jokes that they live as outlaws when they have committed no crime. Corrie confuses crime with sin. A whole congregation she can never again look in the eye.

Sharing the narrow mattress with Simon is a wicked delight. She could have done none of this alone, would still be sharing a meal table with her unbearable father were it not for this handsome boy. Six inches taller than Corrie and still not a tall man. Slight, thin chest but strong of arm. It is the blue eyes, beneath unruly fair hair, and the expressive lips she most enjoys to look upon. And she makes sure he bathes. After working all day in the garage, Simon reeks of oil.

She's found the nearby Catholic church—Our Lady of the Apostles—big and austere. Victorian red brick; the largest circular stained-glass window she has ever seen. Two minarets rise up each side of the principal arch. It could be what she needs but looks like what she fears. And the boy is worth the confession time. Corrie is unsure whether to reconcile her actions with God. She has a growing respect for Simon's indifference to all things religious. This new sin is a good one.

The precursor to her momentous and life changing decision—skip school, run, share a home and a life with the son of an impoverished Yorkshire smallholder—was an assault, swear words shouted into her face, her father's nose barely an inch from her own. The stink of his fetid breath has etched itself into her memory. The buggering bastard—a name Vincent first allotted and one which suits Farmer Dalton all too well—had raised her school skirt with his left hand when hitting her legs with a coarse stick, so proprietorial is he of his children. He's always been the owner of their humiliation, hers and Vincent's.

She thinks she could have stuck it out. She was not surprised by the beating. Such events were infrequent but far from unknown at Low Fell. The same and worse had occurred three months before. It was obvious to Corrie that Simon was the one who couldn't take it even though he was not present when it occurred. Never visited her on the farm, save for a single moment on the doorstep. The couple have fled Cumbria to prevent the boy's transmogrification into a murderer. She thinks he would have done it; tried, might have succeeded. His thin frame bristles if the topic of Jeremy Dalton invades their conversation. Cordelia feels loved that he would contemplate such a selfless act for her.

Being a runaway has its downside. She hoped to go to the conservatoire. Failing that she might have read history at university. After winning the prize last April, she had started to believe a musical future beckoned, and now she will never learn if her piano playing is really good enough. Will never know if a girl similar to her in all ways but the father to run from, would have made her way into the music academy, fulfilled the dreams which Corrie has shed. She passed exams,

A Mere Waitress

ran out of grades to study close on three years ago. Such discipline is only a single strand of the brilliance which those hothouses seek. She can get nervous in front of an audience, might have let herself down at the assessment. She really should stop thinking about it.

Simon has never heard Corrie play piano, knows her as Vinny's younger sister from Broughton Young Farmers. They had a few furtive dates. And then this. He tells her that she would have got in easily, says music is on hold only so that they can escape from the crazy Daltons. She doesn't like him saying that; there's nothing wrong with Vincent. Even drunk, he is the gentlest soul. It's the others she cannot stomach.

Simon wants to buy Corrie a piano. He says that he will and she believes his intention while knowing how much good fortune it will take. It'll not happen in the nineteen-seventies, not by her calculation. It could be years before she plays again. She loved practice more than performance. Doing neither is a hole in her life; she must let it go, knows it and still fingers Clair de Lune on the kitchen worktop. She'd figured it would be this way— piano-less—when she told Simon she was game for his plan, his ruse. Agreed they should lay down their get-out-of-Cumbria-free card.

At night, when the tired boy is sleeping and she fretting, she fears fate might trick her back to Ulpha. Corrie cannot quite believe she will never again see the damp hills, the wooded glades. She pictures herself back inside the slate-grey farmhouse. How such a comeuppance might befall her is not revealed, in her fears nor in her dreams. Last night, he roused her. First, he was sleeping and she not, and then he was waking her up, said that she was shouting. In this poky little flat—just around the corner from a brush factory, close to junk shops the like of which she never saw in Cumbria—Corrie awoke with the smell of the stables in her nostrils. Wet straw, dung. She thought her blue-grey jodhpurs were upon her legs, only the grey-flecked stallion missing. Her horse no longer living even in her dreams. 'I'm sorry, Si,' she pleaded through tears. 'You need the sleep before work.'

'Corrie...' He spoke her name tenderly, kissed the lids of her eyes, '...you're bathed in sweat. Are you sure you're well?'

'I am now,' she said, her arms around the back of the boy who has delivered her from that place to this. Found her sanctuary, anonymity, a new beginning in Stockport. This funny corner of the world.

2.

I saw the advert, the postcard in the shop up the road,' she told the moustachioed man. 'I can do it, wait on tables.'

He leaned forward, touched her left cheek with the tip of his right index finger. 'You very young girl. You work in restaurant before?'

'The Boar in Broughton. English food but waiting on tables is the same in any language.' The man was looking into her face in the way that Simon likes to. Corrie has never carried plates of food to customers, remembered orders, or given out change. The Boar is the only pub she has ever been inside. Worked there not a minute. She knew that Mr De Luca would not doubt her; his enjoyment of looking into her face had already secured her the position, this conversation merely a staging post. She thought it the most mature of things to have spotted.

In the evening, Simon is delighted. 'You can do anything, Corrie,' he says. It must be the extra money that he is so upbeat about; she doesn't explain the excessive role her smile played in the interview. And a girlfriend waiting on tables doesn't sound much to Corrie's ear. She doesn't begrudge it him, wants to contribute. He works much harder than she ever has. In Cumbria he milked cows every morning, and again late afternoon, while she attended school. Nothing pooled back there, Corrie dependant on family. This need for money is a new experience. Food, rent. She feels light-headed knowing they are beholden to no one. She and Simon making their own way. Material wellbeing was never in short supply at Low Fell,

A Mere Waitress

not by a distance. Its absence is a release.

She thought today, before walking down Hillgate, looking for and finding work, how much money her father must be saving now he no longer needs to pay her school fees. He told her how much she was costing often enough. If there is any justice, he should remit these monies to her and Simon, give them a helping hand. Not that she'll be asking for it. Won't be communicating with the Dalton family for a long time. For all the time there is.

Simon asks about the interview.

'It's only waitressing, he didn't ask much.'

'You must have answered really well; you've never done the job before.'

'He thinks I have. Won't know differently unless I spill the soup or drop a pizza.' She sees Simon's expression stall then lift back up. A facial yo-yo. 'Are you shocked that I lied?'

He's smiling now. His ears move forward the tiniest fraction as his mouth expands. 'I think I am. You never lied to Sister Thingy, did you?'

'We're in this together, Si. I did what I had to, couldn't miss out on the chance of a job.' He beams back at her, a smile wider than she knows how to. 'And every girl lied to Sister Carmel. She demanded purity, Simon, but no one really is.'

Simon frowns again, the lined forehead. 'You're pure to me.'

Corrie thinks they are talking at loggerheads. Simon's blank page of dogma allows him to ignore her fallen state. It is very sweet, and he could be right, every pope an idiot.

* * *

For the first time, they leave the flat in the evening, walk a short distance to The Grapes, a pub just beyond St Georges church. She can see the narrow church steeple from the back of their flat, the small bedroom window. She likes its outline. It's not Catholic, same God most likely. Every inch of masonry covered in soot: lovely shape in a dirty town.

Simon leads her into the tap room, tells her drink is cheaper that side of the bar. Corrie is the only girl in the cramped and smoky little space; half a dozen tables up against the whitewashed brick wall, a plain concrete floor. He buys a pint of mild and half a cider. She has her hair in two bunches, not her usual style. No one asks if she is eighteen. No cause to, the answer couldn't be more straightforward.

While the couple are quietly drinking, the laboured push of piano chords carries to them from the lounge bar. A woman's voice begins to sing an old song.

Oh, oh, Antonio

She sees Simon grimace, thinks it a little ironic given his bland musical tastes.

Left me alone-e-o
All on my own-e-o

They sing along in the other bar, ladies voices mostly. The gents on this side—a couple with flat caps still on their heads—throw darts, stare into pint pots. She asks him why a pair of card players have matchsticks stuck in the holes of a small wooden block placed between them.

'Playing cribbage,' says Simon, surprisingly familiar with all things Stockport.

He tells her she should be playing the piano, Corrie shakes her head. 'I don't play the songs they like.' He looks puzzled, and she sees his point. It sounds like child's play.

The rough piano continues but a man's voice is singing now, crooning a song she recalls from the radio a year or so back.

I thought I saw my brother
Last time I walked into town
Just a man of a similar build
Just a man whose hair was brown

Simon whispers, 'Johnson Ronson.' The American rocker's sparse and haunting hit song. He might have it on cassette. The original involved only a single acoustic guitar accompanying plaintive singing. This piano rendition is quite funny, an approximation. Corrie listens more intently; her boyfriend has drawn himself upright, strains to hear the sound which carries from the neighbouring lounge bar. His lips move in synchronisation but he makes no sound at all.

> *I kind of saw my brother*
> *In a dream we were off to school*
> *He walked up ahead of me*
> *I had something stuck in my shoe*
> *There's always something*
> *Absalom, my brother*

Corrie tries to picture the way the pianist's hands strike the keys, contemplates the progression of harmonies produced. She is sure the piano player mistimes a chord change, does so at the same point in every verse. She asks Simon if he has noticed. 'Here,' she says. 'It shouldn't have gone to the major so early.' Simon shrugs: doesn't argue, doesn't know. Corrie has only heard the song two or three times, it is enough. Music imprints itself in a certain corner of her brain.

She is only days out of Cumbria, spent last Friday in the girls' school she has attended for three years. No goodbyes. She alone knew that the forthcoming weekend would be the longest, would never end for this one girl. She must be the talk of the sixth form; they can say whatever they like. She expects that her family will have quickly linked her disappearance to that of the boy beside her, Simon Tripp, although when he gave notice to his employer, collected his P.45, he told them he would be hitch-hiking to France. Smoke and mirrors. She worries that the plan is flawed: neither know themselves to be skilful at such deception.

When Simon asks her if she'd like another drink, Corrie shakes her head. 'We must be careful with money,' she tells him.

'Both working,' he reminds her.

'We are but I feel giddy, rudderless.'

He drains the beer at the bottom of his glass. 'I'm the pilot.'

Corrie smiles. She has jumped ship, left the mad captivity of that great steamer, Low Fell, launched herself upon the wild ocean in the tiniest of crafts. With a boy who loves her. She takes a hold of Simon's hand. 'Home.'

He rises from his seat, defers to Corrie. She likes that about him.

A short walk across the litter-strewn streets.

* * *

In the flat Corrie tries to play the grownup. Worries that it's a charade. On the way back here, Simon said they should save for a television. 'It's all rubbish on it,' she told him, then wondered if she shouldn't have. He wishes her a piano. In the kitchen she makes two cups of tea, brings them into the lounge. The boy looks bored. Corrie did not pull him from the pub just to make him despondent. 'There are plenty of other things we could do,' she says, opening the top buttons of her light-blue blouse, still wearing as she did when seeking work earlier in the day. She sees Simon's eyes alight upon her, smiles while not taking her eye. Slowly she undoes a couple more.

'Oh Corrie,' he says. She thinks his voice sounds smug and pleased. The sofa is old, wooden arms, he pulls her onto it, hands under her skirt, stroking her thick tights. She recalls a school assembly, Sister Carmel's warning. 'Boys would like to defile you.' The nuns were against it, she and Millie agreed it sounded all right.

The flat has barely warmed, although Simon lit the gas fire when they first arrived back from the pub. Corrie has allowed her impatient boyfriend to remove most of her clothing and there are goosebumps on her every limb. 'Back in a minute,' he says, stepping away. Goes to fetch what they will need from the packet in the cabinet beside their single bed.

He returns in no time but Corrie is crying, uncertain in her own mind quite what these tears are reporting. The flat still smells of previous occupants, of cigarettes. The couch is old, coarse to touch, stains upon it from which she recoils. Most of all, she hates the blotchy redness on the skin she seldom exposes, the bruising, the raised welts upon both her legs. The desire to tell Millie Green about life in Stockport produces a

A Mere Waitress

commentary inside her head, but she and Simon have agreed they will contact no one. Bridges burned. She has secured a job in an Italian restaurant. She is convinced that what she feels for Simon is true love. And still she cannot stop the flood.

'Have I done something wrong?' he says, 'I thought you wanted…'

She puts a finger to his lip; Simon is not the cause of her tears. A rescuer, and she fears appearing ungrateful. 'Sorry about this,' she says as he looks inquisitively at her. 'So much has happened.' Corrie wipes her cheeks with the heel of her hand, then curls herself into a ball. Her thoughtful boyfriend lifts her skirt and blouse from the floor, places them as if to protect her modesty. She smiles at him, at his kindness. Far from rejecting the boy, she is becoming comfortable with the outlandish intimacies they share, her newfound nourishment.

Simon leans down and picks his own underwear off the floor, places it upon himself. Hides the evidence of his intentions. 'Did I do something wrong?' he asks again.

Corrie guesses he can't begin to understand her emotions. She struggles, and they're hers. Back in Cumbria—weeks before this compelling physical dimension was appended to their friendship—he told her that he doesn't cry. Not when his mother died, not when his father hit him before that. He conceded that there was a time when he did, as there was a time when he wore short trousers. She has cried too many times in front of Simon, has struggled not to feel that she is drowning in her tumultuous life. Until this flat, she only ever lived in that imposing farmhouse on the hill. Attended a private school for three years; cannot remember when she first started piano lessons, so ingrained in her life did they become. A horse of her own at the age of six. The sadistic father is the stumbling block. Disfigures every picture. Within Cordelia Dalton the water table is high. She thinks that Simon avoids both the joy and the despair with which she is daily acquainted. She would like to accept life with the certainty he has, the boy fearless exactly where she is apprehensive. Corrie stands, letting the clothing upon her fall again to the floor, takes his hand and leads him to the tiny bedroom. As they walk, she stoops, kisses his naked chest.

* * *

She is still unfamiliar with them, the post-coital feelings that tingle within. She had thought he was sleeping. His eyes appeared closed but now he is watching as she runs a hand under the covers, nervously touching her naked body.

'Is it why?' he asks.

Corrie wants to agree with this boy, to affirm his assumptions. She is scared of falling out with him. Not of how he might treat her, she trusts him while still learning who he is. Simon Tripp, now her only friend in the world, the only person she knows for a hundred miles. At school she was not a popular girl but she had a set. A close friend in Millie, others with whom she got along. At home she and Vincent were thick. She has severed the cord—childhood incomplete—time yet to fashion her into an adult. Corrie was one of the cleverer students at St Aiden's School for Girls. For a time, she thought herself the very cleverest, modified that opinion after a heart-to-heart with Sister Carmel. A conversation which took place just a few hours before winning the piano prize in Carlisle. She saw then that book learning or musical performance are but single strings, she was far from the most mature: an honest self-appraisal, assisted by her insightful head teacher. She doesn't grasp the meaning of Simon's question, nor really wish him to fathom her tears more precisely than she can herself. Drawing Sister Carmel to mind while lying in bed naked with the boy feels all wrong. A nun wouldn't have the foggiest idea what she is doing here. 'What why?' she says. 'I'm not sure what you're talking about, Si.'

'You never told me why he did it to you the last time.'

Now Corrie connects Simon's ideas to the tears she shed before they made love. He is mistaken. She was not thinking about her father at all. Not as she recalls. She looks into his face—thin curtains, the light of a street lamp keeping the dark

A Mere Waitress

at arm's length—waits for Simon to tell her what is on his mind.

'Did he find out. I thought he might have found out what we'd done. That you'd given yourself to me. That could be a horrible association for you.'

She shakes her head. Her father beat her on a Tuesday, two days after the very first time they made love; Simon should know that the events are unconnected. 'He never found out,' says Corrie. 'Never found out about us at all. He believed I was at Millie's house. Doesn't know I've ever been to Sark Farm.'

'Didn't,' Simon corrects her.

They both believe Cordelia's flight from her family home will have prompted her mother—father even—to ask around her friend's families. They are bound to have uncovered that she and Simon continued to see each other. Her father thrashed her for associating with the boy back in July. Both Corrie and her brother Vincent led their father to believe Simon no longer in her life. A duplicity. Jeremy Dalton may have telephoned John Tripp. Not that he has heard of Corrie, they expect him to confirm to Farmer Dalton that Simon has no girlfriend. None which his son has seen fit to mention by phone or letter.

And this—Simon's failure to mention her in phone calls to his father—was a matter of consternation to her for a short time. An insecurity she has overcome. Almost. It is more than a month since Corrie asked him how much he had told his father about her. She felt hurt, an irrelevance, when he replied, 'Nothing.' It is the only time he has disappointed her and she has since come to think it a misunderstanding. She asked if this meant she was too young, not a proper girlfriend in his eyes. 'No!' he protested. 'My dad doesn't give a shit, so why should I pour my heart out to him?' Corrie struggled to understand this answer, tried to believe it was a fault in Simon's dim-witted father, not a reflection upon her.

Later the same day—perhaps with a point of her own to prove—she said that she wished to make love to him. It was more than a week before the opportunity arose, when she could

129

meet Simon alone at Sark Farm. His place of work and sleep. That it happened two days before the beating is a coincidence. She feels that only good has arisen from her decision to let him inside her. Their shared destiny.

'What was it then? What made him go so crazy?'

'I'd spilt ink in his little library when I was looking for Tippex. He said it stained the antique desk, not that it's worth anything. It's not a proper antique. That was his pretext.'

'Spilling ink!' Simon sounds shocked. 'It's insane. Why would he hurt you over a thing like that?'

Corrie guesses that he's not understood the pretext word. 'It was an excuse, Si. I've not spoken a word to him since he had my horse murdered...' Corrie begins to cry. She cannot talk of this matter—the most terrible event of a heady summer—without reliving the upset, her helplessness at that time. '...he can't stand my resolve, my determination. I can be as hard as him, Simon.'

He has wrapped his arms around her. 'You are not,' he tells her. 'You're gentle and caring, not hard. I get the resolved; it's a different thing. You put your mind to things. Piano or schoolwork. You aren't hard.'

She doesn't argue, nor does she know herself to be gentle and caring. It is her face which men misinterpret. Read into it whatever pleases them. It secured her the waitressing job this very afternoon. She thinks even their hightail from Cumbria must feel more romantic for Simon than for her. It is two weeks since the beating. When she was out of her father's clutches, Corrie ran briefly from the house, tears yet unquelled, she called Simon from the public phone next to the post office in Ulpha. The farmer's wife, Carol Browning, picked up—they don't know each other—went and fetched Simon. Corrie cried and cried on the phone, perhaps Simon imagined then that it was their act of love which caused her father's wrath. His explosion of rage. Beaten because she had given him her virginity. She sees how that might have been more explicable to him. Not that he would wish her hurt, Simon would never think that way. The act was the momentous thing. Deflowering, say the poets. A bottle of ink that the twisted old curmudgeon had forgotten to put the lid back on. For the nudging of it, Farmer Dalton beat his teenage daughter. A stick to her legs. For not speaking to him for over three months. She told herself that she was awaiting an apology for what he had done to her horse, yet no contrition on Earth could right that wrong. She was never speaking to the old bastard again. That was the decision; she could stand him no longer. Done with each other: her view, if not his. The exponentially rising bitterness of that father-daughter relationship tautened the arm that thrashed her. This kindly boy, her lover, has absconded with her. Pulled her from Cumbria for a better life. Poorer and better, definitely both. She did not tell him any detail, only that it was unbearable. And the antecedents might stretch back further than the girl can remember. Simon doesn't know the half of it.

'We have to sleep,' says Corrie, 'we've both got work tomorrow.' And she turns her back. It is a single bed; their flesh is never anything but connected when they lie together. She is trying to be more like her boyfriend. Trying hard not to cry.

3.

Corrie is surprised to find herself so nervous. Mr De Luca told her she is to work a trial shift, in her mind it's a piano exam. She never failed one, and still would find herself with trembling hands right up until she started playing. Only the sound she made finally convincing her that she has what it takes. Carrying plates should be simpler. Not that it was ever touched on in school lessons. He also told her to call him Antonio but she doesn't like to. He is old, older than her father. His face is kind; however, he has twice put an arm around her shoulders, and she has known him for approximately no minutes.

She carries two plates of lasagne to a pair of men at the corner table. The lunchtime special. They look like office workers, well-attired, one wears a broad floral tie, a splash of colour against his black pinstripe. Corrie finds herself smiling about the boss's name, the words of the song last night. All on his own-e-o. Serves him right, stupid octopus' arms. She wants to tell Simon all about him while fearing he will stop her working with the tactile Italian or, worse still, come down to Ristorante Ventimiglia and punch him.

The two men sitting at the table have a small graph in front of them. One is explaining its meaning to the other. Corrie used to scrape by at maths: good at fractions; logarithms were a slog. As she holds the plates of lasagne over the paperwork, gestures a landing request, the older man slides the diagram aside, keeps talking to his companion. 'I don't think we've got a chance of making the deadline.'

'Enjoy your food.' She says it brightly, hopes Antonio De Luca, standing at the rear of his restaurant, hears. Appreciates the skills that she feigns. Neither customer looks up, bonhomie wasted on this pair.

One other waitress serves alongside Corrie today. The volume of custom is not high: they see diners to tables without making them wait; call in orders promptly. Mr De Luca pours the drinks from a small corner bar. The kitchen is a nightmare. She cannot recall the chef's name, Mr De Luca introduced him but spoke very fast, she didn't grasp it. His name is Italian; everything about the place is Italian except her co-waitress, Kath. The chef is an ugly man and—far, far worse—a bottom pincher. When she secures a better job, she will think seriously about setting Simon on him. De Luca treats her well, he's just more tactile than she is comfortable with. That's Italians, she assumes. The nameless steak fryer disgusts her. When she was standing by him, as he sliced a pizza into its eight segments, he looked up, finger on his own cheek and said, 'Kissy.' She shook her head. It was sufficient to ward him off this time.

She ferries drinks to tables. Businessmen like red wine, she learns. The waitresses make discreet eye contact with any silent table. Pave the way for further drinks orders, the dessert

A Mere Waitress

menu.

When there is a lull, she and Kath stand together at the back of the room. 'How are you doing?' says the older waitress. She's much taller than Corrie, thin and wide-shouldered, a similar build and age to her sister, Thomasina. There the similarity ends: Kath wears green make-up around her eyes, flecked with silver, her lipstick a brighter pink than Corrie thought good taste back in Cumbria. Her opinions are currently undergoing modification, adapting to the urban.

'Is he always like that?' Kath looks bemused, doesn't seem to register what the rookie is referring to. 'Chef. Does he pinch your behind too?'

'Oh, him. He'll feel your titties if you let him. Just the thing if you're between fellas.' Kath laughs quietly, Corrie hopes it is a joke.

* * *

By two-thirty, Ristorante Ventimiglia is empty, the chef is having a cigarette round the back, Mr De Luca counting money and another old Italian—who has yet to lay a finger on her—is washing pots. While she is in the kitchen, Kath takes off the deep-red dress which the waitresses wear, her jeans and sweater on a coat hanger hooked to the back of the door. The washer-up does not so much as turn around. Corrie thinks he would have, had he guessed a near-naked woman was stepping into clothes behind his back. She is more discreet, takes her carrier bag of clothing into the ladies' toilet. Requires its privacy if she is to change her clothing. The cubicle is the tiniest space, makes a simple task difficult.

When she returns to the restaurant, Corrie sees that the chef is back from his smoke. He and Mr De Luca talk together in Italian. The owner switches to English, clearly intending her to hear. 'Teodoro, you must have the last word. Do we hire the girl—this Corrie—you like her?'

She feels insulted that the molesting cook is having the final say, thinks it might be a joke. Cannot yet read Mr De Luca.

'I like-a the face but she no kissy-kissy,' he says.

133

'Ha,' smiles Antonio. 'The job is yours, Cordelita. Now give the chef a kiss or he downs the tools.'

Cordelia stands frozen on the spot. There has never been a kissing culture amongst farmers. It took Simon weeks to find the courage. The cook stinks of frying oil and cigarettes, he is more than twice her age. More than twice her weight.

Mr De Luca smiles, stands still, does not change his expression. Teodoro laughs, points at his cheek. After an age, the manager says, 'Do you a-want this job or a-don't you?'

She and Simon need the money. Corrie kisses the revolting cook quickly on the cheek, in and out like a cuckoo clock. The ugly man laughs. Antonio De Luca pulls money from his jacket pocket, a couple of notes, and passes them to her. 'Tomorrow, no need to kiss,' he says. She nods, feels a palpable relief. 'Tomorrow lunchtime please, then lunch and evening the day after. And again, on Saturday. Both of the shifts that day, please. Double pay Saturday, very nice. Busy and nice. Remember to tie the hair back before you come inside. Thank you, Cordelia.'

The girl nods again, vigorously this time, says not a word. She leaves by the front door; as she steps onto the pavement it swings closed behind her. Corrie spits into the kerbside. There are hours to kill before Simon comes home. She wanders up Hillgate, stops at a newsagent, scours the postcards in the window. Advertisements. Might there be a less humiliating job that she can pretend to have the skills for? They tell of caravans to rent in North Wales, second-hand bicycles for sale, a lost cat. Antonia De Luca of Ristorante Ventimiglia remains the only employer using this obscure pitch to secure his workforce, his waitresses.

She continues up towards Charles Street. Treads on damp newspaper that litters the way. Her shoe slides upon it; not much, she steadies herself, retains her balance. Greasy old chip paper. She looks into a display window, sees second hand electrical goods staring back at her. A food blender, a hair dryer. Even through the dusty window pane she can see a loose wire or two. The price tags reveal that her trial shift could buy her a lot of faulty goods. Extraordinary. Does Kath really let the revolting chef touch her chest?

Stockport is not a sheep farm.

4.

She nicks the inside of her index finger with the potato peeler. It rankles that she is not more skilled at this. Corrie has no piano on which to practice but damaging a finger in so mundane a pursuit feels careless. Vegetables to boil, some liver to fry, not tasks which should get the better of her. The glistening meat looks disgusting, she expects it will improve with cooking. Her mother would prepare it with apple; Corrie thinks Simon's preference lies elsewhere. He got a bit self-righteous when she described how Honoria served gammon. 'Pineapple is for pudding. Tinned cream or custard. Normal people don't eat fruit with their meat.' She has packet gravy for him today, may introduce him to finer things when she is surer of her ability to prepare them. She can manage this before his return from the garage. Potatoes mashed in advance, the frying of liver will be done while he bathes, transforms himself. His aroma swings between car oil and carbolic soap. She thinks that Carol Browning—the awful farmer's wife at Sark Farm, Simon's Cumbrian workplace—might have prepared him nicer food than she has yet managed. Her own mother's cooking was a cause for celebration; dinner parties rare but successful. Honoria rolled pastry, hung pheasants in the kitchen in season. There could be three or four strung up there right now. Corrie never ate them. Not birds shot for sport. She runs her finger under the tap, keen to have no excess blood upon the food but that of the calf it came from. Her boyfriend likes his meat, although she feels a little sickened by the handling of it. With her undamaged hand she pushes back her hair. The Alice band she usually wears is on the small vanity unit at the foot of their bed. She thinks how she and Millie laughed when—aged fourteen—the two of them took biology and chemistry options, leaving the lower-stream girls to their so-called domestic science. 'Preparing themselves for a life chained to the kitchen sink.' It was Millie who said it, and Corrie believed it a truth. She clings on to her world view but the skills she lacks have a certain currency. Might have kept her hands scratch-free.

She lights the ring with a match, puts the pan on. The potatoes may take an age, they are very large; she halved a couple so they sat properly under the salted water. Cuts the cauliflower as carefully as she is able. Tries to keep the shape of each floret, then fails to attain even that small domestic goal. At least she does no more damage to her hands while butchering this vegetable. Corrie is unsure how long it takes cauliflower to cook through. Puts it on the hob, boil and hope. She will push a knife in to check. She used to help her mother with the cooking now and then. It's hardly Rachmaninoff.

The doorbell sounds. Corrie steps very quietly to the top of the stairs, glances down from there. She can make out a figure waiting on the other side of the frosted glass. She knows no one in this town and nor does Simon. It could be a knife grinder or one of the Jehovah's Witnesses who pester people down here. Kath laughed about them during a lull in the shift, said it happens often; none knocked at Low Fell, a little short of a mile from the next property and an ill-tempered Catholic within. She steps lightly back into the kitchen. Does not resume her work, wants the caller to leave without guessing her presence. When she hears the exterior door opening, she feels confused. Only Simon has a key and he would not have rung the bell. She goes back to the top of the stairs, her heart thumping. At the bottom stands a fat little man. She feels terrified; her mouth goes dry. Corrie heard no wrenching of the door or breaking of the lock but a man has been able to enter. She hasn't shared her worries with Simon, that they appear to be living in an unsavoury side of town: chip papers on the roadside; every other person shabbily dressed and not because they work with sheep or cattle. The farm where she has lived her life until now

A Mere Waitress

is remote, she expected to be the poorer judge of these matters, trusted Simon's composure. This is the worst confirmation of her fears.

The unasked-for visitor looks up at her, the hint of a smile coming to his lips.

'I'll scream,' Cordelia calls down the stairs at him. 'I really will.' She ratchets up the volume as she expels these trite words.

'And who are you?' asks the man, his voice quiet, gentle. The opposite of her blasted bark.

'I live here.' Her voice stays loud. Call-the-police loud.

'Not to my knowledge,' he replies. Then the little fellow touches the side of his head, doffing a hat he does not wear. 'Bob Curry, landlord. Your name please?'

She feels flustered by the calmness of her intruder, by the apparent logic of his entry. It is the man's house, not hers, and a scream will not alter the fact. 'Mr Curry,' she says, buying time, trying to think how to deal with the situation. He must not discern that the two of them are on the run, hiding from parents and she still only sixteen. 'I'm visiting, preparing food. Would you prefer to come back when Simon is here, please?'

He stares up at her, his half-smile does not indicate whether he might fulfil her wish or not.

'I'm sleeping on the settee,' she adds. Unnecessarily, she quickly realises: a landlord is not a priest.

He continues to look at her from the hallway. 'I'm renting it out for one,' he finally says. 'May I come up and look around my property, please?'

She says nothing until the man starts to ascend the stairs, then the right answer comes to her. 'Be my guest.' She must act like nothing's wrong, encourage him to think the same. It is barely a plan, just the best she can come up with.

The man arrives at the top of the stairs, he is shorter than she, not even five foot three. Corrie finds herself trembling, her fear obvious. When she realised a stranger was in the flat, she thought of the murders and muggings which Cumbrians associate with Manchester, with urban life. Now she fears only being outed: a schoolgirl masquerading as a housewife. The fabrication she has given him—lounge-dwelling cookery enthusiast—sounds implausible even to her. She steps from the landing back into the lounge, Mr Curry does not follow. He slips into the backroom, their bedroom. She suspects he is collecting evidence of her deceit. The bed is presentable, she does that much each morning. Tucks in the corners. The pyjamas and a nightdress which snuggle together between the two pillows are out of view. Just so long as he doesn't rummage. On the small mirrored vanity unit, a man's deodorant, a girl's lip balm. Sleeping on the sofa was a stupid thing to say.

'Mister Tripp and yourself are…?' The man has entered the lounge, addressed her vaguely. Corrie says nothing, rearranges trinkets that stand on a cream-coloured shelf above the gas fire, a make-do mantelpiece. They are his, not hers, the flat's more inessential furnishings. A small porcelain tea cup and matching saucer, a plate, cutlery, all the size to suit a doll, not that they are for children. Mary Donnelly, in the tied cottage back at Low Fell, has the same on every ledge. Collectables, she calls them. 'What is your name?' he tries again.

'Cordelia Judith Dalton,' she states. A reflex: registration time at St Aiden's. The fear that her name might be known to him jumps into her throat. But their flight from Cumbria has not made any radio news she has heard.

'Well, Cordelia Judith Dalton…' There is a faint loosening of his broad accent, a corralling of his diction as he pronounces her first given name. '…what is your relationship to Simon Tripp.'

'Brother…friend. He's like a brother to me.'

Bob Curry steps a little closer, looks into her face from six inches distance. 'I don't share a bed with my brother,' he says.

Corrie holds her non-committal expression, knows that a little extra blood has moved up to her cheeks. In her mind she feels proud to be Simon's partner, he looks nice, looks out for her. She is embarrassed by it only in real life. Having the world know you are doing those things for which expulsion from

A Mere Waitress

school, the ire of Father Benedict, would inevitably follow.

'More than a brother,' says Corrie. 'Please believe me, we need to live here. We only have each other.'

'I'm a landlord, Miss Dalton. People living here is good for business. The place is in a better state than I expected. Clean. You're a house-proud girl, Miss Dalton. I like to see that in a tenant. I set the rent for your Mr Tripp. The rent is set for one man to live here. Now I find myself renting to a young couple, I think a small rise is in order. Would you like me to discuss that with Mr Tripp?'

'Sir, please let us stay. Stay at a price that's fair to us. Simon works hard, and our jobs earn us only a little. We'll get more when...' Cordelia's plea tapers away. She does not wish to boast but Simon is more than a farmhand. She thinks him very capable, only cleaning a garage to get a foothold in Stockport. She secured seven A grades in her exams last summer. Waitressing is her first job, just getting the feel of work. She tells none of this to Bob Curry, this funny little posity with an unwelcome hold over them. She wants to tell him to have a spray of Simon's deodorant but it would be of no more benefit than her initial impulse to scream for the police.

'Shall I come by in an hour. Will your Mr Tripp be home then?'

She nods, she would like Simon here. He's wrong about gammon and pineapple but he's still the more practical of the pair. Wouldn't have let this fat little man rattle him.

* * *

Simon praises her cooking and Corrie wonders if such ordinary fare is all he expects from life. She loves his honesty and certainty. Cannot explain how he endures the lustreless music on the tapes he has brought all the way from Cumbria, his funny penchant for science fiction over proper literature. Is her life to be one of following his lead now? She thinks this question may overrule sleep tonight.

'I shouldn't have told him my name,' she says.

'It's okay, Corrie. No one can make you go anywhere. I

reckon your parents know it.'

She thinks about this. It is not how they have talked before this moment. Told themselves that they are only a clever step ahead of an ensuing posse. This second week feels different to the first, Simon might be on to something. 'Mummy will have told congregants that I've gone to the convent.'

Simon laughs. 'Sent away to mend your ways and you so sweet, Corrie.'

She ignores his comment, has no feelings towards her father that fit under the guise of sweet. Few towards Cumbria. 'She will say I found my vocation. It must be unthinkable to Mummy that I would do what I've done…' She looks him in the eye, the faintest of smiles upon her face. '…done with a man to whom I am not married. Beyond her comprehension. She will never break her marriage vows, never speak ill of Daddy. And I sometimes think he might have treated her worse than he did me.'

Her smile slides away; reflecting upon those she has left a hundred miles to the north is a sombre act. He stands from the table, hugs her, repeats her name quietly, 'Corrie, Corrie.' There is a loud rap upon the door below. 'Do you want to leave this one to me?' he says.

Cordelia shakes her head, instantly composed. 'We're in this together, Si.' Rising from her seat, she gently pushes him back into his. Still food upon his plate. She skips to the top of the stairs, shouts, 'Coming,' and takes them two at a time, slows before the bottom, remembers she is no longer a child. 'Mr Curry, do come in. This is a good time for Simon and I. Perfect, I'd say. Thank you so much for coming out of your way.'

The tubby little man looks bemused by her performance. He shakes the girl's hand but it is she doing all the pumping. He might be meeting a different girl: she has ambushed him this time.

Corrie takes the stairs back up, beckons the landlord to follow, a crooked finger and a smile. In the lounge-diner Simon rises and Bob Curry extends a hand which he takes. 'It's a fine

A Mere Waitress

flat, Mr Curry,' says Simon. Corrie loves this lie. Flattering the self-important little man. They are vying for a little purchase in the world. Will not slip from this first rung.

'Yes, it's one of my better ones,' he states and Corrie has to look away. Her lips have upturned at the thought of the other dross he must let out if this is his finest. She would like to share the thought with Simon, fears he would hear criticism of what he has brought her to, and she intends none.

'Look, I need to apologise. I always hoped my girlfriend would move in, it's just that when I was signing...' Simon doesn't finish the sentence and Corrie thinks him very crafty for not doing. Why explain when the man can surely visualise the circumstances. A girl may once have turned Bob Curry down, or may even have accepted him. Who knows what prospects he offered long ago, before his waistline took on the profile of a hula-hoop.

'I have flats for two but they're a sight more expensive, Mr Tripp.'

'We've no wish to move, sir. We like it here.'

'Yes, but I can't fit a double bed in that room...' His eyes glance out of the doorway, towards the back of the flat. '...and they're darned expensive, you know? Doubles.'

'We're okay. Corrie's a thin one, me too. We're okay with everything as it is, sir.'

Bob Curry looks directly into her eyes; something Simon said has piqued his interest. 'Corrie, eh? That's not what you called yourself earlier today, is it?'

She points at her own breastbone. 'My full name is Cordelia Dalton, that is the name I gave you. Please call me Corrie, Mr Curry.'

He turns back to Simon. The man is a fool who can neither recall a name nor recognise an abridgement. 'As I said, Mr Tripp, it was let out for one, so I think there needs to be a rent rise seeing as how two of you are living here.'

'Mr Curry...' Cordelia will not be ignored. '...you said earlier that it is tidier, cleaner, than you expected. It's the same flat whether one or two live here and you will see that my meticulous upkeep bodes well for its long-term maintenance. I think…' She waits, Simon says nothing, and in due course the landlord turns his head to the girl doing the talking. '…I am good value. My presence, my housework, is beneficial to your asset, and we are already paying the expected rent.'

Bob Curry looks from one to the other, she detects lightly panted breaths. The man is running out of steam. 'I've come to speak to Mr Tripp, not to argue with you, love. It's irregular, having two in this flat. Not the way I've done it up until now. You clean it nice enough, I have to grant you that.' He turns to Simon. 'Ten shillings, not a big increase, ten shillings.'

'An extra fifty pence?' Simon has a smile on his face. Corrie touches his shoulder. She feels they almost silenced the little money-grabber, and now the expression on Simon's face will have confirmed what he needs to know. Fifty pence will not break them.

The two men shake hands. Mr Curry says he will drop off a revised contract in the next few days.

When he has gone, let himself out, Simon casually seated at the table as he was throughout, excepting the brief handshake with the fat man, Corrie kisses the top of her boyfriend's head. They feared a far more troubling outcome than this. Eviction. And they took the flat before she had secured any work at all; they will be better off than first thought. Twenty-five pounds a week better off if the tips are as good as Antonio De Luca says.

5.

'It'll be forty minutes before the doctor can see you,' says the receptionist. And this after Corrie has filled out a long form, written out her full name and date of birth, completed a short history of her health. Box ticking and crossing, vaccine confirming and tuberculosis denying. 'There are a lot of bugs about,' adds the woman on reception by way of explanation.

Corrie picks up a couple of magazines from the central table.

A Mere Waitress

They are not pointed at her generation. Women's magazines describing the art of table laying, the baking of scones. She looks at the front covers. Wonders if her mother subscribes to them, cannot recall seeing either title at Low Fell. The old farmhouse was awash with magazines. Farming, horses, flowers. Even a body-building monthly that Killian took. Not that you could tell from the look of him: strong of arm but never toned, her eldest brother; corduroys and a chequered cap; an old man at twenty-five and a farmer to his core.

She sits beside a small play area, a low table strewn with plastic bricks showing a different letter on each face, several picture books in an open wooden holder at floor level. There are no children in the waiting room, she sees, then ponders if there is actually one. Does she still qualify for the description? So many thoughts stuck in St Aiden's School for hidden-away Catholic girls. And she really isn't going back, not after today.

When it is time to see the doctor—after a full hour of day dreaming, page turning, feeling her nerves tighten and contract—her tongue dries up. In a squeak of a voice—far from the confident, 'Would you like to see the wine list?' with which she regales the customers at Ristorante Ventimiglia—Corrie says, 'I've come for the contraceptive pill.' She wonders if Dr Jay picked up the word contraceptive at all. Cannot confirm if she heard it herself. Her lips went around it but she neglected to expel air. 'Contraceptive,' she tries again and reddens from the saying of a word so unambiguous in its intent.

'You're a new patient to us, Miss Dalton…' He looks closely at his notes, studies something on the front page of the lengthy form she has completed. '…I must tell you, we are never keen to prescribe anything before we've established a few baselines about your health. Understood your body.'

Cordelia stares back blankly. She saw the doctor in Broughton-in-Furness a time or two, has no recall of the man singling her out for unique appraisal. She presumes her body behaves as the textbooks predict. Corrie says nothing at all and the old doctor finally glances away, back at the form she

143

completed earlier.

'I see you've just moved into Charles Street, Miss Dalton?'

'Yes.'

'With your mother and father?'

'No. I've left home. I'm working now.'

'Really? I imagined you were at school.' He glances again at her form. 'Very neat handwriting,' he mutters. She has heard teachers tell her the same. Guesses it will have little bearing on today's quest. 'What is your work, Miss Dalton.'

'Waitress. It's on the form. I'm a waitress in a restaurant.'

Dr Jay has grey hair, a thick head of it. Eyebrows still black. Lines of age criss-cross his face. 'I think it is wisest to examine you before we prescribe anything, Miss Dalton. We have no prior knowledge of your health. Are you happy to undress for me?'

To her horror, Corrie's cheeks colour deeply. He's a doctor, not a chef, and they can make such a request. Her thoughts are exclusively of the welts and scars upon her legs. Thick tights hide them; they are fading slowly. 'It's only a prescription. Not for being poorly. I'm not sick, doctor. I'm fine but…'

'I see.' The doctor puts two fingers to his own brow. 'I think it might be best if I asked Dr Machin to examine you and talk to you about the prescription. She's a lady-doctor, Miss Dalton. Would you rather she examined you? You can discuss your request with her.'

Shyly, Corrie nods. She is not sure how it might prove better in practice. Her legs will reveal the same story. To let this grey-haired man examine her would be an unbearable intrusion. His tone and demeanour are not unkind; she knows the problem is within her mind. Attached to a past she has no wish to speak about.

'Can I go to see her?' She wonders if it will be any easier to persuade a lady-doctor to prescribe this needed pill without seeing her unclothed. Perhaps she will be happy to listen only to her chest, the most the doctor in Broughton-in-Furness ever did.

A Mere Waitress

'I'll just call reception,' he says lifting up a telephone on his desk. Dr Jay speaks into the phone, requests the appointment. 'I see, I see,' he says. As he puts down the receiver, he arranges his face into a forced smile. 'Tomorrow evening,' he states. 'I'm not familiar with her working hours. Dr Machin isn't here today, I'm afraid.'

'I'm working tomorrow evening,' says Corrie. 'Can you prescribe it, please, and I'll see her when I...' She lets her request fall to nothing; the old doctor is shaking his head. Corrie concedes the matter is not urgent, not life or death. 'I want it soon,' she says. She has already exchanged Cumbria for Stockport, St Aiden's for Ristorante Ventimiglia. This pill is a part of the plan. The doctor calls reception again; Corrie's shifts prevent her from seeing the lady-doctor for three days. On the plus side, the delay affords time for her bruising to heal. 'I hope I haven't offended you?' she says, lifting the small handbag she carries from the floor beside her chair.

'Not in the slightest. You will like Dr Machin, she's closer to your age than mine. Thank you for your forbearance, Miss Dalton.'

* * *

Simon listens carefully. She thinks he is disappointed, must use shop-bought prophylactics a little longer. 'Well done,' he tells her and Corrie looks up at him, eyes narrowed. She is not a schoolgirl, not for more than a week.

This conversation takes place as he walks her home from the restaurant. He has come out at ten-thirty, a mile from the top of Hillgate to the bottom, to collect her. He said that it is unsafe for her to walk back alone at that time, promised he will always be there at the end of her evening shifts. 'Fetch you home until we've got you a job more fitting.' She liked that turn of phrase, has yet to pinpoint what such work might entail.

As they approach the Red Bull, she sees a large gaggle of men on the pavement. One or two hold pint glasses in their hands. Corrie nudges her shoulder into Simon, points out that they could cross the road. He puts an arm around her and guides her through the throng. The men part; there is no argument, no disharmony. Pavements are for everyone, Stockport no less hospitable than Broughton-in-Furness, than Coniston. She thinks it a sight bigger though.

'How was it?' asks Corrie, Simon's after-work task coming into her mind. Pete, the garage owner, promised to take him out, a first driving lesson and at so nominal a charge he jumped at the chance. Simon has handled tractors since turning eleven. Baled all the hay at Sark Farm for the last two summers. He says cars will be easier, more responsive.

'He thought I was good.'

'Did you find it the same?' Even Corrie has driven a tractor—not working day after day as Simon has—across the fields, towing a trailer to take animal feed up to the sheep and cattle. She has done so only with her brother, Vincent, perched in the cab beside her, teasing her. 'You've squashed a rabbit, Corrie. And another one.' She'd squeal when he said it, hated the thought that she might have, while knowing her daft brother was only teasing. Corrie the only Dalton to spare feelings for every creature in the fields.

'Cars go much faster,' Simon intones.

'I've spotted that.'

The smell of cooking oil and vinegar assaults them as they pass a fish fryer. Corrie feels slightly sickened, the same harsh scent emanates from Teodoro's kitchen, the bottom-pincher's lair. 'Have you eaten?' asks Simon.

She has. The entire shift eats thirty minutes before they start work. It is the Italian way, she has learnt. Manager, chef, waitresses and washer-up, all eat something hot that Teodoro has rustled up. No one labours on an empty stomach in Ristorante Ventimiglia. 'Spaghetti Bolognese,' she confirms.

He pulls a long face, looks closely at hers. 'Really? You've no tomato sauce on your chin. Don't fancy a bag of chips, do you?'

'Have you not eaten?'

'Tinned soup.'

'I put out corned beef and pickles. It was plated up in the

fridge.'

'I missed that.' He smiles at her as he steps over the threshold into the shop. 'Are you sure?'

She shakes her head, follows him in. Simon asks for steak pudding and chips, adds gravy when the girl behind the counter suggests it. Corrie knows they can afford this indulgence. The rent is no trouble now they both earn. Driving will open up horizons for her boyfriend, and he reckons he can take the test in March. Once the girl has served him—an acidic smelling newspaper of food passed across the high counter—they walk rapidly back to the flat, a further half a mile. Corrie like a limpet on his left arm, supper keeping warm inside his coat.

6.

'Mangiare!' says the ever-groping chef.

Kath has failed to turn up for the evening shift. It is only a weekday but Christmas is in sight, many tables booked. At the staff's pre-shift meal, the men are tucking into their steaks. It is a small extravagance which Mr De Luca allows his employees from time to time. Corrie finds the bloody pink in the centre of the meat off-putting. She is feeling a growing disdain for everything Teodoro Massimi touches except her own person. Even a little of that for not fighting back.

She eats the broccoli spears and a little of the strange potato concoction that he has put on her plate. It smells sharp, rosemary she thinks, garlic is in there too. Inevitably. Corrie tries a piece of meat, a thin slice cut from the edge which she thinks less red. Properly cooked. Then she cannot bear it in her mouth. Feels foolish removing it with her fingers, putting it on the side of the plate.

Teodoro laughs himself red in the face. 'As crazy as Kat,' he says, unable to accurately pronounce their missing colleague's name. Cordelia, he rolls around on his tongue, as he might if she were his dearest lover. She resents his every utterance. The chef is a toad with status only in his sweaty fiefdom: the kitchen where he caresses the dead meat. Corrie apologises for leaving food, tells him she has only a small appetite. 'And I cook it for you with a-love,' he declares.

She regrets smiling back at his ridiculous phrasing, at finding his Italianised English as funny as he is odious. Her grin prompts the man to point suggestively at his cheek, to pucker his own lips as he invites her to kiss him. Hardly quid pro quo for the undercooked steak. 'Not from me,' says Corrie, 'I only wait on tables.'

Antonio De Luca is watching her, listening to the exchange. He looks untroubled by it: kissing the chef is not in the contract. The cash-in-hand outside-the-books contract that she doesn't have.

* * *

The shift is the busiest she has worked, or perhaps it is Kath's absence which makes it feel that way. Corrie writes each order in her tiny note pad. She learnt all the Italian spellings for food by her second day. Teodoro says that she is the best waitress he's worked with in this country. Praise she can live without.

It appears to be a romantic night in Ristorante Ventimiglia. Couples occupy every table except the large round one in the front window. There, a family busy with children—a lone grandparent looking bewildered by their antics—sit together. Many tables have candles upon them, not all. At a table without, the gentleman asks Corrie to fetch one. She asks Mr De Luca where she can find a spare candle, and he makes it his business to fetch it. Light the wick. He flatters the lady diner, promising her a 'dinner fantastica.' She smiles at his words. 'You will see,' he says. 'Dinner fantastica, you will see.'

Most customers order the pizzas no matter what pep talk Antonio De Luca gives them. A few older diners will go for steak but it's pricey. Corrie is starting to think her writing pad a distraction, unnecessary. She could be a clairvoyant waitress. Pizza, pizza, lasagne, steak. If Kath were here, she would spend time at each table saying how lovely the food is, describe dish after dish until the customer finally bags a Four Seasons. She

A Mere Waitress

must enjoy the chat, limited as it is. And Kath only picks sparingly at the staff meal, same as Corrie. Textbooks and music scores she studied diligently just a fortnight ago, now these mind-numbing transactions over food are the sum of her occupation. Corrie knows these thoughts may detract from her performance. Tries to concentrate.

'Due birra,' she tells Antonio, pointing at the corner table. 'Una grande, una piccola.'

Her boss answers in Italian. It goes over her head but he laughs. 'You a clever girl, Cordelita. Waitress in Milano in no time, si?'

She smiles back; the boss's appreciation lifts her mood. He matters as the chef does not. Pays her wages; keeps his hands to himself for the most part.

Tonight the work is relentless; she never stops, never sits. The old washer-upper has a 'grazie' for each pile of dirty plates she brings. The chef sings her praises, pinches her bottom, sings her praises some more. The tips are a plus. She shows Mr De Luca the pot at the end of the evening. It contains almost six pounds. There is no Kath to share it with and the owner counts the money and then opens his palms—'very nice work tonight, Cordelia,'—and passes it straight back to her. She tries to take it nonchalantly. Fails. The grin on her face too wide for him to miss. 'You like to work in my ristorante,' says her employer. His tone does not require an answer, it is an observation.

'Mr De Luca,' says Corrie, feeling emboldened by the weight of coins in the bowl of her fingers, 'I don't like being touched. Having my bottom pinched.'

He holds up his hands. 'Miss Cordelia, I don't a-do that, do I?'

She finds herself laughing at him, not unkindly. 'The chef does.'

'Teodoro? I speak to him, yes. He has gone home. I speak to him tomorrow. He has a wife. You think I should speak to her? Yes? Mrs Massimi. The wife of Teodoro. She have important opinion about a husband a-touching the girls' bottoms, I think. I speak to Mrs Massimi. Yes?'

'If you could speak to him, please? It isn't necessary that you speak to his wife. Not yet.'

Yesterday evening she was telling Simon that she agreed with the CND movement, the campaign for nuclear disarmament. Just getting rid of the weapons is the most conclusive way to ensure they are never detonated. Don't kill those who have done no wrong. He tried not to turn it into an argument but clearly wasn't on board. He said maybe the country should keep them 'just in case.' This has given her a glimpse of his viewpoint: no deployment of Mrs Massimi, she remains the merest push of a button away.

When she steps out of kitchen door, up the side passage to the road—Simon waiting in front of the restaurant for her—Corrie is in fantastic spirits. She shows him the plethora of coins, retrieves them from her coat pocket. 'Six pounds and that's just the tips.' He takes that as reason for the bounce in her step. Corrie had feared she would cry about the chef. Give Simon a reason to punch him, or stop her from doing the job she's found. Now she has enlisted Antonio De Luca to sort the problem. No hullabaloo required. She likes Hillgate, likes it enormously. The display windows of all the closed shops they pass are cluttered with the most fascinating junk.

The second-hand world.

7.

She has removed everything except her underwear and Dr Machin is frowning. 'I bruise easily. I tripped on a style before we came to Stockport.'

The doctor looks at the girl's notes. 'You've only been here twelve days,' she observes, and the girl nods at this truth as best she can from the prostrate position in which she lies. 'The marks look weeks old, Corrie, but you didn't trip.'

She introduced herself as Cordelia and this young doctor

A Mere Waitress

asked, 'What do your friends call you?' A simple question and one which implied she was angling to join their number. Now she is frightened that Dr Machin will prove no friend at all. Will want to interfere in a problem that Simon Tripp has more than solved. She and Simon together.

'It doesn't hurt,' says Corrie. 'I came here for the contraceptive pill.' Earlier—this morning, after Simon had left the flat for the garage—she contemplated how to approach this important appointment. The phrase, "it's my bloody right," had sounded an attractive way to show she was a woman not a girl. Now, with the fair-haired and serious doctor—who has listened to her chest in the time-honoured fashion; asked a question about sexual partners that made her blush like a traffic light; took her blood pressure; made notes about her menstruation; and advised that her health is excellent but for these bruises on calves, shins, knees, even a long red welt upon her right thigh—she finds no wish to swear, worries she will again go home empty handed. She can see no connection between the marks on her legs and the prescribing of this pill, but Corrie is not a doctor.

'Have you been coerced into coming here?' asks Dr Machin. 'The man you live with, he hasn't registered with us.'

'Simon? He will but he's so healthy. He's not needed a doctor. I've not needed one either, except....' Her voice tapers away, she has no strategy with which to make this lady relent.

'But he sent you here to be prescribed the contraceptive pill?'

'Yes... No. He didn't send me. I...' This is a disaster. The adult world remaining stubbornly beyond her grasp. '...I'm almost seventeen. It's my right. We talked about it. Both wanted it.'

Dr Machin takes Corrie's hand in her own. 'Simon. What is his full name?'

'Simon Roger Tripp,' says Corrie.

'Did Simon Roger Tripp inflict these injuries upon you, Corrie?' The timbre of the doctor's voice deepens for the saying of the boy's name.

151

Corrie is wide-eyed, Simon no villain. 'He would never do that, doctor.' She looks into Dr Machin's searching face, sees her smooth white skin, fair hair tied back into a narrow pony tail. 'He would never harm me.' She feels frustrated; the doctor would trust her boyfriend if she met him, anybody would.

'Somebody has done this to you, Corrie.' The doctor places a hand upon the back of her calf, a thumb grazes over a still-raised welt on her shin, red from the bleeding of four weeks past.

'We came to Stockport to get me away from the man who did.' As she says the simple truth—still avoiding talk of Low Fell, of the place she fears this doctor will wish to send her back to—the assertive voice in which she practised this conversation breaks completely. She turns her face away. 'My father's a bastard,' says Corrie quietly. She has never spoken such a phrase in front of an adult before. Said it feebly and yet it feels a bolder step than asking for the contraceptive pill.

'Your father?' Dr Machin inches closer to her patient. 'What did he...?'

'A stick. He has a lot of sticks.' Corrie explains both the sporadic and the ornery nature of the beatings she has received. She went almost a year without enduring such an event. Then there were three. It all proved more than could be borne. 'Simon saw it more clearly than me,' she tells the doctor.

Dr Machin nods keenly at this. 'He sounds like a good boy,' she says.

'Man.' Corrie has found her voice. 'It will never happen again. Can never happen again. Simon has helped me get away from there. From Cumbria.'

'A good boyfriend,' observes Dr Machin. 'And the wish to have relations, sexual relations, it is shared?'

'I look young doctor but I know what I want. I've always spoken for myself.'

The doctor advises that she may re-clothe, talks through the implications of the form of contraception she will prescribe. 'Other precautions will be needed until the required point in your cycle is reached,' she tells Corrie. This is not a surprise, a magazine told her the same.

On leaving the surgery she feels taller, grown-up, the Catholic church losing its traction upon her. The euphoria of running away with Simon almost two weeks ago is again coursing through her veins. Her choices validated and by a doctor, a concerned and educated lady. Corrie has told her the whole story, no wish to tell another soul but it felt right. Final.

Dr Machin did not ask for the names and phone numbers of those she has left behind. She filled in the box on the form for next of kin, one Corrie had left blank. Wrote Simon Tripp's name in there although they are not married. Corrie could have cried. Dr Machin requested the name of the doctor who saw her last, in Broughton-in-Furness, spoke the single word, 'Confidentiality,' when Corrie raised the need to keep her whereabouts private. It has been a fairground ride but this visit couldn't have gone better. 'Simon Tripp must register with the practice,' says Dr Machin, adding 'when he's ready.' Corrie would like the doctor to meet him, to see for herself how wise she has been to throw in her lot with that boy. He cleans up in a garage right now, she thinks he'll get his full driving license in no time. She doesn't like to boast but he loves her.

8.

At the owner's insistence, Corrie brings Simon to join her and nine others who will all eat the pre-shift meal at the Ristorante Ventimiglia today. There are a couple of other partners present, although Teodoro Massimi's wife is not one of them. Antonio De Luca is at the helm, a radiant silver-haired woman by his side. Corrie never guessed him to have a wife, unsurprising as it now seems. He is a most personable man. The gathering will enjoy an Italian Christmas dinner—just the main course— before donning aprons, wine-red waitress dresses, working the Boxing Day shift. Every table is booked: a single sitting, fixed menu.

'Very good food, a-lovely food,' Antonio confirmed when she asked him what they would be eating. His comment only repeated what Teodoro had already said. She has never trusted the chef; cannot stomach his steak.

Corrie asked around, learnt that it would contain no turkey breast, no roast potatoes. Not a sprout. She explained this to her boyfriend, he only laughed. 'You're kidding.'

Simon slides into the chair next to her, having shaken the hand of everyone present. There is an air of expectancy through which Teodoro brings forward dish after dish, each reeking of fish, and many of a shape and appearance which Cordelia finds a little scary. She worries about what her boyfriend makes of it all. The tiniest octopi scattered among a salad. Black shells with colourless squishy clams inside, butter and garlic vainly trying to make them palatable. Strips of unnamed white fish sporting capers like a rash. When questioned by Corrie, the sweating chef tells her it is swordfish. This prompts Cosmo—a waiter who arrived from Naples only a week ago—to hold a table knife in his right fist, and direct it outwards from the bridge of his nose. Entertaining only himself with this childish display.

The Italians around the table love the food, it is their Christmas fare. Corrie and Kath only pick. She watches Simon; Teodoro has joined the table in the chair next to him. She fears the chef may say something inappropriate. His alternative to bottom pinching—which stopped once she raised the matter with Antonio—is to murmur mildly obscene suggestions. His tone never expects compliance; he has learnt his place but not how to cease venting the lewd thoughts which occupy him. When he said, 'You see me naked, I think you no like,' and she replied, 'You've hit the nail on the head,' he made her waste five minutes explaining the idiom. Only later did it dawn upon her that he was searching for some sexual meaning which the phrase does not harbour. She keeps telling herself to say nothing, holds her tongue most of the time, but his pleas and observations are so pathetic they can draw an involuntary smile. She has told Simon none of this, imagines he would be

A Mere Waitress

furious, insist she must withdraw from his pernicious company. The restaurant has become a haven to Corrie, a source of income and a little self-esteem.

Teodoro explains to Simon what is on each plate. She hears her boyfriend complimenting one of the white fish dishes, watches as he loads his plate with pasta and greens. She doubts that he will sample anything from a shell. Ate no such aberrant creatures in his Yorkshire childhood.

Antonio asks Simon about yesterday—Christmas day—asks if he visited his family.

Corrie quietly forks food into her mouth. This Christmas she and Simon made love three times on the same day. Like no yuletide she has ever imagined. Their love for each other was the principal reason, while having nothing else to do ran it a close second. She enjoyed what they did, likes how Simon treats her physically. The day's most unexpected turn—valued for the insight it afforded her into the boy who is becoming her soulmate—was the twenty minutes they spent entwined inside a telephone box. It is a space intended for one; their close proximity was unavoidable. They were both clothed in the kiosk, it provided respite from the love making.

Simon said he was going to phone his father and then his sister, unless she was at the farm and he could talk to her there. Corrie was silent for a moment. They have avoided all contact with family for fear of giving away where they are, exposing a chink of light which Jeremy Dalton, or his sidekick Killian, might latch on to. There must be no avenue down which they might drag her back to Low Fell. Unknown to Simon, Corrie sent a seasonal card to Millie Green, the friend who played a role in keeping their relationship on track without her parents' knowledge. It was a last-minute decision, she has yet to hear back, but Millie finally has an address to write to. Her new home on Charles Street. It feels liberating, no longer beholden to her volcanic father. Still the season turns her thoughts to Christmases past. Simon's too, she realised.

Her boyfriend turned the dial, pulling the number of Penton

Farm, Aysgarth, not from his memory, it seemed, but from his fingers. She used to twiddle out early Mozart pieces in that manner, that effortlessly. She felt a little trepidation looking on. John Tripp has played no role in Cordelia's life whatsoever, may not know of her existence. Simon has told her that his father is 'thick.' How he might appraise his son's conversion from farmhand to garage labourer, countryman to town dweller, from single man to the keeper of a lover, she could not guess.

Simon bent his legs, lowered his torso, allowing Corrie to put her ear next to his, to hear both sides of the conversation. They are together in this world.

'Six, one, seven, oh.'

'Dad, hi. It's me, Simon.'

There was a brief pause before the man said, 'Simon. I expect it's happy Christmas then.'

'Yes. Happy Christmas to you, Dad.'

'I was just thinking about your mum, son. It's been four years, you know? Four years and a week.'

Corrie tugged on her boyfriend's sleeve, her other arm around his waist, under his open windcheater. She never sees his grief, never senses it. Feels certain that it is in there, nonetheless. She thinks incessantly about her own mother, who never raised a finger to protect her and enjoys the kind of rude good health that Simon's probably deserved more.

'We all miss her, Dad,' he said. Corrie felt it was a cliché, a phrase he has used before, not that she has ever heard him say it.

'Now, Simon, lad, you've been out of touch.'

'Sorry. Yeah.'

'I heard that you'd gone to France. Couldn't believe it. My boy in France, that doesn't sound likely, is what I said to myself.' Cordelia tried to look into Simon's face; they were so close to each other in the tight space she could not gather his expression. She thought it might be deft to confirm the lie, to say he was calling from there. 'I even hear you might have a

A Mere Waitress

young lady in tow. I'm not sure whether to believe that one, Simon. Or what to think about it come to that.'

'Who have you talked to, Dad?'

'I can talk to whoever I like, can't I? My last call was to your William Browning. A fancy farmer, I call him. A lot of funny ways, that man. He told me you'd gone to France and he didn't think there was a girl involved. He said that he'd had a mister Killian Dalton come to his farmhouse to talk but he's never seen you with no girl. That pushy what-have-you, he phoned me every day for a week, as I recall.'

'Who was pushy, Dad?'

'The Dalton man, Killian Dalton.'

'Do you still talk to him, Dad? To Killian Dalton?'

'Oh no. I told him many times, I don't know where you've gone and it's your business not mine. Had me worried, mind you.'

'Why? Why worried?'

'Taking a girl out of school sounds a bit rum, Simon. When the chappie finally told me she was sixteen, I felt quite relieved. You can do as you wish, Simon, but I'm not one as wants to be visiting prisons at my time...'

'Please,' the boy interjected, 'we're almost the same age.'

'Aye, you're both very young and I gather you're with her then?'

'She's called Corrie, Dad. I'm with her...' He turned his face into hers, so close their noses met. '...I love her. I wanted you to know. But please, can you promise me...'

Corrie listened—the declaration of love was the sweetest melody—but, broadly, she did not enjoy hearing Simon being a son, something short of the stalwart on whom she has leant so heavily. He implored his father not to pass any information to the Daltons, awaited the modest promise like wheat asking reprieve of the scythe. It was simpler when they cut themselves off. That Killian did the visiting, the phoning, not her father or mother, took Corrie quite by surprise. Last night, while Simon was sleeping, she worried that her parents may have had strokes or heart attacks. Poor Honoria.

That notion resurfaces, as she picks half-heartedly at the Italian Christmas dinner—most of the noise in the room is a language she cannot understand—an event of great contrast from all this will be unfolding at the fellside farm from which she has fled. Provided their health has held.

Simon tells Mr De Luca that his family live too far away to visit. He says that he had a little chat with his father and his sister. Spoke to them by telephone. When questioned, he confirms that his mother passed away some years ago.

'I'm so sorry,' says Antonio. 'I think you grow up quickly, become a man, just to cope, when this terrible thing happens to a child. God bless you, Simon.'

He accepts the comment graciously. In these short weeks since arriving in Stockport, Simon seems more mature than the boy she first met at Broughton Young Farmers. Just turned eighteen and he has a career as a farm labourer behind him, quickly learning the motor trade. What losing his mother has done to him, she thinks to be far more complicated than Mr De Luca's simple equation. It is not grief but running away which has forced him to grow up. Grief has buried itself within him: it is a box in the attic, the unexamined contents awaiting a time he might have the fortitude to look at what he has lost.

When all the staff, Simon too, have finished their meal, and Corrie and Kath are clearing away the plates, Teodoro asks Simon to follow him into the kitchen. Cordelia worries something untoward will happen between them. Thinks the dirty old man might ask questions about their sex life, or for a photograph of her in a swimsuit. Questions she has already batted off but the chef is persistent. She follows them in, saying she has left hair grips on the side and then pretending to search for them.

'Simone,' he says, Italianising the name as he likes to do with hers, 'these people must work, not sleep, you will have the trifle, yes? Very finest Italian trifle.' She knows about his sweet tooth; Simon will not refuse. Corrie has to go back into the dining

A Mere Waitress

room, lay tables before the paying guests arrive. While doing this—wine glass, water glass, two knives, two forks, soup spoon, dessert spoon plus tiny fork, serviette—her heart is pounding. She cannot recall a conversation with the greasy man in which she mightn't have punched him, were she the kind of young farmhand with little restraint which Simon is proving himself not to be.

Mr De Luca opens the front door, greets the first diners. A couple with teenage children, the mother is Italian-looking to Corrie's untrained eye. She uses their arrival as an excuse to dash back into the kitchen. 'People to serve; you have to go, Simon. You mustn't get under Mr Massimi's feet.'

'No hurry, what-a the hurry,' says Teodoro. 'They look the wine list. Talk, talk. Soup is starter, all in a-this pot.' He places a fat finger on top of a gigantic saucepan. Withdraws it hurriedly so hot is the lid.

'Have you heard his funny stories?' says Simon. 'The stuff he got up to when he was our age?'

She shakes her head, leaves him eating his pudding. The chef befriending Simon was not a development she ever anticipated.

The shift proves to be enjoyable; the mood is buoyant. Corrie takes plates back and forth from the kitchen, finds Simon alternating between drying pots and eating more of the bottomless trifle. He has nowhere else to be this bank holiday.

After they have served desserts in the restaurant, Kath leads the singing.

We wish you a merry Christmas
We wish you a merry Christmas

All the staff have come to serenade the guests. Corrie is surprised how good Kath's voice is, she matches it while being careful not to exceed, not to show off. Still, she notices eyes upon her; Mrs De Luca, who has been as cordial a host as her husband, beams at her youngest waitress. They do not know she was once conservatoire bound. Not a racing certainty but she might have made it. Teodoro stands with the staff as they sing the song. His food has pleased the diners but he does not move his lips. Cannot sing.

Simon pops his head around the door; she glances at him while singing demonstratively. Feels it is her voice that has drawn him away from his trifle.

* * *

In the evening they watch an Ealing Comedy—black and white—not that their TV could facilitate other colours were there any to show. Simon bought it for five pounds from one of the second-hand shops on Hillgate. It sort-of works. He's relaxing with a tin of beer; her feet are across his lap. Simon gently rubbing her calves.

'He said the Italian navy was full of queerios. Sailed backwards and forwards to Buenos Aires about six times. Moved into the kitchen because the work was easier. Spent every journey keeping clear of the queerios.' Simon laughs as he relates all that the simpleton chef has told him. 'He said, in port, half the Argentinios were just as la-di-da.' He makes a hand-flopping gesture, implies that a vast proportion of men from the Argentine are effeminate.

'It's just silly boys' talk,' says Corrie. 'Just because he wants to belittle everybody, doesn't mean I want to hear about it.'

Simon stops stroking her legs, looks at her then quickly turns away, back to the television.

'I don't like hearing you talk that way.'

Simon is silent, appears to be concentrating on the film. 'Uh-huh,' he emits after a pause. It might be concurrence, it's a little vague.

She wonders if it is a mistake to put her foot down. They've had no arguments before now, and this is her only home.

Simon rubs her calves once more. Glances across at her, an initially serious face, raises his lips into a smile when she meets his eye. Corrie returns it, feels exceptionally grateful for his continued warmth.

9.

Early in the new year, on a Sunday night—the restaurant closed this day of the week—they have a pre-arranged social engagement in the White Hart on Shaw Heath. Simon's employer, Pete Conway, is at the bar when the young couple arrive. Corrie invited Kath, sees her sitting alone at a table, not known to the others in the party. She gives her colleague a wave. They get drinks at the bar, pull a couple more chairs up to her table. Kath is drinking rum and coke. Asks for another when Pete offers.

They chat a little, the two girls together, although Kath and Corrie have little in common beyond waiting tables. Pete and a mechanic from Chapel Motors talk cars with Simon; the mechanics wife seems to be listening into Kath and Corrie. Before they have done much more than sip their drinks—crisp packets still unopened—a man in a sharp grey suit comes to the table. He looks even older than Mr De Luca, ruddy cheeked, an army haircut. He says—directed quietly at Corrie alone—'I don't believe you're eighteen, young lady. I have to ask you to leave.'

This gathering is not to celebrate it—Simon and Corrie keep themselves to themselves—but the Wednesday to follow will be her seventeenth birthday. He shouldn't quibble about a single year and doing so in front of these new friends is embarrassing. 'I'm here to play the piano,' she tells him. Always an eye for them, instinctively aware when there is one to hand.

'It's the first I've heard of it,' he says. 'I'll ask.' Without waiting or debating, he steps away. Goes to speak to the lady with her hair in a bun who works behind the bar. She must be in charge, the person who can confirm the lack of substance in Corrie's assertion.

The others around the table look at her with surprise.

'Are you?' asks Pete.

She gets up from her seat, walks to the piano and tentatively lifts the lid. Sitting on the stool, she touches a couple of keys, hears that it is serviceable.

Corrie begins to play the Moonlight Sonata. The pub is too noisy for so languorous a piece, however, one or two people sitting close to her stop talking, watch and listen. This piano is not as responsive as the grand piano she used to play in her Cumbrian home, or even the school and church hall pianos she performed and won awards upon. She bashes the keys more than any tutor of hers would have approved. It is the wish of this pub piano.

Simon has come to stand beside her. A page turner perhaps, although the music is all within her head and "Thump It Out" not an instruction Beethoven wrote upon the original notation. With her increased vigour, the noise rises above the conversations. As she glances at her boyfriend, she notices several drinkers turning around. Corrie brings the piece to a natural but premature close. Simon applauds, his table do the same and so do a few others in the pub.

The man in the grey suit is walking towards her but Corrie goes straight into another tune. One she has never played before; her knowledgeable hands have fingered a likely arrangement upon her kitchen table when it played on the radio.

I thought I saw my brother...

She projects her voice quite powerfully, as she long ago learnt to do. Pub-goers look up from their tables. The song was a big hit a year ago. Corrie struggles to remember the words; she sings the first verse twice before Simon joins in, only very quietly, prompting her to sing the second and third verses correctly.

Although I don't know where he is right now
Last I heard he'd gone to sea
Trawling shrimp off the Greenland coast
October nineteen sixty-three...
...Absalom, my brother

A Mere Waitress

It is music and not words which she attends. Only now, as she tries to put in the feeling that might befit a pub singer, does the image of Vincent enter her mind. He is the only member of the Dalton family whose absence hollows her.

The man in the grey suit waits, a frown on his face, as she sings the song to completion. Her note-perfect singing cannot melt this stern man. Many of the drinkers look enthralled, attending this pop song far more closely than they did the classical piece. When she brings it to an end the pub applauds, a couple even cheer. They can see that she is a child, a talented child. The clapping takes time to diminish.

The man steps in closer but looks around when he hears a call. 'Wait!' The woman from behind the bar—glasses with a thick black frame, face heavily made up, a bun of black hair dyed the same shade of charcoal as the frame of her glasses—puts a hand on the man's arm. 'She's very good,' she tells him. Then she addresses Cordelia. 'We never booked you, love, but I wish we had. Play a dozen songs and we can give you a couple of pounds.' As the lady from behind the bar speaks the man is saying something to her in a low voice. 'And obviously you can't drink. Only soft drinks.'

'And I can stay all night with my friends?' she asks.

The woman glances around; the grey-suited man points to their table. 'Alright, no alcohol.'

Corrie asks if there is any piano music in the pub. The woman disappears through a door marked private, returns in thirty seconds carrying a couple of books. Corrie scans them, smiles to herself and then begins an extravagant rendition of Daisy Bell, adding tremolos that do not belong. Her embellishments sound funny, accentuate the corny tune. She thinks it bubble-gum music. Radio One for pensioners. She sings only quietly, the ladies in the pub—the older ladies in particular—join in. Let rip about a bicycle made for two.

When, after several more songs, she finally comes to sit down, the table give her their own extra round of applause. Corrie feels embarrassed. She ended with Claire de Lune and the pub lost interest. Simon says it was her best; Pete contradicts him. 'No, it was Absalom.'

Kath agrees, her enthusiasm etched into the higher pitch at which she confirms, 'Absalom, My Brother: that one was simply fantastic.' Corrie sees her boyfriend nodding, knows that Johnson Ronson and Templeton Ca. form the core of the music he chooses to listen to. It was kind of him to praise the Debussy.

Kath asks her a lot of questions about music, where she practices.

'I've not been able to since we came down here. I don't have a piano.'

'But you must have played them before?'

'Only the classical ones.'

Kath wears a look of astonishment, near open-mouthed. 'She was just making up the tunes,' she tells the table. 'Absolutely fantastic.'

Corrie tries not to grin. She put a lot of work into this performance, not lately, but a lot of work none-the-less. Music was her haven before the discovery of Stockport.

10.

They are not really huggers and kissers but at Stockport railway station, platform three, Corrie will not let go of Millie. There are tears in her eyes, so long has she craved this reunion.

'I've missed you,' says Millie, although it is Corrie who has clamped herself upon the other girl, hugging her as tightly as she ever has Simon.

Millie has brought a small suitcase which Corrie offers to carry. Deploying a little insistence, she takes it from her friend. Finds it heavier than anticipated. 'We'll take a taxi,' she says. In the past both girls were ferried to each other's houses in their mother's cars. This visit may prove an education to the visiting Cumbrian. Leaving school in a hurry has been one revelation after another for Cordelia. They take turns carrying the case as

A Mere Waitress

they walk through the small tunnel to exit the station, emerge into the bright sunlight of the early-April afternoon. They say nothing to each other as they walk this short distance. The catch up will come, they are reacclimatising to the once-familiar atmosphere of each other's presence.

Corrie feels sophisticated, ushering her friend up the taxi rank. 'Are you free?' she asks, and the driver leans across, flicks his sign over to occupied.

'Need a hand with that?' The driver is eyeing the suitcase.
'Please.'

He emerges from his taxi, puts the case in the trunk. The two girls sit side by side on the rear seat. Millie wears a long red skirt, pink blouse and smart black jacket. Corrie pinches the skirt between finger and thumb. 'We're a bit scruffy in Stockport,' she says, although she has been wearing denim since turning twelve. Town or country, unless school, church or ristorante demanded better.

Millie can only stare at the crowded urban thoroughfares. The taxi makes the short journey up Wellington Road, turning onto Higher Hillgate, then Charles Street. 'Is it all like this?' she asks.

Corrie nods, unsure what the quality is of which Millie discerns there to be too much. It is drab, lacks the beauty—the seasonality—of South Lakeland. She and Simon have made it their own. He has, since Tuesday last, been the owner of a full driving licence. Training to be a mechanic in the garage he previously only cleaned. She's a fixture on the piano in two different pubs, three paying nights every week, no practice required. Still a waitress, mostly lunchtimes; evenings if Antonio is short-handed. She has told Millie all this, written it in letter after letter.

When the taxi drops them at the flat and they enter, climb the stairs—Corrie still carrying the small and heavy suitcase—she feels her mood flatten. This is a far cry from the well-heeled Cumbrian homes in which they met before her abrupt departure. Her friend walks around the small flat, a few paces take her into every room. She picks up one or two of the trinkets on the mantelpiece above the wall-hung gas fire. No words come, and Cordelia has no idea what Millie makes of her new life.

'Simon won't be home for a couple of hours.'

'You really did it,' says Millie.

They listen to the drip of a tap. Corrie steps into the kitchen, twists it tighter.

'I did as you said, never told a single girl in school.'

Corrie nods as she returns to the lounge. She trusts Millicent Green implicitly. Millie was instrumental in the deceit of her parents, helped the couple meet without her father suspecting it was occurring. Corrie chose not to burden her friend, worry her unnecessarily. Never shared with her the plan she and Simon were hatching. One Monday morning, months ago now, Corrie simply failed to arrive at school. The detail was in the Christmas letter Corrie sent to Millie. Probably figured out the broad sweep when she saw the empty desk.

'They all said you were shacking up with a lad. It's what all the girls guessed. I said you wouldn't do that; trying to throw them off the scent. Before you started seeing Simon, I'd have never guessed you'd be the first one from our school to live in sin.'

Corrie frowns at the phrase. She has confessed her living arrangement to a priest, did so before her seventeenth birthday. A quarter of a year has passed. She is moving around to Simon's view: love cannot be wrong. The puffed-up farmer masquerading as a pillar of the community, a patron of Coniston Catholic church, while treating his daughter like a gun-dog, that is the deviation. There are some sins in there all right. She doesn't suppose her father ever confesses them. If he started, he would never leave the booth. 'What I've done isn't wrong. Not to me it isn't.'

'I wasn't being religious,' says Millie, 'it's just how we say it, isn't it? My parents know it's what you've done.'

'And they've told mine?' asks Cordelia. A furrow of the brow,

A Mere Waitress

worry back in her tone.

'No. They're on your side. Mostly.' Millie pushes both hands through her jet-black hair, shakes her head a little as if trying to loosen something in her mind. 'They know how your father is. They're just surprised that you started...' Millie hesitates, looks away from her friend. '...living in sin.'

She seems unable to find another term, although Corrie liked the shacking-up phrase Millie attributed to other former school friends. 'Do you still see that boy?'

'Patrick? Yes, funny, isn't it?'

In her letters, Millie has told her that she is dating Patrick Vulliamy. Corrie remembers him from church. He and Simon seemed to get along at Broughton Young Farmers, the very group in which Corrie first met her boyfriend. Patrick is a couple of years older than Simon. She's wondered if Millie's relationship might also be a physical one, hasn't tried to pry, to force her into the light. Not by letter and they have yet to find any of their former intimacy. 'Why funny?'

'He thinks that the two of you have disappeared together. He knew Simon was after you at that club you all went to. When I said I thought it was a coincidence you'd both left the area on the same weekend, he laughed. "Lovers in the south of France," he says.'

'So you told him?'

'I'm keeping your secret, Corrie. I said I would and I am.'

Corrie has an uncomfortable feeling; it is as though her friend is living a shadow life because of her, not committing or sharing with this new boyfriend. All this pretence because of a past promise. The need to keep secret something as ordinary as Cordelia Dalton and Simon Tripp moving to Stockport, making a go of living together. It feels convoluted now although secrecy was Corrie's opening plea in that Christmas letter. Over time she has been telling doctors, restauranteurs, pub landlady's and even their overweight landlord. Cumbria is the unforgiving place.

Corrie is disappointed to learn that Millie's parents—

attendees at the same church as her own father and mother—are judgemental of her decision to live unmarried with her boyfriend. They might be the only other Cumbrians who know it is true. They must have understood the reasons why she left. Millie told them very honestly of the beating Corrie received, her father's disposal of the horse she loved. They were entirely on her side last autumn. If they do not approve of her lifestyle, it's the dogma of church that's diverted their good sense. At least they understood why she didn't honour her father. Allowed her that much selectivity in her obedience to the tenets of the church.

The two girls share anecdotes: Millie's are mostly of life in Hawkshead, Coniston, St Aiden's School. There is nothing really new in them but Corrie loves to hear about the places she now visits only in her dreams. Corrie tells her about Simon's job, goes over the story of Bob Curry visiting the flat in December. Describes her work in the pizza restaurant, piano playing in the pub. In January she wrote Millie a detailed account of her first week or two at Ristorante Ventimiglia, told her more than she ever did Simon about how she enlisted Mr De Luca to intervene, free her from the unwanted attention of the ugly chef. How proud she felt when Kath Palin said, 'Well done,' on learning that it was through Corrie's intervention that Teodoro no longer pinched her bottom either. The intimacy she enjoys with Simon is rich but she and Millie Green have the longer history. There was nothing left unsaid in their school years.

Millie fiddles with her suitcase, must first remove a grey cardigan before extracting a hefty wad of sheet music.

Corrie is delighted with this trove. As she leafs through the pages, she sees the stamp on the inside front of each piece.

St Aiden's School for Girls
Swartmoor Hall Lane
Ulverston
Cumbria

A Mere Waitress

'Oh Millie, you stole them for me!'

'You'd do the same for me. And no one at school can play a quarter as good as you.'

Corrie finds herself humming the top lines of one or two pieces, not speaking to her guest. Even without a piano these are beautiful; the notation sings inside her well-trained head.

'You're in the middle of town.' Her friend is looking from the window, staring at the identical properties across the road. Fifty feet wall to wall, road and pavement. Cumbria has no such regimented rows of red-brick housing, certainly not in Hawkshead. Nothing remotely like it on desolate Ulpha Fell.

Corrie looks up, notices that tears are in Millie's eyes. She thinks her friend is pitying her, feels insulted by it. She is proud of what they've done. She and Simon building a life together one brick at a time. 'It's alright. I like it here,' she tells her guest. She wonders how this visit will play out. Nurtured such high hopes.

Millie nods, doesn't dispute her point, just looks deflated. She offers to help prepare food.

'Do you need to freshen up?' asks Corrie.

Millie takes this offer up, uses the bathroom. She returns wearing a green pinafore dress. It's quite short, an unfashionable choice but she carries it off. Millie's black hair sits as opened curtains beside her face. She looks well-sunned although it is not yet Easter. A runner on the lanes and fells around Hawkshead; Sports Day winner at St Aiden's, year in and year out. Her richer complexion is a contrast to Corrie's Stockport pale.

When they are cooking together, Millie is very helpful, speaks kindly to her, but something has changed and Corrie feels uneasy about it. Feels as judged by the daughter as by Millie's parents. And when she lived in the Lake District, the Greens' household was like a second home to her.

Simon arrives back from work. He shakes Millie's hand for want of a better greeting between them. Speaks nicely to her, says that she is the only one who has been in touch from the whole of Cumbria. The couple didn't really give anyone else a chance.

They eat cauliflower-cheese with bacon, bread and pickle on the side. Simon praises the food, thanks Millie when Corrie explains that its preparation was a joint effort. Corrie feels criticised by Millie's limited interaction. The meal is gastronomically short of the high teas at Low Fell Farm which her friend joined her for on occasion but the company is the same. Better bearing in mind who is absent. Simon suggests they all go to the pub, not the Adswood Hotel or the White Hart. Corrie plays piano in these pubs each week. It's hard to avoid tinkling out a few extra tunes should she stray into either.

Millie whispers, 'Can you and I stay in,' down Corrie's ear.

She conveys this to Simon. 'Is it okay if Millie and I catch up? You can shoot pool out there if you like.'

Simon makes a joke of it, that he is being elbowed out of his own home. Seems keen enough to go, to drink a beer or two. After washing up—which he insists on doing the bulk of—he pops into the living room to wish the girls a good evening, and then he heads for the stairs.

Millie is on the sofa, watching Simon leave, listens to the click of the latch as he pulls the front door shut. On cue she bursts into tears. 'I'm late, Corrie. Very late.'

She looks at her with both puzzlement and concern. Millie sounds distraught, Corrie doesn't understand the short and cryptic phrase.

'I'm pregnant.'

'Oh God, Millie.' She slides across the sofa and consoles her crying friend.

'A week ago, I was still telling myself it would be alright...'

'And who have you told now?'

The girl is silent for a moment, struggling with her tears. 'You.'

Corrie has no idea how to help, feels upset on Millie's behalf. She enjoys living with Simon in Stockport; since playing piano in the pubs—he, training as a mechanic—she has started to

A Mere Waitress

believe that they are flourishing. Avoiding the accident that has befallen Millie was always part of the plan. Central. She knows full well that she is a kid, not yet a true adult. Never a mother.

She asks Millie questions, tries to be calm, helpful.

Millie has seen no doctor, taken no pregnancy test. Her expectant state is unproven but there has been morning sickness, eight weeks have passed since last she endured a period. Millie's best guess is far from a stupid one. Corrie is shocked when she learns that Patrick has no inkling of her condition.

'I told him I was on the pill. You said it was easy to get.'

Corrie tries not to look astonished. It is absurd that Millie should do such a thing, allow Patrick Vulliamy to think the most important consideration is taken care of when it is not. She even feels a smidgen of responsibility: it's as if Millie has copied her actions without understanding the blueprint.

'Millie, they don't work after the event.'

'Oh, I know...' Millie is sobbing again as she explains herself. '...it was only the first time. I thought fate would be kinder.'

Corrie tries to run through the options with Millie but she doesn't listen, has got herself in a state. Crying and crying, repeating, 'Why me!'

'You must tell him, Millie. Phone and tell him. I'd do anything for you, but he made this baby.'

Millie is ashen faced at this demand. Involving Patrick in her troubles could ruin their relationship, she reasons. 'What shall I say? Tell him he must marry me?'

'There's termination, Millie.'

'Shut up; there is not. I'm not doing that and nor should you!'

Corrie ignores the accusation. She is not the one who is pregnant. 'Okay, what then?' Her friend stares blankly back at her. 'Millie, I think Patrick needs to know, and I expect you should tell Teresa and Michael too.' She gives her friend's hand a squeeze.

'They'll kill me...'

'They will not. They will not kill you, Millie. I'm sure your parents are not perfect but you know how much they care. They'll be better than me at helping. What makes you think they'll take it badly?'

'I'm ruining my life; I'll have to leave school. It's the end.'

'A beginning,' says Corrie, although Millie's point is not lost on her. Without so much as a baby in the offing, Corrie is missing out on the conservatoire, university. A beginning and an end.

'My mum likes you, Corrie. She understands you had no choice. She isn't happy for you—running away—she says your dad has ruined your life.'

'Well, she's wrong then,' Corrie snaps back. 'My life is fine. Simon always got along without school and I'm doing the same. Teresa shouldn't judge me when she's not seen me.'

'She shouldn't but she does. And now they've got me to worry about. They'll blame themselves. Dad said he regrets letting you spend so much time with Simon. Encouraging you.'

'We didn't need encouragement. Everything Simon and I have done, would have happened one way or another.' As Corrie argues, she wonders if it's even true. They faced some obstacles in Cumbria, would've struggled to meet outside of Young Farmers without Mr and Mrs Green.

'They'll think it's all something I learnt from you.'

'Millie, I never taught your Patrick a thing. All boys know that stuff. Know what they want. And…' She pauses, fears sounding insensitive. '…I told you that getting the pill was less embarrassing than I'd feared. I never said you should chance it without.'

Millie draws herself up, doesn't argue. 'They'll think me a coward if I phone from down here in Stockport. I should have talked to Mum last night.' She looks at her hands. 'I am a coward…' Tears are streaming down her face. '…I'm scared of what's inside me.'

'Millie, I would be too—frightened at the prospect—but you can learn. You're a coper. Teresa loves you, Millie. They need to come to terms, your parents. They'll support you once they know, figure out…'

Millie is on her feet, risen up from the sofa. Then she stoops to the floor, takes a small purse from the handbag she has by her feet. 'I'll need a lot of change for these phone calls,' she says, as she stands up straight once more. Wipes the back of her hand across her tear-laden face.

* * *

Simon arrives home just before eleven o'clock and the girls are still up. Both have changed into pyjamas; they sit upon a tartan blanket on the old settee. A blanket Millie is to later sleep beneath. The boy has had a few beers, jokes about having to remember which bed to climb into. His idea of what might be funny deteriorates when he drinks. Millie laughs, and Corrie guesses she is just being polite. She has Patrick now. Might need him more than she has yet to contemplate.

Cordelia joined her friend in the phone box earlier but heard only the girl's side of two conversations. Millie called Patrick first, as she advised. What she said after the call was confusing to Corrie: he is in shock; he always wanted to be a father. The latter is not an aspiration Corrie has discerned in Simon, and she is pleased she hasn't, they are so young themselves. Now Millie has brought Patrick's wish crashing down upon him. 'He said we only dated a few times.'

Corrie felt a chill in those words: the protestations of a cheated man. 'He should have thought about that,' she replied, knowing as she said it that Millicent Green was the reckless one. Failed to apply everyday domestic science.

Corrie stayed in the phone box while Millie rang her mother. 'Why didn't you tell me before you went to see Corrie?' said Mrs Green, and this at a volume the listener-in could hear. Everything else was obscure, too faint to be certain of her words. Millie went through the physical reasons why she believes herself to be with child—turned away from Corrie—talking about menstruation is embarrassing.

Nothing in Millie's reactions led Corrie to think the call a poor choice. She could not hear the spoken words but the conversation was calm, possibly intimate.

When Millie hung up, she pushed on the door and set out.

'Alright?' asked Cordelia.

'Yes and no.'

Corrie furrowed her brow, looked at her friend for explanation. There is little for a mother to do but support her daughter. Unless she's a total wash-out, and Teresa Green is no Honoria Dalton.

'She said Daddy will demand Patrick marries me, say that he must. Then she said she thinks I should too. Said it all the wrong way round, do you see? She's just following what she thinks he will think. It's not an opinion at all.'

'You don't want to marry Patrick, do you Millie?'

They walked back to the flat with this question lolloping along behind them. Unanswered, dragging its heels.

Corrie has not asked Millie if she may share this evening's talk with Simon. She wishes she had, should have made clear that they do not keep secrets. She wants to know what he thinks. Simon still speaks of Patrick now and again. She thought he was a decent sort. Not clever enough for Millie, that's the drawback; a farmhand from uncombed hair to muddy old boots. It is awkward, Millie is their guest but she is not herself.

'I'm brushing my teeth for bed. You as well?' she asks her boyfriend.

He shrugs a sort of yes. While she is in the bathroom, she can hear her visitor talking to Simon. Can't tell if they're talking pool or Patrick.

A little later, snuggled under the blankets, Corrie whispers that Patrick Vulliamy has gotten Millie into trouble. 'In the family way,' she says, and tipsy Simon giggles at the dated term.

'She told me,' says Simon, 'while you were doing your teeth. Hoping for a girl.'

It's a turn up. Millie didn't tell Patrick, Teresa, not even Corrie until she could restrain herself no longer. Now she's refashioned herself as the Angel Gabriel, proclaiming the glorious birth to come.

* * *

The following evening Corrie is preparing to play piano in the pub on Shaw Heath. Flexes each of her eight fingers in turn, no exercises for thumbs. It's a ritual of little function. Simon and Millie and a friend they have made called Sue—whose boyfriend has yet to arrive—are there to listen, to encourage. Millie has put on the smart red skirt, done her hair. She can pass for eighteen far more easily than the piano player.

Sue works at the checkout in Lipton's, Great Moor. Lives around the corner from the White Hart, met Corrie and Simon in the pub. She and Dave laugh about the songs Corrie performs. Constantly suggest others to play in their stead. Corrie has developed a particular repertoire. Absalom, My Brother usually features—it's doleful but everyone listens up to the hit song about the lost sailor—plus lots of singalongs from the landlady's music books. Simon teases her about them, the singing-along-with-old-folk music which dominates every set she plays in these pubs. She's learnt a couple of other chart songs, any young people who chance to be in the pub like to hear them. Corrie remains dismissive of popular music, seldom says as much in the company she now keeps. Even from Simon, she hides many of her real thoughts on this narrow topic. She imagines that all conservatoire-bound girls think like her. Value the classical above the frivolous. Friends and rivals from the life she'll never lead. She drops in Beethoven, Chopin and Satie if the mood takes her, vainly hopes the audience feels elevated by it. There is another tune she often plays, lodged itself in her head a couple of years ago when she and Vincent watched the film version of Making Do, the West End musical. They saw it at the cinema in Barrow-in-Furness, Corrie travelling on the back of his moped for the very first time. That one gets cheers in the pub just so long as she hams up her singing. Pretends to be the cockney wot she ain't.

Dave is not in the pub when she draws herself up to the

keyboard. She sings well, plays the right notes without really trying, feels preoccupied with Millie's worries. She will go back to Cumbria tomorrow, to the biggest change her happy family home has ever known. Changed by her own foolishness, Corrie thinks. If her own childhood home in the hills had not been a violent one, she would have stayed, studied, may have gone on to perform proper music. Played it on a piano more pliant than this old wreck. Corrie has no idea what her former teachers would make of her bashing out simple singalong. It serves a purpose. And pregnant she is not. It might be all right at the right time but poor Millie hasn't really experienced being with a man. Corrie thinks the first time must always feel bewildering. Hers did. Simon was kind—embarrassed actually—paid her compliments that she could not attend. Feelings of foolishness for being naked with a man are normal until you can forget the oddity of it. Fearing you look wrong, wrong in the places you've never shown anyone else. It's funny looking back, terrifying at the time. And Simon saw the marks on her legs, welts still visible from September's beating. She didn't want him to see that; unhurt in her mind, seeking love not sympathy. What Millie and Patrick do is their own business. Why a clever sixth-form girl should be so ill-prepared, allow herself this life-changing happenstance, Corrie expects never to comprehend. She fears her letters to Millie—telling how she found the nerve to see the doctor, get the pill, throw aside the teaching of their church—put notions into Millie's head. But she was only sharing the extraordinary turn her life has taken, she wasn't giving advice. Never foresaw this consequence for it was not a chance she took. And now it will have a name. A boy or a girl; a treasure or a millstone.

My fella buys me flour
So that I can bake us bread
Although we've 'ardly got enough to go around
He wants to buy me diamonds
Says 'e would do if 'e could
But cha don't get many diamonds to the pound

A Mere Waitress

The pub is rapt by the sweet-voiced young girl who can phrase a cockney accent without ever having been near the East End. It's the same skill with which she holds the tune: the acuity of ear, the clarity with which she hears musical sound. Even this sentimental nonsense.

> *He don't 'ave much, it's true*
> *But 'e's got me*
> *So long as he wants me*
> *'e's got me*

Give the punters what they want to hear: Cordelia Dalton, able and improbable pub singer.

* * *

He has quietly slipped in beside Sue; Corrie never saw him arrive. As she approaches, Millie is standing, clapping her return to the table. 'Brilliant,' she says. Millie is a longstanding fan, in the audience for her prize-winning performance at the Cathedral School in Carlisle. 'Brilliant,' she repeats.

Dave tells her she has the listeners around her little finger.

'I thought you missed it?'

'Never would,' he says.

'It's funny though,' says Millie, sitting down again. 'I think they're more excited whether Daisy will marry the lad in the song than anything else that's happened since the war.'

Corrie thought the same when she began playing in the Stockport pubs. She has come to realise her audience is not so old, no more so than Mr and Mrs De Luca, the kindly restauranteurs at her other workplace 'I'm starting to enjoy the corny songs,' she tells the table. 'Everyone knows the words; the tunes are easy to pick up.'

Millie looks at her with surprise. 'And you played that one from the sheet music I brought you.'

'Haydn, yes. I think I lost them a bit. Singalong works best here.' Corrie is confused is confused by her own argument. She loves the pieces Millie has fetched from St Aiden's, had to slip in some of the Sonata in G Minor just to hear it again, feel her

177

fingers share the sound. Her friend was generous as ever in her applause but she dislikes hearing Millie contrast this halfpenny cabaret to her past exploits. Musically it is all she has.

'The one that makes us feel like crying was brilliant, Corrie,' says Dave. He has stepped around the table, placed a hand on the pianist's shoulder.

'Feel like crying? Absalom, My Brother.'

'Not that one, you know...' Dave starts to sing.

My fella buys us flour so that I can bake...

He stops when he sees both Corrie and Millie stifling laughter. His voice is tuneless.

'I throw that in because the old dears love it,' says Corrie. Gently she pushes Dave's hand off her shoulder. 'I like singing it, dropping the way I really speak. Being someone else for a few minutes.' As she says it, she wonders if the persona she adopts is her real self, minus the three years in a private school. And the song isn't meant to make anyone cry. It's about being poor and also about it not really mattering. The singer has someone to love, someone who loves her back. Dave Wright doesn't understand the point, can't get a corny song.

Later Corrie plays eight more songs. She begins with Le Prisonnier Maussade, a Satie exercise from the music which Millie kindly stole from her old school. The pub-goers allow her the indulgence; however, there is far more chatter through this than when she sings a Templeton Ca. hit which Simon suggested she learn; he has it on cassette. She gives them a couple of the old singalongs—Pack Up Your Troubles—then finishes with the song from Making Do, plays it for the second time of the evening. The piano is a faint accompaniment as she warbles the words extravagantly.

So long as he wants me
'e's got me

Her voice is expressive, beautiful, controlled. Amusing too, when she pulls the reins to that side. As she finishes, Dave is beside the piano, pecks her lightly on the cheek. 'Was that for

A Mere Waitress

me?'

'Get back to Sue,' she says, pushing him away as she stands up from the piano stool.

* * *

The girls can hear Simon snoring through two doors, wafting away the fug of more beer than he should have drunk with a working day tomorrow. Millie is giggling, telling Corrie it was a brilliant evening. They each have a cup of cocoa, no alcohol for the underage, the pregnant. Cordelia stretches her fingers, keeping them dextrous. She thinks Millie will have fewer fun nights back in Hawkshead or in Coniston. The quieter pubs up there isn't the half of it. Encumbered with a baby, responsibilities greater than those her own flight from Cumbria have placed upon Corrie. It crosses her mind that she should be talking congratulations on a baby's imminence, the unbridled joy only the experience of childbirth can bring. She cannot. When Millie has talked of it fearfully, Corrie has thought her at her most sensible.

For Corrie, it is the piano which brings her the greatest joy. Entertaining allows her access to one, and there is neither money nor space for such an instrument to find its way into their flat. Pianos are not babies, not so easily come by. In the pub tonight she threw in a couple of complex and subtly layered pieces that she could feel through every pore of her body. Deirdre—the landlady with the black-rimmed glasses—has a tendency to watch her through narrowed eyes when Corrie plays a classical piece. She might just as well be describing the dream she had the night before. The pub-goers are polite, some might pretend to listen, but it holds no real interest for them. She has not spoken to her friend and they have almost finished their cocoa. The giggling unreciprocated.

'I think he's in love with you,' says Millie.

'I love him back,' says Corrie.

'You do?'

'I really do. We're a bit different but I've made my choice.'

'How will you get rid of him then,' she says, pointing towards the back of the flat, the room from which snoring sings off-key.

'What? I love Simon. Me and Si: partners in crime. What are you talking…?'

'Sorry. I thought I'd said. That Dave bloke—he's really got the hots for you—it's kind of obvious.'

'Millie! He's with Sue.'

'She's a dullard, Corrie. And Dave is way better looking than Simon.'

'He is not.' She feels affronted by Millie's dismissal of Simon's worth. Dave is okay. Or maybe not. He was a bit irritating tonight; she never pays him much attention.

'He looks really fit, a broad chest. Don't you think so?'

'I don't know. Or rather, I do. He's of no interest to me, Millie. And you shouldn't be looking at him either, you may be marrying Patrick Vulliamy before you know it.'

Millie leans forward, her hair falling over her face. 'Don't remind me.'

'Sorry,' she concedes.

Millie's smile has fled. There is a flatness to her voice when she says, 'You're not married. He'd go out with you in the wink of an eye.'

This is insane. Corrie thinks Millie looks lost, helpless. She, of all people, should know what Simon's done for her. Means to her. He has turned his life over to her, coming down to Stockport. Let go of farming. He chanced the lot, did it for her and her only. 'I don't care for Dave. Can't say I like him. Sue's fine. A very pleasant girl.'

Her friend looks away, draws a handkerchief from her sleeve.

'I think I'd best go to bed now.' Corrie feels sad that they have not got along better, doesn't wish to continue with this foolish talk.

'It's alright for you…' Millie's voice is soft but there is a bitterness to it, she doesn't bring her head up. '…you can do it with them both now you've got your pill. It's alright for you…'

'You're upset,' says Corrie, 'I'm sorry if I upset you.' It's nothing like Millie seems to imagine. Cordelia shares a bed and a life with Simon Tripp. She'll be doing nothing whatsoever with Dave Wright. Keeping him at a greater distance maybe. Treating him like she has a certain Italian chef. Millie might have noticed something about him that she hasn't spotted. Might be looking too closely at boys she should have no truck with.

It could be Patrick Vulliamy is one of them.

11.

This Wednesday lunchtime is to be Cordelia's final shift at Ristorante Ventimiglia. She has secured a position—a job more fitting—at Stockport College. She was one of six interviewed for an administrative position; guessed herself to be the youngest by far. All six waited together in an unused classroom, called forth one by one, Corrie second to last. Then, waiting over, she convinced a panel of three that she was the one amongst them best suited for the role, without quite knowing what qualities they were seeking. Being young and nervous, perhaps. She is unsure what tasks she must perform. Admin, that was what the lady who sat in the middle said. Today—still doing the job she knows well—Teodoro Massimi is in Salerno, Italy, burying his mother. Mr De Luca works in the kitchen. He did this back in March, the chef unwell for a week. Knows about pizza, risotto, all that. Mrs De Luca is front of house. Corrie likes her.

Since the weather has turned warmer the establishment has placed four tables out front, on the pavement of Hillgate. The lunchtime sun is an attraction, customers sitting at every roadside table. It is Corrie's job to wait on the outside seating, plus the indoor tables closest to the right-hand windows. The ladies sitting around the final outdoor table occupied have yet to order drinks or food. Corrie walks out; she wears a wine-coloured dress with a narrow white collar, the restaurant's name embroidered on the right breast pocket. No tights today, it's over twenty degrees: over seventy, Vincent would call it

Ghost in the Stables

from a couple of school years down the line. Her rich-brown pony tail tumbles down her back. Four women sit around the table, not old, smartly dressed. Working women or rich housewives. Corrie always speculates, seldom learns.

She addresses the blond-haired lady who faces her; they all have menus in hand. 'Have you chosen?'

'I think so,' she says, squinting back at Corrie. The sun is in the lady's face as she looks up. 'I'm going for the Four Seasons, please...'

'Me too,' interjects the customer to her left.'

'Scampi fritti, please,' says the third.

'And Tommie?' enquires the blond-haired lady of the only one in the party who has yet to speak, whose back is to Corrie, face not yet seen. The name alone gives her a jolt. The lady glances around, her hair looks slightly different, the nose is unmistakable. The sisters' eyes meet.

'Hello, Cordelia.'

'Hi, I'll give chef the order.' She turns away. Her smile has simply evaporated, it was only ever decoration. She waits tables for the money, not the love of the job. Not for her sister to find, unmask, and take her back to Low Fell. Corrie feels she must flee, miss out the kitchen altogether, run away from Restaurant Ventimiglia, it's her final shift, leaving now will make little difference. But might Killian be waiting around the corner? Or is he already on Charles Street—the girl's heart is thumping—could her every move have already been anticipated? She wants Simon here but he is at work. In a pit beneath a car where no telephone rings. She runs a sweating palm across her distraught face, draws the small toggle off her pony tail letting her hair hang loose. As she does so, doubt enters her mind. She shouldn't be letting Mr and Mrs De Luca down, not because of her noxious family. They can't simply kidnap a working girl, shame her into returning. Low Fell, farmhouse full of secrets, that is the shameful one.

A hand rests upon her shoulder, exceptionally gently. She is only at the door of the restaurant, has not fled the first five

A Mere Waitress

paces yet. 'Corrie, you haven't taken my order and...' Corrie turns her head, looks up into a face she never expected to see again. Thomasina looks quite serene while the younger sister's heart thumps out a polka beat. '...Corrie, can we talk?'

Thomasina takes both her shoulders, wraps her in the briefest of hugs, then steps back and looks into her eyes. Forehead furrowed. 'Don't be scared of me Corrie. I've always been on your side.'

Corrie doesn't think this to be true. Thomasina has been a most distant sister, twelve years her senior and out of the house, living somewhere in the Manchester area since Corrie turned eleven. She and Simon didn't really pick Stockport, it chose them. Far enough without spending too much on their train fare. She always thought Manchester too big to accidently come across Tommie. Never thought the sister might stray to the shabby side of Stockport.

'Have they sent you?'

'Corrie, no. I'm here with friends. I had no idea you worked here. I live miles away.'

The small writing pad in the young girl's hand is shaking, she clutches it to her chest to arrest the tremor. Cosmo, the waiter on shift with her, has come to assist. He waits just inside the open door, gesturing to his colleague.

'Everything is all right,' Thomasina says in the young man's direction. Cosmo narrows a single eye. Doesn't take his direction from the customer on this matter.

The blond-haired lady, a friend of Tommie's, has come to stand next to her. A puzzled look on her face, enquiring but perturbed. Perhaps the scene feels confrontational despite the hug. It could still prove that way: Corrie feels more fearful than she has at any time since leaving Cumbria.

'It's a little family reunion,' says Thomasina to her friend. She takes hold of her sister's hand. 'I expect you need to work, Corrie. If I stay, can we catch up when you're done?'

'You weren't sent?' the girl reiterates, withdrawing the hand from Thomasina's, reluctantly scrunching her hair together to replace the small toggle she has temporarily removed. Her eyes take in her sister's face only momentarily, flittering backwards and forwards between her, Cosmo and the table she has given a poor service to.

Tommie stoops her tall frame to whisper into Corrie's ear. 'I wish I'd run away from the old bastard. You're my hero.'

The blond-haired woman turns away as if shocked by the term used. Corrie finally smiles at her sister. Then she waves at Cosmo who has waited patiently. 'It's okay, we've to work.' After a pause, Corrie looks around at the nearby tables, all seem oblivious to the drama they have unwittingly been witness to. Played out entirely in her stomach, clever Cosmo noting her disquiet.

Tommie returns to her table, Corrie to the restaurant door, and then she backtracks, stands at her sister's side as she is sitting herself back down. 'Two Four Seasons pizzas but I've forgotten the other two, and you'll be wanting drinks.'

Tommie raises a hand to the table, indicates that she must speak. 'This girl is my wonderful...' She opens both palms at Corrie, who lets her own head drop in embarrassment, hiding the small smile on her face. '...long-lost sister. I cannot describe how pleased I am to have found her.' Thomasina's friends start to ask questions, Corrie turns, leaves it to older sister to tell whatever part of the tale she thinks fit for their consumption. She has no sense of who her dining companions are. The warmth of her sister's accolade surprises her. The Daltons were always visible in church at Coniston; Cordelia sang solo there several times, won a piano prize at the Cathedral School, Carlisle. The family's underlying disharmony was not for public disclosure. Upsets and failures swallowed back down. She is a runaway, a mere waitress. Corrie has felt, throughout her time in Stockport, that the anonymity she and Simon sought was also an expression of that need to keep quiet about everything that had driven them down here. A spiteful father with a will of iron.

'Cordelia,' she hears Tommie say, 'Corrie to friends and

A Mere Waitress

family.' She tries to smile at them, cannot hold the expression. They must see that her role in life is a lowly one: serving food. Even this new job in college is poorly paid and she doesn't yet know what duties it entails. She won't speak of it, so idle a boast would it sound if she were to try. Then she hears Thomasina explaining her disappearance. 'She's making a better life for herself, better than can be had on a remote sheep farm.'

Corrie checks she has written each lady's order on her notepad, a smile of concurrence nudging its way back on to her face.

* * *

Cosmo, Mrs De Luca and later Mr De Luca, are all concerned for her. They can see that this is an unsettling final shift without quite knowing why.

'The boy told me you were crying,' says the owner, chef for the day. He has left the kitchen briefly, squinted through the glass window at the customer who has disturbed his young waitress.

'Not crying. It was a surprise to see her.'

'She has come from your faraway farm to meet with you? She doesn't look like a farmer, Cordelia.'

'No, she's not on the farm any longer. I don't really know where she lives,' confesses the girl.

* * *

Antonio De Luca says that he has to clean the kitchen this afternoon. His wife is going shopping. The Merseyway precinct, far from the second-hand shops of Hillgate. The restaurant is closed to paying customers, he insists that the two sisters must stay. 'Please, it is a good place to talk. Everybody a-talks in Ristorante Ventimiglia.' As he says this, the congenial man pulls an open bottle from behind the small bar, pours two large glasses of red wine. 'On the house,' he declares.

He goes into the kitchen and Corrie and Thomasina seat themselves at a round table near the back of the restaurant. They sit side by side, both looking at the condiments. Avoiding

Ghost in the Stables

each other's faces. Could be strangers. Beneath their idle hands a freshly laundered red and white chequered table cloth tries to frame their mood. Corrie spread it upon the table an hour ago; there have been no further customers sitting here since then, no food served upon it. She likes the cheery design, always has. She turns her face towards her older sister.

Tommie smiles. 'I won't tell Mummy and Daddy that I've found you, Corrie. Not without your say so.'

The younger sister looks closely at Thomasina; it is still only spring but the sun has brought colour to the taut skin of her face. Her nose is the longest of the four siblings, both narrow and prominent. Corrie feels like she doesn't know her, although she is the same sister who has been a part of all her life thus far. A small part, easy to miss.

'You look very well, Cordelia,' says Tommie. Then she adds quietly, 'I spoke to Vincent, he's a big fan of your young man, your boyfriend. You are together with him, aren't you?'

Corrie feels momentarily thrown by the question. Thomasina spoke to Vincent. When was this? It comes back to her how very much time has passed since she fled Low Fell. The family will have gathered one short: Christmas, Easter. 'Where are Olivia and Terence?' she asks.

'We've a nanny, Corrie. We hired a nanny. It gives us greater freedom...'

'And they're well, Olivia and Terence?'

'Fine. Fine and growing. You must come...'

'Have you had a nanny long?'

'Two years. When I was expecting...'

'I never knew. Why did I not know?'

'Corrie, I don't discuss much of my life with Mummy and Daddy. Our lives, John and I and the children, in Macclesfield. It's not a secret but you know how Daddy is. He would just judge. Have a rant about us wasting money, most likely...'

'Do you still go to church?'

'We do.' Neither Thomasina nor Cordelia have touched their wine glasses. 'The boy, Tripp, Vinny calls him, are you still together?'

'Yes,' says Corrie.

'And he treats you well?'

'The best. I had to run away, Tommie. I wasn't allowed a boyfriend in Cumbria; Daddy couldn't have made that plainer.'

The older girl touches her own wedding band, glances down at the eye-catching table cloth then turns her face to her young sister. 'Vincent told me about that, Cordelia. Said Daddy turned worse than ever with you. Said it was simply marvellous that you ran away.'

Corrie listens, it is nice to learn the opinion of the brother she misses.

'Did you hear that he took his job?'

'I've heard nothing, Tommie. Whose job?'

'The Tripp boys. Vincent is working at the farm your boyfriend used to work on. Near Coniston, I believe…'

'He's left Low Fell?'

'Yes, doing dairy at which ever farm your young man used to work at. I don't know the name.'

'He's at Sark Farm?' Corrie's face erupts into a smile. 'Oh Tommie…' She places her hand on top of her sisters, rubs her palm slowly across it. '…I hope he never goes back.' When both have contemplated their brother's free state, she adds. 'I hope he's given up the ruddy church.' As she says it, Corrie is unsure what she even means. She has not stopped believing. Prays when Simon is not in the flat. Tried Our Lady and the Apostles in Edgeley but hasn't been since March. The Father, the Son and the Holy Ghost are a tricky bunch to keep on the right side of. 'Sometimes I want to, want to have a God watching over me, but Simon says it's all indoctrination. He says he'll watch over me.' She removes her hand from her sister's. 'I said, "What if you turn out like Daddy?" Do you know what he said?'

Thomasina shakes her head. 'No.'

'He said, "Throw me out." Can you believe that? He's not bothered about marriage. We're not. He says we'll never split up because we rub along.'

'He sounds a sensible boy, Corrie.'

'He can be an idiot sometimes, Tommie. We're still kids. He listens to me.' She lowers her voice to a whisper. 'Loves me.' Then Cordelia draws herself up, still far shorter than her sister, rises an inch, her face even darkens. 'At Low Fell, Vincent was the only one who listened to me. Ever. Vincent and Mary Donnelly, and Mary isn't family. Mummy doesn't know how to care. Killian pretended to be Daddy. Sickening.' She finally picks up the wine glass, gulps down a surprisingly large draft. Coughs lightly then throws her marbles before the horse. 'I never saw you, Tommie. You were nice at Christmas, when Grandpa came, all that. I never saw you day to day. You practised cello nicely; I remember listening to that when I was small. Not talking. We never did that. I thought you were on their side: Daddy's mission to break Vinny. Break me if he thought I wasn't practicing piano enough...' Corrie stops talking, puts her hand back on top of her sisters. Thomasina is crying silent tears.

'I'm glad you got out. You were always smarter than me,' says the older girl.

Mr De Luca has stepped into the empty restaurant. 'It's alright,' Cordelia tells him. 'We're just talking.'

He scrutinises both girls from across the room, says the single word, 'Families,' his inflexion pure puzzlement. Returns to his cleaning.

'And I think you're right, Corrie,' says Thomasina, waving away the younger sister's offer of a napkin. 'I've never known how to stand up to Daddy. How to do more than keep my own head down.' They sit in silence for a few moments. Corrie takes another sip of her wine, watches Thomasina cry. She has no recollection of seeing her sister shed a tear before today. 'Daddy wasn't so angry when I was young. It all changed when Killian went to grammar school...'

Corrie has no memory of such a time: she was only three years old when Killian moved from primary to secondary, from the tiny village two-room to the boys' school in Millom. She

A Mere Waitress

has always sensed that there was a world before her father mistreated Vincent. Mistreated her. It is a world within her imagination alone. Every memory of her father is laced with fear.

'Killie hated school from day one. He wasn't strong at that age. Other children bullied him, I'm sure of it. Thought it then and I still do. Killie wouldn't say of course, it was all in his sullen behaviour. Tried to farm instead of attending school a time or two. Daddy hated seeing him struggle, so he just did the only thing he knows.' Thomasina has picked up a wooden pepper mill, turns it over and over, then grips it more tightly. 'You know what I mean?'

'No.'

'He beat him senseless. Thought that would solve his problems. Stupid bastard.'

Corrie nods. 'The buggering bastard,' she mutters, a dawning realisation that she and Vincent were not the first to direct such a term at the hateful man.

'I don't think there was any buggering, Corrie. Daddy is quite against that. I think it may have been Killian's other difficulty.'

Cordelia's face flushes; she knows it is possible. Killian has always been odd. She hated Simon making jokes about supposed homosexuals. Vincent used to do the same. She sometimes thought Vinny's speculation might have hit the mark, her older brother twisted inside out by Catholic shame. It saddens her where she is mostly just angry, makes sense and makes no sense. Killian acts as if he is Jeremy, that's how he presents himself to the world. What he was like at secondary school she cannot visualise, has retained no picture of him at that time. Vincent at a young age is clear in memory; Killie only starts with his chequered cap. That he was violent, she knows full well. Not in pictures. The sound of fists on Vincent's ribs. If he was bullied at school, so be it.

'Do you know?' says the elder sister, '—and I know you all had it worse—the only time Daddy ever gave me a proper hiding was when I told him that Killian fought me. He was a lot smaller than me, of course, so perhaps I should have fought back. I didn't really know how. My brother had broken one of my teeth, that's why I told Daddy. He was livid. "Never tell tales." Used his horsewhip on me. I was to be Killie's punchbag: if the boy could trounce me, he'd manage at school…'

It is unbearable to Corrie. She'd thought this sister favoured, has no sense of this earlier turbulence. Thank Christ Tommie got out: it is not an impiety but an answered prayer. Thank Christ. 'What did Mummy do?' she asks.

'Bought a new hat for church, I expect.' Thomasina puts her wine glass to her lips, tips a small measure into her mouth. Swallows. 'I love Mummy, Corrie. Standing up to Daddy isn't something she does. Can't.'

12.

Simon is working another Saturday. He is keen on them, on the time and a half. Puts himself in for every weekend he can. Corrie has learnt that he is the only mechanic at Chapel Motors this morning and he is far from qualified. When she asked him how it would work, he said, 'We don't get many that won't wait until Monday.' She gave him a funny look, thought the garage must be open for something. 'And I'm pretty good,' Simon added. She loved that answer.

Corrie has long gathered that Pete Conway trusts him. Gives Simon more responsibility than he does his long-standing workers. Trusts him with the new cars too, the ones they've started hiring out. He did a drop-off at a large house in Woodford yesterday. Pete gives him every sort of task: under the bonnet; meeting customers; cashing up. Simon thrives off it. And she once worried that she had torn him away from farming life. She doesn't say it to Kath—who comes around their flat now and then—or to Sue, friends who watch her play pub piano, but she is enormously proud of him. Corrie doesn't think they would see the point she is making. Kath never keeps a boyfriend more than a fortnight and Sue's contented with brush-factory Dave. She picked herself a bright one back at Young Farmers.

She called into college yesterday. A meeting with the head of administration, Mark Appley, before she starts work on Monday. He had her curriculum vitae in his hands. Spoke about her schooling, her excellent exam results at the end of fifth form. Said it might be possible for her to resume the education she abandoned precipitously. They could spare her a few hours and she'd still keep her full-time wage. Corrie felt momentarily ruffled, wonders if she is still clever enough. No textbooks opened in five months. She thanked him, of course, kept her options open.

In the evening Simon said it was brilliant, said he never intended that she remain as stupid as him just because they had to leave Cumbria. And she doesn't think him stupid at all. He is more practical, works with what is to hand. Corrie thinks her head is in the clouds most of the time, not the cleverest place to park it.

Mark Appley apologised that Stockport College does not have a comparable music course she can join. But then he held up her application form. 'You don't need a music A-level,' he laughed, 'you're a professional.' That's not quite how she regards the singalong she tinkles on clapped-out pub pianos; she simply cannot give it up. Must push fingers into the teeth of the thing one way or another, seek out harmonies in the most unlikely places. A Windmill in Old Amsterdam. Craves it like Simon does his pie and chips.

* * *

Her boyfriend is still at work when she goes to the phone box, makes the call. Millie's mum answers, Corrie doesn't catch any disdain, any disapproval in her tone. Maybe she only imagined it for a call or two after Millie's visit. The misstep.

When her friend comes to the phone they pick up as they used to before Corrie's flight. As they were.

'I'm always thinking about you playing piano in the pub,

Corrie. You were brilliant. Every type of song. The singing too. If you cut a record, everybody would buy it.'

'How's…you know?'

'How's being up the duff and everyone can see it? It actually gets you a home tutor, Corrie. That's how it is.'

'And…Patrick?'

'I'll be his wife in two weeks, Corrie. And I understand why you can't be my bridesmaid. The service will be at Our Lady of the Rosary and that isn't good for you. If you'd made a record, I'd play it while I walked down the aisle but you haven't so I can't. Oh Corrie…' Millie's voice deepens as she changes tack. '…all that aside, Honoria cornered me on Sunday. I thought she was going to tear a strip off me for getting caught out doing what I shouldn't have—me and Patrick and what have you— then she never said a word about that. She asked after you. I…' Millie's long pause frustrates Corrie, produces a feeling of anxiety within her. '…I've never seen your mum like she was on Sunday. Tears. She was standing next to your horrible father. She was in tears; he didn't even try to listen in to our conversation. Made a point of not doing. Him and old Mr Thorpe talking without looking at her and he must have known she was crying whatever way round he faced. Honoria said she missed you, could hardly get her words out. Wondered if I'd heard anything. I said not, of course. She said she was so worried. But Corrie, I know she did nothing when your worries were staring her in the face.'

Corrie cannot say a word, simply listens.

'You're better off down there, Corrie.'

She agrees with this sentiment of Millie's, agrees but the thought of her mother has prompted her own tears to flow. She struggles to feel anything tangible for Honoria. Sometimes a little crying is the way of this life.

'I always imagined you'd play the piano at my wedding. When I was twenty-one not seventeen, obviously. Now you can't and I know it's Honoria and Jeremy's fault, Corrie. I want you back here too but it's for the best you don't come. I'll pretend it's you playing when I walk down that aisle. In my head it will be you, Corrie. It really will.'

13.

On Sunday morning they walk to the railway station, buy tickets, board the train. Thomasina will pick them up from Prestbury, drive them out to her home in Rainow. Place names new to Cordelia, to Simon. She has told him of her chance meeting. Talked about little else four nights ago, when he returned from work.

She perceives a nervousness in him. They sit side by side in a small closed carriage. Only a mother and son—assuming the boy in short-trousers is so related to the older woman he sits beside—share it with them.

'No one else will be there,' she tells him. He looks back at her, eyes slightly narrowed, as if squeezing out a thought. 'I wish Vinny could be there, Si. I'd love to see him again.'

Simon has never met Thomasina. He says all the Dalton's are nuts except her. She takes issue with this, does so on account of Vincent only. Simon concedes that he likes him, met and liked Vinny at the Young Farmers' meetings before he ever met Corrie. She has told him a couple of tales of Tommie before. Nothing favourable, not before this week. She hopes Simon will walk with her upon the shifting sands.

She feels guilty for the bile she spat at Thomasina when they first sat at the round table, wines untouched. Corrie pushed her sister to tears, did not regret it until the burden of Tommie's own childhood became clearer. As they talked in the closed restaurant, they found themselves survivors of torments a decade apart. Thomasina got out more conventionally than her younger sister, married a congregant from their church in Coniston. Did so after a courtship Tommie now thinks regrettably long. She told Corrie that she was foolish not to trust John Stapley from the word go. Tommie recalled feeling certain that he would take his leave if he got any inkling of how their family really functioned. Or if he learnt her father's opinion of Tommie: her worthlessness. Over time, she came to understand John felt only that she was holding back. Not telling him honestly how she felt about anything at all. It was how she coped with life at the time. 'Putting everything aside for later isn't living,' she told Corrie. And then, squeezing her hand she said the sweetest thing. 'Run, girl.'

'I'm not like you,' she told Corrie later. 'You're passionate and you always were. I could hear that when you played the piano. Looking back on it, I know I just froze myself over. Felt nothing. I dreamed of being elsewhere, while never expecting it could happen. John needed to move to Manchester for his work. I had no opinion when he asked me. Agreed anyway and, honestly, it's been a life saver.'

Corrie wonders how Tommie lives now. A life away from Low Fell.

As the train rattles down the tracks, passes Cheadle Hulme, Bramhall, Simon continues to voice his reservations. 'I've told you, Si, Tommie likes you before she's met you. You look out for me and she cares about that. She can't help herself from being civil with the bugger...' She stops mid-phrase, shouldn't be using such terms with a child in the carriage. '...with you-know-who. She thinks the same of him as you and I, for the most part. She was critical of Mummy too.'

After a short silence, Simon says, 'I don't want you going back.'

Corrie picks up his hand, squeezes it gently. 'Not a chance, Si. This is us. A good life on Hillgate.'

As the train pulls in to their stop, Corrie sees Thomasina on the platform. She wears a leather coat, all buttons open. The day feels to be warming up beautifully. Corrie points her out to Simon, worries that suspicion lurks within him still. 'Tommie,' she calls as she opens the carriage door. Her sister already waving.

'Simon, it's truly lovely to meet you.' Her voice projects down the railway platform, it is an announcement. 'The man

A Mere Waitress

who helps my sister live the life she chooses; you are dear to me.'

Simon looks taken aback, laughs an embarrassed, 'Ha,' and then he adds, 'Thomasina, it's great to meet you.' He has been learning good manners since taking on his new role at Chapel Motors, talking with customers every day of the week.

The older sister initiates a quick hug with the younger. Corrie is barely comfortable with this intimacy, wishes it came more easily. 'My car is this way,' says Tommie, leading them out of the station.

Simon is silent during the drive and Corrie thinks him a quiet boy in general. He seems to have relaxed, felt the warmth of Tommie's greeting.

'You're back in the country,' says Corrie. The car is passing rolling fields, even a few tell-tale drystone walls. The foothills of the Peak District.

'John works in finance, city centre,' says Thomasina. 'Didsbury was far better for him, I'm afraid I couldn't stand it.'

'What does he do?' asks Corrie.

Simon thought it odd—said so yesterday—she attended their wedding in Coniston, saw them every Christmas except the last one, other times too, sang solo at their children's christenings, yet she has barely exchanged a word with John Stapley in her life. The Stapley family were at church, his father farmed at Haverigg. When John first dated Tommie—Corrie still a primary school child—Vincent told her all he learnt about the Stapley's farm, the father's arrangement with the neighbouring prison. The incarcerated provided labour for seasonal tasks. Vinny would spook young Corrie with tales of a farm awash with bank robbers and murderers. The image stuck, true or false. When they married, the couple moved away, never a night on the farm. Thomas Stapley retired, sold up. Haverigg was worth a tidy sum. Corrie understands that the old man moved to Kendall, never seen again in church. How John makes a living, besides distinctly not farming, is as unknown to her as the plight of the convicts who once snagged turnips and gathered hay.

'Stocks and shares, wheeling and dealing. I don't understand it.'

'You must,' says Corrie.

'I understand that they go up and down and John turned his family farm into quite a few. Why other people invest in his guesses eludes me completely. I don't grumble, it affords us a pleasing lifestyle.'

This barely adds to what Corrie gleaned on Wednesday last. Thomasina does not work, has her own car, a nanny, friends who lunch out any time they choose. John Stapley is six years her senior, terribly good with money. It is obscene in a rather admirable way.

* * *

At a corner in the quiet village, the car pulls onto a small gravel hardstanding beside a three-storey house. It is large, not grand, attached to its neighbour. A townhouse marooned in a tiny village. Mullion windows, sandstone brickwork. Corrie gets out of the front seat, Simon the rear.

Tommie takes them through a wrought iron gate into a small yard behind the house. 'The front door is kept locked,' she explains. 'Little ones and a main road.'

'Where's the garden, Tommie?' asks Cordelia. Then she winces at her own words. It sounded condescending and she lives in the upstairs of a tiny terrace on Charles Street.

Thomasina points to a small gate at the back of the yard. There is a row of cottages which this gate leads behind. A few stone steps, Corrie can see the top of a plastic slide up there. 'It's enough,' says Tommie. Corrie dashes quickly up the steps, looks over the gate at her sister's tract. The slide is by the entrance, the lawn goes on and on. 'You could keep a flock of sheep in it,' she shouts down.

Thomasina shakes her head and beckons her sister back to the house, leads the pair through the kitchen door, into the family home. Simon shakes hands with John, a balding man who Corrie knows and doesn't know. She is reappraising everything.

'Here she is,' he says, holding two arms out to hug his sister-in-law. She returns the greeting while glancing at Simon. His hug is tighter than any the greasy chef stole. 'We're so pleased you're well; we were worried about you.'

Corrie pulls away from the older man, looks once more at Simon. Thomasina has a friendly hand upon his back. 'We had nothing to worry about, we know. It's just that families do worry, Simon.'

Two little children are peek-a-booing around the interior door. Corrie goes down onto her haunches, strokes Olivia's face, her dark hair. The little girl seems to remember her. 'It's Olivia and Terence,' she says to Simon, 'the only family member's you've yet to meet.' Terence is barely a toddler, podgy. Walks as though expecting to fall.

'I've never met your mother,' he reminds her.

Thomasina glances at the two, looks surprised.

'I've barely met any. Been met with hostility,' he adds.

'That kind of meet,' says Thomasina. Her husband, John, looks perplexed. 'Don't ask,' she tells him. 'You've known my family for years. This fine young man has everything going for him but his religion.'

'That?' he replies. 'Well, we're RCs, can't quite shake it off, but you, Simon, are always welcome in our home. And Tommie, at Easter that girl Sarah was around, Killie's girl. She's not an RC. I'm not sure that she's anything.'

'He's still seeing her?' Corrie asks of Thomasina. And when her sister confirms it with a nod, she feels slighted all the way from Cumbria. Her eldest brother first dated Sarah Pollard just two or three weeks after Simon was rebuffed on the doorstep for being of the wrong religion. Corrie cruelly chastised for so much as forging a friendship with him. It ended the life of her horse. She thinks her father a hateful hypocrite, allowing Killian to date a non-Catholic and not her. She puts a hand in front of her face, hiding the tears that have welled up.

'I'm a nothing,' says Simon. 'Not catholic, methodist or any of them.'

Corrie listens as she pretends to be clearing something from her eye. She admires her boyfriend's honesty. Doesn't say so but she is thinking of converting to his simpler creed: work it out for yourself.

'Good for you,' says John. 'We've been brainwashed. Priests and popes. Steer clear of men in dresses, Simon. You're a wise man.'

Corrie giggles at this, follows it up with a slightly manic laugh which enables her to brush her eyes more fully. Pretend she sheds happy tears.

Thomasina is grinning wryly at her younger sister. 'Don't be shocked by him,' she says. 'We have a church here...' Corrie has drawn herself up; she was not shocked, simply feels that she's meeting new people, family who take it all so lightly. '...always go if we're staying up at Low Fell. Are you still attending mass? They won't like it if they learn you're living over the brush, you know?'

'It is none of their business,' Cordelia snaps. 'They're to know nothing. That's what you agreed.'

John Stapley laughs now, puts an arm around Simon's shoulders. 'Brave boy,' he says. 'I took on a Dalton but I've been too timid by far. Married her before I learnt the half of it. You're doing it the modern way.'

Simon nods at that, then says bluntly, 'You've not told them, have you?' He looks pointedly at Thomasina as he says it.

The older sister again puts a hand upon Corrie's shoulder. 'No Simon. No Corrie. We will not. Not for as long as you wish it so.'

Corrie slides onto a kitchen chair. 'Is there a way...' As she is speaking, tears are running down her cheeks again. '...you could let Vinny know where I am? Where we are. Just him and no one else.' She and he were not on best terms when Corrie left, not a falling out but he can be a fool. Say the daftest things at the wrong times. It caused problems between them. Not how she would have left him were there another way.

A Mere Waitress

Tommie gives a small affirmative nod. 'I think Mummy is the most worried, Corrie.'

Simon takes the seat beside Corrie, takes her hand in his. A look of concern shrouds his face. Corrie squeezes his fingers. 'But I'm not worried about her, Tommie. That's just the way it is.'

The little children stare at the adults. The one who cries freely and the one they've never seen before.

'We're not going back,' states Simon.

'I've been to church,' says Corrie. 'I've been but I've stopped. Simon says it's all nonsense. Do you think it's alright to stop?'

Thomasina has seated herself opposite her sister. 'Do whatever you feel to be right.' Corrie sees her sister's furrowed brow. Something more to say. 'If God doesn't cut you a bit of slack, Corrie, then He's really not worth a hymn or a prayer. You're always welcome here whatever you do...' Then she pats Simon's shoulder. '...both welcome here.'

John picks up Terence, holds him in his arms. He seems an undemanding child, takes a hold of his father's ear, all the while watching the visitors. The father turns the toddler towards Corrie. 'It's Auntie Cordelia,' he says.

'Snake eyes,' says Corrie, from across the table, and the little boy giggles at the face she makes. As she does it, Corrie also squeezes Tommie's hand, mouths a thank you, then addresses John. 'You're back in the country.' She knows that he is as steeped in farming as she and Simon. Wonders if they too may choose to leave Stockport in time, seek out the smell of wet fields. Being out here feels familiar, although countryside has little pull for Corrie Dalton.

'City boy, now. No tweed in this house, Cordelia. I like how the land looks, long ago found that working it wasn't my idea of fun.'

'I thought it was okay,' says Simon. 'Milking cows was real work. Five, six, seven hundred pints of it a session. Way past a thousand collected by the tanker each day. Now, I just try to keep cars on the road. I'm being trained up as a mechanic and the boss has me taking car rental bookings as well, organising, invoicing. Most of the lads he's got can't do that stuff. I think I'm getting more money because I can read, write and add up, than for all the proper work down in the pit. The taking apart and putting back together of cars and engines. And there's more money in the lot of it than there is in milking cows. Money makes money: farmers are getting left behind.'

'I'm with you,' says John. 'The motor trade fashions something fresh every ten years. Dairy's a bit stuck, isn't it? Milk will always be the same, wet and white.'

Simon argues. 'We need it, a real shame that it can't compete. It shouldn't be this way round but it is. That's what I'm saying.'

'A nice car adds value to a person's life. Milk we all take for granted, like we do air and water,' says John.

Corrie feels relieved that the conversation has moved away from Low Fell. She isn't going back, knows that she will wish to speak of it with Tommie again and again. She's not heard Simon defending dairy farming until today. He might miss rural life more than she thought. She misses a horse, pushes it from her mind whenever the fine animal strays across it. She misses Vincent so much. It's nice to hear Simon putting the world to rights. Not for the detail but the normality of it. Then she asks Tommie about the brother she loves.

'He phones me now and then. And I've the number of his farm of course. I'll give it to you. He still visits Mummy and Daddy, two or three times a week. Says her food is better than any to be had where he works. The farmer's wife is quite hopeless, apparently.'

Corrie nods, must still have the number in her pocket book from Simon's time there. She nudges her leg against his under the table. He is speaking with John, looks at her but she looks away, doesn't voice her thought. Odd that Vincent should be living where Simon used to. Sleeping in the very bed where she and Simon first made love. She will say nothing of this in front of Tommie and John. Cannot possibly.

'A month or so back,' says Tommie, 'he was pulled over and

failed the breathalyser test. He was on his moped. The policeman agreed not to record it, let it be a warning to him. Apparently, they shared pints in an Ulverston pub the weekend before. Vinny reckons the policeman was worried that he could have reported him for driving away from the pub that previous Saturday night. Lucky boy, I think.'

Corrie smiles at the story. He's a fool. That is what Vinny is, and she is pleased that a little good luck fell his way. She misses her lovely fool. Doesn't miss her father, nor Killian: their absence is the elixir. As the two men talk and Tommie is speaking quietly to little Olivia, she recalls a conversation she had with her mother around the time she started at St Aiden's. The private school. Honoria very discreetly boasted that she had breast fed all her children, took real pride from the fact. Explained to Corrie that she had read more recently that it is the perfect nutrition for a baby, helps them build strength, immunity from infection. It might have been the first and last thing she did for each of her children. And her mother drew pride in the telling. No sense of shame for the long and fallow years that have followed.

Now in her sister's kitchen, Corrie finds she doesn't trust her own judgement one jot. This big sister, Thomasina, is warm, kind, funny. A list of qualities Corrie has been oblivious to for all her years until now. Low Fell is an unkind glass through which to view anyone. A couple of evenings back Simon told her that she brings out the best in him. She loved the phrase but doesn't know what she has done for him in any direction. Leaving Low Fell has brought out the best in her, she can see that. Surely the best in Tommie too. John took Tommie away. Very, very wisely. Simon brought Corrie down to Stockport, threw in his lot with her. She owes him everything. As she listens, she senses that her boyfriend is relaxing, giving her sister and brother-in-law a chance. Warming to them. He is establishing to the wealthy stockbroker that he is both a mechanic and a herdsman. Someone who can look after her. Cut a path. Then he tells John about her. 'She's working at the

Ghost in the Stables

college now, found herself a better job than waitressing.' When John nods sagely, Simon adds, 'I don't really mind what she does. Anything that makes her happy.' He loves her whether he's worked out who she is or not, Corrie concludes. And in Stockport, out here in Rainow too, away from the bitter atmosphere that permeated her childhood home, she believes herself changed. Perhaps she is becoming the pleasant girl he surmises her to be, not the bitter oddball of her fears.

Chapter Three

Unbridled Joy

1.

'I don't really think I can any more, Si,' says Corrie.

'That's okay. We'll get by.' Before Christmas I shared too much information about the car hire firm. How much I've had to borrow. It's called Tripps. I'd favoured Tripp's Trips and my wife outvoted me. Called trumps in a one-all draw. With hindsight, she's right: the name Corrie chose is classier. Says the same thing in a quieter way; Debussy to my Johnson Ronson. I've plenty of custom and I'm less than a year old, interest rates my only enemy. The Ford contract which I'm in is basically Pete's from Chapel Motors. It helped me to keep all his existing custom; I'll be changing to Volkswagen at the first opportunity. Their vans are the best, and it's virtually a new market for rental.

'I can try another couple of weeks,' she says.

'Corrie, I mean it, there's no need. Look at you. You'll slip off the piano stool.' She looks hurt at this and I apologise—kiss her—I think she's pretending, shouldn't take offence at a little joke about the weight gain. She knows that I love her pregnant. It's probably wrong but I find I need sex more than ever. She just drips something I can't resist. Her belly is getting big, not her. It's Tommy Tripp in there knocking out the extension. Elspeth Tripp if Corrie's gender hunch is correct. I try not to think about what is inside her when we're making love—the baby—just me and Corrie in those moments, plenty of time to think about another mouth to feed when the loving's done.

'Phone them tonight. Cancel what's planned. We really don't need the money.'

Piano lessons pay well. Corrie turned twenty-five three months ago and she's the best teacher there is around here. Bar none. The others know it, reluctantly concede their top students to her. She used to say all piano teachers were old. 'So what,' I replied. 'Be an exception.' She's popular, with her students if not with the other piano teachers. She charges more than most, does so following my suggestion. I've done a course about this stuff: she offers what others cannot—some of them are little more than pub pianists—high class equals high value. All her pupils are studying for the top grades. Sevens and eights and she's got a couple beyond that, kids playing piano for the beauty of it. Performing too. She teaches four or five adults, slips them in during school hours, one of them is in her sixties. The old one has been learning piano for years and years and she's Corrie's biggest fan—truly she is—gave us a hamper last Christmas which beats an apple for teacher, hands down. And Corrie could've passed for a teenager herself until this pregnancy. You might imagine older musicians wouldn't take her seriously. No one can think that way once they've heard her playing Beethoven or Chopin. Or Absalom, My Brother for my money. She doesn't do enough of that: tunes we all like. She's getting known though, played a few recitals. I've watched her in Memorial Hall, Stockport Town Hall, The Rexworthy Hotel. People pay to hear her, and then she lets the money go to charity. Says they wouldn't come if it was for her to keep. I don't argue, don't agree either. She's exceptional, and word of mouth has brought her the excellent tally of students. Her performances the best possible advert. If I talk that way, she says I'm being vulgar. It's culture and art that count for her. I tell her she shouldn't have married a grubby businessman. 'I didn't,' she replies. 'I married a know-nothing Yorkshire farm boy. Didn't expect you to wise-up like you have.' She says it sweet and funny. Never was after an all-brawn-no-brain. Corrie would have hated that, and there were a few of them at Young

Farmers, Broughton-in-Furness, Cumbria. All except me, I like to think.

She protests a little longer but I can hear in her tone that she is relenting. I think she's finding this pregnancy harder than she did with Leo. 'Keeping you healthy is all that matters. The students will all return when you're ready to teach again. They'll not find another Corrie Tripp wherever they look.'

We spar for a few more minutes. I try saying, 'Rest,' over and over. Not in quick succession, ten second gaps. It might hypnotise her into doing it. She looks gorgeous but a bit top-heavy. Her breasts are never this big in normal times. I think the little one is pushing them up—adding to the illusion—like Atlas holding up the world. Two big spheres for this little Titan. If it's a girl, she's going to be a strong one. The big landing is about a month away. We both think this yet-to-be-born was conceived in the bed and breakfast in Broughton-in-Furness. My wife was inebriated after starring in her oldest brother's overblown wedding. I took advantage, I suppose. Corrie was bloody keen too. I recall every detail of that day: how she wound up her despicable father, made friends with every normal person there. The lovemaking has stayed with me too. Afterhours, just she and I, little Leo sleeping in a single bed beside us.

Judging by Corrie's size, this one might be ripe early. That's what I think but I'm no doctor.

* * *

Earlier this evening she made one of her phone calls. She's not a secretive person, simply her habit to close the lounge door. Our telephone is in the hallway, rests on a small understairs table. The staircase is not enclosed, it comprises wooden steps on a metal frame, each open backed. You cannot help looking between them as you go up and down. No understairs cupboard, just storage space the untidiness of which might shame us. We work hard, we've a young family—Leo starts school this coming autumn—so we let it be. Mess is actually the by-product of endeavour. I can prove it: my desk at the car lot in Offerton Green is worse than the understairs.

Corrie likes to make calls from there if I'm watching an action film—or sport—that stuff bores her. She can talk for hours once she starts. For a while it was Kath, the girl from Ristorante Ventimiglia, who she'd natter to. Quite funny that they kept in touch for so long, they have nothing in common. That's Corrie: not a big circle of friends but gets along brilliant with the most surprising people. She might still speak with Kath on the phone for all I know; she's in London now, or somewhere near to it. Moved away last year; I forget the name of the place she went. And that of the guy she went with.

It's only been in the latter stages of this pregnancy that she's started to phone Honoria again, her mother. I wondered if it was the first time, back in February. I'd had a beer with the football, was just popping upstairs to the toilet when I overheard her saying something about Sarah. It struck me as unusual. The only Sarah we know is Killian's wife, unless she has a pupil of that name. And this was not a conversation about playing piano. Sounded gossipy.

When I came back downstairs the call was over. 'Were you speaking to Tommie?' I asked.

'To Mummy,' she answered.

To the best of my knowledge, they had only the most fleeting of conversations at the wedding, those many months back. The big Dalton shindig after which I got her in this family way. I don't understand my wife's relationship with her mother; she can be very dismissive of her, say she failed. I brought Corrie to Stockport before her father could kill her. She says now that it was never that bad, he only ever hit her on the legs. He killed her horse: mad as fuck, I'd say. Honoria couldn't stop him. Corrie has no hatred for her, none at all. Maybe I've blamed her mother for Corrie's grisly childhood a little unfairly. I know it was all about navigating Jeremy. All about that for both of them, for everyone who came within about a hundred yards of the nasty sod. I should be pleased if Corrie and her mother are getting onto a better footing, everyone needs family. Quite frankly, it confuses me: even the Daltons I do like have a screw or two loose. All except Corrie.

'How is she?'

'Complaining about Sarah for not leaving the kitchen as she found it. It's crazy. The poor girl hasn't any other kitchen to leave her coffee cups in. Killie should finally play the man and get his own place—buy a house—do like you did years ago, Si. Mummy blaming Sarah is tragic.'

I agreed with her, thought I might pursue the conversation in the morning. I was hoping to catch Sheffield Wednesday's game. They're having a decent time of it this season. As I settled back in front of the television, it struck me how the need to hear family talk about family has never left Corrie. Talk about other local families up there too. We only know four or five neighbours on the estate here in Marple, I think she can recall the occupants of every farmhouse in South Cumbria.

Never did pick up that exact conversation. A few days later, she said, 'I'll just give Mummy a call,' as if it was the most natural thing she could do. And perhaps it is. So many young mums can take it for granted: a mother as a source of support. I shouldn't wish different for Corrie.

Later that evening I asked her about it. 'How's Honoria? What do you talk about?'

'Oh, that. I think she's finally growing up. We talk about absolutely everything. Except Daddy, of course.'

I can't say I understood the growing-up comment. I tend to think that Honoria Dalton is old before her time, worn out. Looks regal and behaves like a pensioner. Corrie sees it all differently, thinks about the mother she knew and I've not yet met—someone with a playful side, a lightness to step and heart—the compensator. I hope it's not a fantasy. I'm not sure if it's purely Corrie's idea or something Thomasina told her, but she seems to think her mother's white hair is all down to she and I skipping out of Cumbria, hot-footing it to Stockport. It's complicated. It dates back to then certainly but my theory is that even Honoria could see who we were running from.

207

Ghost in the Stables

When you realise that you've married Satan, your hair turns white. The new look is hardly the worst part of that bleak epiphany. I had to run away with Cordelia Dalton, wasn't letting the old bastard kill her. She thought I'd kill him. Says I talked about nothing else in the autumn of the year we met. I don't remember it being quite like that and probably we'd have neither killed anyone. Corrie should never have had to put up with what he did to her, that's the bottom line. She agrees it's been a better life down here. The snag is where Honoria fits in, and my view is that she actually doesn't.

'Do you want to see her?' I asked. 'Go up?'

'Simon...' Her voice became thinner, reedy, more insistent. No longer explaining but a quiet demand. '...I'm done with Cumbria. With my fucking father. I can't see them again—never—it's just nice to hear her voice, pretend something is back even if it isn't.'

This idea makes me intensely sad. I've never thought of Cordelia Tripp—Tripp or Dalton—as a girl to pretend. I recall when she was only sixteen or seventeen and told the barman in the pub on Shaw Heath that she was not an underage drinker, had come in by arrangement to play piano. She was making it up—lying—while speaking to a higher truth. That moment was a Corrie masterclass in twisting a misfortune into her triumph. She is always here, always being who she is. Corrie does not practice life: she gives the greatest performance. That night in the White Hart she sang the doleful Johnson Ronson song that became a staple. Warbled out Absalom, My Brother. She'd heard it on the radio, never played it before. No one knew that it was unrehearsed. I didn't know either, not until later that evening. No practice is required for Corrie Dalton, Cordelia Tripp. I fear I pulled her out of her childhood five years early and she has regrets I've never contemplated. It isn't simple. She wants to be here and not there, and just wishes to dwell upon what might have been now and again. She might have gone to a conservatoire. Become a concert pianist rather than a piano teacher. I don't see her regretting this life but it might be in there. A concert pianist might have found a classier partner than a hire-car hustler.

I have wondered if Honoria has become more important to her since she became a mother herself. 'Corrie,' I asked, after this evening's call, 'she's had four. Do you ask her...you know...pregnancy or baby advice?'

I may have said something stupid. My wife laughed at me. Not unkindly, and not for the first time. 'She's had four, has she? I'll try to remember that. We talked names tonight. Probably should have included you in on it, Simon. I wasn't trying to exclude, honestly.'

'It's okay, Corrie. I like it if the bitterness has gone.'

'I don't know if it has, Si. I just like that there can be mother and daughter too.'

'So, will this one be a Simon or a Cordelia?'

'I like Elspeth, Mummy agrees. I came up with it.'

'Elspeth.' I ran my hand over her stomach. Her womb. Directed my voice there. 'Elspeth.' Teaching the little one its own name.

2.

'Did you watch it or didn't you?' says Kerry.

I know that I'm distracted, running over last night's conversation in my head. I'm particularly worried that Corrie's pregnancy isn't running to course. She's a bright and breezy soul, always has been, and there is a tiredness within her today that was never evident when she was carrying Leo.

'Sorry, which programme?' I don't know why I apologise really. This girl is on the Youth Training Scheme. All my calls would go to answerphone without her. She's a bit weird but an improvement on the no-hoper they sent me first time around. Kerry, Gerry and I always try to get a mid-morning coffee together if all is calm. Good for morale, to my thinking.

'Shoes and Slippers!' she says. It's the seven o'clock soap opera, flagship of the new channel.

'No.'

'No one knows if she's dead or runaway.'

She seems quite aerated about it, gets a bit wrapped up in the problems of fictitious people. I want to tell her that we've all been there—Corrie and I have a similar story but it isn't made up—could be the best lesson a YTS girl could get from a boss. I look at her: Kerry is skinny as a rake, her face made up crazily with green eye-shadow, rouge on the points of her cheeks, sandy-coloured hair in two bunches. She dresses pretty odd, safety pins as a fashion accessory. I had to pick her up on it in the first week but we've come to a compromise. She says nice things about her mum and dad; I expect that they love her which would make the running-away lesson superfluous. Even a little love is worth sticking around for.

'I've not been watching, been a bit busy, Kerry.'

'It's rubbish,' says Gerry. He turned sixty-three last week, a Victoria sponge in my tiny office. Had to eat a third each, so small is my workforce, and a piece that big takes it out of you. Gerry lives in a blue boiler suit, knows his way around a piston engine and he's still happy to valet cars for most of his working day. Clearly not a fan of Kerry's favoured television viewing.

'It's not. Stuff just like it happens all the time.' She looks keen to argue it out, angry with Gerry's dismissive assertion. I think I'm more with her than him. Corrie and I watched Shoes and Slippers for the first few episodes, it's all right; this pregnancy and my business have distracted us. Not kept it up. And I don't take sides in employees' disputes, not unless they're work-related: they're all grown-ups. I learnt it on a training course, the value of keeping neutral: sound advice which I'm sticking to.

The phone rings. Kerry gives it an adversarial look. Don't they know she's drinking coffee? That one. I look at the phone and then back at my employee until she gets the hint, picks up. 'Tripps.' Kerry listens carefully to the voice on the other end. 'Of course, Mrs Tripp.' She hands the receiver to me.

'Hi, love.'

Unbridled Joy

Corrie talks very fast, sounds worried.

'I'll be right there,' I say. 'Love you.' I put the phone on the cradle. 'Gerry, Kerry, can you keep it afloat today please? I need to take Corrie to the hospital. I may be back. Can't say when.'

Kerry's face lights up. 'The baby's coming. Aw. I wish I could come with you.' I ignore her comment but it doesn't stop her from babbling on. 'Don't even think about us. Babies are just lovely. Lucky you, getting another one.'

'Are the booking sheets up to date?' asks practical Gerry.

'Spot on. Just two to go out this afternoon. Can you chase the pick-up that was due back yesterday?'

'Will do,' he answers. 'Now get yourself off to your wife, where you belong.'

* * *

She is standing on the step clutching an overnight bag as I pull onto the drive. A pregnant wife is always prepared.

'Where's Leo?' I ask.

'Harriet will pick him up from nursery. I've written her address and phone number down for you.' Corrie has a slip of paper in her left hand.

'She'll look after him for however long we're there?'

Corrie nods—she's made arrangements—young mothers help each other out. As we are driving to Stepping Hill, she says again, 'I saw blood, Si. I'm really worried.'

I want to say something reassuring, tell her that she's not in labour. Fear it will miss the mark. I really don't know the first thing about this. I saw calving go belly-up a few times in my formative years. Twice at Sark Farm, Cumbria, when there was only me on hand until the vet came. It's a stupid comparison, and I'm smart enough to keep my mouth shut. 'We'll be there in minutes.' The traffic is pretty quiet in the middle of the day.

* * *

I am astonished by the youth of the doctor; looks as young as Corrie and she can't be. I really hope she's passed her exams. My wife doesn't seem bothered at all, talks with her quite freely. I know she's anxious about the health of the baby. Worrying herself sick that something has gone wrong.

'You can still feel movement, Mrs Tripp? That was what you said.'

'Yes. Please call me Corrie.'

'I think we should have another look. A scan, ultrasound. You are pretty certain though?'

'I don't feel her now.'

'Her?'

'Him or her.'

'You said that you felt the baby moving on the drive here?'

'I did.'

The doctor ponders this for a long time and then she says, 'Let's play safe, Mrs Tripp. Will you have the ultrasound?'

'Please stay, Simon.'

'I'm going nowhere.' My wife thinks I'm wedded to the car hire firm, thinks I have been since I put my name on the sign. It's her name too, she's who I do it all for. Corrie, Leo and little Elspeth who has yet to see the light of day. I'll only ever be wedded to Cordelia Tripp, that is the plainest truth.

The young doctor walks with us as we go along the corridor to the suite hosting the machine which she believes able to throw some light on my wife's predicament. It's busy, plenty of others walking these tunnel-like corridors. The strip lighting shows how filthy the walls of this hospital are. I painted up my office one Sunday, I suppose it's harder to find a time when this place is not in use. 'Will you need to admit her, Dr Baker?'

'It's too early to say,' she replies. 'I am still trying to confirm what caused this early show. If it's safe for your wife to return home, then she shall.'

'But it's not normal?' I whisper. A porter is in front of us, pushing Corrie in a funny wheelchair. She walked here from the car park; the enforced laziness is just hospital etiquette.

'There isn't much we haven't seen before. Usually this would be the start of labour, it seems not to be this time. We need to investigate a little further, Mr Tripp.'

Unbridled Joy

I'm not sure what it is about her words that bother me. I'm as worried as Corrie now; thought the doctor would know and she doesn't. I ask what it might mean, what she can do to ensure mother and child will be okay.

'We have plenty of options at our disposal,' says Dr Baker. 'Let us first hear from baby.'

* * *

The nurse comes quickly when she sees Corrie crying.

'I'm okay, sorry.'

I think she is quite astute. She stops three or four paces away. I tell her that Corrie's just coming to terms with the decision: Dr Baker is keeping her in.

'I'll be here if you want me,' says the nurse.

The young doctor told us that it looks like a breech baby. Had to explain to me what the phrase means, to me, Corrie knew already. Head not engaged. It's a funny phrase; my own heads been a bit floaty since last night's conversation. The doctor said that labour hasn't started but it could at any minute. There seems to be some complication because Corrie has bled some more. The doctor sweated when she was examining her. I don't like to think on this stuff. If they need to operate the little girl out, then I don't know why they wait. Corrie is sure this one's a girl; I expect she's right, don't mind either way.

I pull the curtain around the bed so that Corrie can change into her nightdress. As I'm doing it the nurse comes back. 'That's my job.' She says it with a smile, not some trade-unionist nonsense, I hope. I want to be doing something and the more practical the better. Don't let myself dwell on what Corrie must go through. Doctors in blood-spattered gowns cutting open my wife—I'm not just powerless to stop it, I must embrace the deed—the only way Corrie will lose what is connected to her, only to find it again as an independent girl or boy. And then I'm overstepping the mark drawing a curtain around a bed. It's nothing, nothing at all.

While she changes, I stay within the drawn curtain. Corrie looks younger than ever, frightened. It's infected me, I feel only worry, and I've got to tell her it'll be all right. I have to go home soon, to collect Leo. Corrie has said that Harriet Jackson will have him again when I need to get back to the hospital, have him anytime, day or night—it's brilliant of her—I hope to be here when the baby's born. I'm not a stay-at-home father like John Tripp. I was just outside the door all through her labour with Leo, and that took forever.

I pull the covers back so that she can climb into the bed. As she does it, Corrie's eyes go up. 'It's not two o'clock yet.'

'Bed rest,' I tell her, sounding like a matron in a black-and-white film. Yesterday we were debating whether she should continue teaching piano, I'm pleased I called that one right. I don't know what's for the best now. Trusting to doctors is my only strategy. Dr Baker said she will come back later and examine Corrie again, determine when they need to take her to theatre. It might be sooner rather than later. This one's coming out the secret panel.

'Kiss Leo for me,' says Corrie. I think she's conflicted. Wants me with her but cannot stand for our son to be spending this much time without either of us. It's already been a very unusual day for him, for our little lad. He would have expected Corrie to collect him from nursery—might think he's been kidnapped—I don't know what Harriet Jackson looks like. Corrie has written down the address, it's in the glove compartment.

After a few more reassurances—from me to her, and I'm just faking it, worried as hell, quite frankly—I leave.

* * *

Driving back to Marple I fluctuate between feeling nervous—so much so that I crunch the gears—and then not really feeling I'm here. Not with it. I drove past Tripps without noticing it at all, without looking to see which cars are out front. I've never done that before. I'm heading straight for Harriet's house which is near the secondary school, heading for Leo. Missing the sign with my name on it feels pretty crazy.

When I get to her house and she answers the door, I find

Unbridled Joy

that Harriet is older than I expected. I doubt if she's forty but it's possible. I've dropped Leo at nursery, picked him up, once or twice, no recollection of her face. Corrie tells me that Harriet has visited our house; not when I've been at home which is the way of young mums, if I can use that term for Harriet. She is great, I must add. Leo looks pleased as pie, sitting in the lounge alongside her little girl. There's a dad in a pair of slippers. An old-man dad, forty and then some, with a soft face, calm. Not really playing with the children—sitting in an armchair while they sit on the floor—speaking with them nicely.

He rises up, walks across the room and offers me his hand. 'Simon,' he says, and I take and shake it.

'Yes, your name is?'

'Simon,' he says again.

Ha! We share a Christian name, and there I am asking him to repeat it. 'Off work today? I ask.

He tells me that he is marking assignments, he teaches at Manchester University. I should have known that already, I expect. A little bell is ringing inside me like I've heard it before. I listen to everything Corrie says but it's harder to retain when you've got no face to fix it to. I think it unsurprising that Corrie knows these university types. She would have gone to one herself except for circumstances. Me being on low pay back then, and her father being such a fucking disgrace.

Harriet brings me a cup of tea, not one I asked for but it's very welcome. 'Would you like a sandwich?' I pause before answering and she says, 'That's a yes. You've had no lunch, have you?'

Leo comes and takes my hand for a second, then goes back and plays with Lucy, the Jacksons' little girl.

'How is Corrie?' asks Harriet.

I explain as best I can. 'It looks like they might do the caesarean job on her.' Both parties of this well-educated couple smile. I probably haven't explained it well. I plough on anyway. 'Labour hasn't started, I don't think, but even the doctor was confused about that.'

215

They continue to smile at me, not unkindly. 'You'll not be sleeping tonight then,' observes Harriet. Her husband starts to tell me how good the maternity services are, nothing to worry about at all. Harriet cuts him off. 'He's concerned about what Corrie's going through, that she has an ordeal to endure. Not that they'll be let down medically. The hospital will look after mother and baby to the highest standard, and it is also true that operations aren't picnics, Simon.'

I think it was her Simon she was directing all that at. And Harriet might be the better professor, or whatever title it is that he holds. Her statement is not trying to stop me from worrying, just placing some sensible parameters on it. A tough night ahead but we're all going to be okay.

When I leave, drive away with Leo next to me on his booster seat, I don't go straight home but nip down the road to Offerton Green. To Tripps, the nearly famous car hire company. Leo has been here several times. I've told him it will all be his one day, a line that he laughed at. Corrie too. 'It will have gone the way of horse and dray before you're ready to hand it down,' she said. And now little Elspeth is near I see the eldest-son nonsense—inheritance Low-Fell style—for what it is. Elspeth can have the car lot and Leo bash about on pianos, I'm easy.

Kerry makes a fuss of the boy, asks after my wife. I find her very sensible: the questions she asks show real concern; she must have dwelt upon all the baby-baby nonsense she was gushing earlier, thought over our uncertainty, our fears.

Gerry has sorted both take outs, assured me the cars were in tip-top order and ready on time. He managed to phone the guy who hired out the pick-up. The customer apologised for the confusion and agreed to pay for two more days. Back with us by five. 'Good work,' I tell Gerry. He doesn't know how touch and go the finances can be. The insurance is sky high, gets worse if we need to make big money claims: major repairs, write-offs, theft.

Leo is acting a bit cranky, which reminds me that Corrie said he might sleep. Often does straight after nursery and that was

Unbridled Joy

ages ago. Maybe I shouldn't have come into work. I thank them again and leave the pair to it. Gerry will lock up. 'I'll get myself back for eight tomorrow. No worries if your girl's a-birthing,' he says. I'm sure he's Stockport born and bred, still it could have come out the mouth of a North Yorkshire farmer. A Cumbrian's too.

* * *

'Oh goodness. I do hope that she's all right.'

'I'm sure she will be. I just wanted you to know.'

I've taken it upon myself to telephone Honoria. Killian answered, fetched her straight away. Corrie has the number in our address book under her mother's name alone, although I'd guess it's little better than a one in four chance that she's the one to pick up.

'It's a big step if they're keeping her in now. One month early, I understand.'

'We think so. Baby's pretty big, looking at how Corrie has filled out,' I say.

'She carries the little one's swimming pool,' says Honoria. I think she's being a bit patronising; I don't need pregnancy lessons. Then she switches track, asks a question or two about Leo. I answer politely and then out of the blue she says, 'Your new house is big, isn't it?'

In my mind it is not new, we moved in a few weeks before Killian's wedding. Coming on for a year ago. A three-bed link detached—I'm proud of it—a shoebox next to Low Fell. 'It's a decent size,' I tell her.

'Can I help out? Come and stay with you when baby comes?'

I am quite flummoxed by the question. Corrie talks about how we don't have anyone to help us and I think she may have phoned her mother more times than she's told me. Letting her into our home, having her handle Leo, Elspeth, that is a bigger step than I want to commit to over the phone. I need to know what Corrie thinks. 'Just you, not Jeremy?' I reply. Quite rudely, I realise, as I play it back in my head, the point simply needed making.

'Oh, he can't abide babies.' Her answer tells me that the old sod is not in the hallway or withdrawing room. Out of earshot from whichever telephone Honoria is currently speaking from.

'I think I need to ask…'

Before I can finish, she has interrupted. 'Do. I want to help Cordelia, not impose myself upon her. Phone me back if I may come. At the drop of a hat, I'll drive down. I love her, you know, Simon?'

That is quite a declaration from inside the Dalton family home. It is a place of ritual and judgement as I recall, not that my brief visits have been sufficient for me to weigh in with a view. I've never thought my wife felt loved by anyone except Vincent while she was growing up. Corrie blows hot and cold on the subject of her mother. We exchange a few more words and then I tell Honoria that I need to go, have to put Leo to bed.

I start to do exactly that but the phone rings before the boy and I have made it to the bedroom. We are mid-stair when I track back down.

'Who have you been talking to, Simon? The phone shouldn't be engaged when I'm in here.'

'I'm sorry, Corrie.' I hadn't expected her to call. I was planning to phone the ward once I'd tucked Leo into bed.

'Caesarean,' she says. 'I'm going down to theatre in a few minutes.

'Gosh. I'll sort it. Be with you as soon…'

'No hurry, Simon. The operation takes quite a while. Settle Leo at Harriet's before you come.'

I agree to this, then she changes tack.

'Who were you talking to, Si?'

'I phoned your mother,' I tell her. 'Just to say you were in Stepping Hill.'

'Oh, Simon. Thank you. I was cursing you, thinking you were inviting a few mates round for cards or something. Thank you.'

'She wants to come down and help, Corrie. Stay with us when

you bring baby home.'

The phone is silent for seven long seconds. 'Help is good. Tell her, yes, Simon. She can come and stay with us. No bastard. Nice to hear she's finally making an effort.'

I feel a degree of relief as we each say, 'Love you,' and hang up. My initial call has not been the miscalculation I feared.

I shout up to Leo who stands on the top stair. 'Baby's a-coming,' I tell him. 'I need to take you back around to Lucy's house.'

Leo is funny-clever. 'Lucy will be in bed now,' he says. His tone of voice implies I'm a bit daft, taking him to another three-year old's house at this time of night. I doubt if he thinks of it as Harriet's house. Funny-clever is not clever-clever; I expect that will come later.

I tell him to make sure his pyjamas and Ted, his bear, are in the small case we have ready. I'll check it too before we go.

I phone Harriet. She is calm, unflustered. 'Thank you so much,' I say.

I head up the stairs to fetch Leo, then turn back before I've reached the top. Return to the phone, call the Cumbrian number once more, Low Fell.

'She'll be going into the theatre any minute. Caesarean.'

Honoria doesn't speak immediately, then says, 'I'm sorry, Simon. I don't think I can face driving in the dark. I'll set off early morning. Should be at the hospital well before lunchtime.'

I'm surprised by her reply, I only phoned to prepare her. It wasn't a summons. 'I expect she'll be kept in for a few days.'

'Yes,' says Honoria. 'I can meet Elspeth. Or the little boy if Cordelia has it wrong. I can tidy up the house ready for the homecoming. You'll be much too busy. That will be all right, won't it?'

'She might be in for days.'

'It's been years, Simon. I can sit out a few days. I don't mind hospitals, you know?'

* * *

Leo is excited when I drive him to Harriet's. Not about the

night in the strange house. He wants to come right on down to the hospital, meet his new sister. I have to say no to that. I can't take him there until I know what's really going on. I'm worried that she, or even he, will be an incubator baby. One we can't hold until a week or more has passed. I think that must feel all wrong. I'll do it but it must be harder to love them through glass.

'In a day or two,' I tell him. 'Right now, Harriet has a comfy bed for you.' I feel like a hypnotist talking soothingly; the boy even yawns after I've said it.

* * *

While I am in her house, tucking Leo into bed, Harriet is hovering by the door. 'Have you got a drink, Simon? It'll be a long night.'

I smile to myself: Vincent would have a hip flask of the strong stuff should the flighty Kat ever bear him a litter of kittens. 'I'll use the vending machine; our outpatient visits have got me hooked on the salty soup.'

Harriet hurries down the stairs. She is clearly a good mother and Lucy no longer sufficient challenge. Adopted me and Leo for the want of occupation.

I step backwards out of the room once my son looks settled. He's okay, he'll know where he is when he awakes. The little girl sleeping in the next room is the one in for a surprise: my little boy around her house again.

Harriet has a flask, cereal bars, a couple of chocolate biscuits for me. 'There's no need for all this.'

Simon Jackson emerges from the lounge, joins the conversation. 'Harriet calibrated what I needed through the night of Lucy's birth. She got it right to a tee.' The little smile on his face tells me I should accept her hospitality.

'What's the drink?' I ask.

'Sweet tea.'

I want to refuse, never sugar my own. Inside my mouth, my taste buds are staging a protest against my own brain. I could drink it sweet right now. 'Thank you.'

Unbridled Joy

The pair wave me off, wish Corrie well. They're a great support to our family; I met both for the first time just a few hours ago.

* * *

The ward sister advises me to wait in the seat next to Corrie's bed, unless I feel restless. 'That's me right now,' I tell her. 'Restless. Need to know—see she's alright—both alright.'

'Until they've come out of theatre, we can only wait, Mr Tripp. We have a visitors' room four doors down. Magazines to keep your mind occupied. Some fathers just pace the corridor.'

I've brought a book with me, one Corrie recommended. I'm loving it, a book about the weirdest wartime childhood. Can't imagine settling into it tonight though. Can't go to Shanghai when I'm needed in Stockport. I thank the nurse, take myself in the direction of the visitors' room. The salty soup. I don't wish to stop her from doing her job.

The room is unoccupied. Alone, I look at the posters on the wall. The horrors of AIDS and drugs, the wonders of immunisation. I'm on board with their messages—nothing to convince me about—the hectoring gives the room a depressing feel. I flop into one of the chairs. It doesn't look comfortable: hard plastic moulded to the curvature of a bum which is not necessarily my own. I realise as I sit that I could fall asleep, although I have called the uncomfortable quite accurately. This makes me stand. I have to stay awake for Corrie. I puzzle over if I'm trying to avoid knowing, running to sleep for fear of what might await us. I've already decided I love this baby, healthy or not. That decision doesn't stop me from wanting healthy, feeling the weight of the alternative. Corrie joked that she wanted a Taurus. Neither of us believe in that nonsense. We'll be happy with an Aries. That's what we're having. We'll be happy with healthy and make-do whatever we get.

I notice a little anger creeping its way up my veins. It's not rational. I didn't care for the nurse, for the way she packed me off to this magazine room. I can see why she might. It may be that I'm angry at my own ready compliance. And yet fighting my way into the operating theatre has never been an option. I'm not stupid; I want to give the doctors the best chance. For Corrie, for Elspeth. Elspeth or Benny. I've come up with that one because Corrie gave up on boy's names when she mystically concluded she's carrying a girl.

I'm not angry with Honoria. Confused by her, maybe. Worried that her presence will upset the balance in our family. Not that it necessarily will. The Daltons are a challenging bunch. Vinny easy company; Tommie's nice but not so laid back. Honoria was always okay with me, not a strong impression made in any direction. I can't understand Corrie's relationship with her. I don't know what it is now or what it was back when, and most of our life together I've thought that I did.

I think over this, a women's magazine in my hands. On the cover a headline reads: I Never Knew My Mother Until I Turned Fifty. Women worry about this stuff more than men. I'll never know my mother, full stop. She looked out for me in her own way, I know that. The cancer wasn't her fault. I lost her before I knew what the word relationship truly meant. I missed her as a kid, nothing to miss now. We never got a shot at having an adult relationship. I thought it was the same for Corrie. She gave up on her mother a long time ago. Now I've learnt that wasn't quite it. Didn't give up, not even when it looked that way. She put it in abeyance. Gave up on her mother's ability to mitigate her father's temper, his calculated sadism. She never gave up the ghost.

A spotty teenager enters the room. A drawn look shadows his face. I wonder if he's taken something. A drug. It could just be lack of sleep. That's a common affliction in the maternity hospital, one which I recall from Leo's birth. The kid is probably only a couple of years younger than I was first time around. And Simon Jackson—Harriet's husband—might think me a kid, even today.

'You don't have a cigarette, do you?' asks the youth.

'Sorry, never smoked. Are you waiting on news?'

'Got a baby girl,' he says. He runs a hand through his hair. It's not long, simply unkempt. 'I'm over the moon.' He sounds dead on his feet, saying the phrase people say in here. After those few words, he simply stares at me, like I might produce a packet of fags that I have secreted upon my person, reverse the first call. I don't and he leaves. I guess he hoped for a boy; that or being over the moon isn't all it's cracked up to be.

I open the magazine, begin to read the headline article. It doesn't go in. Extraordinary that Honoria is coming down. I understand that she stayed in Cumbria until Thomasina was well enough to travel up there with each of hers—Olivia and Terence—when they were newborns. Corrie was living at Low Fell back then. She said it was very formal, both children baptised in the church in Coniston even though the Stapleys lived in Manchester, in Didsbury at that time. She certainly didn't drive down to help her older daughter, and I've never thought Corrie favoured within the family. It's never once looked that way.

I think something must have changed. Honoria never struck me as having the gumption to file for divorce. Catholics seem to be against all that. It might be that Jeremy's lost his bite. Could be marooned in an upstairs room, speechless from a stroke or God finally smiting him with a bolt of lightning. It's a longshot, you'd think she would have told Corrie in one of their calls. I do find, when I try to interpret other people's behaviour, I get it wrong unless it's about what type of car they'll be happiest to hire. I've fathomed that little corner of other people's brains and no other. Corrie will tell me what it's all about when the lady's been and gone, or my mother-in-law could tell me in person tomorrow evening. That would be a first. The couple of times I met her, she said little, and the more I thought on it afterwards, the less it amounted to.

The tall nurse pops her head into the room. 'Your wife is on her way back to the ward.'

'She's okay?'

'I believe so.'

'And baby?'

'You've got a boy, Mr Tripp.'

She is holding my eye. No bad news to impart, it seems, and I feel inordinately thankful for it. 'Brilliant. A little boy.'

Then the nurse looks down at the polished floor. 'The baby is going down to special care.'

Special care, this is a shock. 'Can I see him?'

'I expect so. Wait until Mrs Tripp is back on the ward, please.'

* * *

I put my arms out to hug her then wait, watch for her acceptance. I am frightened that I might hurt her. I don't understand what it is that she's been through. A doctor has been in and out of her since I left in the early afternoon. It's remarkable. Corrie doesn't respond as spontaneously as usual, looks a little bewildered, lying back on the bed. I think she has only just come around from the operation, the caesarean.

I air kiss her. 'We have a baby boy.'

'Don't say it like I'm an imbecile, Si. He's lovely. I held him, cuddled him to my breast.'

I find myself welling up. She is herself. 'Sorry. I wasn't sure what you knew.'

She gives me a strange look like I'm not making sense.

'Did you come around in the operating theatre?'

'Simon, did you read the book I gave you?'

'Yeah,' I protest. Pregnancy book she's talking about; didn't read the chapter about having a caesarean. Never thought she'd need one; it was my dearest hope that she wouldn't. Only skim read the more digestible chapters.

'I had a local anaesthetic. I was in the room, heard his first cry.'

I'm still welling up. I like this but I don't get it. 'How could they only give you a local. It's not a tooth. The baby was pretty much inside all of you.' Then, gesturing her stomach, I add, 'All that bit.'

Unbridled Joy

Cordelia has a beautiful face; her eyes are alive and she is finding some humour in what might prove to be my stupidity. At the very least, my failure to make the most of an easy-to-read guide to pregnancy. It's mums-to-be who need to read that stuff but I'm starting to feel unsure of myself. I've been picturing it all wrong.

'They can numb pretty much what they like. I was conscious; the anaesthetist talked to me throughout the op. He said that earlier today—in the afternoon, not a middle of the night baby—the husband was sitting in throughout the operation. You missed it, Si. I didn't know that they let husbands in theatre up here. I'd heard it was being done in London.'

I feel a bit faint. 'You watched them lift the baby out of you?'

'If you don't want to know the result, look away now.'

I laugh but that would have been me. I could barely bring myself to look at all the afterbirth and whatnot on Sark Farm. The messy calf deliveries. I'm relieved Corrie has got through it so well. I lean in and kiss her again. Properly.

'Little Benny,' I say. 'I want to go and see him.'

'You want to see someone else's baby? I mean to say, mine's not called Benny or anything close to Benny. That, Simon Tripp, is a racing certainty.'

I don't want to argue about it—she's just been operated on—Benjamin really isn't such a bad name. Even sounds like a Dalton if you say it in full. Not that having a posh-sounding name bothers me either way. Before I go to see the new-born, I tell her about the last call I made before I left the house, that her mother will be here in the morning sometime.

She doesn't say anything about that but squeezes my hand which she happens to be holding. 'Find out what he weighs. If they told me, I forgot.'

* * *

Our new-born son, who has yet to acquire a name for himself, is in a kind of propagator. I don't know if that is what the doctors call it. The nurse tells me it is only for observation. He has a little lead monitoring his heart rate. I ask her why: are they worried about it?

'It's just what we do in here,' she says.

I glance at the other baby stations, the glass cots. Tiny babies, strained faces. More than one has a tube leading into a nose, or connected to a vein. Someone must love each one of them; I think that this is what these tiny ones need most just to stay alive. Then I wonder if I'm being as daft as Kerry was first thing this morning. Going baby ga-ga. Their helplessness does something to us, makes us sentimental. My little boy is on the big side to be in here, and when I glance across the lot of them, I laugh. Do it silently but the picture is amusing. Each of the funny cots and fish tanks has a new-born inside. I think that our big fella looks like a fifth former sitting in nursery class.

I remember the question Corrie had, ask it of the nurse.

'Five-thirteen,' she says. 'It's a good weight for a baby born so early.' I remember that Leo was only six-something-or-other and he had the decency to wait out the term.

The nurse is not keen that I handle him. 'If you stay with your wife, he should be on the ward in two or three hours. We don't see any reason for him not to be with mum very soon.'

'So why is he here?'

'The doctors are always cautious straight after theatre. They need to know he's acclimatising properly. It's all very strange for a tiny one, first hours off the umbilical cord.'

I don't really understand what the nurse has told me. I'll remember the weight, and he's coming up to the ward soon. Going to be okay, whatever his name is.

* * *

On the ward Cordelia is still awake. I tell her our boy is looking well, that the nurse said, he's big for early. Give her the pounds and ounces, worry aloud that I've got the figure wrong. Corrie says, 'Think!' and 'Are you sure?' I'm tired and not very sure at all. Tell her it makes no difference, we're not planning to cook him. She laughs at that. 'No, we're keeping this one.'

I sit. Corrie tells me she's getting sensation back following the anaesthetic. When I say, 'Good,' she corrects me. I haven't

Unbridled Joy

thought it through, should have read the book. The doctors have rummaged around in her innards.

She tells me in a hushed tone, 'It's fucking agony.'

I fetch a nurse who nods solemnly, speaks briefly to Corrie then turns back to her nurses' station. I pace down the ward after her. 'Aren't you going to do something?'

She looks a little exhausted but not cross. I think I may have spoken rudely. I didn't mean to but Corrie's in a state. I try to look contrite; the hospital staff are our lifeline. 'I'm phoning the doctor,' she says. 'I should have explained. I expect she will give your wife something to make her comfortable. It takes time for everything to get back into place. It's a physical trauma. Nothing unexpected but she feels it acutely. A lot to deal with.'

'Thank you.'

I return and hold Corrie's hand. She's crying now; I think there is some joy mixed up with all the pain. 'I want him here,' she says.

After a little silence, I ask if she is disappointed not to have a girl. Corrie says, 'Don't be daft,' and I agree with her one hundred percent. She's been through medieval torture to bring this boy into the world—hurting not complaining—I wish I'd not asked.

The young doctor is back—Dr Baker—I'm surprised she's still on duty, over twelve hours since first we saw her. She pulls the curtain around the bed, talks quietly with Mrs Tripp, as she again insists on calling her. I try to pay attention, feel excluded. I hear the doctor repeat the phrase, 'I know,' when Corrie tells her of the intense pain. I wonder if she does, if she has a baby or two to go with her medical degree. I doubt it. She seems to have won Corrie's trust, so I should stop bothering myself about how young she looks.

'Would you like to step outside the curtain.'

I do as the doctor asks. I presume she wants to tell me something without Corrie hearing. It feels ominous that she wants to talk about my wife behind her back. I wait and wait and when Dr Baker finally emerges, she begins tugging back the curtain. 'What is it?' I ask. She looks puzzled. 'You wanted to speak to me out here.'

'No, Mr Tripp. I was just ensuring your wife had some privacy for her injection.'

When the curtain is open—no hiding anything from Corrie—the doctor exchanges a word, runs a hand down my wife's forearm.

'Has it made the pain go?' I ask when the doctor has left.

'It will,' says Corrie. 'I've been morphined.'

I feel uncomfortable about this, a wife on Opium. 'How will you get off it?'

'Simon! You didn't read a word of that book, did you?'

I think this strange day may actually be normal for a maternity ward. The bank insisted that I did a preparation course before they would lend me the money to start up my business. Three days it took. I thought it would be boring: book keeping, financial ledgers, that stuff. Turned out money was only the smallest part: there was employment law, how to track economic projections, managing people without making a drama out of small disagreements. I learnt so much. Christ-knows why I didn't read the having-a-baby book. Just below the surface lurks an idiot farmhand.

'Did I say,' I ask, although my wife is looking drowsy now, 'Honoria is coming tomorrow? Really keen to see the baby.'

She looks back at me. 'I won't be home.'

'She'll come here. See you here.'

'Tidy up, Simon. Try to get along with her.'

I tell her that I will. I know that I may not tidy all that Cordelia would like. Her mother will have to take us as we are. She even said she'd get the house ready for Corrie and baby to come home to. As I'm thinking about this, there is a quiet commotion on the corridor. Little no-name has arrived on the ward. Two nurses accompany him; I recognise one from the special care unit, the other is a youth, a girl with spots and glasses. Swapped her school uniform for that of a nurse, by the look of her. 'Here he is,' the young nurse whispers to Corrie.

Unbridled Joy

My wife takes our new baby from the girl, holds it upon her. Opens her nightshirt a little just to feel flesh upon flesh. The two nurses stand back. I place a hand on the little one's outstretched leg.

'His name is Mortimer,' says Corrie.

'Is it?' I ask. I think he was knocking about with King Arthur, Sir Mortimer of Gadfly or something like it. I don't say so just in case she's serious.

Corrie nuzzles into the top of his head, repeats the name Mortimer quietly into him, permeating his still-soft skull with the sound.

'It is,' I correct myself. 'I like Mortimer.'

'I love him,' she says. 'Love you.' She directs a gentle kiss onto his wisp of fair hair, the very top of our newest family member's head.

* * *

Driving home, I see from the dashboard display that it is five o'clock. I need sleep. I've no idea what to do about work in the morning. It is morning. I suppose Gerry and Kerry will have to manage; I'll be back at Stepping Hill at lunchtime. I want to hold Morty in my arms. I must.

In the house I go for the breadbin. It comes to me that I've left Harriet's flask by the bedside in the hospital. Forgot to eat more than a cereal bar. I grab a piece of dry fruit bread, eat it while climbing the stairs. I put my head in Leo's room, look across the empty bed. I think that tomorrow will be me and him. Corrie will be a few days on the ward, a week maybe. It's probably in the book. Then I remember my mother-in-law will be here too. I've no worries about that, if Corrie's good with it, then so am I.

In my mind, Honoria Dalton is a benign stranger, I have no more met her than I did the nurse tonight. We've had transactions—Christmas two years ago, Killian's wedding— this visit will be an opportunity, we can start over.

Her household and ours are miles apart. Philosophically, I mean. Corrie hardly eats meat, no beef, less chicken than she

229

used to. I'm not fussed but I go along with it. She is adamant that she will consume nothing from Low Fell, and her sure-fire way to achieve that is to eat no red meat at all. Not a sliver in the last four years. She gives all cows and sheep a wide berth. I thought it tasted good when we were up there. The second-best thing to come from the farm after her. She doesn't like me joking about it; she's started up with a bit of animal-rights talk lately. It's rubbish but spot on from the cow's perspective. We'll have to see what Honoria makes of all that. She might nip out to the Wimpy bar the odd lunchtime for a sneaky beefburger, do like I do.

I get into bed trying to imagine how to show her that I've always been the right one for her daughter. We have a decent house. If she's snobby about Cumbrian farmhouses—wants wood beams on the ceiling—I'll have to tell her some home truths. I don't think she'll be like that though. I expect her to be complimentary about our place. We've even got an eight-hundred-pound piano, it has a mortgage of its very own. I'll not show her the books, the debt. I've got it covered, know what I'm doing. It doesn't keep me awake.

And so, sleep comes to me. Why wouldn't it? I am a father of two.

3.

It is after nine o'clock when I awake. I feel groggy. Before dressing I phone my own office. Kerry answers, sounds a little flustered. I often wonder what the place is like when I'm not in, when me and Gerry do deliveries, have to leave her alone. The first YTS girl got her boyfriend in when that happened. I had to let her go, couldn't have her canoodling when she should have been working.

'A baby boy!' exclaims Kerry. 'What did he weigh?'

Again, I say five pounds and quite a lot of ounces, have a stab at a precise number. It's written on a chart for the nurses and makes no difference to anyone else. Surely.

Unbridled Joy

'Lovely,' she says.

I tell her that I'm tired, the baby came late. I've been at the hospital all night.

'Don't mind about you,' she says. 'How's Mrs Tripp?'

Kerry has asked exactly the right question. Corrie's the one who has been through the ordeal. I say, 'Okay.' Hope it's the truth. I thought in the night how the return of feeling to parts that have been numbed, anesthetised, must be horrible. I used to hate the feeling coming back to my frozen fingers during morning milking at Penton, January and February when I was a kid. Everything in the parlour was icy and I'd run them under the hot tap to get a bit of sensation, to be able to use them properly, but the tingling was diabolical. Having that happen to all your innards must be tonnes worse.

Kerry asks me what baby's name is.

'Mortimer. Cordelia chose Mortimer. I like it too.'

'It's lovely,' she says.

I tell her that I'll pop in on my way to hospital.

'No need,' she insists.

I will. I want her and Gerry to meet a father of two. I'm not so bothered about the business, that more mercantile pride is for another day.

Next, I phone Harriet Jackson. She is equally thrilled with the news, expresses it more conservatively. When she asks the weight, I try to sound authoritative and proud. I think it the done thing. When I finally get to ask about Leo, she is all reassurance. 'He can stay if you need to go back to the hospital. To see Corrie.'

I explain that I want him to meet Mortimer. 'We're a family.'

'Of course, you are,' she says. I really think Harriet Jackson gets us. And that says a lot about Corrie too: her friends can be a bit unusual, always good people.

I tell Harriet that I will be around to pick up my son once I've eaten a bowl of cereal.

Then I phone the ward. 'Mrs Tripp is sleeping,' says the nurse.

Ghost in the Stables

I ask about baby.

'He's gorgeous.'

'Are the doctors still worried about him.'

'Keeping an eye, Mr Tripp. His first hours so we must, but he's bright as a button, your Mortimer.'

I recall from his older brother's birth, maternity hospitals are all anxiety before, euphoria after. We've been lucky, two healthy boys. Leo never needed it and this one saw off special care in the blink of an eye.

I stick a bit of breakfast cereal into a bowl, splash on milk. The kettle boils: instant coffee. I take a couple of spoonsful of the mush, two sips of my hot drink. I don't want to be alone. I leave it on the side, maybe I'll eat it later. Go to the car, need to fetch my firstborn. My Leo.

* * *

Harriet wears a navy-blue dressing gown. It surprised me when she answered the door, not yet dressed and it's around ten o'clock. She's decent though, her hair is well-groomed. I expect she's been up longer than me. A ledger is open on the dining table, an array of receipts spread out beside it in small clusters. She's working in some fashion or other and minding youngsters. Dressing is not so important when you've no office to go to, I suppose. The two little children are busying themselves on the floor. Playing with a pretend zoo. Plastic bears and lions, green caging which they've shaped into big and small enclosures. I like how old-fashioned Harriet's toys are. Lucy's toys, I suppose. It's the stuff I had and Leo hasn't, not that he's short of things to play with.

'Where's Mummy,' says my boy.

I explain that she is in hospital and that he has a new brother. We will see them both shortly. Harriet brings two cups of coffee into the dining room. It's pretty similar to the one I rejected fifteen minutes ago but Leo and Harriet make a difference. I stay to drink.

'Having a caesarean can take some getting over,' Harriet tells me. 'I don't suppose you can get time off work, can you?'

Unbridled Joy

'Her mother is coming to stay. And I can be flexible; I'm my own boss.'

Corrie must have told Harriet a little about her family. She's interested to hear that Honoria is visiting. 'She's not bringing her husband, is she?'

'He wouldn't be welcome.'

She looks back at me gravely. I don't think it is our impertinence towards the older generation that motivates it. I'm guessing Corrie's told her quite a bit. 'I hope it's not upsetting for her, for Corrie.'

Harriet makes a very good point. My wife seems okay with the arrangements, it's tricky to guess how she'll get along with her mother after all these years. Even visiting Tommie can bring all sorts of crap up for Cordelia. Honoria might be much worse on the childhood-reminders front. I ask Harriet about her husband's work. I don't like talking about Corrie's family with strangers, she's sensitive about her gruesome past.

Simon Jackson is not at home—out teaching at the university—'He's a published poet,' Harriet tells me, 'however, that could never pay the bills.'

'Poetry? I thought it was a science university.'

'I work in the sciences,' she says. 'Simon teaches economics. Poetry is his passion.'

This sounds a bit girly to me. Corrie would say I should read a few before I snipe at it. Very strange that he teaches economics too. Head not entirely shrouded in mist. 'I don't understand that stuff really. I got my English O-level without reading the poems, just blathered on about how good they were. Never meant a word but that's what examiners want to hear.'

I realise that Harriet is looking at me as if I've produced an audible fart. Warily, while knowing I couldn't help it. Her husband is a poet and I've been rude: it could all be a digestive problem. 'You're not an A-student, I think, Simon?'

'I guess not.' I gather from her tone that she finds it amusing. I suppose my confession—not even reading that guff in

233

school—is not one generally made to a poet's wife.

'It's quite a trick passing the exam without reading the set pieces,' she notes. 'It will have made you feel cleverer than the examiner and rightly so, after a fashion. Simon and I—my Simon—love poetry. It moves us. You passed the exam but missed out on the bigger prize, I fear.'

I think about Corrie's passion for music. See it puts her right up there on a par with these university types. I might be the missing link between these refined people and common humanity. 'What are his poems about?' I shouldn't have professed to having never read one by anyone; I recall sitting outside The Boar in Broughton-in-Furness and telling Cordelia Dalton, as she was then called, that Templeton Ca.—my favourite band aged seventeen, still a bit of a fan—were better than Beethoven. I was wrong then as I might be now; my sixteen-year-old wife-to-be put me straight on the musical order of things. Not that becoming my wife seemed at all likely when we first met. Young Farmers. Corrie read poetry back then, I recall. I think she still has a couple of books of it in our house. I don't know why I give it such a wide berth, I just do.

Harriet is still smiling, not trusting that I am genuinely interested. I fear she understands me too well. 'Exactly what you wrote in your O-level, I expect. Anything and everything. Nothing at a pinch.'

I try again. 'War poetry?' It sounds manly but implausible. Poetry should be sweet floaty words and war must be absolute hell.

Harriet shakes her head. 'Just observations,' she says. 'Carefully crafted.'

I nod, vigorously. I get that. Your own take on everything you see, your personal experience. My mind has been buzzing for days with Mortimer coming into the world, wife having the op: I could write some poetry of my own but I expect it would be useless.

I thank her for the coffee, for caring for our son. She waves it all away. 'Interesting to talk to you,' she says. And perhaps it

Unbridled Joy

was. I like Harriet Jackson while fearing she might regard me as more suitable for anthropological study than friendship.

Leo and I head for the car.

* * *

I call in at Tripps. Leo tells Gerry that he has a brother. He says his mummy thought it would be a sister. 'She was wrong because you can't see inside your tummy.'

Gerry tells him that a brother will do nicely and I concur with this.

We are speaking outside and I see through the glass door that Kerry is on the phone. She beckons for me to join her. When I do, Leo at my heel, she puts her hand over the mouthpiece. 'This gentleman wants six new cars in June, to keep on hire until the end of the year.' I am astonished by the size and duration of the request. Puzzle over the who and the why; whisper a question to her. Kerry doesn't answer me. 'I'll just hand you over to Mr Tripp,' she says down the mouthpiece.

'I didn't catch your name,' I say.

'Mr Rathbone. Chatterton's.'

I know this name. Not the man, just the company in Davenport. There's a big sign on an old converted mill. It's very close to where Corrie and I lived when we arrived in Stockport. Upper Hillgate. He tells me he's expanding his salesforce, short-term contracts. Can I help him with their vehicles? This makes no sense to me. I get mine from Ford, why would he use an intermediary? I don't say this; indicate that I could supply him with some figures if he gives me minimum durations. In the corner of my eye, I see that Kerry is occupying Leo. I wonder if she should be handling the call. It would have all been down to her had I not dropped in. I try to make notes; the details of the man's plan have not solidified yet. Then he asks me—Mr Rathbone who must manage a large salesforce—'Shall we talk it over in a wine bar tonight?' When I pause to think how to answer, he adds, 'On Chatterton's.'

I don't want to appear rude, it's simply that I don't conduct my business this way. Never have, never will. There will be no wine bar tonight: I have a wife and baby in Stepping Hill Hospital and a mother-in-law I scarcely know coming down from Cumbria. 'I need a day or two to look at all options, come up with a proposal that suits us both. This is an unusual request for Tripps.'

'I see,' he says. 'Is it your company or your father's?'

I sense that he is impatient with me. 'My father has no role in Tripps,' I tell him. My father is a dullard who wears bailer twine to hold up his trousers, still scratching a living from a few acres of tarnished Yorkshire soil. I think this fact makes my success more remarkable, choose not to share the insight with Rathbone. 'We usually only do short term rentals. I'm happy to supply you with costings for any duration you like. It might be easier if you fax me a specification in writing. Say what engine size you prefer. Two door, four door. Any automatics. The more detail, the more precise I can be with my figures. I hope I can make it attractive to you; calculated promises that I won't deviate from.'

'You're not a chat-and-shake man then,' he says.

'I like to shake, there needs to be a contract first, substance to it.'

'Yes, yes,' says Rathbone, 'I've nothing prepared to fax. Shall we fix a date to discuss how we might work together, or shall I try other car companies, Mr Tripp?'

'Would you like to meet at my office, Mr Rathbone. Monday would be good.'

No reply comes from the other end for fully thirty seconds. 'Monday. I can do ten,' comes out grudgingly. The man may yet phone other companies. The prospect of losing this windfall might bother me more if I were not so preoccupied by a wife in hospital, Mortimer Tripp's homecoming to prepare.

* * *

I gather from Gerry, and perusal of the notes that Kerry has made, that all our planned rentals are going smoothly. Gerry tells me that the vacuum with which we clean all our cars when they come back from hire is faulty, won't suck. He's going to try and fix it later today; we can't do without one.

Kerry seems grateful that I've called in. 'That man phoned before,' she says. 'Asked a lot of questions about you.'

'Extraordinary.'

She made coffee while I was on the phone. We all have one, Leo just the biscuits. Gerry tells me that he can cover the work for the rest of the week.

'My mother-in-law is on her way; I may not be needed at home.'

'Best come in here if she's back there,' he sniggers. Gerry is a good worker, reliable. I'm not a fan of his old-style humour. I wonder whether to put him straight, tell him Corrie's mum is all right. I'll be spending more time with her than I ever have before. Truth is, I don't know if she is all right, haven't an opinion about her either way. She's never been a laughing matter, that's why his comment irks me.

A car pulls into the driveway, parks in front of the office. It's one of ours and I caught sight of a problem before it even turned off the road. The passenger side front wing has been crumpled. I don't want this today. It looks to be driving okay, no untoward noises. That doesn't necessarily mean the engine is fine, it will need a proper appraisal. Damage is a big problem, copious paperwork, insurers to contact. We don't do bodywork repairs here. Any stuff that Gerry and I can fix keeps the insurance premium down. This is not that. Metal to be straightened out, replaced most likely.

'I'll sort him out,' says Gerry.

That's good for me. Nice to have an employee show initiative. He goes to meet the driver, find the story. Even from inside the shop I can hear the driver saying it is not his fault. Gerry says, 'Forms to fill, I'm afraid.' Good tactic: don't get into a debate. He brings the man into the office.

'I can take it from here,' I say.

I trust Gerry completely but this is my chance to get a view of the driver, the customer. His name is Roscoe, a regular. I don't want to put him off using Tripps unless he's a total liability. Of course, he might be accident prone and that sort are more trouble than a visiting mother-in-law.

It's only a car-park shunt, a lot of damage for low-speed. An old story: two poor drivers each blaming the other. I take his name and telephone number, although they are already on my books. He gives me the names of two witnesses. He and the lady in the other car both wrote them down. This one will be a doddle for the insurers: independent witnesses bring objectivity.

Kerry is earning her money simply by playing with Leo. She might be better at minding kiddies than reception duties, okay at both, I suppose. Or I'm going soft. At twelve-forty I decide I'm done. The customer left a few minutes earlier. I'm giving him one more chance, shared that with Gerry.

A big heartfelt thank you for my two employees and I'm off with Leo. He's about to meet Mortimer Tripp. Car prangs are soon forgotten, he'll have this brother his whole life long.

* * *

'Sweetie!' says Corrie to her eldest son. Leo hugs her, looks around the ward. He was a new-born himself last time he was here, Stepping Hill Hospital. Corrie calls out, 'Susan.'

A nurse comes across. 'Yes,' she says, going to the small cot at the side of my wife's bed. She reaches in and picks up Mortimer, carries the precious baby the two steps to Corrie.

I indicate that I would like to take him. Corrie and Nurse Susan seem to communicate without speech. The nurse passes him to me and I bundle my baby son closely to my person. Crouch down to Leo who looks into Mortimer's face.

'He's funny,' he says. 'It's an old man.' It's true that this one has a few long wisps of hair on a mostly bald head, the nose and eyes of a hedgehog as he struggles from sleep. Funny folded eyelids too. I nuzzle over the top of his head, kiss my second son.

'Not an old man, sweetie,' says mother to son. 'He has the wisdom of living in a cave for a few months.' Leo looks puzzled. Laughs when Corrie points at the bedcovers, at her abdomen.

'The cave inside Mummy.'

I sit on the chair beside her. Leo stands beside his mother, turning his head back and forth between her and baby Mortimer. 'How are you feeling?' I ask.

'It's a whirlwind. Did you see her?'

'Who?'

'My mother only just left. She held Morty before you did, Si. I didn't really want it that way round; have to hand it to her, she was pleasant first to last. Everything I needed.'

'She's not gone, has she?'

'Yes,' says Corrie.

'Back to Cumbria?'

'No, to our house.'

I have a finger inside Mortimer's little hand, he has rolled his tiny digits about it. Makes a little gasping noise, not uncomfortable, just trying the lower gears on his lung-mouth engine. 'She can't get in,' I say. 'I'm here.'

'I gave her my key, Si. Did you tidy up?'

'Of course.' I have just lied to my wife; it is the rarest thing. 'Harriet's been brilliant,' I tell her. 'Did you know her husband, Harriet's Simon, is a poet?'

'Started on his collected works, have you Si? Can I tell you about Mummy?'

'Sorry. Do.' Leo clambers on to the bed and Corrie flinches, experiences a pain that might be related. He has tugged the sheets. 'Let Mummy lie, please. She's been through a lot,' I tell him.

With Mortimer cradled in one arm, I drag a second plastic chair next to my own. Leo scrambles up. Corrie asks for Mortimer, takes him gently against her breast. 'I think I can feed him,' she says. The nurse, Susan, is hovering. Corrie does as she thinks fit, an instinctive mother. 'She drove here.'

I feel distracted by the openness of Corrie's feeding of Mortimer. His head is squashing a very visible breast. I glance around the ward; it is clearly the way they do it in here. Don't feel a need to pull the curtains. That makes sense, I suppose, all

239

at it sooner or later.

'Never done more than thirty miles or so alone at the wheel before, she told me that. Said she's tired of missing out on grandchildren. Sounded a little down on Tommie. The thing is...' Corrie adjusts the baby's position, places a finger on her nipple, very carefully bringing his mouth back to it. Leo looks away as though it is socially unacceptable; he won't remember having the same done for him. '...she kept repeating, "Father wouldn't wear it." She may have just meant that he was the obstacle to her visiting Tommie. My sister has always seen them up north, they've never come down. I asked if he objected to her coming now. "Too late for that isn't it?" That was as much as she said on the topic. I think something's happened between them. I wanted to ask, just never quite got there. It's a minefield for both of us. I hate him and she didn't the last time I could vouch for her allegiance. And now she's here...' Corrie adjusts Morty's mouth again, fingers her own nipple to help him. When she's sorted the baby, resumes talking, the subject has slipped away. 'She was over the moon with this bundle of loveliness.' She looks to Leo. 'Mummy will love you, sweetie. Grandmama to you. Remember? From the wedding.'

'Grandmama,' says Leo.

Two boys form quite an obstacle to a serious conversation, even when one is only up to a little breast-suckling, a little handling like a fragile parcel. After twenty minutes with us, I place my sleeping child back in his cot. Mortimer is a cracking name.

Corrie takes a hold of my hand. I can see from her face that she is in some pain. I don't wish to alarm Leo, try to express my concern with my eyes, glance between her and Susan. 'I'm okay,' she sighs. 'It's like a wave inside me.'

Susan comes to the bedside, feels Corrie's forehead. Nods sagaciously. 'An hour or two more,' she says.

I look at my wife intently, I guess I look worried.

'Medication,' she says. Then she turns my palm over, runs her fingers across it. 'Mummy said you have a lot of

Unbridled Joy

initiative...' Corrie sees my questioning face. '...for phoning her.'

I am too worried about my wife's visible discomfort to laugh. I ran away with her daughter when we were too young to vote, started a business a year ago that looks to be on course to make a decent profit, and yet it seems telephoning her a couple of times yesterday—to say no more than that Corrie was in the hospital sooner than we expected—is the exploit that gets her nod.

'Really. She likes you. Try hard to get on before I come home. Don't go out, none of that wetting the baby's head rubbish. Get to know her better.'

I tell her that I will. I wasn't going to leave Leo with such an unknown quantity anyway. When he was born, the first of our two sons, Corrie seemed unconcerned with wider family. I phoned Tommie and Vinny within an hour of his birth; Corrie didn't phone her mother at all. Honoria rang us when Corrie and Leo had been home for three or four days, after hearing from Thomasina. Vincent came down from Cumbria the first weekend after the boy was born. Not Jeremy, not Honoria, not Killian. The rift hasn't lessened but it seems there are only two still stuck on the dark side. That's how it looks like from here, quite a turn up to my way of thinking.

'She told me about giving birth to Killie. It was long and difficult. I didn't know; mothers never told their daughters about these matters when I was a schoolgirl.' She looks into my face. 'Not my mother, anyhow. And earlier, quite out of the blue, she said to me, "Jeremy can't express his love." I told her straight that he doesn't have any, never has had. "You might be right," she said straight back.'

As I look into Corrie's face, I can see her eyes glistening; I do not know if it is the pain of family, of the awful operation she's yet to get over, or a little happiness that her mother's finally seeing sense.

'I really don't know what has gone on up there,' she adds.

'Do you think she will stay for your first week or two out of hospital?' I'm thinking firstly of support, companionship for Corrie. Enabling me to crack on with work, keep Tripps shipshape, could be a bonus.

'I think so. We'll have to see how it goes. She might want to stay and...' Corrie lowers her voice, barely more than mouths, '...leave the buggering bastard.'

I kiss her; Leo does the same. At the cot I put a hand on little Mortimer's knee. He is thin but has a fold or two there. Still to grow into his own skin.

* * *

I am surprised that her car is not on our drive when I pull up. I imagine Honoria has gone back to the hospital. Our paths cross out of sight of each other, it seems. I unbuckle Leo, lean across and open the car door. He slides himself from the booster seat, trots to the front door.

I open it up. No suitcase in the hall, no evidence that she has been and gone. Leo takes himself up the stairs, singing a song from children's television. I look in the kitchen. My undrunk coffee still sits on the side. Touch the kettle: cold steel.

I suspect that she has checked herself into a hotel. She kindly appraised that I have initiative, still has no wish to share our house until her daughter has returned to it. It comes to me that she might be frightened, uneasy. May think I will tear a strip off her for being such a washout for all of Corrie's twenty-five years. I won't be doing that; however, I can see why she might worry. Jeremy, I would gladly give an earful. Neglected to tell him what an arse he is on the two trips we made to Cumbria when Leo was small.

I start tidying up. It is what Corrie has sworn me to, whether her mother is here tonight or not. I start to wonder if she drove down our road and decided the houses are too close together, too small, too utilitarian. Low Fell is one on its own, literally: a grey slate cube halfway up its own Cumbrian hillside. I don't especially care what has prompted Honoria's decision not to come inside, I care only how it will affect my wife. Childbirth is an emotional time. Her mother has mostly been an obstacle to

Unbridled Joy

us. Nothing she has done in eight years has really told us she doesn't agree with her husband. Whatever she said to Corrie this morning, it scarcely tips the scales. In my recollection, she doesn't really offer anything. When we—Corrie really, I don't think that I matter significantly in Dalton circles—signal our dislike of Jeremy, by running from Cumbria first off, or Corrie's magnificent performance at Killian and Sarah's fellside wedding, we have to unwittingly kick a blind dog. Hurt Honoria because she comes with the package. I've never felt good about that, never felt we had a choice either. The journey today, her visit to the hospital, is an exception. Corrie thinks her mother is switching sides, but she has still to come over our threshold, enter mine and Corrie's home. Raise a flag on our side of the barricades.

My own family are a bit shit but they are simple souls. The Daltons are like Roman emperors, so deep does their intrigue run. Except for poor Vinny, long ago fed to the lions. Well, Kat is his lion of choice and he deserves a little good fortune.

I start to fix some cheese on toast. I'm no cook and maybe that is what annoys me most about Honoria's absence: she serves up top nosh. Leo will eat my cheese-on. I only use mild cheddar, it's kids' food really. I call him and he comes down clutching a girl's dolly. I don't recall the toy at all. It looks new. I think Corrie may have bought it for the never-to-be Elspeth.

'Give me that,' I say to him sharply.

'I like it,' answers Leo. He has a timid look on his face.

'It's a girl's toy, Leo. You're not a girl, are you?'

'But I like it.'

As I go to remove it from him, he looks like he could cry. I dislike this—his wimpishness, and myself for coming across as an ogre—and then I stop mid-stride. I realise that I am reacting against a boy with a girl's toy. Cordelia reckons she is still ironing stupidity out of the odd crease in my brain. This would be one of them. Leo can play with what he likes, be who he likes. I think it over. John Tripp, back on the farm where I was raised, is ignorant, unreflective. I know that he would have taken my sister's dolls off me if I ever played with them, hit me if he thought it would stop me from repeating the offence. I really don't recall such an event but it could have happened, there were things in that ballpark. I don't even think about those times today. I am not a simpleton but without Corrie nudging the tiller now and then, I just might have turned out that way. 'Play away,' I tell my son. He and Morty can be anything they like. Concert pianists, poets. We've needed them for centuries; car hire is the most fleeting of enterprises.

* * *

When we are lounging on the sofa—a plate of breadcrumbs on the floor by our feet, a girl's dolly sitting in the chair opposite, 'Watching us like a mummy,' in Leo's words—the phone starts to ring. I slide myself up the cushion, get to my feet. It might be work, they don't close shop for an hour. I hope it isn't the hospital; from what the nurse told me, Morty's fine and the pain Corrie has experienced is to be expected after a caesarean. Everything under control, even the drugs.

In the hallway I pick up the receiver; the door is open through to where little Leo plays. 'Hello, Simon Tripp speaking.'

'Cordelia Tripp, please?' I recognise the caller straight away and yet the pitch at which he speaks is also too high to be him. He sounds upset. His voice oddly strangulated, as if breathing itself is a struggle.

'Is that Killian? Simon here.' I don't actually think it is Killie, nor can I picture his father—Corrie's father—to be as weak, as broken, as this man sounds.

'I know who you are. It's Jeremy. Can I speak to my daughter, please?'

'She's in hospital. We've had a little boy.'

'She can't come to the phone?'

He sounds desperate. I am annoyed that he is making himself a part of this day. Nice to hear him cracking up now that Honoria's off the farm, yet I'd much rather he didn't call at all. Mortimer was born yesterday, in its final hour. Technically we are still experiencing my son's first day in the world. Farmer Dalton has no part in that. Not a lead, not a speaking part, not so much as a walk-on extra. 'She's in the hospital. Would you like me to pass a message on? Honoria isn't here.'

'Strewth,' he spits down the phone. 'I know she isn't there. Can you tell me what's happened? Were you there, young man?'

'I'm sorry, I don't understand. What are you talking about exactly?'

'The police have been here, told me she's dead. That can't be right. I wondered if you knew different, knew more about it all.' The man is spitting the words at me faster and faster. They mean nothing.

'Cordelia's in hospital. I was with her a short while ago. She's not dead.' Can't believe he's trying to tell me otherwise. 'She's had the baby. A boy...'

'You sound like you've been drinking, young man. And my wife dead. Dead in ruddy Stockport. What happened, young man? Will you tell me that much?'

'Honoria,' I stammer. 'The police came about Honoria?'

'The police aren't interested in babies. What went on, young man? What did you do?'

'I know she visited Corrie. She spent an hour or more with her this morning. Saw Mortimer, the baby.'

'And you were with her? The policeman said she was driving.'

'I...' My head is swimming, can't fathom it at all. I recall a police accident sign. An ambulance at the traffic lights, couple of police cars, Offerton Green, about a quarter of a mile after my little car lot. A bobby waving us through. I never took it in—tried to ignore it with Leo in the car—no interest in a tragedy for an unknown person, not on this joyous day. I don't even know what car Honoria drives. '...I'm so sorry for your loss, Mr Dalton. This is the first I've heard of it. The police haven't been here. I think I should speak to them.' I'm thinking aloud, trying to make sense of what has happened. The accident which I passed is coming back to me. A car on its roof. An absurd sight at that crossing. Someone or other was reckless as hell, flipping a car in a thirty-mile-an-hour zone.

'You're sorry now. Were you in the car?'

'I was not, Mr Dalton. Like I said, this is the first I've heard about the accident. I was expecting her to arrive at our home. Did the policeman not tell you what happened?'

'He didn't say much. That's for why I'm phoning you. You've never been much to the Daltons, I must say.'

'I'll need to tell Corrie. She'll be in pieces. Poor Honoria...'

'Yes. And Killian and I up here, the ones who stood by her. We've been running the farm, the family's lifeblood, while you're racing cars in Stockport. Why she...'

I hear him break up into a coughing fit. His anger might be grief, and he still seems to point it at me. I don't race cars—never have—can't guess what he's on about there. 'Are you able to tell me what the police told you, please?' I ask this quietly. There is no reason for this heat. For the first time in my whole life, I feel sorry for the uptight bastard.

'They thought the other driver was at fault. It's a young woman as crashed into her. Not killed, not as I've been told. Gone to the hospital, I presume. It wasn't our Cordelia, I asked that. My wife got the worst of it, they said, on account of not wearing the belt.'

'She wasn't wearing a seat belt?' As soon as I've said it, I wish I hadn't. I know I sound scornful. Everybody wears them, absolutely everybody. Thomasina told Corrie and I that he won't wear one. She said that Jeremy boasted—over a mealtime during the Christmas just gone—that he would do no such thing precisely because it's the law. He said the adverts convinced him it might be sensible but he's not for doing anything if he's forced. It's a principle with him. I laughed about it when she told me, laughed at him for being a bloody fool. Said it might get rid of him quicker. Tommie never said that their mother followed his example. So stupid. A couple of years back, when the law first came in, my father sounded just as daft.

Unbridled Joy

He changed his tune when he learnt the police had pulled over a farmer two properties along from Penton, fined him for failing to buckle up. Dalton is so self-righteous nothing will change him, not even this, I'm going to guess. 'It might have been the excitement of seeing the baby,' I tell him.

'The other driver. That's who's to blame. And you weren't there, young man?'

'I was not. And I am so sorry for your loss, Mr Dalton.'

'Right.' Then I hear the click of the phone. The man has hung up. He's impossible. A cantankerous fool who can't even accept condolences with civility.

'Leo,' I call.

He slinks his head from behind the open lounge door. The little boy has been listening. My own side of the conversation must have sounded strange. I hope he didn't hear the old git. Can't see how he could have. I do feel sorry for Farmer Dalton and that's a first for me, feeling anything but anger toward him. There's a bit of that in me still, it's just that this was never in the script. He relies on Honoria for everything that isn't agricultural. I even think she is the one for whom church has real significance, it is simply not his style to play second fiddle. He gladhands the priests, gulps down the communion wine. God is a Mafia boss—a dodgy father-in-law—and Jeremy runs His Low Fell syndicate.

'I need to make some phone calls, Leo. You might see Lucy again this evening. Would you like that?'

He nods but looks pretty indifferent about it. He and she are not the biggest buddies. It is Harriet's hospitality that Corrie has tapped into. Couldn't have planned it better.

'Would you find some clothes, Leo? I'll bathe you before we go.'

He looks a bit blank and I indicate he should go up the stairs. When he is away from the hall, I look in the phone book, find a number for Stockport police. Not the nine-nine-nine. The emergency has passed.

When I explain my purpose, the lady on the other end is very

247

helpful, sympathetic. Connects me to a station in Hazel Grove that is responsible for traffic in East Stockport. The next woman I speak to tells me her name, Sergeant something-or-other, I don't take it in. She confirms for me what I already know: Honoria Dalton died in an accident at the top of Offerton. She tells me that the victim has yet to be identified. They presume it is her only from documents found on her person, from the registration of her car. An ambulance took her to Stepping Hill Hospital but she was never admitted to a ward. There was no reason; a doctor pronounced her dead. Came into the hospital car park to notarise what the paramedics already knew. The sergeant asks me if I would be able to view the body, confirm if it is or is not Honoria Eve Dalton. Sounds daunting but it's the least I can do. I am devastated for Corrie. My wife will not be able to comprehend this. I'm stunned myself and the more I picture it the more I recall what a state the upturned car was in. A wreck, a terrible sight. No seat-belt. I even find that I sympathise with Jeremy Dalton, he can shout at me all he likes, this snatching away of a life is unbearable. It will leave Corrie in bits.

I learn that Honoria rests in a mortuary at the same hospital in which my second son awaits the all-clear before entering the wider world, coming home. Where my wife feels the joy of having a new-born along with the pain of her inner organs returning to their regular positions. What she will feel when she learns of this? I wish Honoria were here in our house. I do not know her, never knew her. It would have been a wonderful thing to have rectified. There is nothing I can do to resurrect the possibility now. Nothing at all.

I advise the policewoman on the telephone that I have not seen Honoria since last summer, that I don't know her well. I will identify her if she thinks me qualified to do so. 'People don't change so much in that time,' says the sergeant. I think her throwaway comment to be wrong, quite mistaken. Honoria is dead, changed irrevocably.

When I have finished with phoning, I bathe Leo. He must be

Unbridled Joy

on my wavelength, although I've not tried to tell him what has transpired. Not unhappily, I bathe my boy in silence. Dry and dress him, ready to take round to Harriet's house. Leo looks at me cautiously, he has picked up the gravity of the situation. I don't know how.

Harriet is shocked when I phone her. Offers any help we wish for. 'Poor Corrie,' are her signing-off words. And that thought has been lodged in the front of my brain like a little piece of stone since I first understood the reason for her father's call. A conversation like no other I've known. I'm struggling to believe it's happened, keep wondering if I imagined the call, imagined the overturned car. I did not. Whatever it is I am feeling, everything is all too real.

* * *

A policeman meets me in the reception area. There is a desk but no NHS clerk behind it. I wonder what goes on here, maybe the police have control over this part of the hospital. I've not thought about it before, who controls what. The doctors' jurisdiction must end when the pulse does.

I worry how Corrie will react to me identifying her mother's body before I've even let her know that such a task has needed doing. One thing at a time is my motto, the best way to through a tight spot, and this feels as difficult as they come.

'First dead body?' he enquires. The policeman looks very old to me. I heard they could retire at forty-five. This one is well past that, didn't get the memo. Balding on top, what hair he has is thin and white; his uniform looks far too large, airy; his face is lined, crease after crease. A slim man inside clothes and skin of a fatter one. He's not retired so I guess he loves his job. And it's a grim one in my estimation; I'd rather be anywhere else.

'I've not done this before,' I confirm. It bothers me, I'm not good with gore. Hopefully there is none. I saw death a few times on the farm. Sheep commonly, cows once or twice. People never. I had no reason to look upon my mother's body after her death, I'm not sure my father did either. She was already in the hospital, identified while living. I did learn, back then in my

249

early teens, that death is always close. The turn of a corner away. I'm not minded to poke my head round, go looking for it. No sneak previews, when mine comes I hope it's quick. Hope Honoria's was and it feels a cruel thought. I wish none of it had happened.

During the drive down here, I thought only of Corrie. Only of her for the first couple of miles. She will remember today all her life. The life before her mother and the life after, they will be distinct. It is surely that pivotal in a girl's life. And she is a girl, a quarter of a century isn't much. It made me think about my own mother and that is the rarest thing. I don't grieve her. Maybe I did when I was still a schoolboy but the time has passed. I cannot remember the child I was when she lived. One or two anecdotes, stuff we did together, sure. But I am a different person. I don't think it was losing her which did that to me although it must have done something. It was finding Corrie that changed me. I have a before and an after pivoted upon her role in my life. All for the good, her presence has changed me for the better. One hundred per cent. It bothers me that I may be unable to rescue her from this loss, as she did me from mine. I am already in her life, whereas her arrival transformed everything for me. Where I lived; how I lived; who I was deep down. There can be no step change for Corrie. I'm already doing for her what I can; I hope it will prove enough.

The policeman leads the way into the mortuary. I expected a smell of TCP or alcohol, not booze but the cleaning, rubbing, disinfecting stuff. Tramps would drink it, I suppose. Instead, I find it like an office, the whiff of an unaired basement. Filing cabinets—big grey metal ones—line the walls. I can't see any damp cardboard but I can smell it. This undertaking is going to be distinctly unpleasant, staring at a corpse, bringing to mind the last time I saw her alive. Identifying that it is my mother-in-law. And I think telling Corrie will be much, much worse.

'We think the husband might come now. He's rung again.'

I don't say anything to this. I know I could not tolerate him in my house, sympathetic as I try to be to his grief. This cruel turn. If it's changed him, it isn't even for the better judging by the phone call.

'First, he said he couldn't, that he is working. Now he can. Do you know him? Mrs Dalton's husband.'

'He's my father-in-law. We don't get on.'

The policeman gives a dry laugh, stifles it quickly. This room must hear little laughter; his is utterly tactless. 'Are you alright, son?'

'Is there a body in each drawer?' I guess that there is and, irrationally, I fear it. The dead cannot hurt us; it is the prospect of joining them which makes us uneasy. The metal lockers in here are more than six-foot deep, cavernous cabinets by the look of them, each with just two drawers. An upstairs and a downstairs. I count a dozen cabinets on each of the two long walls. Two times twelve times two again: this place can accommodate forty-eight dead bodies. Counting is better than contemplating. If they have old medical files in them, I will be pleased to learn it, yet I feel certain that every drawer prefigures a tragedy. May house a body but no longer a soul. This is not a gateway, not heaven's waiting room. It's not even lost property: the depository of discarded bodies. They'll each get identified but no one's taking them back home to share a supper. They're done.

'Most,' replies the policeman.

I have only ever attended this hospital—Stepping Hill—for the birth of children, for Leo and Mortimer. It alarms me to find death so close at hand. 'Let me see and go,' I say. 'Will the husband identify her as well?'

'If he turns up. We need to be certain about who's who. I had a case one time, a chap we identified by his wallet. Brother did the viewing, confirmed it were 'im. Then the dead man turned up in this hospital, on a ward, alive but without his wallet.'

I look at the old policeman, wonder what on Earth he's jabbering on about. The dead aren't always dead, seems to be the gist of it.

'You've not grasped it, have you? He was the victim of a mugging. That's how his wallet ended up on a different corpse. Mugged by a lookalike in the brother's reckoning. Couldn't see it myself once we'd had a squint at both.'

I watch a lot of crime series on TV but can't fathom the point of this. I think he is implying my identification of Honoria may be meaningless. 'Who died?' I ask. 'The mugger?'

'That's it. There might have been two. One killed the other. The first chap was found alive, brought in. The hospital patched him up. We found the victims two miles apart. Both knife wounds, only one fatal.'

'Wouldn't the second stabber have taken the wallet?'

The policeman shrugs. I don't think he had anything to do with solving the murder case. Not by the sound of it. He just opens up the drawers of the dead, same as the traffic police mostly check driving licenses. The man has a ledger beside him on the only desk in this office. I think he's looking up which drawer number we require, which one houses Corrie's mother. Unless I am to view a stranger, killed while driving her car, carrying her documents. I can picture no version of reality where that will be so. Even the failure to wear a seatbelt has started to sound exactly like something every Dalton would do. Every one of them except Corrie and Tommie. Even Vinny's daft enough for it.

'And you'd think a man would know his own brother. We can't have too many identifications, not when we need to get to the bottom of it...' I think he's talking on and on because I am so quiet. '...can't make mistakes here. Not in the long run. We need to be sure of the who and the how. Every exhumation is a failure.' This policeman is hopeless, makes his mortuary sound like an old sock drawer.

He opens the cabinet that his paperwork has directed him to. The sound of a metallic scrape goes through me. Like a whispered shriek. The drawer is long, wide and heavy by the sound of it. I want to get this over with but also fear going too close. Mustn't touch anything, not if it has been in contact with a dead body. I look into it, the enormous filing cabinet of an ended life. The policeman draws back the plain sheet. The first thing I see is her white hair, it is not as neat as I expected. Several strands are loose, not in line with the majority. The poor lady has been in a terrible traffic accident; there is bruising too. The colouring of her skin the lightest grey. I scrutinise her forehead, the closed eyes, regal nose. Might this, by some yet-to-unravel mystery, be a different white-haired lady? She was driving Honoria's car. A car thief? Everything I see tells me it's her. Everything except the unworldliness of her flesh, its gelatinous appearance as if this is a waxwork of my mother-in-law. I know that no such muddle has been made. A doctor in a hospital car park will not mistake the absence of vital signs on a dummy for a dead lady. Such an illusion could only work the other way around. A mannequin with a pulse, soft flesh, that might fool the lot of us. I realise I am not concentrating, letting myself drift into a morbid daydream. There is no flight from this. I can wish for all the explanations I like, wish Honoria was not really dead. I cannot will it, powerless to make it so. The drawer contains the woman I expected to cook dinner for tonight. Would have let cook for me if she'd offered. It is her in the drawer, the most helpless and expired arrangement of her. She lies a hundred yards of corridor from her youngest, sometimes-estranged daughter. From her fourth grandchild. I tell the policeman that this lady is Honoria Dalton of Low Fell Farm, Ulpha, Cumbria. I think the most forlorn look might be upon my face. The policeman has certainly stopped wittering. I look at her for a few seconds more. The man closes the drawer.

'It's Honoria,' I say again.

'Alrighty,' says Plod.

* * *

I walk so quickly up the corridor that I can hear my own feet smack the vinyl flooring. Believe that I hear the sound echo back off the hospital walls. I have an image in my mind, a false image. She was frighteningly dead, not how I should have been seeing her today. Still, in those last few seconds looking into the drawer that housed Honoria, I heard—not literally but inside my own head—the same voice which chatted amiably on the telephone just a day ago. 'Dining alone after all.' That was all I heard. I confirmed her identity and left before accidentally blurting out this madness to the burnt-out police officer. It wouldn't have made a difference; however, I've no wish to be the subject of that man's idle chatter the next time he is opening up a drawer for a grieving relative.

I don't see why the woman would say so trite a comment should the dead speak. And I also know that they do not. I am not in two minds about it. The voice was inside my head. Shock: that is what people say, so shock it is. Today I have had my share and now I must pass it on to Corrie. I fear that it will not diminish with the handling, that the jarring I have felt since her father's phone call—that has stirred some sort of auditory hallucination in my churning brain—is but nothing to how my wife may react.

And I shan't be dining alone. I will collect Leo. I need to remove the thought of it, the apparent reality of what surely did not happen, the disembodied voice of Honoria Dalton, from my strained mind. I need to help Corrie over this. It may prove more painful than the realigning of her internal organs.

And Honoria has truly been displaced, can never get back to where we'd all wish her to be. That she cannot, that she is stuck where she lies, is the one thing I can see clearly. She is in the other place, the wrong one. No place at all.

* * *

I go directly to Corrie. She is awake. I am too focussed on what I must do to think of going to Mortimer, aside in his cot. I try to give my wife the most sympathetic look I am able. I fail, can't arrange my face in any way that communicates what I need to; appear only as harrowed as I feel.

'You've not argued already?' she says.

'What about?' Then I correct myself, arrest this drift from the point. 'She's not there, Corrie. Your mother didn't make it.'

'I told you she did. She was here much earlier today.'

Unbridled Joy

'No, she never got back to Marple...' As I dither, try to form words to say what really happened, I see Corrie's face change. The notion that I may have upset her mother, argued, or even that Honoria may have caused me annoyance, these have given way. She is listening most intently. '...there was an accident.'

'Simon, what kind of...'

'A car-crash. She wasn't wearing her seatbelt. Corrie...' I take both her hands in mine. '...your mother was killed soon after she left this hospital.'

The nurse, not one I recognise, must have fathomed the import in our conversation. She comes across, stands a little to the side. Listens discreetly. Whatever happens on this ward it is her business and I feel glad of the support.

'Killed?' says Corrie. 'I'd not seen her until today. Never talked like that...'

'I know,' I say wrapping a careful arm around her shoulders. Since hearing this awful news from Jeremy Dalton, I have pictured this, breaking it to Corrie. Now I do so she does not dissolve into tears, wail with grief. My visualisation missed the mark. She looks bewildered, falls quiet for a moment.

The nurse says, 'Should I give you a minute?' We both nod our heads, and she walks up the ward.

I step aside, lift up my sleeping son. When I glance at Corrie, she pulls her eyelids together tightly, longingly, as if trying to squeeze out tears that will not flow. She is not a baby, not one to cry without good reason. I've never known my wife shed tears in the cinema or while watching a TV film. She dislikes the mawkishness of that stuff. But during conversations about her family, childhood conflict, our leaving of Cumbria—of which she remains as proud as me—or two or three years back when she still used to mull over the loss of her horse, tears were frequent. Coming to terms with the seismic shift these events conjured beneath her feet. This news about her mother is as large as any, maybe larger. I think tears will come.

I cradle my baby son briefly in my arms, quickly pass him to Corrie, as she has gestured for me to do. She is sitting up now.

255

Asking me how, what happened. When I say I had to identify the body, she gasps. 'Oh Simon.'

The nurse walks passed us again, says nothing, sees that Cordelia needs this baby in her arms. I realise Mortimer is the greatest comfort and I am pleased for that, felt overwhelmed by the prospect of trying to help her get through this trauma alone.

'Your father phoned. The police were at Low Fell within the hour, from what I gather.'

'Amazing,' she says. I doubt if this is her intended word. Corrie is far more articulate than me. She will be astonished, surprised, shocked; her amazement she will surely reserve for Morty.

'He hadn't taken it in properly. He thought I was in the car. Asked me to explain it, when his call was the first that I'd heard.'

Corrie runs her lips across our baby's wispy hair. 'Morty, Morty, Morty,' she whispers. Then she turns to me. 'It's so unfair.' I nod and she repeats the phrase. 'So unfair.'

'The policeman told me he's coming down. Jeremy will be in the hospital in a couple of hours.'

As I say this, her demeanour changes, shoulders sink a little. 'Nurse,' she calls.

The same nurse comes around for the third time in as many minutes. She is Harriet Jackson's age, I guess. Ten or fifteen years older than Corrie or I. Her uniform is light blue, carefully ironed. She has black hair tied back, a single narrow pony tail, clasped at scalp and tail's end, a neat and proper nurse.

'I need to go home,' says Corrie. 'We must take Mortimer to safety.'

'No, Corrie,' I say firmly. 'You're not well enough; they're still keeping a close eye on Morty.' I didn't expect this reaction. Her father is a broken man and I might need to make that point.

'Me and baby, we've got to go. Simon, you're driving us.'

'Cordelia,' says the nurse, 'you cannot discharge your baby. Not until doctor says.' She draws herself up a little taller before adding, 'And I strongly advise you to stay with him.' I think it a pretty confrontational way to speak, after which the nurse looks at my wife pleadingly. 'Can you tell me what has upset you?'

Corrie turns her head away. I try to assure the nurse that Corrie will stay but I don't seem to be in charge of anything right now.

'He's ours. It's my right to leave with him.'

'Corrie, Corrie, it's better to stay. I can stay here with you.' I turn to the nurse. 'She's had some upsetting news.'

'I gathered,' she says quietly to me, not excluding Corrie but angling for elucidation.

I start to say that her mother was in a car accident this morning, killed between the hospital and our house. My voice breaks as I say it, I find a splutter of tears coming from me. I swear they are Corrie's. I don't cry. Ever. I feel ashamed that I can't even tell the nurse the facts she needs to know without making a spectacle of myself.

My wife picks up my hand, holds it in both of hers, Mortimer held in that cradle between us. 'It's awful,' she tells the nurse. 'My father is coming now. Simon has already identified my mother—her body—in the mortuary. In this hospital. He needn't come but he's on his way. He will try to see me. I won't have it; I have to go, go with Morty. Simon will drive us. It's what we have to do.'

'You don't wish to see your father?' asks the nurse.

'Can't. There is no wishing about it. I can't.' She has raised her voice, not shouting, simply letting the nurse understand there is to be no debate.

I see the mothers in the beds closest by looking intently at us. I put an arm around my wife's shoulders once more. 'Stay. There's another way. I can stay with you.'

'You've to look after Leo?' she says. I am looking at her with bewilderment, I suppose. She is usually so calm, never overreacts. Plots a sensible course. 'You don't see it do you?' Her voice is louder still, I think. Talking fast. She's like a

257

different person. Not in looks but in manner. 'I don't know what Mummy has done. Why she even came to Stockport. That man will blame me. Take it out on me. He might do anything to our children. You know that. I've told you exactly what he's like.'

I see that one nurse has had a quiet word with another. The one who has been watching us has stayed, the other walked up to the ward office. They're up to something.

'Corrie, he can't do anything. This is Stockport, not Low Fell.' As I say it, I feel like I'm describing some ancient law. The buggering bastard has no jurisdiction here. It makes no sense—boundaries within which he may or may not do as he pleases—and yet Corrie looks at me keenly, like I might have a point. 'He's only coming to identify the body,' I try. Her fear is infecting me. I don't think I could drive her from this hospital, make her suffer without the support, even the medication, which she needs to get over the operation, and nor can I say no to her. I never say no to Corrie.

'You did that Simon. He's not needed and he knows it. He's coming to wreak some... ...vengeance.' Her lips moved, mouthed the word, fucking, mid-sentence, but she has the control not to let it be heard. There are babies by every bed, it is not the language of the maternity ward.

The nurse is nodding at me. She wants to have a word. Corrie is still on her bed. However much she might want to leave the hospital, I don't think she physically can. I hope she starts to see it for herself; if I argue with her, she always wins.

'Leo is at Harriet's; your father can't possibly know where that is. I'm staying here, I'll watch over you all night, Corrie. Won't let him near.'

I put my face to hers, hug Corrie close. We remain united in our thwarting of him, never have we given an inch to her terrible father. It could have been in our wedding vows. I think it is animal instinct that has held back her tears. She needed to fathom the story, that is the way with her family. Until she understood how the land lay, she could not indulge in frivolous emotion. I feel a surge of anger inside me; it could be fate that

Unbridled Joy

I'm raging against. I didn't know I was at odds with anything until the feeling swelled. Corrie holds on to me tightly, Morty still in her arms, to the side, he evades the crush. Her shoulders convulse in two bursts of tears. She starts to push away from me. 'Thank you, Si,' she whispers. I release her and she me. Corrie's eyes are a flood. 'I'm sorry to have been sharp,' she says to the nurse, blubs it but her point is clear. 'My baby and I are staying with you.'

The nurse nods. 'I am glad,' she says very quietly. I feel unsure if she trusts us yet, nor did she flinch as Mortimer bobbled in my wife's arms, our unrehearsed choreography. She has at least understood that Corrie loves the new baby. Can do him no harm. Even her threat to leave was her way of putting him first, I hope the nurse can see that.

And Corrie is not one for changing her mind. I want to tell her that Jeremy sounded helpless, even feeble, when we spoke by telephone earlier, don't because I know it would be futile. She has prior experience of him: the thrashing man of the fell. That will not fade to nothing, not on the basis of a phone call she was not even party to. The baby upon her breast moves his arms slowly as if learning to swim. We smile together at these meaningful gestures. I take Mortimer from her, again kiss the top of his head. As I step towards the cot, the nurse intervenes, takes him from me, gently places our son in his bed.

Then I hold my wife's hand, not tightly, lovingly. The simplest gesture. We are very tactile, perhaps more so now than those early years on Hillgate when we were just children thrown down the road too soon.

'And Mrs Tripp's father?' asks the nurse, turning back to me. She has gathered what is at the nub of the problem.

'I will stand guard,' I tell her.

She walks up the ward, indicates that I should follow. Quietly the nurse asks if the man—'Granddad' she calls him—is a security risk. I tell her that I can handle him. 'The hospital has procedures,' she says, but I shake my head. 'And Mr Tripp…' She is looking around, ensuring that we are far enough from

Corrie's hearing. '...has your wife had these episodes before?'

I don't really know what she means, tell her as much. 'She's alright.'

'Childbirth is an emotional time but this seemed very irrational. We can get her assessed. Psychiatrically assessed. Although I can see she is calming now.'

I raise a hand, a flat palm. 'Nurse...' I scrutinise her badge. '...Nurse Cooper, her father put her through hell. Flogged her with sticks as a child. Don't tell me that she's crazy because she doesn't like the idea of him visiting. What he's going through, his wife dead the moment she finally chose her daughter over him...' I cannot go on. I have an insight which overwhelms me. Everything that Corrie has just done—her panic, her raised voice, her wish to flee from the hospital, from where Jeremy Dalton might find her—leads the nurse who doesn't know the man to think she is going mental. Corrie is sounder of mind than me; her father's return has loomed within her fears like an unerring tide. We would all run up the beach, take ourselves beyond its reach, had we been put through a quarter of the torment she has.

* * *

A little later I telephone Harriet Jackson. Explain as much as I can. She is the most understanding person. 'Not him,' she says when I raise the matter of Farmer Dalton's imminent arrival. I go on to tell her it is to keep him and Corrie apart that I must stay. 'Do you want my Simon as back up?' she asks.

I tell her it will not be necessary. Inwardly I wonder what use a poet could possibly be in a fight. I have no wish to put him down, do not let my dismissal of the offer come into the communication. 'Thank you, no need to trouble him.'

Leo comes to the phone. He is still very unsure of this contraption so infrequently has he spoken into one. He confuses it with an unsatisfactory toy which he similarly chunners into.

'Who's that?' he starts with, although I heard Harriet tell him it was to be me as she passed across the receiver. I ask if he is happy at Lucy's, if he's being good. I tell him I must stay at the hospital tonight. Leo gets clever, says, 'Are you poorly?' I think he means it; I assure him I am not. When I come to hang up, tell him I love him, that his mummy loves him too, he says the breeziest, 'Yes.' Within our tight little family, it goes without saying.

* * *

Tonight, I do not sleep. Not close. I do not wish to do it and so I shall not. I have a purpose: I am soldier, sentry, homesteader, all of these rolled into one. A father and a husband, my kinfolk safer for my presence.

I wander periodically between the ward and the room full of magazines. It is where I spent a little time just one evening ago while Mortimer was being skilfully evicted from that first home within his mother. I drink two black coffees and two salty soups, spaced out with military precision. I look closely at the face of every visitor to this ward, step out of the room onto the corridor with each new arrival. I try to underplay my investigation of their identity, although it is my sole reason for looking upon them. The number of arrivals, visitors in the night, is very small. Jeremy Dalton never one of them.

My wife sleeps fitfully. I think it is the discomfort in her stomach—or close by—which causes her to rest flat on her back. That is not her usual posture, not for sleeping. I have known her curl up as tight as a ball. Now I can watch the rising and falling of her breast, more ample than at any time in her life. She has a lovely face, no smile upon it in her sleep. All our life together I have considered her troubled by childhood, struggling to put it truly behind her. The death of Honoria might have complicated that. I have loved her since we chanced to meet—at the Young Farmers meetings in Broughton-in-Furness, a nothing little village in beautiful South Lakeland—I think this feeling has intensified, multiplied, grown deeper and stronger and I already loved her more than I knew how to feel back then. Back when I was the tongue-tied farm boy who couldn't ask her on a date.

Morty's chest also rises and he too sleeps on his back. I wish

Ghost in the Stables

I could look in on Leo, as I have done so often in his almost-four years of life. These are my family. I am sorry for Honoria's passing, even for Jeremy's loss, although there cannot be a harder man with whom to sympathise. Cordelia is the only one from Low Fell for whom I would go to war.

* * *

I thought it would be a long night but it has proved otherwise. I have loved gazing on Corrie, on Morty. Spoke to her reassuringly through a single sleepy feed. I had more purpose in my discreet appraisal of the nine visitors who have entered the ward than I do for most activities in life. I like car hire but know it is only a game. In that small cohort—coming to the ward in the nighttime—only a junior doctor spoke to me. He said he was waiting for his girlfriend, one of the nurses soon to be off shift. I appreciated his need to explain himself, assure me he was not part of the problem. Not that he will have had any inkling of the drama playing out in my head. At no point did the hated man show his face. Now—after a quick word with the nurse on duty—I leave my post. She understands who she is to keep an eye out for. Whatever these nurses write down it must add up to something; they're on our side and I will always be grateful for that.

It's back to the mortuary for me. A bit creepy but at least I shall chat with the living, not perusal of a vacated body beneath an off-white sheet.

I tell the girl on the desk who I am, that I identified Honoria Dalton yesterday. I say that I expected her husband to come; that her daughter, Cordelia, is on the maternity ward. I say nothing about the rift between them, the chasm. History written in a horse's blood. The receptionist is young—like Kerry in my office—too young to spend her days just outside a room containing drawers full of cadavers in my layman's opinion. I am not this girl's careers advisor and nor is she as unsuited to the role as the policeman yesterday. Very helpful, and she doesn't stray from the point, in fact, if they keep her and sack the bumbling bobby, the place would run more smoothly.

'Mr Dalton viewed the body with police in attendance at twenty-two forty-five last night,' she tells me. 'I don't know where he is now. A Cumbrian undertaker has been booked to take Mrs Dalton to Coniston once the coroner has agreed to release the body.'

He has gone, come and gone—driven a hundred miles or more to assure himself that the knock on the door was not a hoax, nobody playing tricks on him, turned around and driven straight back—perhaps he came to assure himself that it is only in death that she has deserted him, however implausible her living flight might have seemed. He has been duped by no one but his God.

My wife was terrified that he would traverse the whitewashed corridors from mortuary to maternity. Lay a claim to her, to his newest grandchild while he was at it, despite eight years of freedom from his insidious patriarchy. As this young receptionist makes a note of my brief enquiry, it comes to me. The man never gave a second's thought to the prospect of visiting Corrie. Has no wish to engage her, me, or even tiny Mortimer Tripp, on any inch of land not owned by him. Land tied to the Daltons in perpetuity. I am surprised he made it to Stockport without vaporising, disappearing, turning to ash. So particular is his belonging on this Earth.

Chapter Four

Stuck-Up Little Runt

1.

Had he gone to the Young Farmer's meetings a few weeks earlier, he would have met Corrie sooner and then he would surely know what's what by now. They might have got themselves onto a proper footing, or he may have learnt it was a one-way crush. That must happen too. A few weeks is all it would have taken, two or three. She never went to the meetings herself until May. Had been only twice before he turned up. He thinks three or four weeks would have made all the difference.

Simon works at Sark Farm. It is nearer to Broughton-in-Furness than the Dalton's farm, Low Fell. Lived and worked on this farm since leaving school a year ago. The only labourer employed by the Brownings, another family of bad-tempered farmers.

He can do the work. They pay him okay: a lot less than he's worth but that's farming. In his first ten months in Cumbria, he barely went out of an evening. Maybe a cycle ride while it was still light enough. Through the winter months he went back home if Will gave him the weekend off but he's stopped that now. His father still expects him to milk and toil on that Yorkshire farm during days off from his real job. Simon is no mug, he stays put.

It's boring for him, he has no friends here. Spends a lot of his free time in his room reading science fiction in the evenings. Or he listens to cassettes which he picks up second hand. By his own reckoning he has everything Templeton Ca. ever recorded.

The bootleg of London Live might be a collector's item. It's no duller than living at Penton Farm, Aysgarth, pretty much the life he expected. If Will Browning gets in a strop, shouts at him, he never takes it personally. The man is an arse but he's not Simon's father. In one ear out the other.

It was Will who suggested the Young Farmer's meetings in Broughton. Simon thinks the farmer and his wife are embarrassed that their employee spends so many evenings in the small attic room that comes with the job. 'I met Carol there,' he offered, as if it constituted an incentive. Having an overweight wife to shout at, one who shouts back with bells on, was not an obvious draw for Simon.

The Brownings met there years ago; Will's memories are of the club in a different era. They—the husband and wife who employ him—have kids in primary school now.

He relented, no real objection to the idea, decided to give the current crop a go. It's a beer and a little company. He's a paid-up member now, the Young Farmers, Broughton-in-Furness, South Cumbria.

His first time was seven weeks ago, and as a consequence, he has only met Cordelia Dalton three times. And now, for the third week in a row, she has not come. Simon feels that she is avoiding him. He briefly thought of her as his girlfriend although no such words have been spoken between them. This three-week absence makes the very notion ridiculous.

* * *

He cannot understand why she is staying away. They never fell out, simply never put into words the interest he thought they each had in the other. Perhaps it is all his and none of it hers. He never told her he loves her, has never spoken such words to another human being. He would like to say it and Corrie is certainly the person he has in mind. He fears sounding helpless or unintentionally making her laugh. So long as she stays away, he can't even do that.

Perhaps she has found someone else? Utterly devastating. Vincent should have said.

Stuck-Up Little Runt

Two weeks ago, fourteen nights precisely, Vincent Dalton was here, in this room, although he did not stay very long. Unusual for him. Simon wanted to ask where Corrie was that night, why she had not arrived on the back of his moped as she had done before. He would have told her, no reason why not. Might have said she was seeing George or Tim. Some lad who plays piano, violin or rides a fine horse. He never asked, so he didn't learn. And he has no notion that other boys are in her life. Seems unlikely. Corrie Dalton attends a girl's school, lives at the back of beyond.

He ventured close. 'Fancy another pint, Vinny?' These were the only words Simon directed at Corrie's brother in the ninety minutes or so they hovered in the same room. He thinks himself a fool to have asked no more than the offer of a drink but it is hindsight. Two weeks ago, he was happy to wait another week. Didn't foresee her absence from the club becoming a permanent state.

'I've to be off soon, my friend,' Vincent said that night, and then he turned quickly away. Simon recalls that it was Janine he turned towards. Vincent was talking to the most coveted girl in the Young Farmers' meeting. He had previously professed no interest whatsoever in the large girl whose father has an even larger farm, has sired only daughters. Simon now thinks Vincent was avoiding him. Can't have been cosying up to Janine Fox; that kind of angling is another man's game.

Vinny leaving early? Very strange, he thought, both then and now. And he called him 'my friend' but that is just how Corrie's brother is. It might have been a consolation prize, contained a hidden meaning that his sister has found a less agricultural boy to spend a Thursday night with. Or it could have been a piano lesson or riding in the summer light that detained her, no one else involved but an elderly teacher or her oddly named horse. But if it were either of those, Vincent would have been more likely to say. A rival for her affections might have made him feel embarrassed, conflicted. And whatever tied his tongue, it really did cut both ways. He gets along well with

Vinny; there was nothing stopping Simon from asking except the fear of rejection. And that is no reason at all unless you let it be.

Simon thinks he should have kissed her when he had the chance. When he wanted to, behind the church. He found himself unable without some clear sign, certainty that she wouldn't laugh or scream. Bop him on the nose. She is not an easy girl to read, Cordelia Dalton, and nor is he a scholar of girls. Never sat a single exam.

Tonight, Simon is supping up his third pint of Hartley's. He might have a fourth but wonders if he'll be in a state should the moped buzz, Vinny bring Corrie to The Boar before the meeting breaks up completely. Gone ten o'clock, it's highly unlikely. He feels wobblier than usual. He'll have to stop on his cycle ride back to Nibthwaite, pop behind the dry-stone wall for a pee. It's what he did last week and the week before. He's still a kid, can't hold down his beer yet. When Corrie was here, he only drank two pints; she and he among the most moderate drinkers at Young Farmers. They shared no beer or cider the third time they met, the time they did not enter the pub, join the meeting. He had no need for alcohol: he was drunk on her, on looking into those lovely brown eyes beneath her unlined forehead, a tartan Alice band holding back her rich chestnut hair. He thinks her the worldlier of the pair even though he works while she sits behind a school desk. She's learning stuff he'll never know, that's the truth. As he sniffs over the dregs of this third pint it hits him again: there is no pair.

'You're a misery tonight,' Patrick Vulliamy tells him.

'Can I get you another?' he asks, raising his own empty glass.

'It's my round.' His friend pats him on the back. 'You're missing the girl, aren't you?'

'No,' says Simon, not wishing to appear so forlorn. 'I'd talk to her if she was here but…'

'Missing her,' Patrick overrules. 'Do you know her friend, Millie?'

'No,' he answers. Corrie has said the name but Simon has

Stuck-Up Little Runt

never met her.

'Both those girls go to my church. I think I'd stop going if they didn't. I've had my eye on them but...' Patrick nods in a highly suggestive manner, enlarges the whites of his eyes momentarily as his head dips. '...you know?'

'What?' says Simon. He cannot imagine they get up to very much that merits the rolling of eyes; prayers and hymns the likely fare in a Catholic church of a Sunday.

'I'd have to watch it until now, both only turned sixteen this year and I've had my eye on them since they started sprouting.' Patrick cushions a folded palm over his own right breast, shows what has been sprouting on these two girls. Simon instinctively dislikes the talk. Not that he hasn't said similar things about girls in the past; Corrie has appropriated a place in his thoughts which precludes speaking crudely of her. He has noticed her every curve, of course, hearing another boy discuss them is the complication. 'I want your opinion,' says Patrick conspiratorially as they head down the stairs from function room to bar. He stops midway, turns back to look Simon directly in the eye. It seems he is to raise an important matter. 'Millie, Millie Green, is...well...I think she's beautiful. I don't really know what I look like, not from a girl's point of view. What do you think? Would a really gorgeous girl go out with me?'

Simon laughs. Daftest question he's been asked in a long while. 'You make me go all weak at the knees,' he says. Patrick has turned back to him, peevishness on his face as he looks up at Simon two stairs above. The younger boy puts both his hands on Patrick's chest. 'And nice boobies,' he announces, in a splutter of laughter.

'Little nonsense,' he is told. 'You just want to do that to the Dalton girl.' Patrick grabs him back, squeezes in to pinch Simon's nipple.

Two liquored-up farm boys cavorting with each other while pretty girls fill their minds. It could be any pub in Cumbria.

* * *

The first time Simon went to the Young Farmers' meeting in Broughton-in-Furness was unexceptional. Corrie was not there. He met Vincent Dalton, had never heard of the family before that day in June. Vincent was nice enough, drank a lot of beer for a lad on a moped.

The cycle down to Broughton was easy, the return back up to the fell farm always going to be the tougher one. The Boar sits prominently in the village square. He realised he had been through here only the Sunday before; bike rides across the Lake District pass his time. He seldom pays much attention to the detail of his meandering tours, gobbles up the sights without seeking to name the many features. Knows which lake is which. It all looks better than the North Riding to him.

On entering the pub he found the light decayed, faint. No electric lights on except directly behind the bar, and the room is big, its windows few. A stark contrast to the low sun which shone in his eyes for too much of the cycle down there. The man behind the bar coughed and Simon expected to be asked his age. That happens. Not every time he tries to buy a pint, but often.

'Young Farmer's meeting?' asked Simon. The rule doesn't apply to clubs and private meetings, he's heard it said. Another six months and he will hit the magic number of years, a visit to a pub become straightforward.

The barman gave him a short stare. 'Room above.' He nodded at a staircase at the end of the far wall of the barroom.

Simon started to saunter towards it, then turned back. 'Is there an upstairs bar, as well?' he asked.

'Not as I recall,' said the man, a self-satisfied smirk sculpting itself onto his lips.

Simon thought his joke stupid. It was his first visit to this pub, couldn't be expected to know. 'A pint of...' He looked at the labels on the pumps. '...Hartley's.' He knows that asking for a shandy or a lager and blackcurrant—sweeter, more palatable drinks—would make him sound like a kid.

'And you're eighteen?' said the barman, finally.

Stuck-Up Little Runt

'Yeah. You have to be to join the Young Farmers.'

'I know that too,' replied the man, taking a pint pot down from the shelf above the bar. 'Handle?'

'Yes, please,' answered Simon, grateful that the enquiry about his age had run its course. And perhaps no one's being fooled. Will Browning told him they'll serve anyone in The Boar.

Drink in hand, he climbed the wooden staircase. The pub is bare—stone walls—feels like the interior of a barn. At the top of the stairs there is a small landing with just two doors, one having a sign advising No Entry and one without. It made for an easy call. Simon pushed the door open slowly. There were more than a dozen men in the room, a couple of girls as well. They were all talking, quietened down a notch at the sight of a new arrival.

'Young Farmers?' said Simon.

The oldest-looking man in the room waved him in, introduced himself with a cordial 'Hello,' asked his name and offered his own, although what it is did not register with the boy, as he took in the roomful of farm labourers. 'You're in for a treat tonight,' said the man. 'I've brought some slides of Charolais. Prepared a little talk about them. They're the next big thing, you know.' He may still be in his twenties, may have popped out the other side, Simon couldn't tell. The hair on top of his head is thinning and he wore a checked shirt and thick cable-knit cardigan, an unnecessary affectation in the warmth of that summer evening. If he is young, it is a youthfulness he chose to hide.

'Great,' said Simon. He hoped his insincerity was not obvious. Talking to farmhands about cattle didn't sound like a proper night out.

He looked around at the gathered few. One or two raised a pint glass in welcome to the newcomer. A large girl shouted, 'Young Farmers rock!' as she raised what he thought to be a wine glass. A dash of red liquid at the bottom. Simon spotted only one other girl in the room. The loud one looked the size of Carol Browning, and maybe only half her age.

'Which farm do you work on?' asked the older man, the slideshow-about-cows chap. Simon told him that it is Sark Farm, Higher Nibthwaite. 'Sheep, eh?' he said. Before Simon could explain that William Browning has gone dairy on that high ground—even installing a modern milking parlour—the man was introducing him to another, handing him on. 'Patrick, you're sheep, aren't you? This is Simon, works up Nibthwaite.' Then he turned back to the boy. 'You are eighteen, I take it? It's a strict rule, what with meeting in a pub.' Simon took a deep breath, prepared to answer. Was mustering up a yes, calculating a pretend birthday several months before the one to come. 'No worries,' laughed the older man with a conspiratorial wink. 'It's Cumbria, nobody's watching.'

The meeting was pleasant enough, young people drinking for the most part. Peter—as he subsequently learnt the balding man's name to be—took centre stage for the slide show, his pictures of French cattle. With the room in darkness but for the projector's beam, the large girl—Janine Fox he learnt her name to be—kept shouting boys' names and saying, 'Stop touching me.' It was all a joke. Almost all. At one point, and in a markedly more forthright tone, she shouted, 'Ben Jones, for real, don't do that!' Mostly Simon thought she was simply trying to draw attention to herself, imagining boys more interested in her than seemed probable. When the lights were back up, surprisingly, she had them hanging off her. The other girl was too shy to hold attention, wore her hair like a pair of curtains. Drank coke.

The young man called Patrick offered to buy Simon a second pint, and he also bought one for Vincent whom he had introduced by this time. Janine shouted, 'Campari, Patsy. Be a love and fetch me one up.' Patrick gave Simon an aggrieved look. No one else called him by that effeminate nickname or demanded he buy them a drink. Janine played the spoiled queen of Broughton Young Farmers.

Once Patrick had gone downstairs, Vincent whispered to

Stuck-Up Little Runt

Simon that Janine is courted by every boy who wants to marry a farmyard. Get their hands on her father's many acres. Simon laughed at that, it all started to fall into place. Then he asked of Vincent, 'Do any pretty girls come here?' He should have thought before he spoke. The room had fallen silent on cue, a rare hush just for his faux pas. He turned crimson to his earlobes knowing that Janine Fox and the girl with hair over her eyes had overheard his casual dismissal of their visual worth. He isn't an unkind boy. Careless now and then.

Peter ignored the remark. 'What do you think of my Charolais then?' he asked of Janine and the others sat with him, deflecting the crass comment quite seamlessly. His slides were clearly the purpose of the evening in his mind, and these two plain girls winsome enough for him.

'Not really,' Vincent replied once there was a bit of noise to cover the indiscretion of saying it out loud. He was looking into his empty pint glass. His voice contained the hint of an alcohol-induced slur.

Ben Jones nudged Simon on the shoulder. 'You should see his sister. She really is worth a squirt.'

'Shut up,' said Vincent, looking crossly at Ben. Simon felt embarrassed for him; the phrase was funny, and certainly not one he would dare say to the brother of the girl so crudely referenced.

'Is she legal yet?' Ben demanded of Vincent.

'She'll be having nothing to do with you, Jonesy,' he stated, as Patrick arrived back at the table with their drinks.

'Oh, you couldn't stop me from nailing her,' said Ben, pinching his bulbous right bicep between the fore-finger and thumb of his left hand.

'My brother bloody could,' said Vincent.

What an odd thing to say, thought Simon. Ben's coarse phrase was funny but Simon knew he would never utter it in company. The bawdy talk put his own indiscreet enquiry in the shade. And a girl better looking than the two plain Janes here tonight really wouldn't go a miss.

2.

As he is sinking the fifth pint which he knows he shouldn't be having, the one that will give him that sickly feeling throughout morning milking, he finds himself rolling with the man's notion. Patrick—who has yet to tell Millie he likes her—wants to double date with him and Cordelia Dalton. Beer makes life that simple.

Corrie has told him a little about Millie: both attend the same private girls' school; Millie doesn't ride but once sat on her friend's treasured horse. 'She looked like she was waiting to be shot,' laughed Corrie.

Simon confirms for Patrick that he has never met Millicent Green, has heard mention of her by Corrie, not seen or spoken to the girl. He suggests to Patrick that she is the more stay-at-home, she certainly doesn't venture out on the back of a brother's moped to attend these Young Farmers' meetings.

'Millie's got nothing to do with farming,' says Patrick. 'She's a runner, likes her sports. I see her in Hawkshead on the footpaths. I couldn't jog as fast as she does.'

Simon realises how limited his knowledge of Corrie is. He's never seen her out running, tries to imagine it. She doesn't seem the type. He has seen her only in this pub, excepting the one evening they bunked off. Talked alone in the churchyard until the summer light faded to nothing.

* * *

His second trip to the Young Farmer's mirrored the first except that Peter didn't turn up. He sent a message via the quiet girl with the funny hair, his sister it turned out. In the absence of any slides or better organisation, they played drinking games. Did so with restraint, for the most part. Janine Fox stuck with Campari and then refused to drink the amounts various boys told her she must if she were not to face a sterner forfeit.

Simon spoke briefly to Vincent. The man was drunk of

course, an odd state in which to ride his moped back to Ulpha Fell, but he was amongst them after a similar stunt the week before. It's a knack of sorts. 'I hear your sister sometimes comes here?' said Simon.

Vincent looked directly into his eyes, gave him a little smile. 'You're her age, aren't you?'

Simon nodded at this, a half-hearted confirmation. He'd yet to meet her; the brother would know the answer to his own question were he not too addled to work it out.

'She came a couple of times, didn't enjoy Ben's pestering. It put her off. And our old man hates her being down the pub.'

'Why?'

'The place for fallen women, I expect. He's got a few screws loose, a funny blighter, you might say. He's okay about Young Farmers, so he blows hot and cold. She'll be back, I expect.' Then after a quick pull on his beer, he said, 'Hey! She's a nice girl, I've to protect her, being her brother and everything. I'll have to fight you off if you try anything untoward.'

'I've not met her. It would be nice to meet a girl here who didn't weigh more than me.'

'Choosy, choosy,' laughed Vincent.

Simon decided to win the man over. He offered to buy him a pint, felt a little conflicted on account of the moped but Vincent was keen.

His new friend—hospitality in hand—asked Simon a little about where he worked. Vincent knew of Sark Farm, the Brownings. 'Aren't they shitty employers?' he asked.

'Weird,' said Simon. 'Decent enough to work for, and then they are at each other's throats all day long.'

'I think it's her. Billy Browning's a misery but no one wants a wife who goes behind his back.'

Simon couldn't understand the point he was making. Looked at him enquiringly.

'You don't know, do you?' Vincent took a long pull on his pint before continuing. 'Carol Browning has dropped her knickers for more farmers than most of us have knocked in fencing posts.'

'No!'

'Don't go there, my friend,' cautioned Vincent. 'Billy Misery won't treat you well if he finds out.'

Simon shook his blushing head. He entertains no wish to lay with the fat shouter who cooks his breakfasts. Her alleged enthusiasm for sex was the surprise. Enjoyed chatting with Vinny, doubted every word.

* * *

His third trip to the Young Farmers put the first two in the shade. And they had been acceptable, more fun than holing up in his attic room at Sark Farm while Mrs Browning berated William down below. Vincent—who had been the flat-out winner of all the drinking games the previous week—arrived as Simon was locking up his bicycle in the pub's car park, a girl on the back of the moped. She swung a short leg over the rear of the seat and bent her head forward to remove her crash-helmet. As it came off, she shook loose her rich brown hair.

Simon said, 'Hi Vinny,' but it was the girl in light-blue jeans, matching denim jacket and a raspberry-red blouse, who he was drinking in.

As Vincent was taking off his own helmet, waving a hello to Simon, this younger, brighter sister had her own ideas. 'Introduce me,' she asked of her brother.

Vincent put on a well-spoken voice, the tone of a titled man. 'Mister Simon of Sark Farm, dairyman and dogsbody to the Brownings of that Godforsaken hole, I introduce Miss Cordelia Fell-off-a-Moped. If she tells you that she's my sister, don't believe it. She's a stray, hangs around our farm day and night. Scares the wits out of me most of the time.'

The girl laughed at her brother. 'You're Simon. He told me there was another...' She dipped her head, lowered her voice. '...rule breaker, young one.' Then she let her volume rise, including her brother once more. 'And Vinny said you're not as slow in the head as most who come here...' She took a breath, beamed a smile. '...although I don't see how he could tell.'

Stuck-Up Little Runt

Inside the pub, Vincent insisted on buying drinks. He gave his sister—who had asked Simon to call her Corrie—a half pint of cider. Refreshment in hand, she glanced around the public bar while walking over to the stairs. Simon saw her raising her head, a stretched neck, maybe trying to look eighteen although she could not. Perhaps she was simply gauging who had noticed her. The barman for one, he looked long and hard. His interest was not to challenge her presence in the pub. Corrie is a girl who's worth a look.

The projector was out again in the upstairs room. Janine Fox announced that she was showing slides of Grenada and Malaga. She went there with her parents and younger sister at Easter, the pictures only just back from the chemists.

The small group, brother, sister, Patrick and Simon all sat together. When they were taking their places, Ben Jones sidled up, tried for the seat next to the pretty girl.

'No Ben,' she told him, 'Simon is sitting here.'

'What's he got?' asked Ben of young Corrie.

'Better manners than you, I'm more than certain.'

Ben muttered a barely audible, 'Fuck off,' and went to sit elsewhere.

'See what I mean,' said Corrie quietly. He'd already spotted Ben's absence of good manners. If she meant the slow-in-the-head comment she made in the car park, Simon disagreed, chose not to say it. Ben is coarse, not slow, his observation of the previous week bang on the money.

While Janine was talking—her slides a mixed bag, some showing Spanish architecture and others of family members posing with odd-looking food—Corrie was attentive while passing occasional dry comments. When a picture of Mrs Fox and daughter Janine in swimsuits upon a Spanish beach shone out, a couple of the young men wolf-whistled. 'The poor things have become beached,' muttered Corrie into Simon's ear. It took him a moment to get it and then for a full minute he could scarcely stifle his giggles.

Janine showed a slide of a grand-looking palace, imposing

curved architecture unlike any Simon has come across in northern England. 'This is a very famous palace,' she said. 'It's called...er...er...something or other and I know it was built by the Moors.'

'Who are the Moors?' asked Ben.

'They were like the Roman's but in Spain,' said Janine. Then she said, 'What?' to Corrie who was audibly sniggering.

'The Moors entered Spain long after the Romans had left. The Romans were in Spain in their day. The Moors were Muslims from North Africa. They were in southern Spain for centuries, conquered the whole peninsular for a time,' said Cordelia. 'And I think it's the Alhambra Palace.'

'Alright, know-all, it might be called that. The old people have gone now, Romans, Franco. Mum says they're like us since they've got their king back, and the past doesn't really matter.' Janine turned back to the projector and put in another slide.

'I think I've offended her,' said Corrie quietly to Simon. 'My big mouth. She's gone to quite an effort.'

Her quiet asides stopped; Corrie led the table's applause for Janine when the presentation was complete. Simon thought the talk was terribly boring, he'd enjoyed the caustic comments far more. When Janine was putting her slides into their plastic box, he saw Corrie go over to her. He couldn't hear what she said but her demeanour led him to guess it was an apology. Janine went from looking cross to patting the younger girl on the back.

At evening's end, Simon was pleased to spot that Vincent had tempered his drinking, a sister to return over the moors. As they wandered out from pub to car park, the girl who he felt had singled him out, securing him a seat next to her—although her low opinion of Ben Jones may have contributed to the decision—said a simple, 'See you next week, Simon.'

'Yes,' he replied, pausing, remembering her term, slow in the head, thinking what to say that would keep him out of that pen. 'It was nice tonight,' he finally managed. Failed to define why, never gave her the credit she had earned by allowing him to sit with her. Simon is a farm boy.

* * *

The cycle back up the lanes to Nibthwaite after that first meeting with Corrie was invigorating. Simon drank only two pints while the girl he sat beside had a single half. He was wise enough not to be foolish. No unnecessary jokes. He doesn't have her sharpness of wit: a little shy, the better way around for a lad like him.

Arriving at the farm he saw the lights were still on, a contrast to his last two Thursday nights out. The Brownings are early risers, not late-to-beds. He shut his bike away in the disused barn, then took the bulky back-door key from his jeans pocket. It wouldn't go in the hole and he realised there was a key still in the other side. Tried the handle. Carol locks up, has a routine. She was hours behind that night.

'Simon, you've been out?'

Will Browning should have known that. He reminded his employer that he'd been once more to the upstairs room at The Boar, the one in which Will had met his wife.

'Ha, I could curse the place sometimes.'

Simon quickly figured that the pair had, in his absence, been rowing. They'd done the same in his presence often enough. Will told him only, 'She's been talking with her mother all night.' He pointed at the telephone, wrinkling his nose as if it were a cowpat.

The shouting and once-in-a-blue-moon plate throwing of this couple are of no interest to him. His father is just as bad-tempered, no longer has another soul in his squalid farmhouse with whom to row. Simon told Will Browning that he'd enjoyed the club this evening. 'A great slide show about Spain,' he said, knowing the adjective 'great' belonged not to holiday snaps at all, but to the girl with whom he'd looked upon them. He didn't mention her, chose not to tell Will about meeting Corrie Dalton. There is a ring of privacy around the boy. He quickly drifted off to bed. Carol Browning still banging around the lounge. There sounded to be a little more arguing scheduled. Simon guessed he would be milking alone in the morning.

* * *

That night he could not sleep. His head was back in the pub: could a girl as clever as Cordelia Dalton—she knows which civilisations have been in and out of Spain, the who and the when of it—see any hope in him? A boyfriend? Not so slow in the head, she'd said, and perhaps he could fulfil this modest expectation.

He had long harboured mixed feelings towards his geography teacher, Miss Lowther. She was his form teacher during Simon's third year at secondary school; his mother died just as the autumn term was ending. Miss Lowther told him that, if he wished to talk about it, her door was always open. Talk about his mother. Three and a half years later, a year out of school, such opening up has yet to happen. Simon talks readily about livestock, tractor engines, will express his opinion about football and virtually every West Coast rock band too. He hates glam rock, will tell you why at the drop of a hat. All the personal stuff he keeps in the vault. A fortnight earlier he accidentally made a fool of Janine Fox when he asked his ill-timed do-any-pretty-girls-come-here question. Apologise for it, he did not. Simon hasn't the vocabulary. Corrie's good manners confused him only because he wouldn't think to be so forthright, to right a wrong without obvious gain. He deplores the rudeness of Ben Jones, then behaves in a similar way by accident. Corrie is kind and generous, it's likely worth a try.

Miss Lowther wrote an awful lot on Simon's twice-yearly report card. Told him it was because his father needed to know how well his son was doing, shouldn't be short changed just because he was too busy to come in for parents' evening. In one or two subjects Simon wasn't doing well at all. Miss Lowther glossed over that, when a normal teacher would have emphasised it. Not that Simon was stupid, passed more O-levels than he failed. In fact, he fared miles better than his sister, Rosie. Doesn't recall if his father ever learnt his results. Simon left the envelope on the kitchen table for two whole days but never mentioned it directly.

He remembers the displeasure which he felt in his teacher's long missives to his father. And in her explanation for them, his supposed need to know. From the distance of his bedroom at Sark Farm he could see that she was simply trying to put his family back together. Trying is not a crime; not that she came close. Miss Lowther should have known that Alison Tripp—the late Mrs Tripp—never went to parents' evenings before she passed away. His father was only continuing the family tradition. Rosie, his elder sister, had been through the school five years ahead of him. No parent ever attended the said evening to enquire about her progress either and Alison Tripp was still heartily alive back then. Miss Lowther hadn't done her homework.

Simon thought he might just be clever enough for Corrie to like. But he also thought he might not. Until this evening, being cleverer than John Tripp was the sole measure he'd bothered with. The imaginary certificate for that one hanging on his wall since the age of twelve. Meeting Corrie has raised the bar. Hoisted it up to the height of Ulpha Fell. During their evening together she was the more switched on, he could see that. This is the nub of it really. He has sleepwalked through the last three and a half years. It isn't that he misses his mother, there simply isn't much that interests him. Found the sense to get away from John Tripp, to move to a neighbouring county. A farm not dissimilar to the one he left. Getting away from a miserable face, a miserly father, is not dumb, but nor is it taking life by the horns. He's not even impressed with himself; Corrie might think him a bit cowardly. Simon's not sure what a girl who knows the name of every palace in Spain looks for in a boy.

He resolved, as he dwelt upon it, to tell this kind and clever girl that his mother has passed away. It could be crazy. Make him sound nothing like a prospective boyfriend, more a child hoping for adoption. But he thought she'd get it; Corrie is definitely sensitive, concerned for others. That's why she made up with Janine Fox. And she hadn't really done anything wrong: Janine is the big mouth; Corrie knew what the slides were about, could have given a better talk than Fox's drivel. He's been through the mill with his mum and everything, and she seemed the sort to recognise it. Understand. It was a funny sort of mill, looking back. Simon didn't really feel its pounding. Any emotional shit and he stands right back. It's the way he's made.

He hoped he could sleep before next Thursday came around. He was making no progress that night and the sound of a pan thrown in the kitchen downstairs helped little. He couldn't imagine Corrie throwing a pan. He saw no bitterness in her face, none at all. She has a lovely face. Being with her made him feel more alive than he has realised himself to be.

A few weeks before his final exams, Miss Lowther tried to discuss Sixth Form with him. 'I like geography a lot.' He knew there was no chance he'd be studying it the following term, even as he spoke those words. He'd been scanning the adverts in Farmers Weekly, applied for jobs on eight different dairy farms. Heard back from four. Simon put Miss Lowther down as a referee without thinking to ask her. Too embarrassed to do so, actually; she would only ask him more rubbish about A-levels.

A while later—a week or two—she stopped him on the school corridor. This was at Swale Valley Comp in North Yorkshire: more thick kids than you could poke with a pitchfork. It was the day of his first exam: English Language. 'I gather you've applied to work on a farm a long way from here?'

Simon bowed his head. Not that he was a contrite boy—not even then—he simply had no approach in mind to this conversation. She should write him a nice reference, had done as much on his report card. 'I need to earn money.'

Caroline Lowther tried once more to comprehend his family

Stuck-Up Little Runt

situation, queried if his father would allow him to enter sixth form.

'He doesn't pay me.' That was not a state unique to Simon Tripp. School boys and girls receive whatever pocket money their parents care to divert their way, nothing more. Simon thought it the greatest injustice: he ploughed fields, milked cows, dipped sheep, rebuilt tumbled-down dry-stone walls far better than his father ever could. Might have worked a job harder than any other boy in Swale Valley Comprehensive School. Might not, but it was a plausible notion. And for all this, money was almost unknown to him. His father gave him but a few coins which Simon saved up to buy second-hand cassettes. Never accrued it. Knew he couldn't unless he left home, worked for a proper wage. Miss Lowther said learning was more important than money but she only thinks it because she's got enough. He could figure that out and he's not even a teacher.

Simon secured the job at Sark Farm—Mr and Mrs Browning driving all the way to Aysgarth to talk to him, interview him in his family home—and finally felt like a grown-up. No evidence on the day of the interview that William and Carol were not at one, that he would be living in a household more tumultuous than the one he was fleeing. Indeed, Penton Farm was already a dull place. It had been a fierce little trap when John Tripp was at odds with Simon's sister, Rosie, shouting at her that she was getting a reputation. Carrying on with different lads the way she was. Rosie would shout back, not coherently but loud as hell. And poor Alison—who offered no opinion one way or the other about the carousel of male company her daughter enjoyed—might have been crying into her home-made jam. All this the summer before breast cancer took her from the farm altogether. Penton, at the time Simon left the damned place, was boring. Rosie was long gone, married in a registry office, living down in Keighley. Alison Tripp, the mother he doesn't allow himself to miss, was in the churchyard, a small marker denoting where the urn is buried.

The better part of his father buried there too: the verve, some of the anger perhaps. He is a pointless moaner now, another old crosspatch. A faint echo of the belligerent man he once was.

Simon reckoned that Corrie would understand him if he told her about his past, his mother and father. Not the how or the why of it. He was there and he hasn't figured that out. Simply having someone who might listen, hear about where he is from and will not be going back to. It would be a nice addition to a lonely life. She doesn't seem the sort to dismiss his upbringing just because it was on an unprofitably small farm, a thicker-than-should-be-allowed farmer heading the household. Corrie's been around screw-loose farmers all her life, Vinny has as good as told him that. Their old man comes from the ranks. There was no question about it in Simon's mind, he would share it all with Corrie Dalton.

He closed his eyes to sleep. Pictured her once more: the white of her forehead; those gorgeous brown eyes. The rich head of hair. A broad smile crossed Simon's tired face. He's never known a farmgirl like her; worth a bit of self-improvement, if that's what it takes to win her.

3.

The week that followed was one of farm work and anticipation. Simon's mind awash with the prospect of fulfilling Corrie's see-you-next-week request. A tingling in his stomach too.

And then there was the occurrence on Tuesday.

At breakfast Carol Browning was fussing. Seemed more bothered than usual about getting her children on to the school bus. They were excitable, term's end drawing near.

'You'll need to move the herd over into Cartmel Pasture,' she said as she put his toast in front of him. 'They can't stay in Garden. William says the water's running filthy there. Clean up the milking parlour first and then move them, please?'

He nodded; the task was not a surprise. The previous evening, it had been Simon who told Mr Browning that the

Stuck-Up Little Runt

stream-fed water troughs in the near field—known as Garden—looked contaminated. Will said he'd take a look, then he never did. And he calls himself a scientific farmer. Simon considered the cattle's access to metallic-looking water to be a more serious hazard than his employer acknowledged the day before.

'We can move them in a few minutes,' Simon offered.

'No,' said Carol. 'I've only just fed the dogs. Hose down the parlour first, then you can take them with you. You'll have to manage alone today. Once you've put them in Cartmel, take the dogs up on the fell for a run. Look over the sheep while you're there, please?'

'You're the boss,' he replied. Carol smiled, might have felt a compliment he never intended. Bossy cow.

William Browning would have helped but he had left early that Tuesday, gone to look at the cattle market in Cockermouth. Simon milks alone often as not on Sark Farm. Did the same with the smaller herd at his father's farm long before venturing to Cumbria. They modernised the milking parlour last summer. It was the first big job after Simon's arrival here; he and Will started the transformation, a team of contractors finishing the job. The boy struggled to tame a hopping pneumatic drill, splintering away the former milking shed's concrete stalls as best he could. Together he and Will dug an enormous hole; the contractors laid concrete, installed the machinery. The morning's milking is a simpler task for it. Placing machines on udders from down in the pit. And even the bringing of cattle in and out is easier than it ever was back at Penton Farm. The animals are keen to enter the parlour for the feed. Batches of five he lets in, using the gate handle at the side of the pit. He needn't go more than ten paces back and forth all milking. Back home Simon must still lead each cow in from yard to milking shed, chain it in the stall, stoop to put the suckling liners on each teat. His father uses an old-fashioned milking stool such is the state of his back.

'After I've seen them on to the bus...' Carol gestured her

breakfasting children, '...I'm sorting out the kitchen. Cleaning it, defrosting the freezer. You'll have to make do on your own today.'

Simon stared back at her, kept his face as blank as he could. Carol's assistance is intermittent at best. She might have had some serious mother-phoning to do. That she only farms when she feels like it has long been his experience. Carol knows the work inside out, the daughter of a farmer in Kendal or thereabouts, spent a year at agricultural college in her late teens. And she's a lazy lump, never a mucker-in. Her husband goes off for the day and the seventeen-year-old hired hand must do the lot.

Breakfasted, Simon went back to the milking parlour, squeegee-ed the cow-shit out of parlour and yard. It's a broom-like tool he uses for this. A concave rubber grounds-piece collected what muck there was as he pushed it over the smooth concrete and down the drop into the midden. He hosed the parlour and cattle yard. Brushed out the fetid water. The job is grimmest when the spring grasses have turned the cows' excrement to slippery cocoa and the rains keep yard, farm track, and every field's entryway the same filthy brown. It's a breeze at this time of year, high summer. Barely even smells unless a warm wind drifts the stench back up from the midden where it ferments while waiting to be spread back across the fields as fertiliser. They talked about it at Young Farmers; Ben Jones calls it the cycle of shite.

When that job was finished, Simon went behind the barn to the small kennels where Baron and Stevie, two half-trained sheepdogs, are housed. Their half-trained status bugs Simon. His father—who is a nonsense-farmer, with his antiquated ways and bailer-twine for a belt—can handle dogs better than William Browning. His employer consults textbooks on soil quality, updates machinery and milking parlour alike, and then won't have his dogs professionally trained. And he possesses no inner discipline with which to manage such a task himself. Shouts at the dogs for no reason beyond his own frustration.

Both are keen runners and rounders-up of sheep and cattle but Stevie, in particular, will snap at a cow's rear hooves. Even a kick to his jaw doesn't deter him. And cows will kick like hell. Baron may come to a whistle if he wishes, or not if his mood guides him the other way. A good sheepdog is not the decision-maker but this pair enjoy more autonomy than most. Simon's arrival at the farm has come too late in their development to make a difference.

As he approached the kennel, Simon heard the constant clinking and whimpering of the dogs as they strained on their chains. He released them quickly, spoke to them in clipped single-syllable commands. The manner his own father uses. The gruff talk does nothing; these are old dogs, stuck fast in their shapeless ways.

* * *

When he arrived at Garden, Simon whistled the dogs. They understand enough, will circle the herd, usher it towards a gate one way or another. Simon waited by the opening, blocking the way onto the lane while the dogs herded the cattle closely together. He noted that one cow was gagging, coughing, making a racket from the depths of its many stomachs. Desdemona: every cow has a name. He knows them well, the personal food supplement of each lodged in his herdsman's head. He gives it to them at morning milking: one, two or three pulls on the relevant lever. Dogs aside William Browning runs a structured farm.

Simon was concerned about the cow's retching. On arrival he'd seen her by the water trough. She may have ingested some contaminant. Could belch it back up if he's lucky. He wondered if other cattle have done the same, were going through similar digestive discomfort. He told Will that the water looked befouled the evening before. Suggested a change of field and the farmer said no. He simply wasn't in the mood for more work by Simon's calculation. For all his scientific hogwash, the man is no better than his sheepdogs. And if the cattle become ill, Browning is unlikely to blame himself. That's not in the grumpy bugger's nature.

When the dogs had done their best, brought the herd close to the entry, Simon stepped away from the gate, allowing the herd to follow him through. He put himself in the centre of the narrow lane so that the cattle moved south, would not try to pass him. From that position a short way above the farm buildings he glanced down the hillside towards Lake Coniston, sunlight glistening upon it on the summer's morning. A couple of tiny white clouds punctuating the bluest sky.

As the dogs came through the gate with the final cows, he left them to hold the rear. Simon tried to hurry past the cattle. The lane is unforgiving, no more than four cows wide. Barely a verge, drystone wall and hawthorn hedgerow enclosing them. He made his way to the front; only from there could he divert them off the road at the turning for Cartmel Pasture. Will Browning would be here to help but for his foray to Cockermouth. A relocation of the herd is a two-handed job without better-trained dogs.

A car tooted its horn ahead of him. Simon grimaced. Impatient motorists unsettle cows. He was passing the livestock in twos and threes; they quickened their step, flicked a tail or neck while letting him pass. His presence is familiar to them; none were spooked as he brushed past. He recognised the car, its driver tooting once more, as if a car horn might hurry a cow. Simon flapped his arms, signalled that he was doing all he could. The driver was Roy Piper, the AI man.

As Simon approached, Piper wound his window down. 'Work to do,' he said, smiling apologetically at the farmhand. They've met several times before. Piper performs his function—the artificial insemination of cows—on Sark Farm's livestock. Browning has no bull of his own and Piper can supply the finest semen in the land. One British Friesian bull in particular—Emperor Grey its pompous name—has sired more than half the calves born here in the year past. Piper the intermediary.

'Then stand ahead and direct them down that cutting,

please?' Simon asked of him.

Roy Piper emerged sheepishly from his vehicle. For a man employed in the agricultural field his impatience with cattle is plain silly. Upon request he made himself useful for a short time. Stood like a closed gate on the open road. It did the trick. Piper turned the cows into the field while Simon went back, ensured the dogs did as they should, no broken jaws from snapping too keenly at hooves. Then the AI man climbed back into his car. Drove off to a cow in need of his services.

Simon, Baron and Stevie headed up to Nibthwaite Fell, the footpath towards the open moor, to check the welfare of the sheep. That was Carol's instruction.

* * *

It was not yet mid-morning and already Simon was feeling hot. The air upon the moor was still, windless. This summer is a record breaker. The narrow diamond of the lake sparkled below. As he headed up the fell, he saw how the dry heather by the side of the path has wilted and crumbled beneath the gaze of the relentless sunshine. News reports say hay crops have failed across England, so sparse has water been. The Lake District has had a tiny bit of rain, plenty before these weeks of high pressure which have come to dominate the summer. 'We've never gathered more grass,' William has told him. Too much rain is the usual lot up here, the ruin of hay and silage if not brought under cover quickly enough. No farmer in the Lake District can have messed up this fine summer. As he walked up the path, whistling for Baron to come back to heel, he saw how all the bog grasses that proliferate on the moor have faded. The usually muddy soil is crisp and flaky, light brown, sun bleached. These are unusual conditions.

When he turned away from the mesmerising lake—Coniston Water, white sails polka-dotted upon it—he could see the car parked by Sark Farm. The farmyard is a mish-mash of grey slate. House, barn, milking parlour, a further disused barn, neglected for so many years that grass and moss proliferate on its unreliable roof. Even from here he could see that it was Roy

Piper's car parked beside the house. Colour and shape.

He neglected to tell Simon that he was going to Sark when he stood beside him twenty minutes earlier. And when the AI man comes, it is Simon who usually figures out how to bring the cow to him, the cow requiring his services. Held back after milking most often. Carol told him what jobs to do this morning, never mentioned this task. May have believed Will told him the night before. Nor did Simon see a cow bulling, at morning milking or yesterday evening either. Cow-randy is the term his sister, Rose, memorably gave to this act: cows mounting each other. Farm boys watch out for signs of bovine love—cow-on-cow action—for the insight they offer. They must learn to spot when a cow stands stationary while another one rises upon it, simulates a sex act although neither has the necessary organ to complete the circuit. Only then is it adjudged ready to meet a bull or a call made for the services of a man with the know-how, a vial of what the bull would like to give it. Roy Piper is an unlikely fantasy for a cow. His fiddling around at the back of them, a sleeved arm where a bull would put its engorged member, is doubtless no fun from their perspective. They get pregnant nine times out of ten, it's a magnificent hit rate.

Simon was still a mile from where he last saw the Brownings' small flock of sheep. Wandering the fell with no greater purpose than checking their health is a nice task; they are really not in any peril, not in summer. He decided to turn back. Will must have called the AI man and forgotten to tell him, might have mentioned the name of the nominated cow to Carol. Piper charges for callouts, even if he never sleeves up.

Simon was wearing lightweight boots, good for summer farming. He trotted back, the dogs becoming excited by the boy's increased pace. The downhill track is easily traversed, and he always watches his footing, avoids loose stones. The boy has been jogging across moors his whole life, a practicality of where he has lived. In little over ten minutes, he was back at the farm. He puzzled over the car being beside the house, not up at the

Stuck-Up Little Runt

milking parlour where Piper usually leaves it.

Simon went round to the back door. As he placed hand on handle, he heard an odd moaning sound. Tentatively, he clicked the latch, pushed open the door. He saw the top of Mrs Browning's head, moving forwards and back as it lay upon her bare and folded arms which were resting on the kitchen table. She was wearing little, possibly nothing. Mr Piper, the AI man, stood behind her. No plastic apron today. With his eyes closed and face contorted in something that looked initially like pain, he thrust himself in and out of William Browning's wife. Slower than made any sense in retrospect, Simon figured the purpose of Piper's visit. The boy stepped straight back, saw Carol Browning's eyes open briefly, got himself out of there, pulling the door to behind him. Softly letting down the handle, the latch.

Vincent Dalton has his ear to the ground.

Simon whistled for the dogs to come, did so as discreetly as he could. A sucked-up trill of a whistle. They came, the odd sound worked. Stevie began to bark with excitement, a response that Simon had not wanted. How could William Browning instil discipline into his dogs when he can do no such thing with his wife. As Simon walked away, he wondered why he'd not figured the purpose of the visit when he spied the car from the fell, when he saw it by the farmhouse not the outbuildings. He isn't normally this slow in the head; thrown by the antics of people who should have grown out of sex at their age. Had enough.

Carol saw him, that's an embarrassment. Maybe for her, certainly for him. Roy—the balding inseminator of cattle— seemed otherwise occupied. He had wedged his nose into the fleshy back of the fat farmer's wife. Far and away the most indecent thing Simon has ever seen. Nasal penetration of the skinfold.

4.

As Simon and Patrick talk in the pub, the older man brings the conversation back to farming. Comparing their working lives—close to two thousand head of sheep, versus the hundred-strong dairy herd and modest flock that Simon looks over—is simple talk. Discussing their aspirations with girls in whom neither are confident of reciprocal feelings is a stretch. Simon, ever cautious, offered only the truth that he would like to see more of the girl from Ulpha Fell. Patrick asserted that Millie is the prettier and Simon couldn't dispute it; never met her. He thinks it highly implausible: cock and bull. Chose not to argue the point, talking sheep is the easier.

Ben Jones is beer-stewed, three sheets to the wind. He circles around them. 'Alright queer boys?' He stands unsteadily next to their chairs. A pint in his hand, he lurches forward—coordination elsewhere—as he leans to place it on their table.

Simon turns away. He is not getting into an argument with this oaf tonight. Not in this pub. He thinks back to seeing Corrie for the second time. She seemed as keen to chat with him as he to her. As keen as he is now to avoid Ben fricking Jones. The second time they were together at the Young Farmers was quiz night. All the questions related to farming. Peter planned it: the man with the receding hairline, the organiser and harnesser of these meetings. He set them, asked them, adjudicated which almost-right answers earned a point. Young farmers need a leader, few having more rebellion inside them than the cows and sheep of their day jobs.

* * *

'Do you like quizzes?' Corrie greeted him with four weeks ago.

He shrugged out an, 'I suppose.' A confirmation containing no commitment.

'Or shall we just talk?'

He nodded keenly at this. An invitation to keep her to

Stuck-Up Little Runt

himself, an even better turn than being on her quiz team. He purchased a half pint of cider for Corrie, two beers, one for Vincent.

'You're trying to get me drunk,' she said quite loudly, and her brother turned and held aloft his pint of ale. 'You go on up,' she told Vinny. 'We're having a chat first.'

They took their glasses and sat at a corner table in the downstairs of the pub. Simon felt as if he was on the date that he is still too shy to ask her to.

'I like coming to the pub…' Then she whispered, 'Us being too young is great,' before concluding in her well-spoken voice. '…but most of the young farmers are simple-minded, don't you find?'

He didn't know how to answer this question; it seemed a bit of an obsession of hers. 'Vinny gets on with them,' he ventured.

'Yes, a lovely brother, but you can see why he works with sheep not in rocketry science, can't you? Don't repeat it to him or he'll make me walk home. Did I tell you I play the piano?'

Simon recalled she had mentioned it last week. Asked what she likes to play. 'Not that miserable Ronnie Prousch stuff, I hope?' he said in advance of her answer. It might have been the strongest opinion he had yet voiced. The most notable pianist to make the charts in recent years, Simon thinks his songs sentimental twaddle.

Corrie laughed. 'I don't listen to pop music. I play all sorts. A lot of Mozart and Brahms. My teacher introduced me to Debussy at the turn of the year. It's beautiful; I could play it day and night.'

Simon nodded, as if in agreement. Everybody's heard of Mozart but Simon has no idea what tunes he wrote. The one used in the cigar advert on television, most likely. Quite catchy but there are no guitar licks in it, not young people's fare. Simon said nothing—the Ronnie Prousch comment was an error—showed himself to listen to the pop music which she doesn't.

'Cat got your tongue,' said Corrie.

293

'I wish I could play an instrument. A guitar or a banjo.'

She laughed. 'I love riding, cantering a horse across the fell or finding my way to the heart of a concerto: those are activities which move me. Foot-stomping banjo music must be a bit of a donkey ride, don't you think?'

He started to say that he'd try and learn Mozart on it, and Corrie simply laughed louder.

'I love my horse more than anything in the world. It's a black stallion and it has a dusting of white hairs across every inch. He's called Ghost.' Simon thought Ghost an off-putting name, had the good sense not to voice it. She told him all about her horse. Not stabled on her farm exactly, kept on Dalton-family land close by. A large stable-block adjacent to a tied cottage. 'All the Daltons ride,' she said, 'but they don't all treat their horses nicely.'

Simon murmured that they ought to. Wondered if his treatment of cows, sheep, sheepdogs occasionally, might be anathema to her.

'Mary is such a lovely girl.' As the tale meandered, Corrie told him that Mary and Derek Donnelly live in the tied cottage where the horses are stabled, Derek a farmhand at Low Fell. The girl, Mary, turned out to be a woman ten years Corrie's senior. Stable hand, feeder, groom, exerciser and mucker out of every horse the Daltons own. 'You don't know my father, do you?'

Simon confirmed that he did not.

'Keep it that way.'

He gave her a puzzled look, then saw how her face had clouded with thoughts of the man. 'Why? What's the matter with him, Corrie?'

'He's not to be trusted and still everybody does. Sister Carmel for one. He told her that I asked for a grand piano and so he bought me one. And it's not true—he just did it to show off—I was happy with the upright.'

'How many sisters do you have, Corrie?' Simon had already heard of a different older sister and another brother beside

Stuck-Up Little Runt

Vincent.

'Sister Carmel is the head teacher at my school. And you'd think someone like that would know better. Father Benedict calls Daddy a saint. I think he gets donations, they always like that in church, it funds missionaries. None of them know what his temper is like...' Corrie covered her face with her hand, her voice went still quieter. '...that he's a vicious so and so.'

Simon nodded a look of concern. His own father has a temper although he has learnt to navigate it. Put a county boundary between himself and the old faultfinder. He asked what she meant by vicious and she shrugged before murmuring, 'How he treats Vinny.'

Simon waited for more.

'Don't tell him I said it. No one wants pity.'

Simon worried that her father vents his temper on Corrie too. Couldn't think how to ask.

He questioned her about religion, having learnt last week that she and Vinny both attend the Roman Catholic church in Coniston. Corrie, holding his gaze with her eyes wide open, said simply, 'I believe.'

Simon doesn't. Unsure how to impart this he tried, 'My father has no truck with religion at all.' Corrie said nothing in reply, waited for more, and he added, 'I don't know myself. I don't feel anything. Don't feel God.' He doesn't think he did wrong, you can't pretend about that stuff. Still fears that he sounded uncouth. Sitting next to Corrie he was finding it hard not to.

He asked more questions about Ghost than he did Catholicism. Safer ground. She relished talking about her horse. 'He's more than a stallion: he's a mirage. Much of his hair is jet black, and then there are whites and greys which create the illusion. Ghost isn't just a name, it's his signature tune.' That phrase sent a little chill through Simon, while Corrie clearly loved the saying of it. 'If the weather is misty, you cannot see him at all. His colouring is exactly rain on the fell, the drizzle that we Cumbrians endure for the greater part of our lives.' Her turns of phrase made him all too conscious of his own clumsy mouth. 'If I was riding by in autumn rain, the sound of his approach would turn your head. Louder and louder and louder as Ghost draws near. Two-four time, for that is a horse's canter. Can you hear it? A succession of thumps—the strange noise on the moor—it's a polka beat, that most insistent of rhythms. The drumming of iron shoes, thudding hollow on the peat track. Echoing up from the very ground you stand on. You can feel it in your empty stomach, can't you? Feel it, hear it. You search the mist only to find the sound fading. Hooves heard, horse never seen. My Ghost can take you by surprise, Simon, always will if you fail to pay attention. Miss the clop-clop-clopping of his arrival. It's easily done, so close to invisible is clever Ghost. Truly, I'd love you to see him, fear you will not. A horse which seldom shows his thoughtful face. It might be only in dreams that I ride, so few the people who have seen me.'

He smiled as she finished her ode to the animal, quite mesmerised by her poetic turn. He didn't believe it but sort of did. Maybe it looks something like she says. He doesn't know anything about musical time signatures. It's easy to imagine horses running. To picture Corrie holding on tight, a rueful smile in his direction. He hopes to be one of the few. To see her often, with or without a horse beneath her.

'Figaro is Honoria's horse...' He looked at her blankly. '...that's my mother.'

'Your mother's called Figaro?' asked Simon.

Corrie laughed. 'She's called Honoria, dumbo.'

He felt embarrassed that she'd seen fit to call him that. It was simply that he'd never heard a name like it. 'Honoria: is she a Roman?'

'She's just my stupid mummy.' Corrie said this through a splutter of cider. Showered him slightly, laughing at his ridiculous question. Apologised with a hand gesture, Simon didn't mind the spittle. Not as long as she didn't judge him unkindly. Honoria, Figaro: how was he supposed to figure out who was who?

Cordelia asked Simon about his interests. That she performed piano in church and school halls and rode a barely visible horse was always going to make his offering sound spiritless.

'I like cycling,' he told her. When questioned he conceded that he has never raced. For him it is a solitary activity.

She said, 'What else?' and he struggled to answer, feared sounding foolish. Slow in the head. He confessed to having a stamp collection, although it resides in a farmhouse in North Yorkshire. Known value: not much. When she teased him about the limited pleasure to be gleaned from philately—a term she had to explain to the supposed enthusiast—he changed tack. Said that he reads science fiction, devours it. He tried to wax lyrical about the American writer, Timothy Spiegel. 'He really makes you think, makes you wonder if aliens could be way more clever than us.'

She took this pastime more seriously than the stamps. 'I've begun to read the Brontes. Mummy said I'd like them now that we're doing proper literature at school.'

Again, Simon saw the chasm between their families. When his mother lived, her choice of reading matter began and ended with the TV Times.

During the course of the evening Simon developed a new hobby of looking into Cordelia Dalton's unblinking brown eyes, listening more attentively to her words than he recalls granting another soul. Watching the graceful movement of her arms, the turn of her expressive lips. He thought he might enjoy hearing a bit of Mozart or the other composers she mentioned, watching music from long ago being played upon a piano. Provided it was this girl tapping out the tunes. Seeing her hands moving up and down the keys, her head rocking gently in time to those slow old pieces.

* * *

When he was cycling back to Sark Farm after this second meeting—a half-moon providing just enough light until the

Ghost in the Stables

high hedgerows on the turn from Water Yeat left him navigating the pot holes in a shadow-world—he worried he might have blown it. Hobbies have past him by; he really must try harder.

Corrie told him that she will study music, literature and history in Sixth Form come September. She hopes to go to university in two years. To Cambridge or to a conservatory. The last she said in French. 'A conservatoire.' He didn't know what it was, didn't ask for fear of making her laugh for all the wrong reasons. He'd done a bit of that. When she added, 'Maybe I'm not clever enough,' he told her she was. Said that she is cleverer than him. She smiled, so it must have pleased her. Out on the open moor—the cycle home—it didn't really sound like a line to pique the interest of a girl like Corrie. Interest in him. He earns twenty-four pounds a week for milking sixty-five cattle twice a day and all the chores which go with it. He has no wish to inherit his father's little plot of land, so limited is its return. He once played on a piano at Swale Valley Comprehensive. He and Stephen Bunce had found the music room unlocked during lunch hour. Bashed about on the ivories for fully five minutes and got themselves a lengthy detention for doing it. They'd made the most horrible racket.

His chances with Corrie seemed very, very slim.

* * *

That evening when they talked in the bar together, and after he'd purchased her a second half pint of cider, the odious Ben Jones arrived at their table with Janine Fox by his side. There is nothing between them, Simon is sure of it.

'Peter says you've got to come up to the quiz,' said the big girl.

'Yeah, quiz,' grunted Ben.

'You're not even eighteen, you two. You're only allowed in here because of our meetings,' Janine continued to lecture.

Simon glanced at Corrie; she seemed not to be for arguing. They'd spent just short of an hour alone. Both went upstairs and joined Vincent's table. The quiz was halfway through.

Stuck-Up Little Runt

The siblings whispered together and then Corrie cupped a hand over Simon's ear, passed on what Vincent had said. 'Janine was asking where you were. Didn't ask about me. She's jealous that I've kept you out of the meeting. She asked, "Why isn't Simon here?" three times before Peter dispatched them. Fancies the pants off you, Vinny says.'

Initially he sat back and looked at her with incredulity, then they both burst into laughter. Janine of the Carol-Browning-sized bloomers is of no interest to Simon. The acreage of her father's farm will not entice him, not so long as this younger, livelier, lovelier girl allows him to sit beside her. 'She's not for me,' he whispered, touching the back of Corrie's hand with his own. He hoped to communicate a great deal with that small gesture.

They participated in the second half of the quiz. Simon was okay, knew a few answers, Vinny and Patrick too. Cordelia is a genius. The questions were all about sheep and pigs and crops, subjects in which she professes no interest, the answers just dropped off her tongue. 'I must have read it in that magazine,' she said. 'I'm just good at remembering things.' An avid reader of the farming weeklies, if not a shearer of sheep.

Janine looked daggers at Corrie Dalton when their table won the prize. The little box of chocolates she hardly needs.

After the quiz he and Corrie talked quietly in the meeting room. He learnt that she doesn't go to a normal school but to a private one. 'The Catholic girls' school in Ulverston,' she told him. He queried that, had spent a couple of Saturdays in the town and wondered where so posh a school might be. 'Out at Swarthmoor,' she said, and the answer confirmed for him that it is not in dirty Ulverston at all. She is schooled in a village a couple of miles out. Half the girls are boarders. Not Cordelia: she said that a taxi collects her each morning at seven-fifteen, an earlier start than school ever got out of him, and he used to bus it to Swale Valley Comp.

It actually sounded improbable to Simon: no farmer that he knows coughs up for private education. Or grand pianos, come to that. 'Four of you. School must have cost your father a harvest or two?'

Corrie laughed about that, prodded Vincent, asked him to tell Simon how much 'the buggering bastard' spent on his education. The epithet used for her father jarred with him, coming from so well-spoken a girl.

'Nada,' said Vincent. 'When I raised the matter, he said it was all I'm worth.'

It turned out that all Corrie's siblings went to state school, and she did likewise until she was thirteen years old. When she brought a boy home, her father took umbrage to her actions. The episode proved to him that she was ill-suited for co-educational schooling. The lad was not even a Roman Catholic; Corrie said that this may have been a worse attribute than his gender. 'He's a mental father,' she told Simon, whispering, 'fucking mental,' by way of emphasis. 'The lad wasn't a boyfriend. I've never had a boyfriend. Not sure if I even want one. Alan played the flute; we were only meeting so that he could practise. He worked out pop songs and I could accompany him on the piano, although I don't really do that piffle now. Pop isn't proper music.'

In bed that night Simon dwelt too long on the obvious: he will never go to Cambridge or any other university. He is not a natural suitor for this gorgeous and clever girl who doesn't know if she wants a boyfriend. He thinks her singling him out might be proof that he really is a cut above the other wellie-chuckers, the slow-in-the-heads. Corrie has quite a few names for farm labourers, hopes she doesn't apply them to him, or only smilingly if she feels the need. He would forgive her that. And she seems to forgive Vincent everything. He's a nice lad but a bit of a wellie-chucker even in Simon's estimation.

He thought he might tell her about his mother's death the following week. It's a difficult subject to raise.

5.

Ben Jones hiccoughs and follows it up with a mouth-made fart, laughs at what isn't even funny. Had as much as Vinny drinks when he's not ferrying his sister back to Low Fell, although the brother has not turned up at all this week or last. Ben is a liability. He is swaying ever so slightly, pint pot back in his hand. He has been slurring his speech for half an hour. 'Hey, Tripp-lad...' The boy turns away, has no wish to speak with him. '...where have you hidden the girl then? The little Dalton?'

Simon shakes his head, won't be talking about Corrie with this lumbering foul-mouth. 'She's not come tonight,' he says.

'Come, you say. I'd make her come.' He says it lewdly, screwing up his own face as if imagining the filthiest of times. 'Or are you poking her already, Tripp-lad?'

Simon shakes his head again, mutters a barely audible, 'Shut up.'

'At least Janine lets you cop a feel,' says Ben. 'Your friend looks okay—I'd put it in her if I had to—but she's just the stuck-up little runt of the Dalton litter.'

Simon stands up, he can feel himself wanting to fight, punch the man. And it has never been his way; only ever fought when somebody started on him at school. He's not had a girl to defend before. Drunk quite a bit himself.

Ben Jones pushes Simon back into his seat. 'You've never even been to Low Fell, have you? Never met Farmer Dalton. He's a hardnosed bit of gristle, take it from me. My dad and him go back years but we can't abide him. We call him Psycho-Farmer down our way. Psycho-Farmer Dalton. That whole family stinks. Vincent's fucking useless, isn't he? Get in the girl's knickers and then get out. That's my advice to you, Tripp-lad.'

Simon stands again, pushes firmly against the chest of his verbal assailant. He feels how firm it is, but Ben is drunk, fails to steady himself and topples over a chair. As he clatters to the ground, he releases his glass, spills his beer. 'I'll fucking get you,' he yells from the wooden floor, head knocking the underside of the table as he tries to rise.

The barman has stepped back into the bar from the kitchen, shouting, 'Glasses please,' before he has taken in the scuffle. Stops in his tracks.

'He fell. Drank too many and fell over,' states Simon. 'I'm off.'

He fears getting into trouble, a glass tumbled onto the floor with Jones. Didn't hear it smash but it might have. He takes to the door hurriedly, heading for his bike. There is laughter in the room, perhaps the scuffle amused some. Patrick follows Simon out of the pub, holding open the door for just a moment, listens out the barman's jibe at the loser.

'You've been bested by a slip of a lad, Jonesy,' Simon hears the barman telling the great oaf on the floor. Laughing while he says it. 'Just a slip of a lad and he's done you.' Others in the room are laughing, no sympathy for Jones.

* * *

He cycles out of Broughton beneath a full moon. The further he rides the clearer it is that Ben Jones hasn't followed. Lives in Broughton, walks to the pub. The drunken oaf can't catch him now. Simon decides to take his time, cycle slowly. He'd like to tell Corrie what he has done, left a man sat on his arse in retaliation for his talk of getting into her knickers. Such a conversation could go horribly wrong, of course. Wonders if he dares indicate that he has thought about the same, what she has down there. It was hearing the words coming from Ben Jones which disgusted him. Not thinking about it silently in his head.

At the first steep incline he swings his leg off the bike. He never usually pushes, fit enough to cycle up. But there is no hurry tonight and he needs to sober up a little. Milking at six-thirty. As he walks, bike in hand, he remembers the third meeting he and Corrie enjoyed. Three weeks ago. Twenty-one days. The last time he saw the girl he cannot stop thinking

Stuck-Up Little Runt

about.

* * *

Her arrival alone was an astonishment to him. Not that she came as she since has not. It is the manner of it which was quite unexpected.

Simon waited by the pub and saw only a lone rider upon the moped. Felt disappointment that she had not come. Waited to learn from Vinny the reason for her absence. As the funny little motorbike puttered into the parking space, he saw that the lone rider wore denim, felt momentarily disoriented. Vincent dressed in the fashion of his sister, Simon's confused initial thought. As she slid off the seat his heart jolted, sent a needed charge up to his too-slow brain. Corrie had come alone, ridden solo. Vinny lending her his vehicle should not have been such a surprise. He knows brother and sister trust each other; however, a moped is not a horse.

Helmet off, chestnut hair shaken as she does, he stepped up to Corrie. 'They're gathering in hay back at Low Fell,' she explained.

This puzzled Simon. At home in Aysgarth, his disinterested sister, Rosie, used to be in the fields at hay time if at no other. Across the country, the hands of every farmer's child over the age of ten come and stack bales, lift them on to trailers, that is Simon's experience. It was a glorious time when he was young: sun-burnt faces laughing as they were ferried back to the barn atop a trailer of stacked haybales. Extra pocket money! He wondered whether the dreadful-sounding Jeremy Dalton might be more indulgent of his daughter than she has thus far implied. Private school fees, a grand piano and permitting her to slope off, however busy the farm. Or could Corrie be so defiant that she might do this, come down to Broughton when her family all have their shoulder to the wheel? Ride off in the face of great ire. She has shown him traces of that, the jarring dissonance within the Dalton family. Simon tried asking—used words that did not accuse her of being lazy—probed only her father's attitude to her absence.

'I don't farm. Piano fingers, you see?' She spread out her hands, fingers a little longer than one might expect on a girl of small stature. 'Daddy insists that I don't. He wants me to win every competition in Cumbria. He shows sheep at the county fair, does the same with me when there's anything musical to be judged.'

Simon was surprised, couldn't work out if Dalton was the most cultured farmer in northern England, or just another show-off.

'Do you know…' This was said when they were walking around the churchyard, not entering the pub, not giving Janine and Ben any opportunity to summon them to join the slow-in-the-heads. The girl had explained to him that she would drink no cider in order to travel more safely than ever occurred when she clung to Vincent for the homeward journey. '…our father leads Vinny a fucking dog's life. That's why he drinks so much. I think my brother wants out, would drink himself into forgetting who he is if he only could.'

The strength of her assertion surprised Simon. Not the basic facts, he had thought of the possible link already; the force of the telling was a serious turn. She doesn't pepper her conversation with swear words; they arrive infrequently always in close proximity to mention of her father.

While the pair sat on a wooden bench by a small and ancient church, looking across the graveyard, Corrie told Simon about her family. 'Daddy puts Killian on a pedestal and he is the thickest Dalton by far.' The story was negative but the strength of feeling had dissipated. That was all reserved for her father. 'He has always bullied Vincent; Daddy knew and never once tried to stop it. Killie could shear a sheep at twelve years old, that has always made him favoured. He might have been whipped a time or two when he was younger, Vinny says he was, I don't recall anything of the sort. And my lovely brother—Vincent—Daddy beat him every week of his school days for one thing or another. He's only now coming out of his shell. Not far enough out yet. Not while he's stuck on the farm.'

'And you?' asked Simon, concerned that her nasty father might spank, slap or whip this defiant girl as he has done to her brothers.

'Don't worry about me,' she replied.

He saw her glance quickly at her shoes, think too long before offering her answer. He knew then that he would worry. Sensed she had held something back; no one likes to share feelings of humiliation. His own father used a strap once or twice. Did it in the past where it can stay. 'My mother…' he began to say. Corrie looked up at him. 'My mother…' he repeated as if waiting for the engine of his brain to bite on this turn of a key.

'You've not told me about her, Simon,' she said, placing a hand upon his own.

'She died. It doesn't matter. When I was…' He hung his head in shame. Tears were escaping his eyes, slowly overcoming the friction of his cheeks.

'Oh Simon,' she exclaimed putting an arm across his shoulders.

'I'm alright,' he said, brushing his stained face clean with the heel of his hand, unsure how tears even came to be there. Might miss her a little but he isn't terribly bothered. 'I'm alright. I just wanted you to know.'

She was silent a moment and then asked him if he wanted to talk more about it.

Simon shook his head.

'I think I've got it bad, Simon, and I haven't really. I should have asked about you, thought more…'

'No, I'm alright,' he repeated. 'It's not right that your dad is like he is. I wasn't trying to compare, I just wanted you to know.' She looked directly into his face, Simon's eyes went down, embarrassed by his tears. 'I think you understand me. That's why I said it.'

Corrie questioned him gently, gathering from him what he needed to say. Simon told her that it was breast cancer, that the funeral was in a tiny church where the coffin was whisked away to be burned. She questioned if it was a church at all. 'Wasn't it just the crematorium? I've heard about those funerals.'

'Is there a difference?' asked Simon. Simon Never-in-Church.

Corrie smiled at his ignorance, told her what she knew. Crematorium funerals are commonplace in many faiths. Her family, however—the departed Daltons—are all interred in the ground. Some in Coniston, others in Carlisle. Simon learnt that night that it is only opponents of the faith who burn Catholics.

'Does all that matter to you?' He worried that he might sound like an idiot on this topic.

'I think it does and then I also think I should pass it up. The buggering bastard is in thick with every priest in Cumbria; I want to be his opposite.'

She held Simon's hand through much of the serious talk. When he told her about school and work, the mood lightened. Corrie asked him if he was ticklish. He said he wasn't but she tested it a little. He tried to return the favour but wasn't able to let himself go as Corrie did. Worried that his more Ben-Jones-like intentions would make themselves known. She didn't seem to notice, played and laughed and told him about her schoolfriends. Which ones were too stupid to move up to the sixth form. She said a little about her very best friend, Millie Green. Simon loved watching her talk. The animation in her face, the depth of feeling he sensed as he watched those expressive brown eyes in the fading light of the summer evening.

* * *

It was only a little after ten o'clock but the moon was behind a cloud as they sat together in the church yard. They could barely see each other's faces in the deepening dusk. As she talked, so closely did they sit together, her breath warmed his cheek.

'Do you know my lot?' asked Simon. She didn't understand what he meant by the phrase. He told her he was referring to the Brownings, the farmer and wife who employ him.

Corrie has never met them, heard the names, and Vincent had told her that William Browning is a conceited man, thinks a land management course has given him agricultural wisdom.

Stuck-Up Little Runt

'My lot only know Catholics,' she said with a disdainful wave of her hand.

'A week or so back...' began Simon. He felt his cheeks flush, hoped she could not see this in the prevailing darkness. He described the scene when he returned to the farmhouse without fulfilling Carol's request that he look over the sheep on Nibthwaite Fell. His voluntary trek to see what the AI man wanted at Sark Farm. He tried to word his story carefully, has thought about it many times since it occurred. By far the craziest thing that has happened to him in Cumbria. He feared getting marooned in X-rated territory, couldn't stop once he'd started, she was listening so intently. 'I'm embarrassed to report that there was nothing artificial about this insemination. The man was humping Mrs Browning across the kitchen table.'

Uproarious. Corrie Dalton clutched Simon's shirt sleeve. Through extraordinarily high-pitched laughter she said, 'No!' and 'Surely not?' When able to again draw breath properly, hysteria abated, she muttered, 'Crikey, what a strumpet.'

The funny phrase reminded Simon that his friend attends a girls' school, may not speak the language of boys. 'I don't think she's a prossie, Corrie. No money will have changed hands. It's her husband who always pays Mr Piper for the service he provides.'

She giggled uncontrollably, put an arm across Simon's shoulder. 'So funny. He gets paid, not her.'

'I don't think he mistook Carol for a cow; however, it's a shadowy kitchen at Sark Farm. Might have been an honest mistake.'

Cordelia leaned into him, spluttering as she spoke. 'There's a way to tell,' she told him, tears of laughter on both cheeks. Simon nodded for her to explain; she could barely compose herself. 'I think...' She paused to let her invigorated lungs settle, allow the faculty of speech to return. '...you're the dairyman, Simon, but don't the AI men put an arm into the cows bum, while lovers do it with their willies.' Corrie hung her head, long hair hiding her eyes, as she erupted into further hysteria. Simon thought it very funny too while something in her ungovernable laughter led him to guess that she is unused to sex talk. It was a first for him in mixed company but, back at Swale Valley Comp, lads talked of nothing else from the age of thirteen.

When Corrie's laughter finally stopped, she asked him, 'Will you tell Mr Browning?'

'I can't,' said Simon. 'Mrs Browning gave me an extra ten in my pay.'

'She's bribed you to keep quiet!'

'I think so. She pulled a weird face when she gave me my money last week. I was about to say she'd given me too much when I put two and two together. The face meant not to talk about it. Then or ever, I suppose. And I was never going to tell Will anyway. That would only start them throwing pans about.'

The girl asked about this side of the Brownings' relationship. She was shocked at first but then said, 'The buggering bastard gets like that. Mummy doesn't rise to it.'

Simon thought again about the unpleasant household the girl must return to, squeezed Corrie's hand, knowing it was no compensation at all.

When he thought they had exhausted the subject of Mrs Browning and the kitchen table, Corrie took it up again. 'What exactly did you see?' she enquired, nudging her shoulder firmly into his. Shunting him an inch up the graveyard bench.

'Her knockers were swinging like a cow's udder. Piper had his head down like he was biting her back. Dogs do that too.'

'Oh, how funny. I shouldn't have liked to see it. I think I would have screamed. I suppose it's better than him injecting her with some old bull's piddle juice.'

Simon creased up laughing at that.

'What is it? What's so funny?'

'I hope there wasn't any piddle involved.'

The girl quietened very quickly. Turned slightly away from him. 'It's not called piddle juice,' she declared, and Simon thought then that Corrie might not get top marks in a quiz if sex was the theme. 'What is it then?' A little tension entered her voice, implying he'd played a trick upon her for which he must atone.

'I don't think I can tell you. It's embarrassing really.'

Then the girl must have dredged up some learning from her biology class. 'Well, it's semen, isn't it? But how is that different from a man's pee?'

'It just is,' he told her. 'It's something else they keep down there.'

They only sat in silence a few more seconds before the girl nudged him, gently this time. 'How can you look at her over breakfast now you've seen the woman's udders?'

'I know, I know. It could ruin my life. I'll be haunted by Carol Browning's titties until the day I see some nicer ones.' As he said this Simon turned towards her, clasped Corrie in a brief hug. Nothing untoward, just pulling her into his chest firmly enough that, through his thin shirt, he could feel her breasts yield to the gentle pressure.

'No one's seeing mine until we're married with a cat,' said Corrie, pushing him away. She wrapped an arm around his back. In the returned moonlight he could see her broadest smile; pretty face streaked with tears that testified to a diverting evening.

* * *

As he walked her to the moped in The Boar car park, Simon took her hands in his. He looked at them as though unsure whether to kiss or shake. He would have liked most of all to feel those laughing lips upon his own. It was within his desire to do to her a little of what Roy Piper had been up to in that kitchen; a truth he did not let find air, sensed the child in her might take offence. He knew he must be patient, couldn't stop thinking about the feel of her in his arms. 'Oh Corrie, I could stay here forever.'

'You're mad, you are,' she told him, before adding, 'See you next week,' while mounting her brother's moped.

He failed to declare his love and cannot know what she feels towards him. Spent much of the evening physically closer to her than he has ever before been to a girl. It is uplifting to recall and all the more confounding that, three weeks on, no satisfactory next week has arisen.

6.

By the following Saturday, the final day of the month of July, Simon has resolved to take a stand. Find out what Corrie thinks of him one way or another.

When he thinks about her, the conversation in the churchyard unfolds before him as if watched within a darkened cinema. Corrie of the captivating looks, he a stumbling support actor. He thinks there was a connection, rapport. Not every second perhaps, something worth grasping nevertheless. Hold on tight and hope it doesn't squeeze the life out of it. He is aware that his plan may culminate in the discovery that she has no wish to rekindle their friendship. His talk of the oversexed farmer's wife might have been an error. Maybe he overstepped the mark when he squeezed her tightly late in the evening. He blubbed at one point which was plain stupid. She could have felt goaded into saying words she would ordinarily choose not to use. Willy, primarily. He didn't intend that, tried to tone down his own language in the telling of the tale. She laughed like crazy at the time.

He hopes she has not forgotten him in the tumult of her piano playing. Become shaken from mind as she canters her horse across the fell. Simon cannot forget and not knowing why she has stayed away is an agony. If Cordelia Dalton was a little less highbrow, a little rougher around the edges like her brother, Vinny, they would have kissed or quarrelled by now. Maybe both. It is her refinement which has wrong-footed him.

Then there is psycho-farmer. Her homelife is unimaginable to him. The angry man who pays her private school fees. Is it purely to keep her away from boys of the wrong faith—or maybe boys in general—that's what she implied. Violent to Vinny. He hopes she has never been whipped; he couldn't bear to learn it. Jeremy Dalton could be the source of Simon's problems. It's the wildest of guesses.

Vincent and Killian, she spoke about. A loved brother and a hated one. That's not a normal family in his book. She hardly said a word about Thomasina, the oldest of the Dalton children. Married and living in Manchester, that was the sum total. Her family is bewildering to him. His own sorry foursome so much easier to comprehend. A sister who got married with a big fat pillow up her wedding dress; a mother in the graveyard at Aysgarth. And then there is John Tripp, his father, still farming for one, wearing bailer twine for a belt, eating homegrown spuds night after night. A shop-bought sausage if he can be bothered to fry it. Corrie's lot are the unpredictable ones. The Tripps do not amount to much and nor do they confuse.

Once Simon has completed his morning chores, he sets off on the long cycle ride to Low Fell. At the heart of his decision is simply the need to see her once more, to learn how the land lies. On Friday evening he pored over his ordinance survey map, found the farm in which she lives. Thirteen miles of country lanes away, up and down hill. He has hardly slept.

The road he cycles on is busy with traffic. Tourists and locals alike squeeze him into the verges. He passes field after field of sheep, knowing it is they alone who will be grazing the higher fells. Neighbouring farmers regard Will Browning's decision to go dairy at Sark Farm as absurd. It was a sheep farm in Mr Browning senior's day and for generations before that too. It is only in the eight years since Will took the helm that it has accommodated greater than a handful of domestic dairy cattle. Will has a theory, an idea. He spends more on fertiliser than many a holding three times the size of Sark. His grass yield is excellent, its quality an occasional worry. Two months ago, two cows had to be put down. They were bellowing in the middle of the night, lolloping around the field without coordination. Suffering from the staggers. Soil testing uncovered a magnesium deficiency in the land, the cause of their chronic ill-health. Veterinary called it a brain disease. This prompted Mr Browning to source yet more mineral feeds, more bespoke fertiliser. Simon can't fault his method, while speculating whether the true dilemma is living so far up the hillside. It sends the cows crazy, Will's a bit volatile, his wife a nymphomaniac. All the Daltons except beautiful Corrie sound like walking fruitcakes atop Ulpha Fell. Up where everybody gets the staggers.

As he climbs Smithy Lane, changing down the gears on his ten-speed bike, the sense of enclosure through the heavy lining of trees overwhelms Simon. It contrasts with the roads around High Nibthwaite or Broughton-in-Furness. Bracken only on that moorland. The wooded vale he now climbs feels ancient, a mixed forest. Overhanging branches by the side of the road make him duck his head. A red sports car overtakes him, shooting by just inches from his right leg, the driver reckless on the narrow lane. The farmhouses he passes are all cottages with an outbuilding or two. Small holdings. From one of them a dog races out under the five-bar gate, causing him to brake, curve his path around the yapping menace. It's a Scottie, a silly dog, though clearly not so daft as to have run in front of the sports car. It is still here.

On a short down-hill stretch within leafy woodland, he thinks he sees deer, pulls on his brakes—outer levers of his drop handlebars—takes a look. Goats, a few of them grazing in the enclosed woodland, eking out some sustenance from the forest floor. He likes the look of goats, enjoys their grumpy and comical cries. Milking goats is a labour of love. Simon has read, in Farmers' Weekly, of bespoke milking parlours, herds of two and three hundred of the funny animals. Back in North Yorkshire he knew of only two farmers who kept them, and those in modest numbers. Even here, where a small tribe graze, he counts no more than twenty. Expects no such technological assistance as an adapted milking parlour. An old lady may pull on the teats of the goat's udders by hand, a lady with strength

Stuck-Up Little Runt

in her fingers from the doing of it down the decades. Goats are more pernickety creatures than cattle. He has read that, and one can sense it from their narrow features. They disclose it with each bleat of discontent.

The downward slope was a cruel trick. The road climbs once more, leg muscles pressing energy through his pedals into the chain pulley of his bike. His wheels grip the tarmac with a sticky deliberation as he rises above the woodland. It feels as if he is pushing through the surface of the road, sending it slowly down the hill behind him. His thighs strain with the effort. The view clears, all trees are below him now. He has found the fell. In the distance he can see the western hills folding out before him, Eskdale and beyond. Dry stone walls draw abstract shapes upon the land. Tumble-down walls which no longer enclose the sheep. And the animals won't leave, nowhere better for a sheep to be. The rocky fields are greener in Cumbria than elsewhere in England this arid summer. By a gate he sees the dark ring of a mineral feed, extra nourishment to enhance their nutrition, compensate for the toughness of the high-ground grass. Will Browning gives no supplements to his small flock who summer on the open fell, in his view it would be a waste. Declares that other sheep with other markings would access such goodness were he to leave it out for his own. The man is tightfisted in his application of science and that might unravel his calculations.

Simon wonders how close he is to Low Fell; could this be Dalton land he cycles across? His current thinking is that Cordelia's father must be a shrewd farmer—he sounds to have money in abundance—and a vicious bastard, rolled into one. The fell he is now on must be theirs for the grazing, the sheep could be Dalton sheep. The map showed him that the farmhouse, hay and grazing pasture, will come when the fell slopes away, a mile or two further north. The bracken-strewn terrain which stretches out before him offers strange challenges. Land so spartan, rocky and undulating, impossible to plough, can yield little goodness. A sheep chewing on the meagre grass turns her head towards him. Trills a short bleat of concurrence.

* * *

He knows that it is Low Fell, long before any written sign shows itself. There were intermittent tiny farms on the way up, and he passed a couple of improbable cottages on the high ground. He has only just begun the descent; as it falls away, the mixed yellows of recently cut fields tumble down to Eskdale below. One large farmhouse shouts its name. Set back from the road by fifty yards; two rows of wind-bedraggled trees line the downward track to its door. A house and an array of outbuildings. The slate-grey grandeur of Low Fell speaks of money, of pomposity, many rooms, surely large and high-ceilinged. An ugly lump. It feels as if he has come to rescue Corrie, to smuggle her far from this bitter hideaway. He has seen farms like it in North Yorkshire: Wensleydale, Grassington, those places. Never been invited inside. Not once.

* * *

At the gateway, he brakes, pulls in, leg swung backwards around the saddle, and pushes his bike down the private track. Walking to her door.

He knows this is the right place, the name carved into an old wooden plaque secured to the open gate. This short walk could culminate in a meeting with his girlfriend. He fears learning that he does not have one. As he walks, he strains his ears. No piano plays. The feeling inside him is an uncomfortable one. It comes into Simon's mind that he might better seek out the stables. She could be there, grooming Ghost, or out riding on the moor. That and Vincent may be the only ones she loves around here. The mother with the extraordinary name barely gets a mention. As he stumbles over these thoughts, he recalls that the stables are a short way away, beside their farm-hand's cottage. He didn't seek it out on his ordinance survey map, never thought to.

The entryway is narrow and a Land Rover has turned off the road, following him down the gravel track. Stepping on to the grass, the leaves of one of the trees which line the route brush the top of his head, he pulls his bicycle closer to his person. The vehicle slows, its windows already open. A ruddy-faced man leans towards him. 'Can I help you?'

Simon's heart stalls for a beat. Resumes. 'Mr Dalton,' he enquires tentatively.

'Yes,' the driver replies, the lone occupant of the vehicle. Simon sees from the man's youth that it must be Killian Dalton. He is more weathered than Vincent but cannot possibly be Cordelia's father. Not as old as Peter, the man who made up the quiz at Young Farmers, showed the slides of his French cattle.

'I've come to visit Corrie.'

'Come to visit Cordelia. And your name is…?'

'I'm Simon Tripp. We know each other from Young Farmers.'

Killian Dalton scrutinises the boy, lets out a peremptory laugh and puts a foot on the Land Rover's accelerator. The vehicle stutters briefly before bumping down the rutted drive, coughing exhaust into Simon's face.

He continues to walk towards Low Fell, pushing his bike, following the diesel fumes which have despoiled the fell air. His stomach churns as he contemplates the sheer arrogance of the man. Ahead he sees him slide out of the four-wheel drive, slam its door shut and strut around the back of the rambling farmhouse. He expected to share Cordelia's dislike of Killian. The man treated him like dirt. Simon has never thought his own name a joke, Killian reacted as if it were. He has no foothold here, not even certain who's who, but they seem to know him. Dislike him even. Simon's not for turning back, simply feels pessimistic about the reception he is to receive.

* * *

As he leans his bicycle against the porch wall and enters the small vestibule to ring the bell, the front door opens. Vincent looks like a different boy than the one he knows from The Boar. Eyes to the floor, shaking his head. He mutters so faintly Simon can barely make out his words. 'Probably not,' that's what it sounded like. Discouraging. When he finally takes his eye, Vincent has an apologetic smile adhering rigidly to his face. Looks unsettled, not himself. Sober, perhaps.

Killian pushes in front of the younger brother, says the word, 'Yes?' It is as if their exchange on the drive never occurred, although three minutes have not elapsed.

Simon looks at this man closely now. He has removed his chequered cap; short black hair scribbled on a sunburnt forehead. His face is angry although they are unacquainted and Simon has done him no wrong. This must be for whom Vincent wordlessly apologises. Even inside the Dalton family home Killian wears wellingtons. A pointless uniform this dry summer. Simon puts his left foot, the one closer to Vincent, over the lip of the doorstep. 'I'd like to see Cordelia, please?'

'You're not coming in,' says the red-faced brother. A more assertive take on Vincent's mutterings.

Simon stands his ground. 'Is it possible to speak to Corrie, please?'

A door opens behind Killian. He hears a woman's voice say, 'Jeremy.' A note of concern in it. The voice is not Cordelia's. A well-spoken voice but not the one he wishes to hear. Simon cannot sense whether Corrie is within this unwelcoming house.

A man of stature, broken red veins across his cheeks, and wearing a green sleeveless jacket—a gilet—over his brown checked-patterned shirt, strides towards the door. 'Out of here, lad.'

'What have I done?' asks Simon.

'Oh, I'm cutting you off at the pass. You'll be doing nothing more with my daughter, whatever you might have done so far.' The pitch at which he speaks is not loud, it is insistent. The man's eyes are all over him but they never meet his own. Jeremy Dalton—no introduction required—is looking through Simon, past him and at the track he came down. It is sufficient to make the boy turn his head. Nothing to see there, he looks again into the face of Corrie's father. 'Off you go, lad,' says Dalton quietly.

Stuck-Up Little Runt

Simon wonders how long this man's enmity has been waiting for him. He has said and done nothing to provoke it. Vincent looks directly at him, winces a little, while seemingly nodding agreement with the father. His strained expression tells of his own discomfort.

Killian shoulders roughly into the younger brother. 'We should count to ten, if he's not cycling, we'll take his bike apart.'

'Manners, Killian. There's no excuse for bad manners,' calls the well-to-do voice from the room out of which Jeremy Dalton emerged. Father and eldest son exchange sly smiles.

'No excuse for plying my little girl with tipple,' says Jeremy. 'She's no need of boys. Never will have a need for boys like you. Now turn around.'

'Can I just speak to her, please? To Corrie.'

'Cordelia is otherwise engaged,' says her father. His voice a quiet monotone now, a grin of no meaning illuminating his severe features. Eyes dart across Simon, up and down, never resting for a second. Spiteful smile.

'Best go,' says Vincent. 'I may see you Thursday.'

'Shut up,' says father to son.

'But you had best go,' says Killian. He is pointing at the boy's bike, the front wheel of which protrudes from the side of the porch.

Jeremy nods his head.

'Is she here?' he asks, stepping backwards off the door step, as if blown by the sustained hostility.

The father slams the front door of the farmhouse shut. It is all the answer he will be getting. His view of the unlikely sentries, the three males of the household, instantly erased. He has been sent packing by shotgun. No such weapon was shown but every farmer has one. The seething-mad psycho-farmer was thinking about it, about his twelve-bore. That's how it feels to Simon.

'Fuck,' he mutters as he takes hold of his handlebars and begins to trudge slowly back up the gravelly lane. 'Fucking nutters.'

317

Ghost in the Stables

* * *

When he is halfway to the road—a long cycle ride ahead after this fruitless pilgrimage—he turns and studies the sombre farmhouse. The sun is behind and to the left, the windows are all in darkness. He cannot see if a soul looks out, it is the effect of the silhouetted light. Corrie might be in there but he never caught a sense of it. She could be a thousand miles away. He waves a hand, expecting it is no more than a grey-stone building watching him. There is no discernible response: no window sash opens and no hand waves acknowledgement of the effort he has made. Farmer Dalton doesn't watch him leave either, surely not. He dispatched Simon with a confidence that requires no corroboration. The boy glances the other way, up at the road ahead, mounts his bike and cycles the remaining few yards to the public lane. Once there he turns downhill. Not heading back to Nibthwaite yet. Takes the opposite direction.

He comes to a small coppice of trees. There is nobody in sight, the three Dalton males are the only souls he has seen in the last half hour. He pushes his bike into the undergrowth beside the road, brings himself back out into the open. He sees a stile by which to enter the first field, the one behind the Dalton's farmhouse. Has it in mind to go stealthily around the back, to seek out Corrie's bedroom window. As he enters the field, he calculates that he is quite visible should Killian or Jeremy come out to the parked Land Rover. Simon hunches himself down below the height of the dry-stone wall. Moving forward in this posture is uncomfortable. He drops onto his hands and knees, makes his way commando-style. Before he has gone ten yards, he stops. Feeling ridiculous. Not a clue which bedroom Corrie sleeps in, or if she is in there at all. Her deranged father might have sent her to a convent. There must be a reason for the fury his arrival at the farm incited. He told the man's schoolgirl daughter how Mrs Browning shags bald men for fun, it could be that. Seems inappropriate now. How Jeremy Dalton got wind of any of it is beyond him. That family has a way all its own: a bunch of lunatics plus Corrie. His own

Stuck-Up Little Runt

set-in-his-ways father disapproved of Rosie liaising with man after man from the nearby villages, said as much at the dinner table and said it forcibly. Never thought he might keep them at bay with a stern face and an olive-coloured gilet. His father's ill-temper has no authority in it.

Simon looks away from the house, the opposite direction. There is a cottage situated two fields lower down the hillside. Stables adjacent to it. It looks right, a tied cottage. She's probably with her horse, Ghost—a spooky name—grooming him in the stables or out riding across the moor. Unaware that Simon has come calling. He desists his futile game of commando. Rises up. With his back to Low Fell, he struts towards the stables. Walking tall. If Jeremy Dalton is watching, he will see Simon's determination is undimmed.

* * *

'What you wanting?'

The man who asks this looks only a little older than Killian Dalton, his hairline receding prematurely, face unlined. What hair he keeps is long and untidy. Simon expected that he might meet Mary, the name he recalled Corrie using for the wife of the labourer, who feeds and grooms the Dalton's horses. This must be that girl's husband, name slipped from Simon's grasp.

'I'm looking for Corrie Dalton.'

'Up yonder house. It's where she lives.'

'I know, I just thought she might be here.'

'Then you thought wrong.'

He feels no threat from this brusque man. Simon is unknown at these outbuildings. He might treat a stranger at Sark Farm, or back at Penton, North Yorkshire, with a similar cold shoulder.

'I'm her friend. Are you Mary's husband?'

The man looks at the ground before answering. 'I am.'

'She likes you...' Simon is stuck for words, not sure where to go with this conversation. This man could be a staging post on his circuitous approach to the girl who has filled his mind through a three-week absence. '...and that's a big compliment coming from any Dalton, I think.'

The man took his eye. 'Aye, boy, Mary's very fond of Corrie, she is. I like her too. She never done me no wrong.'

'And she's not here?'

'Not seen her in weeks,' he answers.

'But she comes to ride Ghost, her horse. Can I see it? Ghost.'

'Not now she dunna,' says the man. 'Not now.'

'Is Ghost here?' asks Simon, confused by the reply. The dishevelled farmhand simply shakes his head. Simon feels disheartened; Ghost was her passion. Ghost and the piano which did not play. It is as if he has come to the wrong farm. Come to it ten years late. 'What's happened to it? Her horse.'

'It's not my business. It's Mr Dalton can explain about that. Not my business to say nothing.'

* * *

Cycling back, up on to the fell and then the long downhill towards Broughton-in-Furness, Simon feels numb. Tries to put aside any anger he feels towards Derek Donnelly. The man at the stables shared his name, spoke only kindly of Corrie. Simon thinks he was holding back a lot more than he said. Knew the whole story, most likely. The girl loves her horse, no explanation for its absence left his lips. Frightened of Jeremy Dalton, that's the most likely reason. Simon tells himself he has no fear of him, the buggering bastard as Corrie aptly calls him, just contempt. It bothers him that he gave in so easily. A few words on a doorstep, it was barely a spat. Embarrassing to think about. He should have thrown a punch, fought for his girl. He won't fear Dalton just because Vincent and Derek Donnelly do.

'If she was out riding, I would have told you so.' That was the phrase Derek said to him. Even the labourers talk in riddles at Low Fell.

Simon's daft convent fears loomed too large in his mind. 'Has she been sent to be a nun?'

Derek scratched his sunburnt forehead, his reclaimed scalp. 'I hope not. Expect I would have heard if she'd done that.

Young Corrie upping and turning to a nun. No, I don't see that at all.' It was at this point in their conversation—and no other—that he saw Derek smile. Simon's fears must have missed their mark, still the reply told him nothing of where she's currently cloistered. He said that Corrie did not appear to be in the farmhouse and Derek only shrugged.

7.

A day later and Simon is not for giving up, not on Corrie Dalton. He milks the cows alone this Sunday morning; William has declared himself 'knackered' and asked his employee to mind the farm for two or three days. It is irritating. Twenty-four pounds a week is all he gets and Will leaves him to it. Perhaps it is only a few days here and there but the man is a hypochondriac, a grim diagnosis for a farmer. He didn't turn up to morning milking for a whole fortnight last Autumn. Carol assisted some days, Simon new on the farm. The Spanish flu, Will called it. A common cold was Simon's assessment; Carol's too most likely. She shouts at the big drip however poorly he declares himself to be.

The cows turn into the field. They are back in Garden, the water-supply pure again. Before this over-egged sickness, Will Browning did a bit of his better work. Traced the watercourse up the fell, found half a dozen car batteries dumped upstream from where it feeds the water-troughs. A fly-tipper must have driven up the bridle way onto the fell, dumped an obvious hazard into flowing water. It caused the farmer a shouting fit. He apologised when Simon calmly pointed out that he was shouting at the wrong person. The boy has no need of car batteries, rides a bike. 'Sorry Simon,' said Will, 'it just makes me furious. They likely put our milk on their Corn Flakes, then kill our cattle with their ruddy stupidity.' Simon didn't disagree, hardly the one for Browning to vent his spleen on.

And Simon managed no such deflection at Low Fell yesterday. Received no apology after the psycho-farmer's unjustified verbal assault. The more he dwells upon it, the more Simon feels responsible for whatever fate has befallen Corrie. The girl he was barred from seeing.

* * *

The milking parlour is clean. Shit-shovelling, he calls the job he has just completed. It's only a little after ten o'clock, no further labour required until afternoon milking. Entering the farmhouse, he sees Carol sitting at the kitchen table with her children, crayoning books out, her husband still in the marital bed, simulating his demise. Simon goes upstairs. In the bathroom he scrubs his hands, checks his face. Hasn't time to wash properly. Back in his room he changes into decent corduroys and a shirt which he usually reserves for Thursday evenings.

Then he is back on his bike, off to Coniston this time, not such a long ride. Arrives before eleven; fifteen minutes to, says his watch. He leaves his bicycle to the rear of the churchyard, not in sight of the gathering congregants. A man in black stands out front, inviting all-comers into his austere-looking church. Simon narrows his eyes, observes the priest from a distance. He has a thin face, the shortest black hair clinging to his narrow head. White collar and cuffs upon a long black garment. An almost-skirt, an effeminate looking garb. He checks himself; his father's fixations need not be Simon's. Can't be all bad: Corrie is a Catholic.

The priest smiles at him, beckons him closer to the church. Simon recalls Corrie telling him that one priest favours Jeremy Dalton. Swayed by his money, his donations. He wanders a short distance away, slides his bottom on to a low standing wall, slouches his shoulders, puts his head down. His hands near but not covering his eyes. It might look as if he is praying in the August sunshine. Furtively, he looks out from beneath his bowed head. Who would self-reliant Simon Tripp pray to?

A Land Rover swings into the car park. He only catches sight of it in the last moment, so fast does it travel. Doesn't see the occupants but the manner of the parking—swung beside a

Stuck-Up Little Runt

tree, at almost forty-five degrees from the marked space—suggests it has been driven by an arrogant man. The family emerge, his inference squarely on the head of the nail.

The tall man who alights from the driver's door is definitely the bastard. He is wearing a tie, a tweed jacket. Must bake in the morning's heat. From the opposite door a tall lady—wine-red dress and hair the colour of Cordelia's, shorter in length, styled—emerges. She smooths her dress down carefully and then leans back into the car, pulls forward her seat. It is a two-door vehicle; from its rear a succession of passengers clambers out. Killian is first, as tall as his father, wearing a strange cardigan, as unfashionable as he is detestable. Stands next to his mother. The next child out brings an enormous lift to Simon's spirits, the first of the weekend. Derek Donnelly is good to his word, Cordelia Dalton not locked-up in a convent in Rome. She is here in Coniston, fifty paces from where he sits, head still masked by his proximate hands. Her tartan Alice band holds her hair in place. A brown rainbow, all shades dancing in the sunlight. Her dress is a rich green, cut to below the knee. Her arms are quite white, she wears long socks, possibly tights. She must feel hot, so attired; it is the first day of August and the sky unbroken. He wants to go to her, resists the temptation. Re-enacting the doorstep row in front of the church seems a poor choice. He keeps his head down, his eyes scanning through the hands which obscure his face. He cannot let her leave his vision. Vincent pulls himself out last. Hair unkempt, he wears a jacket and tie. Good effort; lost his comb.

Simon watches the family trek to the entrance. Corrie remains unaware of his nearby presence. He would like her to see him, while being similarly keen to avoid detection by Jeremy or Killian Dalton. Even Vincent might inadvertently give him away to the odious ones should he espy him first. The woman, the mother, does not know him, never saw him yesterday. He watches her for a moment, she stands erect, far taller than her daughter. Then he returns his gaze to Cordelia, to where it belongs.

The priest at the door of Our Lady of the Rosary Catholic Church greets the Dalton family, one after another. Farmer Dalton is the first, shakes his hand, exchanges words as each holds the other in their grip. The tall lady doesn't linger, nor the boys. They have entered the church as Cordelia—last up the shallow steps—speaks to the man of the cloth. Simon sees her look into the priest's face, chin pointing upwards. He cannot hear what words she enunciates. Maybe this is a different priest to the one she scorned, the confidante of her father. Or maybe he didn't understand the point she was making those weeks back. Simon doesn't know who's who around here. Forgiveness is the problem: Simon doesn't believe in it. Then she is through the stone doorway into the hidden interior. He wishes he could have stood where the priest stood, shared a conversation with Cordelia. Looked, as he did, into her earnest face.

The priest remains outside to greet a late arrival—an elderly lady whom a younger congregant is helping from a car—he turns towards Simon who remains sitting on the wall and waves a hand. 'Don't miss the service now,' he shouts.

Simon arises, feels both trapped and excited. He wonders what his own father would say if he knew what denomination of church is temporarily to devour his son. His father's views are stupid, first to last. 'Bombers,' he calls all Catholics, even says it of the nuns at Settle market. It's not a way to think. Sharing a roof with Corrie Dalton, it has to be worth it. On entering the church, Simon is astonished by how ornate it all appears. Nothing in the grey exterior prepared him for this. Velvet curtains of the deepest blue dominate the front; lit candles are in abundance, each secured upon a shiny brass knob. It is Christmas in August. He slips into a pew towards the rear, strains his eyes in this grainier light. It is a well-occupied church but he sees them quickly enough, the Dalton family, on the same side of the aisle as he has chosen. Much nearer the front. Then his eyes rest on the chestnut hair, the lowest head in the line. He can only imagine the dancing brown eyes; the back of her head is all he can see, more than nothing, scarcely enough. He speculates within himself that his gaze will penetrate her consciousness. Corrie, Corrie, Corrie, he mouths silently. She does not turn.

* * *

The liturgy and the bible readings pass him by. Simon has no feel for religion. Aliens must be out there somewhere, disappointing they do not show their faces; the saints and the resurrected, pure fantasy. Signs and miracles are seldom seen by the faithful, not at all by those with a pinch of scepticism. He cannot lend himself to it, may change his mind should Corrie choose to explain it all.

When she sings, her hair moves. Not excessively: a less perceptive onlooker might miss it. Not Simon. It's the subtlest swing. Then the priest has them all bow their heads in prayer, many of the congregants kneel in front of the pews, hands on the back of the bench in front. Simon doesn't: taking a look is far from converted. He spots neither Corrie nor her mother have knelt, all the Dalton men have. Perhaps it's a penance handed to them at their last confession. Or the dresses which the ladies wear may exempt them, unseemly to have them hitched up above the knee. He can apply no such reasoning to himself, nor find the ear of a God to whom he might excuse himself.

As the priest intones well-worn phrases, Simon finds himself filled with an unchristian diatribe. He should punch old Dalton. Punch him like he's never before done to anyone. That man has whipped poor Vincent, may have done similar to Corrie. He fears that his association with her—fledgling love, a boy and a girl giggling in a moonlit churchyard—has brought wrath upon her from the father she always hated. He felt its resonance at the farmhouse yesterday. How the horrible farmer even knows about him is beyond Simon's understanding. 'Plying with drink,' he said yesterday—accused—and last time he saw her they drank none. He's a madman. Eighteen months ago, his English class went by coach to York on a snowy winter's evening, saw a performance of the Shakespeare play which had been set for their 'O' Level. Only now does he grasp what it was all about. If he killed off Farmer Dalton it would make for a proper conclusion, the consummate final act: justice. And his moralistic church might be the right place for it. However, Simon carries no sword; this cannot be the day. He clenches his teeth together, rises quietly from his seat, glances one more time at her lush brown hair. Out the door, he slips away. Back to his bike with the proof that she is here still, Cumbria, living at Low Fell. That she wishes him to pursue her is but a hope. He has seen but not heard from the girlfriend he doesn't quite have.

8.

It is with meagre expectation that Simon cycles once more to Broughton Young Farmers. He waits outside, feeling no real kinship with the run-of-the-mill attendees. Wellie-chuckers, Corrie has said it many times. His pulse quickens at the buzz of a moped—incredible—and then it does not. Vinny has arrived alone. Not a terrible return but the sister is the one whose presence he craves.

'No, I'll buy,' says Vincent. He places a proprietorial hand on the young man's back. 'All my fault, I fear. You're sweet on her, aren't you?'

Simon dislikes being asked personal questions. He stood for several minutes on the doorstep while Jeremy and Killian treated him as a barbarian to be repelled. It is barely an observation that he is sweet on Corrie, lovestruck. All the words he never uses. 'I want her as a friend,' he tells Vincent. 'Do you think she wants to see me?'

'I'm sorry about Saturday,' he says, not answering the question. 'I should have talked to you weeks ago. When I was last here. I thought it would blow over but it's getting worse.'

'What's getting worse? Will she see me?'

'I think she'd like to, it's just that she can't. Her and the old man. A terrible situation…'

Stuck-Up Little Runt

'He's not beaten her, has he?' This question might be giving away what he shouldn't, his knowledge of Vinny's struggle to find self-respect in that man's shadow. Simon is desperate to know.

'Eurgh.' This is not an answer. Vincent shakes his head after expelling the strange noise. It might have been a no, didn't really sound like a word at all. 'Other stuff mostly. Corrie should tell you...'

'...but she's not here.'

'No. And she's stopped speaking to him. To the nasty old arse who is our father. I'm not sure if that's really the solution or just creating another problem. You see, Corrie's ever so headstrong...'

'What happened, Vinny?'

'Well...' Vincent has bought two beers, the pair have wandered outside, seated themselves on a wooden bench that overlooks the pub carpark. '...my fault, like I said.' He looks directly into Simon's blue eyes. Chinks the bottom of his pint against the glass of the younger man. 'I really should tell you, owe it you. I think it was the Sunday after she was last here. The time she came alone. You see, we finished haymaking and I saw Patrick at the Horseshoe Inn for a few jars that Saturday night...' As he listens, Simon draws back his head, can't see what any of this has to do with it. '...he told me that you and Corrie never joined the meeting. I decided to get a little rise out of her at Sunday lunch. Just ribbing. God, I wish I hadn't. Teased her rotten really. Something along the lines of, "Was that a boyfriend who kept you out of the Young Farmers meeting all night?" That was the gist of it.' He holds his pint pot between his knees and places a hand on Simon's shoulder. 'I know you wouldn't do anything off limits. And Cordelia would have none of that anyway. She's strict, takes church far more seriously than I do, you know? I wasn't really thinking, teasing her that way. All my fault. Daddy never minded when I used to rib Killie about getting stuck in a shooting cabin with a girl in the rain. Never bothered at all. I'd say all the usual. "Did she have to take her wet clothes off?" And Daddy would laugh, no matter whether Killian squirmed or laughed about it himself. It's only Mummy who tuts at that kind of talk. When I poked this little bit of fun—nothing X-rated, just about keeping a particular young farmer for herself—Corrie went bright red, face like a three-bar heater. I think everyone at the table could see I'd struck the jackpot. You were romancing her in some fashion or other. Well, you're no Ben Jones, if I can't trust you with my sister, what hope is there? It would all have been pretty funny in a normal family.'

'Why? What did Corrie do?' asks Simon.

'Corrie? She just stayed red. Told me to shut-up, I expect. It was Killie and the old arse who got uppity.'

'What has it got to do with them? With Killian.'

'Killie started saying daft stuff. "You're still at school, Cordelia. Not ready for boys." School never put that bugger off the boys, Simon. He can be such a ruddy arse sometimes. Ingratiates himself with Daddy before I even know what the game is. Corrie tried to say you were just more interesting than all the other dimwit young farmers. Being a boy was incidental, she said. Funny, eh? Like she'd barely spotted it. Crimson in the face when she said it. Big fat crush, I was thinking. This started...'

'Do you really think she likes me?'

'Oh, she plays her cards close to her chest, does Corrie...' Vincent took another drink from his glass, put it back between his knees, smiled directly at Simon. '...but we all saw her face turn the colour of love.' Then he dropped the smile. 'She's a bit all or nothing, my sister. Still a kid. I don't know for certain but you might be her first crush. The thing is, her evasion of Killie's daft question and her face turning tomato coloured got the old arse asking questions.'

Simon feels light-headed. He wants to attend Vinny's words, the knowledge that Corrie likes him is a substantial impediment. Blushing at mention of him, he can picture that. They both went a bit red last time they spoke. Indiscreet talk about a randy farmer's wife. 'We did nothing. Whatever your father asked, we did nothing but talk.'

'Look, you know he's an absolute arse, don't you?' Vincent takes another long glug from his Hartley's, wipes his mouth with the back of his hand, while Simon nods. It has been noted. The man gave a two-minute showcase of exactly that on the front doorstep of Low Fell five days ago. 'Thing is, he picked up that Corrie had gone this astonishing shade of red. She's a cucumber in normal times. Even the old arse could see that she has a thing for you, Simon. Lucky you really. She was quite standoffish with the chappies who approached her the first couple of times she came to Young Farmers. And her being so flustered got him asking questions. "Who is he?" and, "Where's he from?" The big one was, "Is this a boy we've seen in church?" I really shouldn't have opened my mouth. Corrie's the best in our family, you know? I didn't mean to make trouble for her, and this is an obvious stumbling block for the big old arse. It's all bollocks if you think about it. He couldn't bear for Corrie to be spending time alone with a proddy dog. Not that you'll think of yourself that way.'

The younger boy rolls his eyes. He is of another religion; the father's dismissal of his worth is both preposterous and unsurprising. Growing up at Penton, the received wisdom declared Catholics to be poorer, more uncouth than their Anglican cousins. Received ignorance. It does not surprise him that, in the Dalton family, the social divide appears the other way around. Mr Dalton may not be a sophisticated man— didn't look that way on the doorstep—however, he must have plenty of influential money. Simon saw the priest shake his hand for an inordinate amount of time. His own father is a peasant, holds his trousers up with bailer twine. Farmer Dalton might have one up on Farmer Tripp; a decent pile of money to look down at him from. Two bigots from a generation with nothing of value to offer. That's as much as Simon can make of the pair of them. 'Did you talk to Corrie? She really likes me?'

'I think she's still cross with me. Opening my trap like I did.

It's all turned horribly sour. The old man's a right bully...'

'What's he done to her?'

Vincent puts his pint pot up to his lips. Shakes his head without a drop passing them. Lowers the drink. 'What hasn't he done? My sister can be her own worst enemy sometimes, Simon. I think she's terrific. Brave. She hasn't said a word to him since...' He shrugs. '...since I put my foot in my mouth, or thereabouts.' He hangs his head down a moment. 'God, I'm sorry, Simon.'

The expression on Vinny's face alarms the younger boy. All his good cheer is momentarily drained, utter dejection lies upon it. Then Vincent rises, says they should join the meeting upstairs.

'I need to know what's happened,' says Simon. 'Did he hit her?'

'It's other crap really. She'll tell you when it blows over. She's terribly upset though. Won't speak to the old arse.'

With that Vincent walks to the pub door. Simon follows, feeling short changed by the abridged explanation.

* * *

Through the course of the evening, and whenever he feels no one can overhear, Simon asks Vincent more questions. This week Peter spends the meeting trying to recruit volunteers to help out at Grizebeck Street Fair. The Young Farmers will have a stall.

'Fun and recruitment,' says Peter.

'Say you're milking,' Vincent tells him. 'It's hopeless through the day, get to the Star Inn for the evening. Live music: it's always packed out.' No surprise that Vinny likes beer more than hoop-la. When asks about Corrie, Vinny confirms that she would like to see him. 'She thumped me. Without my stupid teasing the old arse would not have known a thing about you. He always blew hot and cold about her coming to Young Farmers.'

'When will Corrie be allowed to come back? If she started talking to him again, would he let her?'

Vincent evades the questions, apologises more than once. He is comprehensively contrite about his actions, his unintended role in keeping the two apart. He confirms, as often as Simon asks, that his sister holds him in her thoughts. 'Besotted,' he says once, and the boy likes the word, realises it is how he has felt since first laying eyes on her. Then, late in the evening, the brother says out of the blue, 'Tell you what, write her a note and I'll ask Corrie to arrange to see a girl after church on Sunday. Millie Green, she lives at Hawkshead. That's up your way, isn't it? A schoolfriend of my sister's, she'll play along. You go to Hawkshead. Presto.'

This is genius, five pints of Hartley's worth of genius. Simon needed a plan and Vincent plus beer have come up with it.

At the bar Simon asks for pen and paper with which to write Corrie a note. The barman has no paper, apologises, furnishes him with a biro. Simon sees a pools coupon left on an empty table. He glances around the room; nobody's claiming it, not a cross in a box. There are few spaces to write on, so busy is it with grids and teams and small print. In tiny lettering he scrawls in the upper margin that he will be at Hawkshead church on Sunday, noting C of E in brackets and writing after it, 'not to attend the service.' He hopes that she won't mind his choice of meeting place, knows not if there is a Catholic church in that small village. He will be there at one in the afternoon. He writes, 'I hope this is all right with your friend, Millie. Thank her from me.' Simon is surprised by his own good manners. Wonders whether to sign off with love but it is an open letter, a pools coupon without an envelope; Vincent will read it. 'All the best, Simon,' he puts, and then adds several X's in the boxes by some of next Saturday's football matches. Imagines that Vincent will think them predicted score draws and only the smarter Corrie gather their true intent.

Besotted, sweet on: he finds himself far more predisposed to these terms than he has previously known himself to be.

* * *

Ben Jones is hovering beside the table in the lounge bar where

Vinny and Simon sit. He has been in meeting and pub all evening; Simon has dealt with last week's fracas by crossing his fingers. Not spoken a word to the great oaf; nothing to apologise for in Simon's book. He hopes Ben was too drunk to remember landing on his bum on the wooden floor.

'You and me, outside.'

There have been no fights at Young Farmer's save his own shove into this man a week ago. Simon fears being the first to lose one. Ben is older, tougher. And not nearly drunk enough to tumble with the barest prompt as he did a week earlier.

'I'm sorry about last week. I didn't mean for you to fall over.'

'Steady on, Ben,' says Vincent. 'What seems to be the matter?'

'Nothing to do with you, Vincent. This is about me and him and that sister of yours we both want to give a poke.'

Simon looks down, says an audible, 'Shut up.' That is not how it was, and nor does he wish to explain last week's conversation to Vincent.

'What's that, Tripp-lad?' says Jones.

'Nothing. Look, we'll both get barred from the pub if we fight…'

'Ha. Comedian, Tripp-lad. I might get barred. You'll be in the fucking hospital, won't you? Jaw wired up, drinking beer through a straw from here on…'

'Steady on. We're not a fighting group.'

'Shut up,' says Ben to Vincent, then he grabs hold of Simon's shirt. He is a strong man, pulls him to his feet with a single hand scrunching the centre of Simon's T-shirt. 'Have you broken her in yet?'

Simon settles himself on to his feet. Brushes Ben's hands off his person. 'What?'

'I don't think I should be the first with one like Dalton's little runt. I might split her insides with what I've got in here.' He points at his own crotch. 'Give me the nod, Tripp-lad, once you've opened her up and then I'll fuck her brains out until she's thick as you and me.'

Stuck-Up Little Runt

Simon pushes against Ben, lets out a meaningless war cry from his mouth, face contorted in anger. Ben is ready, laughs, holds Simon in both arms. It could be a wrestling hold. Vincent stands up from his chair, seeming quite uncertain how to assist.

The barman is quickly around from his counter. 'Oy, stop that!'

'Friendly talk, friendly talk,' says Ben, momentarily releasing his arms from his adversary.

While Ben is distracted, Simon uses a leg to trip him. The big man is over it, the younger one stumbling upon a judo move he didn't know he knew. Ben Jones crashes to the floor with all his weight, an outstretched hand brings the small circular table down with him.

Simon steps aside. Mouths an apology to the barman.

'Look at you. Look at you,' the barman laughs at Ben. 'You'll have to fight at the school gate, Jonesy. You're losing in here every week.'

A woman is coming purposefully down the staircase. Simon doesn't recognise her; she walks straight towards them. Must have come from the private quarters, wasn't in the function room where the young farmers met.

'Fighting on the premises: I'm barring you,' she says. The lady is old, hair pinned back, creamy pink make-up lathered on her cheeks, nose and forehead.

'Not me,' says Vincent, 'and he started it.' His finger points decisively at the oaf beneath the table.

'Started it, lost it,' says the barman.

'Okay. You're out and you're not coming back.' Then the lady scrutinises Simon. 'You're not even eighteen, are you?'

'Young Farmers,' he says tentatively. 'It's a private meeting.'

'Well, you're in the public bar now and I don't think you should be.' She glances at the barman. He is smiling back at her, dancing his eyes comically towards Ben who still lies sprawled out upon the floor.

'Any more fighting and you're barred too. And keep to the function room only, mind. Have you got that?'

'Yes,' says Simon. His eyes are on the feet of the vanquished Ben.

'Up and off with you,' says the lady. The pub landlady, Simon realises. She stoops and takes an ear of Ben Jones in between two fingers and a thumb. Pulls on it.

'Ow,' he says, rising to his feet.

'No coming back. I heard that you caused the same ruckus last week.' He offers no resistance as the landlady leads him by the ear to the pub door.

Simon cannot look at Vinny, feels mortified by the words Ben used before the scuffle. Then a different thought floods him. 'I should have done that to your father,' he says. 'Your pompous brother too, when they wouldn't let me in the house.' His friend smiles back, it might be disbelief but he must see why Simon might. He flattened Ben Jones, seems to have the knack.

9.

Simon is sitting on a bedroom floor with two girls. The one beside him he is meeting for only the fourth time—he can recall every moment of the previous three—a feeling that she is his oldest friend pervades: the most important person in a life he is beginning to enjoy. The second girl seems good-natured, friendly, time and again she gives him a winning smile. Millie Green, jet-black hair, wearing summer shorts; she sits cross-legged, in what he thinks of as a school assembly posture. The tan of her well-toned legs reminds him that Patrick spoke of her as a runner. Sporty, outdoorsy, it's her bedroom they occupy.

Sharing this time with the two girls—they are talking casually, joking with him—does not feel like his life. It is a better one than he has ever known; he thinks he may have willed it. Everything before now—Broughton Young Farmers, the indignity of being pushed off the doorstep at Low Fell—a staging post to this destination.

Throughout their short talk together, Corrie has repeatedly

touched the back of his hand. No reason, she just seems delighted to have him close. As he does her. Then, inexplicably, the girl whom he only wants to please has tears running down her cheeks and in seconds her shoulders are shaking and a wail accompanies her cry. Simon puts the palm of his hand onto the back of hers, covering all but the tips of her fingers. Millie, her schoolfriend, is not inhibited by false proprietary. Shifts her bottom across the rug on which they sit, hugs her friend closely. Corrie's head upon her shoulder and her own on Corrie's. Simon wishes he were Millie in this minute. Wishes he'd comforted the girl as fulsomely as her friend has done, for no other reason than to stem her tears.

* * *

Earlier, Simon leant his bicycle against the railings outside Saint Anthony's Church and waited near the vestibule as his scribbled note advised he would. The service was over, congregants dispersing. He was early, gave himself twenty-five minutes of waiting. He even exchanged a word or two with those leaving. 'You just missed it,' an elderly man told him with a smile. He knew Corrie couldn't possibly have arrived so soon, that a similar service at her own church in Coniston would only now have finished. Waiting, anticipating: Simon enjoyed these activities, bathing in the certainty that he would see her soon.

When a car pulled up just before one o'clock—the shortest, politest toot that a car horn can give—it nudged the boy out of his reverie. He had expected Cordelia to come on her own, or possibly with her friend, Millie. The other girl's parents and sister were not in his mental picture of how the day might unfold. Parents generally play for the opposition, that is his experience. His father is a simple enough obstacle to navigate, Corrie's less so. The Greens are a different matter entirely: he was greeted warmly by a car full of them.

The rear door opened and Corrie—her best dress again upon her—ran in short steps up the path to the boy. They did not hug or kiss; he has not the confidence with which to illustrate the feelings he holds for her. They looked at each other eye for eye beneath the bright August sun. 'Come back to Millie's house,' said Corrie. Looking over her shoulder—which he did without allowing her cherished face to leave his gaze—Simon saw a thin, black-haired woman step out of the driver's seat.

The girl tugged lightly on his sleeve then they clasped hands and stepped towards her. 'Teresa. Teresa Green,' said the lady. Simon saw that her face was unlined, quite youthful, although she was clearly Millie Green's mother. She did not look as other parents do, not so careworn. Nothing like Alison Tripp, the mother he inadvertently cried about the last time Corrie was in his company. 'Please come and eat with us,' she said.

He shook her proffered hand but looked only to Corrie for guidance on how to react to the request. He had scoffed down a corned-beef sandwich and a portion of yesterday's leftover rice pudding before setting off from Sark Farm. When Corrie said 'You must,' he nodded like a puppet. Doing as Cordelia Dalton asks is the sum total of his plan for this reunion. And farm labourers can eat day and night.

Teresa introduced each person in the car. Her easy manner enabled Simon to relax, ignore the formality of it. In the front passenger seat sat a man with grainy lines upon his face, he appeared far older than the driver. When she said, 'My husband, Michael,' the lines raised up into a kindly smile.

'I've never given you a prescription,' he declared, reaching out a hand to shake through the open car window.

Simon took it while turning to face Corrie. 'What?'

She explained to him that Michael Green is the pharmacist in Ambleside.

'I don't take medicine. I'm never ill.'

Michael looked back at him, a raised eyebrow of disbelief.

'Sorry. Is that bad?'

Both Michael and Teresa laughed at that.

Millie and her older sister, Joan, introduced themselves from the back of the car. Spared him the handshake. The younger was excited. 'Hiya Simon,' she said, her face animated, beaming.

Her restlessness—head bobbing up and down—as she

looked at him from the backseat, contrasted with the reserve of her bespectacled sister. 'Pleased to meet you,' said Joan, looking quietly amused.

Simon and Corrie went by foot to the Greens family home. It was very near and he had a bike to push. On the short walk, the couple asked questions of each other in a manner more polite than anything which occurred during their last two meetings, the times they'd monopolised each other to the exclusion of other young farmers.

'I hope I haven't caused trouble by befriending you,' said Simon quietly.

Corrie shook her head but did not expand upon the matter. 'I like your shirt.' It is white with thin blue lines giving it the appearance of graph paper. Rebellious when he wore it to school two years ago—the rule was plain white—hardly rock and roll.

Simon felt his breath catch as he asked her, 'Has your father done anything to you?'

Cordelia looked down, pulled her right hand into a fist. 'I'll tell you about it later.' Simon didn't press.

When—after pointing out the house just yards away in which Millie Green lives—she said rather grandly that it was good of him to go to such trouble to see her, Simon laughed. 'I've thought about you every minute since we talked in the churchyard.' Corrie smiled broadly, then she embraced the boy—a lop-sided hug, Simon holding on to his stationary bicycle—only to let him go as quickly as she had clasped him. In that moment he felt loved. Entering a stranger's house is a departure from his normal life, an unpredictable activity. Being one half of a couple more so: completely uplifting.

Simon found the Greens to be good company. Through a meal of cold meats and salad, they asked questions about Aysgarth, about Swale Valley Comprehensive School. Simon told them he enjoyed one or two subjects but he wasn't sorry he left. This contrasted with the three girls present. Corrie and Millie await promising O-level results, will waltz into sixth form. Joan plans to study physics at Newcastle University, so confident of the grades that her parents have already put down the deposit for a room in halls.

'What was wrong with school?' asked Teresa.

'The other kids,' said Simon. 'A nutty form teacher.'

Joan gave a brief soliloquy about the benefits of St Aiden's School for Girls. The crux of it was the absence of the opposite sex. She said the distraction causes a lowering of behavioural standards. Neither benefit.

The younger girls glanced at each other. 'We…want…boys,' they chanted at Joan, who laughed. Didn't argue her point further. Simon was happy to hear Corrie sound so buoyant, guessed himself the boy she wants.

When they had eaten the meal, Corrie said they would talk together in Millie's room. Teresa said—directed at Cordelia with whom she is clearly familiar—'Then have an hour by yourselves before I run you home.' Simon did not thank her for this, he stared open-mouthed. Never anticipated an adult being so considerate towards him. The Greens should be Corrie's family, he thought. She doesn't belong in forbidding Low Fell.

* * *

Now, in Millie's tidy bedroom—having waited briefly downstairs while the two girls changed out of their church wear—the three of them have been sitting on the Afghan rug and talking. Millie is tanned, face, arms, legs. Her fawn-coloured shorts ride up, the faded outline of a Johnson Ronson album cover printed on her T-shirt. Corrie is back in jeans, a plain white blouse beneath her denim jacket. He finds the new girl—Patrick's fancy—to be a lively soul. Her black hair is long, frequently shaken away from her eyes. She was mid-story, telling them about her mother, Teresa, telling off some uncouth London children for pouring water across the floor of their dormitory. She's the assistant warden at Harrowslack Youth Hostel apparently. For no connected reason Cordelia has started bawling, sobbing, consoled a little by Millie's immediate hug. Still Corrie is absolutely distraught.

Stuck-Up Little Runt

'I know, I know,' Millie repeats. Simon realises that these two girls will have met many times since last he saw his precious friend. The conversation with Vincent last Thursday has given him cause to worry over what has occurred up on the fell farm. Corrie's father: it all centres on him.

Simon takes a hold of Corrie's hand, as Millie releases her from the wrapped hug. Tugs her gently and she leans into him. 'What happened?' he says, an arm around the crying girl.

'He's a buggering bastard, like Vin always said.' Simon strains to hear her, so quietly does she speak. 'He's sent Ghost for cat food, that's what the buggering bastard's done.'

He keeps his face away from her line of vision, Corrie's head hanging down. Something in the way she swears—the assertion that her horse is now cat food—has drawn a smile upon it. He knows that, whatever action her father has taken, it has undone her.

'He wouldn't do that?' says Simon, composed. Intonating it as a question, not disagreeing.

'Would. Has. Fucker,' says Corrie softly.

Millie is nodding seriously at him. She has heard this story before. Heard it in some detail, probably.

'What a thing to do.'

'I've told my dad to have a go at him,' says Millie. 'He should tell Father Benedict or something. It's an outrage.'

'Corrie...' Simon takes a hold of her hand, rubs his work-weathered palm over her pianist's fingers. '...has your dad hurt you? Physically? Did he beat you?'

The girl bows her head, does not speak. Behind Corrie, he sees Millie nodding purposefully, her own bright face suddenly clouded and bitter. 'You should see her legs.'

Cordelia splutters a fume of tears. 'Ghost! It's Ghost that matters!' she shouts.

Simon feels that he has caused a world of trouble. Regrets his smile at the cat-food assertion. Wants to atone; thinks killing Jeremy Dalton could do it. Michael Green, the kindly pharmacist, can't bring himself to tell the parish priest.

Families live behind closed doors. Simon never told others of the malign parenting of John Tripp, by age fourteen he was out of its reach. Bereaved of a mother also, no one left in whose eyes the dumb ox might have imagined himself the big man. If Jeremy Dalton kills horses, then he really is of a different order.

Corrie picks herself off the floor, says only, 'I need the bathroom,' as she gently pats the hair of the boy from whom she has extricated herself.

When she is out of the room, Simon turns to Millie. 'Has he really done away with Ghost?'

Millie tells him that the man is a monster. 'I don't get how her mother puts up with it. Perhaps she has stick marks on her legs too.' Millie says that Corrie has told her everything, tells him what she knows. When Vincent unwittingly implied that Corrie had a boyfriend, Mr Dalton asked her brothers and his wife to leave the room. He demanded that she tell him what had gone on. Cordelia initially said she had no boyfriend but he shouted directly into her face. Said she would not be turning red about it if her denial held any truth.

As he listens, Simon feels burdened by Corrie's ordeal. Responsible. He was scarcely a boyfriend at that point. Hadn't asked her on a date. Wished to, the words are still to emerge. He lacked the courage to make his feelings clear during their churchyard conversation. Now he worries exactly where his feelings really run. He feels elated seeing Corrie but cannot bear this upset. He loves her—he's been calling it that in his head since arriving at Coniston—and yet it is bound up with the hatred he feels towards Jeremy Dalton. It's the more concrete emotion.

Millie tells him that Corrie confirmed to her father only that she spent an evening talking with a young man.

'Unchaperoned!' her father shouted at her.

'What difference would that have made,' Corrie shouted back.

Millie says her friend is headstrong. 'I love her but she'll never be a diplomat.' A cryptic way of speaking but Simon understands her.

'I let you go to the Young Farmers club. Not courting at your young age,' Jeremy Dalton had shouted back at Corrie. 'While I know you were only talking,' says Millie.

She tells him that—contrary to anything she or Corrie, or even her own church-going parents, think—Simon is not of the faith required should he wish to court the Dalton's daughter. For blushing about a boy, one who does not, nor ever will, have his approval, Jeremy let his youngest know that he would have to teach her a lesson. 'That means a beating in their house,' Millie explains. 'Corrie told me that she began to cry when he said it. She's been through it before and he's a really vicious so-and-so. When she cried, he went quiet, said, "Come with me." She followed him into the library, Corrie thought he might have changed his mind on seeing how upset she already was. When they were in there—it's a small room full of old books, a writing desk where he does his bookkeeping—he just said, "What's the lad's name?" I think Corrie was trying to keep the peace, get him to calm down. She said, "We didn't do anything, Daddy." Something like that. "What's his name?' he said again, said it much, much louder second time. "He's called Simon, Daddy." And that's when the nasty brute leaped on her. He took up a stick that she'd not seen in over a year. It was snuck between wall and bookshelf, hidden away where only he knew. 'Simon!' he shouted as he struck her with the stick. "You've introduced your mother and I to no Simon." He thrashed her madly, legs high and low. Corrie fell to the floor.'

'Oh Millie, it's all my fault.'

'It's not you. He's a monster. He was just using your name, frightening her with it. "Jeans off," he shouted when she was lying on the floor. Corrie didn't say it to me but I think that's when she saw red. She's dead brave, you know. She shouted at him. I don't know what she said; "Old bastard," probably. It's the name that best suits him.' Millie has lowered her voice to accommodate the swear word. 'She wasn't taking any clothes off for him. As Corrie rolled on the library floor, she heard her mother shout, "Can I come in?" only for her father to call back, "Off with you, woman." Corrie continued to shout back at her father. She knows some proper names for swine like him, I can tell you. But he shredded her clothes, shredded the fabric around her calves, knees, thighs. Cut her on both legs: bruises and wheals. He was slicing the air and it's like a thin bit of birch, that's what Corrie told me. A stick with nobbles and knots on it. In the melee her mad father toppled on top of her. He pulled himself up saying 'Sorry.' She said she spat at him when he said that. He calls it disciplining but Corrie reckons he's a pervert.' Millie turns her face from Simon's, doesn't drop the intensity, the propulsion of her speech. 'He doesn't do sex or anything. Corrie says it's only the violence that he likes. And that's worse than liking the other, if you think about it.'

Simon feels close to tears just hearing what Corrie's bastard of a father has done to her. He holds it together while regretting leaving the man on the doorstep without kicking him in the crotch, lamping him on the jaw. If he had known then what he knows now, he would have gone totally berserk.

'When he got up from the floor, from lying on top of her, he must have realised that he couldn't decently grapple with a sixteen-year-old daughter. He lowered his face down next to hers, waited for a pause in her heaving sobs. "Like that, is it?" he said. "Like that, is it?" and he left the room. Corrie went to her bedroom, stayed there all evening and most of the next day. Her legs must have been agony. Her mother asked if she wanted help bathing them, cold water and a balm? Corrie said, "Fuck off," and she's never spoken like that to her mum before. Honoria let her be, Corrie cried about it after. It's her dad needs swearing at, not the other one. The mother's hard to make out but she doesn't like her husband's nasty streak, that's what Corrie thinks. She was worried that Honoria might tell Jeremy how she'd spoken, create more trouble. The next day, Vincent came into her room. Said it was very odd, Jeremy had taken the Sunbeam, the families second car, and gone to stay at his brothers. Corrie came down for the meal. Apologised to her mother for how she'd spoken. There was real solidarity with Vincent. He smuggled her up a bottle of cider and they toasted the departure of their mad father. The other brother was home; he never really bothers with her...'

At this point in the telling, Corrie re-enters the room. Millie's face reddens, she is telling the boy of Cordelia's most private experiences: the thrashing; the shredded jeans. Corrie's eyes move back and forth between the two on the floor. She slides down next to Simon; red eyes, tear-dirtied cheeks. 'Whatever she's said, he's tonnes worse.' She shuffles herself on the floor, Simon feels her thigh against his own. 'I love that horse.' She slides the back of her left hand across her cheek although tears no longer flow. 'Loved.'

'Corrie,' says Millie tentatively, 'I've not got to that part. Just what he did to you.'

She pats Millie's hand. 'I'll recover. He's done that shit before. I'm not cat food.'

'Corrie,' says Simon, 'we'd done nothing. It's not normal to go for your kids...'

'Normal for the buggering bastard...' She spoke over him. '...normal for him alright. The terrible thing, Simon, I didn't know for nearly a week. The bastard, my bastard father had gone away. I still don't know what that was about. I thought he was ashamed, banishing himself or something. But he doesn't know shame, the fucking bastard. He came back. Two days he was away, two days and two nights...'

A knock on the bedroom door, the handle turns, and it opens slowly. Teresa stands before the three children and then goes down on to one knee, places a hand on Cordelia's shoulder. 'You're upset, Corrie. Please? We don't use that language in this house. I do understand how upsetting it is.'

'I'm sorry,' she says, placing a hand on top of the one Mrs Green has on her shoulder. 'So sorry.'

'I don't mean to intrude,' adds the mother, rising. Leaving them as quickly as she arrived.

Simon wonders if she has been listening all along. Corrie

couldn't help raising her voice; horrible terms for a man who deserves worse. Simon wants to kill him, can't stop thinking he should. And Teresa was entirely sympathetic to Corrie, intervened only to maintain Sunday decorum.

'It was a week later, when I stopped feeling sorry for myself and went to the stables. Probably the first day I could get my riding boots on. He did my legs worse than he's ever done them. When I arrived there, I went frantic. There was no sign of Ghost. Mary was in the house; I shouted at her, made a fool of myself really. She said she couldn't tell me where my horse was. "Your father must tell you," she said. I couldn't wait. I thought I was going to thump her. I still think she knew but poor Mary is as scared of the...' Cordelia lowers her voice to a whisper. '...buggering bastard...' And then it rises. '...as Vincent is, although she's not had to put up with any of the shit he has.'

Millie gestures for her friend to quieten, her last expletive at the old pitch.

'How do you put up with me?' says Corrie.

Millie Green—so confident a short time earlier—appears overwhelmed by this story. Her parents are the kindly ones, a comfort to friends and family alike. The mere contemplation of cruelty looks an agony for her.

'Did I do something?' asks Simon. 'I hate that all this has happened to you because you spoke to me.'

Corrie pushes her head into Simon's chest, says, 'Shut up,' before giving the boy the quickest kiss on the lips. 'You did nothing wrong, did you? I've always had a madman for a father. It's for me to deal with, not you.'

'I'm not Catholic. That might matter to a lot of people. People at your church.'

'They can all go to hell. I think that's where he's bound anyway.' Quietly she adds, 'The bastard. I don't know what to think about it anymore. I don't share a religion with him.' He sees her nose turn up, as if a malodour is detectable from the subject of her utterance. 'Mummy has said I can make friends with anybody...' She looks away from Simon. '...marry anybody. She says that we're all the same really. It's just different ways of worshipping.'

'The thing is,' says Simon, 'I don't really believe any of it. I don't worship anyone, not a God that I can't see.'

'That's alright with me,' says Corrie, again placing a hand upon his. 'Idiots like my father have been fighting about it since forever. Pretending their lot is more important than all others. Your angle is cleverer by miles.'

* * *

An hour to themselves, Simon and Corrie walk around Hawkshead together. It takes no time, so tiny is the village. At the side of the children's playground, they sit beneath a spreading tree. 'I should talk to him,' says Simon. He thinks he will sound vulgar if he says punch, kick in the nuts or stamp on his face, but these are the actions he pictures.

Corrie shakes her head. 'Michael Green said he would talk to the police but I can't have it. I can't. I'm not letting Vincent, even Mummy, get caught up in it, they'd hate me for it. The man knows everyone. There's no stopping him and they'd hate me forever.'

'I want to help...' The boy has more to say but Corrie's lips are on his, resting on his. They share a moment. '...I'll do anything.'

'What can you do? You don't know the people around here. Are we a lot worse than Yorkshire people, Si?'

'I could punch him. Like I did Ben Jones.'

'Simon! Vinny told me about that but he wouldn't say what it was about.' She gives him the quickest kiss. 'You tell me?'

Simon doesn't know where to begin. 'It was about you.'

Corrie narrows her eyes. 'I hate Ben. He has nothing to do with me. My father and his father used to be friends but not any longer. I never learn why the buggering bastard falls out with people. No end of possible reasons. Why did you fight with Ben, Simon?'

'He was rude about you. Horribly rude.'

'If it was silly boys' talk, I don't care. You shouldn't get yourself hurt over me, Simon.'

'It wasn't silly, it was awful. I can't tell you, Corrie. He's an animal. I only gave him what he had coming. If you want me to do that to your father, I will.' Cordelia pulls away from him, looks down at the grass they are sitting on. 'I really will.' Simon says it loudly. 'Kill him. I don't care what happens to me.'

She pulls him back to her, places a careful hand over Simon's mouth. 'Don't fight. Not Ben Jones. Not my father. We're better than that, Simon. You are. You must see that? We'll get through this without broken noses and…' Simon is holding her in his arms, would do anything for her, cannot navigate the choices alone. '…getting sent before the magistrate.' After she has said it, Corrie starts to laugh. She kisses Simon on the lips. 'Of course, in a better world, we could just push him in the midden and that'd be that.' Her lips linger upon his; their tongues explore each other. 'And you are helping me, Si, just being here. The buggering bastard isn't getting his way.'

* * *

They have moved across the park to sit next to each other on stationary swings. No one else in the play park.

'Did he actually tell you where Ghost has gone?'

'You'll get me upset again, Si, and I'm being driven home in a few minutes. Back to where the buggering bastard lives. I don't talk to him now. Not a word since he's done what he's done.'

Simon shuffles his feet, edges his swing over, links his hand under her elbow, as intimately as adjacent swings allow. He doesn't wish for her to go back to dreadful Low Fell. Feels powerless in the face of the obstacles. 'If we were older you could live with me.'

'And I would!' she says without hesitation. 'When I left the stables and went back to the farmhouse and saw Daddy sitting with Killian, watching a horrid war film, I shouted at him. "What have you done with Ghost! Where is he!" My brother just smirked; I knew he knew. Killie's an arse. Likes arses. That's what Vinny says. That he's one of *them*. "We're watching the Battle of Britain." These were the old bastards first words to me since he beat me. "Where?" I think I screamed it at him. "You wouldn't let me teach you the lesson that needed learning, so I've sent him for cat food. Your horse is now in tins, Cordelia." I ran out, not just the room, the house. I ran back to the stables. Screamed at poor Mary. She told me he'd said the same to her.'

Simon has stood up from his swing, pulls Corrie from hers and hugs her more tightly than he ever has. Tears are rolling down her cheeks. 'I'll kill him,' Simon tells her. 'If you want me to, I'll fucking kill him.'

'No Si, don't. I'm not worth ruining your life over. Will you see me next week after this?'

He kisses her quickly on the lips. 'Tomorrow, next week, anytime, Corrie.' He thinks he probably could kill for her. Doesn't have a plan but it's in him. Kill Dalton before the bastard kills Corrie, turns his girlfriend into cat food. His girlfriend, Corrie Dalton.

10.

'Something has changed,' Corrie tells Simon.

They are in Hawkshead once more, it is the most practical way for the couple to meet. Millie has left them together, they walk over fields, smell the late summer, the moisture in the evening air. This is precious time, Will Browning milking the herd at Sark Farm, Michael and Teresa Green at vespers, reassuring Cordelia's mother that she is with Millie. The half-baked truth that is now a lie. The boy feels trepidation in her words, worries that she means her feelings towards him have changed. 'Nothing's changed for me,' says Simon.

'Not us,' she looks at him carefully, eyes scanning his face. 'Don't change, I like you this way.' She turns and faces ahead as she walks. 'He smiles smugly. Hums silly tunes. Even treats Vinny better.'

Simon takes this in: the change is in the horse murderer. It is too little, too late. He hates Jeremy Dalton like he never has another soul. All that Millie told him—the violence he meted out on Corrie for no reason that will ever make sense—dwelling on it sends the bitterest juices coursing through Simon's veins. He will always hate him, from now until forever. Hitting a girl with a stick, it's obscene. Always hate him.

'Last weekend,' says Corrie, 'Killie got so drunk on Saturday night that he didn't make it to church. Kind of unheard of in our family. I thought he'd be in big trouble. Thing is, when I got back after seeing you here, Vincent filled me in. A friend from Killie's college days—agricultural college—stayed over, probably equally drunk. Vincent doesn't think our parents knew that the friend was even in the house, not until they got back from church. Me and Vinny didn't, certainly.' The couple come to a small kissing gate; Corrie leads the way, pauses when she is in the centre-pen turns to Simon and kisses his lips as the entryway's name suggests they must. She squeezes herself back as he joins her in the middle, hugs her close, then he lets her out and she turns and kisses him again. Then both are in a field of dairy cattle, recently milked Simon sees from their slackened udders. 'I'm not allowed to have Millie stay over; having some odd-ball college boy in his room without so much as asking could be big trouble. My father is mental-crazy—I've mentioned that already—yet he didn't have a go at Killian. Quiet words were all they had. In the library, no stick this time. Maybe he can't go at him like he does me; Killie's a grown man, it's years and years since he was last chastised. But I don't think it was even like that. I wonder if Killian made Daddy see a bit of sense. Accept that all his children are growing up. It's hard to imagine but it could be what's happened. That's just my feeling about it. No one's said.'

Simon doesn't know this family well enough to read their behaviour. Both Killian and Jeremy were foul to him on his only visit to Low Fell. 'You're not going to forgive him, are you?'

'Never,' she snaps, clasping both hands into fists. She takes long slow strides as they walk, long for her short legs. 'Sorry,

Si,' she says. 'Sorry I shouted at you. No forgiveness; he can hum all he likes. No forgiving what he's done to Ghost.'

This evening, as they talk and walk, Simon explains to Cordelia why he'll never live back at Aysgarth, at Penton Farm. 'I've finished with him. I'll phone now and then, I might go for a weekend if Rosie will be there, see her little ones. I'm not farming with him, spending time. I know it's different for you, for girls, but I don't know how you stand it.'

'I can't stand it,' she says sullenly. 'The most I can do is not talk to him. The cold shoulder. He hates it, hates me, but I think he always did. I don't enjoy the iciness but I'd hate any warmth more. I'm not much good but I'm no hypocrite.'

Simon takes her hand in his. It's a clumsy gesture, he pulls her to himself, hugs her as they walk, inducing both to stumble. 'You are so good,' he tells her, very unclear in his mind what has prompted her to say otherwise. 'I still don't know how you stand it.'

She takes his head in her free hand, as if to kiss him again, and then the uneven ground makes her topple into him. Simon holds on to Corrie, breaks her fall. 'Daft thing,' she says. The grass is dry enough and she permits him to roll her on to her back, hover above her like a press up. Kiss her on the lips.

'If you want out just tell me,' he says.

She kisses him harder, pulls him down, accepts his weight spread across her. When their mouths are briefly apart, she says, 'Sixth form—I'm stuck at home—got to complete sixth form if I'm ever going to get on.'

Simon did okay at school, knew when enough was enough.

11.

A week later they spend the Saturday afternoon in Ulverston. Vincent brings Corrie down on the moped; her parents believe that only she and Vinny are spending time together. The brother knows some people, some bars. He's more than happy to leave the couple alone. Corrie slips an arm under Simon's elbow; they look in shop windows for a short time. Then he takes her into a tea room. The warmth of summer has fled; it's an overcast day. Simon wears a navy-blue sweat shirt; Corrie is forever in denim jacket and jeans. They order tea-cakes with their drink.

'Is he treating you alright?' asks the boy.

'No,' she replies, and he immediately places a hand upon hers. 'It's like he's suddenly happy, and that makes no sense. Not to me.'

Simon spends many nights worrying what happens in Low Fell, within the family he cannot fathom. 'You don't speak to him at all?' Corrie nods her head. 'Do you talk to Killian?'

'He's as weird as the bastard,' she mumbles. 'He was out two evenings last week, Vinny said he was with a girl. That never happens. Frankly...' Corrie bows her head in order to sip from her tea, speaks before her lips touch the rim. '...I used to think Vinny might be right, that Killie's a queer.'

Simon leans back in his chair, recoils from the idea. 'I thought he was tough. Isn't it just something mean your brother says?'

Corrie looks at him directly now, her brown eyes intelligent and alert, white forehead crossed by the stray brown hairs which have evaded her tartan Alice band. 'He's a lot tougher than Vinny but he's abnormal. No friends.'

'He must hate Killian for...'

Before he can finish, she has interrupted him. 'Vin says Killie has started seeing Sarah Pollard. Her dad works for the Collins at Beckfoot. You must know it? The big sheep farm.' Simon shakes his head. 'They've got land stretching all the way to Wast Water, thousands of sheep. The Collins are at church...' Cordelia raises her head, looks a little down her nose, a frown distorts her appearance. '...but Sarah Pollard certainly doesn't attend our church.'

'What do you mean?' asks Simon, confused by the change in her demeanour.

'I don't know what she is, she certainly isn't a Roman

Stuck-Up Little Runt

Catholic.' Disdain in her voice, eyes narrowed in disapproval.

Simon laughs—hesitantly—a guarded insecure laugh. 'Nor me, remember. Is it so bad?'

'Oh, you're a wodwo, you are. And that, Simon Tripp, is why I treasure you. Sarah Pollard is more of a lame hare, not a wodwo at all. I've nothing against her, she's quite sweet, I expect. My gripe...' Corrie stops talking mid-sentence. 'Catching flies?' she asks, looking intently at him.

Simon closes his gawping mouth. 'I treasure you,' he says, then mouths the words, I love you, without finding sufficient air to expel the syllables outward. She can lipread that much, surely. 'What's a wodwo?'

'That? Did you not read the poem for your O-level? It's usually on the syllabus. Wodwo by Ted Hughes.'

'I don't know it...'

'I remember now, you said you got a C-grade without reading the poems at all. The clever Tripp way, less work all round.'

Simon feels a little laughed at by the girl with straight A's. Her brown eyes hold him captive; loves her smile. And at least he passed the exam.

'A wodwo is a creature that doesn't know what it is. It just keeps looking for signs. That's you, Si. Exactly you. And yes, I think I do. I love you.'

Simon leans forward, kisses her on the lips, leans back and glances at the tea shop counter. A lady behind the till is squinting at the pair of them. She does nothing, hasn't a kissing-prohibited sign at which to point.

'Now we've cleared that up, back to my gripe. The man I hate—refuse to speak to—went swivel-eyed mental when he heard that I talked in a churchyard with you. And you being something other than a Roman Catholic was his stated reason. Now, all of a sudden, Killian goes on dates with a girl who's not at church and not even terribly bright. Goes with the bastard's approval by the look of it. That's what's wrong. I can't stand it.'

'Can you talk to him?—your father—make him see it's unfair.'

'I've told you, I've sent him to Coventry. I won't ever speak to my father again. Not since he did what he did to Ghost. I think he laughs about it every day.' She turns away from him. 'I'm not crying over all that again.'

He takes hold of her hand momentarily, then rises from his seat, ventures an arm around her slender shoulders. The woman behind the counter is eyeing them once more.

* * *

The couple leave the tea shop and walk the streets of Ulverston; they pass a couple of rows of white-washed terraced houses and then come to a small park. Sit on a bench together, facing the climbing frame and swings. It's approaching five o'clock, the park is empty of all but themselves.

'Back to normal' is how Corrie describes entering sixth form; she is enthusiastic about the subjects she studies. He likes hearing how much she enjoys her lessons, can't really credit what is so good about them. Tries making a joke about the pupil-husbandry which teachers practice, classrooms more regimented than Will Browning's milking parlour. 'Simon,' she says, 'you'd be in sixth form but for your slow-in-the-head father. We're kids really.' He puts an arm around her shoulders, pulls her head carefully against his own. 'When you do get a job with a cottage—a tiny little one will be alright—will you take me out of Low Fell, give me a home with no buggering bastards in it?'

He hugs her, clamps her to his person with wrapped arms, moves his head so that he is not shouting in her ear, speaking in the direction of the empty swings. In his clearest voice, he says it, the matter that has been on his mind three months without let-up. 'I love you, Corrie Dalton.'

Chapter Five

Our Stairs at Night

1.

Leo and I are pallbearers. My brother-in-law, John and his son, Terence, behind us; Paul and Sean, fathers of two of his school friends, make up the six. As we come down the aisle of St George's, it feels to me more like a school assembly, a show that is being put on. All Morty's friends are here, they have come in droves. Teachers too, the lot of them by the look of it. I will be grateful when I cease to feel only numb.

Mrs Leigh, the head teacher of Marple Wood, sits with Corrie. They know each other well; my wife has taught piano to all of the school's most talented musicians. She looks at me as I come around the front of the church, our son perched ridiculously on my shoulder. Nothing whatsoever has prepared me for this moment. My only coping mechanism—the proven ability to cry no tears in any situation this life assaults me with—is an inappropriate one for this day. Teachers cry while Mortimer Tripp's own father does not. I make no sense to myself. Not even by being here. It should be me inside a coffin, hoisted upon the shoulders of Leo and Morty. It is a part of life's logic that it must one day happen, and now it cannot.

I have spent more than half a life time telling myself—one or two others along the way—that my wife is beautiful. I may think it again, or I may not find the strength. Today it is not even true. She looks anguished, her face transformed. Youthful, alive, those qualities which she has exemplified throughout our life together, have left her eyes. Her hair has whitened in just three months. Not in its entirety. About four weeks ago she said, 'I look like a badger,' and there was levity in the comment; our son still lived at that point. Not that we laughed out loud. We could not allow her self-deprecating observation to refocus our thoughts away from the misfortune which educed it. Today, inside St George's—Church of England, a kindly vicar named David White at the helm—I fear she and I are as lifeless as the dead badgers we may see on the roadside up Mellor and beyond. Saw many more of in our rural childhoods. Inside our hearts we have gone the way of Morty.

As we place the coffin on its bier, a silence like ice resonates in my head. I pull on Leo's hand for a second, a gesture that we are in this together. I think it is his strength that I need, even as I pretend to offer him mine. The church is bedecked with flowers, deep reds and whites. A line of scruffily dressed boys—grungers, as they call themselves—are arrayed behind Corrie and the head teacher. They were his closest friends. Mrs Leigh moves aside by one seat; Leo slips between her and Corrie. I go to sit the other side of my wife and take her hand. She cries my tears and hers. Leo leans forward, puts his head in his hands—I hear the strangest convulsion from him—Mrs Leigh has an arm around my eldest son, comforts him as I wish I could.

The Reverend David White begins the service. I liked the man the moment I met him; he could not have been more straightforward with us. I had earlier suggested to Corrie that I might phone the Catholic priest. Brought it up a day or two after the terminal diagnosis, the stark and truthful prediction of two or three weeks, made by Doctor Tetteh, the specialist. The doctor spoke sensitively although she might as well have sprayed us both with machine gun fire. It is not news which gets better through the kindness of the telling. Corrie just shook her head at my suggestion, murmured, 'Not that outfit, please.' I had not expected this late conversion. She is the Roman Catholic: is or was. Neither of our children were baptised, confirmed or indoctrinated into any religion but the love of their closest family, of each other, Corrie and I. They

Our Stairs at Night

have been true to our faith; we always thought it would be enough.

It crossed my mind that choosing this contrary church to hold the service for our son—saying this impossible goodbye in a structure sanctified by a God other than the one the Dalton family pray to—was a final withholding from them. From the ones in her clan for whom these symbols matter. Over the days I have come to think it far more complicated: Cordelia Tripp is losing touch with who she is.

David White, now leading the service, spent hours in our house, answered questions and offered comfort to both of us. Particularly to Corrie. I would like to be that comfort; I love Corrie as much as I ever did. Cannot trust myself to disguise the anger I feel at this injustice, the theft of our beautiful boy.

Corrie is artistic, magnificent; she has a caustic side, can retaliate to slights that the giver hasn't noticed. Leo is clever, brilliant even; sometimes cynical, it can be deflating. I have not made money my God, I might have venerated it a bit more than best play; not pretty but several notches short of full-blown worship. Morty is the sweetest Tripp there has been. Is, was. My life without him is unknowable; not a life I want to live, though doing so has become my fate.

Before I even sit, this vicar has us praying. I am happy for the distraction. I don't attend his words; I think about the idea of prayer. Am I asking Him to look after my son now He has taken him from me? Requesting peace, a coming to terms, for Corrie and Leo? I think I want to give Him a piece of my mind. What to say, how to square it all, evades me. Many people have been through this before me, had youngsters taken from them, my pain is not new. This nice chap's God dishes it out time and again. Engineered it into creation.

As we bring up our bowed heads, I see both Thomasina and her husband, John, turning towards me. Or perhaps it is Cordelia's expression they hope to gauge, her eye they wish to meet. I fear I have looked through them; it is not intentional. It is where I am.

The vicar thanks the Lord for the life of Mortimer Benjamin Tripp. I don't dismiss this meditation at all. I am richer for his life, richer in a currency which I fear being unable to ever again exchange. It is no longer available to me, the capacity to swap my morose introspection for that boy's joyous presence. Then I believe I can feel it even as I think it impossible; Morty is not exactly here. I am conjuring him up. As I do this, the Reverend David White, talks about my son, about our family. He says that the loss of Mortimer is one we may never feel properly reconciled to. Our consolation is memory, and as he says it, I believe it to be true. Every square inch of our house will reverberate with Morty. Every paving stone in Marple.

As he started this eulogy for my lost boy, I felt an itch to turn around. To stare down Jeremy Dalton, whom I know to be sitting three rows behind us. Killian by his side. Sarah Dalton, the incomer, inexplicably not here. That was my impulse but the vicar's words have captured me. It is true that Morty is in our home, although he is also in it no more.

I find myself thinking of an incident just over three weeks ago. Before he went into the hospice, before he came back from there to our home. His final return was a heartbreak. Barely more than a day after going into the hospice, he was back home. Corrie insisted and we all agreed. The staff in that hospice were near perfect, it was just that they were not the Tripp family. Morty belonged with us, with our upset and our many imperfections. By the time of that final homecoming, our twisty, turny, wriggly boy—never really an athlete, more a sail in the wind—had become bedbound, lost his flight. We loved him dearly, though I struggled to see it was truly him, so much had been taken by the cancer. Mortimer died in our house, with Corrie and I each holding a hand. We had sat so for hours; Leo there with us when the time came. The night I am thinking about, before all that—the two journeys we put him through and wished we hadn't—Mortimer was still a vibrant child despite the diagnosis hanging over him like a curse. At three or four in the morning I'd stepped from our bedroom to look in on him, on my son. It is a reassurance I have been taking his whole life long.

'Hi Dad,' he whispered from the stairs.

He was sitting three or four down from the landing. It reminded me of a time before, not that I stopped to dwell upon that other time. Not then.

'Can't sleep?' I asked him. It is a state that has overtaken me since the turn of the year.

'I don't really want to,' Mortimer replied.

Only now, in the light of the vicar's well-chosen words, do I see what Morty meant. Understand my late-son's thoughts on a plight he never deserved and from which no good could possibly come.

I sat beside him on the stair, an arm across his thin shoulders. I am thankful that he was not alone for those minutes. It is not a lot, and I can take nothing more.

David White acknowledges Morty's popularity. Quotes teachers and pupils who have only good things to say about him. I do not know if Marple Wood School has the same miscellany of bullies that cropped up in every class at Swale Valley in the nineteen-seventies. I wish his cancer upon no one, though justice would have been better served had some belligerent thug suffered its scourge, not my angelic boy. I glance across, behind Corrie's hunched-forward back directly into Leo's brown eyes. His face is a question mark. I feel as though he has unmasked me as my merciless calculation clatters to the floor of the church. He winces, and I see that my left knee has dislodged a hymn book from its shelf.

* * *

Corrie stands—her full five foot three—on the spot from which the vicar has addressed us. She is braver than I, infinitely so. She felt she must bear witness to her love, her loss. I am sure that similar feelings to hers are within me; I cannot lay them out in front of others. I am pleased she is saying this piece, letting Marple know that we are grateful for Mortimer's life.

'I thank you all from the bottom of my heart. Thank you for

keeping in touch with our son wherever he is now. His memory is dear to us.'

Two nights ago, she and I went through the speech she wished to make. David invited me to speak; however, I could not imagine stringing two or three coherent words together. Not with this number of people before me; not in these circumstances. Corrie's family are here in full; excepting Sarah, of course, the in-law. My sister and her family are here, Morty's grown-up cousins, Jane with husband and an unborn child visible in her profile. I don't think their presence—not even that of her despised father—is putting Corrie off. But nothing she is saying quite chimes with me. I don't think it is the speech she showed me on Wednesday evening. Those words may have slipped my recall—these are difficult days—or she may have reworked it entirely. No words can satisfy in this moment: it is his living flesh we both wish to feel.

'My son was a typical teenager and one on his own.' She looks into the congregation, speaks directly to Morty's peers. 'Maybe that's how you all are. It has been a source of wonder to me. Morty could get cross and angry and frustrated, all the things that people say teenage boys get, and yet I have to tell you...' My wife brushes her hair back with a hand, keeps it out of her face, the rivulets of tears which continue to seep from those forlorn brown eyes. '...he was mostly serene, content, saw the funny side of his own problems. He was the lightest company...' A quick glance up and back down. '...put my own family to shame. Morty felt loved. He loved us and we loved him; there was no other way it could be around Mortimer Tripp.' She pauses, takes a deeper breath. 'I feel that was how he went about his life wherever he was. I feel the love that you all gave him and must have felt back from Morty, our Morty, all of ours; yours, mine. It was his way of doing things.'

I don't disagree with a word she says, still I worry that it is maudlin. That it is the sanctification of the dead which we neither wished to partake in. We said everyone was welcome, not because we wanted to tell them what we think they have lost, simply to allow them to remember him in their own way. Even the vicar understood this. The service has been heartfelt without any excess. No sentimental pop songs over the PA system, no teddy bear on the coffin.

'I thank you from the bottom of my heart,' says Corrie. She glances at David White. I see him smile calmly back. Her address has been briefer than the one we worked upon, said what she needed to say.

Now music comes out of the speakers, a tune I knew would play although it has slipped my mind until this, its juddering undercurrent, reminds me. Butter Melts, the title: a song by Mortimer's favourite band. I have heard it played many times in our house. Not in recent weeks, long before then. Corrie and Leo said it fitted. The lyrics are neither poignant nor apt in my view, saved only by the difficulty the singer has given us in hearing them at all, so jarring is the grunge music he traipses his voice across.

> *I can't teach*
> *Because I know there's nothing much worth learning*
> *Can't quell fires*
> *Because I love to watch them burning*

I think the whole thing sounds like a justification of failure. A strange theme to celebrate in song.

> *Butter melts in my mouth, I cannot lie*

The singer's not-quite saving grace: he's useless but won't try to hide it. What it has to do with my son, other than the tragedy of him dying at the point in his life when he was still seduced by this nonsense, evades me completely.

As the song plays, Corrie stands back from the small wooden lectern, slightly to the side of it. Makes herself seen. She raises her arms out to each side and begins to dance ever so slightly, swaying and moving to the dirge-like rock music. With a simple hand gesture, she signals that we may all stand, join her as she moves to the music. The tears still flow while a smile takes residence on her lips. I turn and see that the boys behind me, a girl or two amongst them, all wearing the very clothes Morty most approved of—the scruffy dressers—are dancing, lowering their heads, hanging their overlong hair down before their eyes as their bodies find the slow rhythm. These are grungers, their dancing not over-enthusiastic, that would be a step too far. They move with only the smallest smidgen of relish; it is no more than the weak push of the sound waves which stirs them. They are dancing for Morty. My eyes begin to water as I consider the approval he would give—the strongest opinion I recall my son commending was that naff is the new cool—if he were only here. I don't know why I hate the song so much: I love the pleasure he took from hearing it.

Leo and I, John, Terence, Paul and Sean, step forward, bend before the coffin, raise it back up to our shoulders. The undertaker walks before us as we take the box to the hearse. Take my boy to go alone to Stockport Crematorium. Religions teem with poetic words which science has long disproved. My sense is that Mortimer's soul flew before this service today. I am unsure what I am carrying, where he is or will be. Worry he is but memory in the paving stones. Our bodies are corn husks.

* * *

I feel weaker than I have at any time in the last three months. In my best suit, I rest my bottom on the ivy-clad church wall. There are gravestones before me, overgrown, mossy. Illegible inscriptions upon tilted headstones. St George's Church has a long history; this suburb used to be an independent mill town, and the mill town once a village beholden to agriculture before the disfiguration of the industrial age. The seeping out of that ugly wealth of which I have snaffled a little.

Vinny is beside me, Kat Mason with him, they are both sober and I appreciate the effort they make. Being entirely here for me. Currently I have no interest in alcohol, in the thought of changing my mental state. I have no interest.

'How are you bearing up,' says my brother-in-law.

Our Stairs at Night

I am not; tell him only that it is tough.

Kat says that Corrie was brave, that she senses my wife has a strong soul. She is being kind, trying to show concern and even a little hope. I think her words bullshit while holding none of it against her. I have not attended the funeral of a friend's child; I imagine I would be similarly clichéd. She mean's well, has dwelt upon my loss, Corrie's loss, as far as she can permit herself. I recall the sense of ill-fortune which used to accompany too close an identification with tragedy, the fear that thinking too intently about the matter might coincidentally will a similar occurrence into reality for oneself. When Mortimer was fighting the illness—the cancer in his stomach that became cancer everywhere—I pictured his illness with the opposite in mind. Thought fate must prove my awful imagining wrong. I believed myself useless and my visualisation of his cancer bound to turn out way off the mark. The more I feared it was spreading, the less it possibly could. With hindsight, I wish I'd just prayed, my mumbo jumbo was more implausible still.

I think Corrie did exactly that—prayed—I don't have the number.

Kat talks about Ulverston, tells me that it is changing. Not for the better is her premise, and by my recollection, it was only ever worth getting away from. I courted Corrie there once or twice. Unnecessarily furtive liaisons which foreshadowed our flight to Stockport. Secrecy because we had to ensure her father never learnt that we met up at all. He would permit me no role in his daughter's life. The stupid edict of a vindictive man. I have never been a threat, an advantage-taker, someone who would do my wife a scintilla of harm. Lately I have been wondering if I missed something, failed my son. I might have called a doctor on Christmas day, or asserted myself a week earlier with our GP. If responsibility for his awful fate is mine, then it is the whole family I have let down, and I am not the benign presence I believed. Perhaps these are normal thoughts when one is struggling to adjust; I do not know how it is done.

I feel mild relief when the pair choose to move on. Vincent has yet to speak to his sister, and I know, like me, he cares for her deeply. If he can console her today it will be a miracle.

Perhaps I should seek her out but the wall upon which I rest holds me captive. Corrie and I must return to our house on Palmerstone Crescent, get drinks out for the youngsters who are all invited back. I fear they will already be congregating upon our drive. Practicality is not in me today. I don't really mind if they have to wait although they are boys and girls who I feel only goodwill towards. There are worse fates than waiting.

My sister approaches me, unaccompanied although she has husband, son and daughter all here in Marple. Come to remember my boy. Celebrate his life, says our little flyer.

'Take care of yourself through this.'

'Thanks.'

'I remember when Mum died. I thought it would be impossible to live at Penton without her. She made Dad bearable.'

I look up into her pale face, her white skin. She has freckles still and fifty is in sight. Her memory is not mine. I recall feeling very little when Alison Tripp left this life, or perhaps that was the catch. It could be that I felt something akin to this back then—in the beginning—and then arrested those emotions. Thanked their scouts for warning me of the pain on the horizon. I cannot freeze out my longing for Morty. It is all I have left of him.

'You'll not have that worry, Simon. Cordelia and Leo are lovely ones. You can help each other through this.'

As she says it, the down-to-earth optimism of her prediction feels like an unwelcome truth. I think, like me, she knows that my youngest son has already gone. She emphasises the living, not the clinging. My pain is that I am not prepared for this. She never really knew him. Rosie tousled his hair once or twice, she never sat upon a stair, chatted with him through the chasm of the night. Not when he was one, eight or fourteen. She can let him go.

I hardly speak and Rosie does not hold this against me. She embraces me, hugs me for a long time, before leaving as Vincent and Kat have done. I do not recall my sister, Rosemary, ever hugging me before this moment. There may have been hugs in my infant years that have not stuck in memory. Probably not. In the last thirty years we have not. The funeral seems to have brought us closer together. Corrie would call this the Morty effect; I haven't the first idea what is going on.

'Circulation not the order of the day?' asks David White. It is a fairly put question, far from a demand.

'I'm not up to it, David.'

'You know where I live, Simon. Come any time, day or night—I mean that—night can be the hardest.'

'It is.'

I am thinking back to Mortimer on the stairs; it is Corrie I want to speak to, I fear we are out of step. I have not understood why she chose this church, sidestepped Catholicism at the point I expected her to need it. I like the undemanding faith that lives here, this man of the cloth's broad inclusivity. His acceptance of my scepticism. He has done so much for me while knowing that I reject the fundamental tenets of his religion. His kindly actions I appreciate, cannot connect them with the teachings of a sandalled mystic two thousand years ago. Perhaps he has disassociated them also, sees it is not kindness itself which I reject. Morty was kind: I'm all for it.

I wonder to myself if Cordelia's speech was off the cuff. I fear the grunge song was disrespectful. Not to Morty; he would have borne that wry smile, his no-one-saw-that-coming face. Perhaps the feelings of a church don't matter, even to David White. It is only stone, a hollow interior, whatever glass and baubles it tries to deceive us with.

David says he can drive us—Corrie, Leo and I—back to the house where he has helped prepare a few sandwiches, stocked the fridge with lemonade, coke, orange juice. This is for Mortimer's friends to eat and drink. I fear it is the last time they will ever cross our threshold, and I wish them long and happy lives. Truly.

'I can't leave my car here in the car park,' I say.

'Oh, you can, Simon, probably should. It will only be a ten-minute walk to collect it. Today is not really the ideal day for you to be driving, my friend. Come back in mine, please?'

His request makes a lot of sense. I have been party to no traffic accidents in my life: a conscientious driver. And yet today I have lost even the ability to be myself and await its return only passively.

I sit in the front with David. Corrie and Leo are in the back.

It's a quiet car, a two-minute drive. The Reverend White enjoyed Corrie's talk. Tells her it was beautiful, heartfelt. 'Isn't that right, Leo?' he tries.

'Yes,' says my living son.

* * *

The house is thrumming incessantly to the beat of the same rock group we heard in church: The Seattle Miseries. It teems with young people talking in hushed tones. Leo's eighteenth was the nearest we've had to this. Alcohol meandered the house that night, today it is only the knowledge that the boy shall never touch a drop, grace that age of independence. Pubs, sex and voting, Mortimer Tripp has been denied them all. Spared the trouble. I am sitting on the stairs, an unlikely hang-out for the boy's father. I have thought more and more about our conversations here. He and I, stair-bound in the middle of the night.

A girl, fair-haired, the metallic line of braces revealing itself inside her smile, tells me that Morty and she sat together in maths. She says the class sit in rows: girl, boy, girl, boy. Mr Wilson believes children are less distracted that way. I ask the girl her name: it is Safia. She looks young, far younger than Cordelia did when I began seeing her, although we too were only children. She tells me it is stupid. Girls and boys have distracted each other since Adam and Eve. I wonder if this is a thought that she has fashioned, or one she has learnt from her

Our Stairs at Night

mother. Or even the self-conscious musings of Mr Wilson. Perhaps she and Mortimer distracted each other. Too young to go together to the cinema, or too shy to do so which is, at the bottom of it, the very same condition. Too well brought up for snogging behind the school kitchens. I'm sure the behaviour in Marple Wood is many notches above that at Swale Valley Comprehensive back in the nineteen seventies. I do not think Morty has ever been party to that precocious sexual teasing. If he pictured something like it once or twice, with this animated girl, entertained stolen thoughts from his obstructed future, I am pleased for him.

'There's someone at the door,' says Safia, and it is true that the bell has rung twice, on this afternoon when half of Marple seems to have entered our house.

I raise myself up, thanking the girl for the kind recollections she shared and which I scarcely attended, and open the door.

Corrie's father stands before me. We advised him of the funeral arrangements, that it would not be in a Roman church. And the reception would be exclusively for Morty's friends. Thomasina, Vincent, they have respected our decision although they are welcome in my house any day of the week. I stare down Jeremy Dalton on the doorstep. I can outstare anyone now that I am made of stone.

'I want to pay my respects, young man. To you, to her. I'm sure he was a fine lad you lost. You don't deserve that.'

My unchanging visage replies, reinforces the disinvitation of Friday's phone call.

'Will she see me?'

'It would only upset her further,' I say. Corrie's thoughts seem to be running like a fugitive today. She told me that everything she said in church was made up on the spot. She kept looking at the paper on which we had drafted her planned speech. Not a word of it was resounding with how she felt. She wanted to ease the pain for Morty's friends; for herself she expects no relief. When she told me all this, I think I just gaped open mouthed, forgot to hug her. And I love that girl like a

Ghost in the Stables

summer storm, shouldn't be forgetting to hug her.

'Then I'd probably best go, so I'll go. You wouldn't walk with me a step would you, young man? I'll not keep you long.'

I am reluctant to leave my son's funeral wake to spend even a few minutes chatting to this ageing tyrant. He has been the cause of all my wife's angst until this most unbearable severing of a better family. I fear creating a scene, my emotions are looser than I've known they could become. How I might conduct myself in any conflict is unknown to me. I've never been a violent man but who knows what is buried deep. I nod my assent, pull the door closed behind me. I've no idea what he has to say but it must be easier to accompany one you hate than to lose one you love.

I used to feel tense, brittle, in this man's company. Today I feel nothing. It is a lukewarm day in April, the world a sour place.

Jeremy is still taller than me, two or three inches, grey haired. He holds a chequered cap in his hand. A thick coat upon his person. A church coat, to my eye, quite unnecessary on this mid-April afternoon. He and I walk up the road; I am the half pace behind.

'We never got off to the best of starts,' he says. We have reached the corner of Palmerstone Crescent, where the larger houses begin, Balfour Way.

'I'm not a young man, Mr Dalton. You've always called me that, frowned at me for a lifetime. What do you want?'

'I dare say you're right. She was too young, mind, when you started doing whatever you did with her—courting—she was too young for any boy back then.'

'You're a bit late saying this. And I don't agree a word.'

He turns his neck back and forth, looking at me and then looking away. His is an old neck, wrinkled now. Thin white hairs cling to it like moss.

'You floored me running away with her like you did. I couldn't hold my head up in church.'

'The best thing I've done in my life,' I say to him, speaking quietly, levelly. More calmly than I have ever imagined I might speak to this detestable man. 'Bar none.'

'You could have waited,' says Farmer Dalton—ex-farmer, living alone in the cottage that once belonged to the stable hand and her farm labourer husband—I can't imagine that he has any role in Killian's agricultural enterprise, he looks frail, spent. 'Perhaps I'd have come around.'

'Wait for your blessing? It was worth nothing to us. Not after what you did to her.'

'My consent, Honoria's approval too. We gave Thomasina and Killian each a tidy sum on their weddings, you know? We never said you were unsuitable; you just didn't let yourself be amongst family.'

The fuck-off phrase is not far from my lips right now. He never gave me the time of day when it mattered; rejected for my deficiency in rosary beads. I fear sullying the final day when Mortimer is in my life. If it is only ritual, it is still a piece of his story. I do not wish to fight this man today. Morty never knew Corrie's family beyond Vinny and Tommie. We shared stories, I'm sure he understood Jeremy Dalton to be a bit of a bastard.

Morty and Leo knew my father, John Tripp, met him about once a year until he passed away. He was not a normal relative for children in suburban Manchester to visit; only ever belonged to a time before their lives had begun. Corrie and I never vilified him. When I was a child, he beat me out of ignorance. Forgiven, forgotten. I expect it taught me a lesson, although it is one bearing no relation to that intended by my hapless father. Taught me to be better than him. Not simply reactive, being so makes us all veer further out of control. That was my learning and I'm not sure my slow-in-the-head dad ever quite grasped it. The old sadist walking the pavement with me today was one hundred percent calculation. That has always been Corrie's assessment, and I defer to it completely.

'I know what I did.' His tone is not confessional, not repentant. His arrogance is sickening to me. 'I dare say I would do a thing or two differently if I had my time over. You and

Cordelia brought up your boys scarcely hitting them I can imagine.' Then he sniggers quietly to himself. 'Corrie wouldn't whip a horse.' I glance straight into his face. He might see my hatred. His comment is casual; a viciousness underlies it. 'He seems a nice boy from what I gather, Leo. The dead one too, I'm told.' I don't say a word. He might think his pronouncement conciliatory, I do not. 'It was different when I was your age. I put a stick to them to make them see sense.'

'Bastard. You killed her fucking horse. I hated you for hurting Corrie. The stick. She wasn't bothered by all that. You killed Ghost—that was the name—she loved that horse and...'

'Now, now. You've lost your lad. No need to get uppity with me, young man. That was all a misunderstanding. If she'd been a bit more civil it could have all been resolved quite nicely.'

'What!' As I shout at the old man, a dog walker looks purposefully at me from across the road. 'I'm sorry I swore,' I mutter to Jeremy. 'Explain yourself.'

'When all that happened, my daughter was still a schoolgirl. Cordelia was concentrating on the piano. I wanted the world for her you know, Simon-lad. With my steadying hand she would have become a concert pianist in London. Not living in a shoebox in Stockport. She was still at school; far too young for dirty teenage boys. You might not know it, you've only sired boys, just try and look at it from my point of view: Cordelia needed to keep her mind free for schoolwork, and more so for all that piano practice. She had a brighter future than this...' He glances over his shoulder towards the house we share. '...but there we are.'

'Bloody hell,' I say. I have stopped walking and the vitriolic old elephant has stepped four or five paces further from me. Turns around and looks back. 'I've loved your daughter every day since she left Cumbria. She never got that from you. Not ever.'

'She got fathering from me, young man. I'm not trying to argue with you, if you'll listen you might learn how it's all been for me. It's only ever been my family's truest concerns that I've tried to look out for. So, when I heard about you, whisking her away from the Young Farmers' meeting I'd agreed she could go to, and not from the right church either, I had to do something. You weren't from any church, Cordelia told me that much. No restraint at all, your sort. And what you did next proved I was right. Running off—not even married—only got married when you'd embarrassed her mother and I once more. Getting our little daughter pregnant; letting the whole world know what you'd both become. Well, you've not had girls to raise so you might not see it. I'm her father, her protector. The horse was a joke; I expected she'd see it when she came around…'

'You had it killed; Corrie was devastated. That's not a laughing matter, not any way you care to look at it, Jeremy.'

'No, you've never understood the story, have you? Collins took the horse for safe-keeping. A good man, may he rest in peace. He farmed Beckfoot, if you recall. He was trustworthy. One of the few. Honoria knew it was a ploy; I couldn't hide it from her. She was a bit horse-soft, like her daughter in that respect, like our youngest. Cordelia stopped talking to me on account I told her I'd had it slaughtered. I was teaching her a lesson, not her horse. I'd nothing against the horse. I don't hurt animals. Ha! Well, I still like to eat a good roast, I'm not in the same camp as Cordelia, but I've never been one for hurting them. She's quite a headstrong girl, my youngest, even impudent, very impudent indeed back then, it was annoying. Not a word said to me week after week. I wanted to give her back the damned horse, not that I was going to crack as long as Cordelia was being uppity. That isn't in my nature, you must know that. When she showed a little courtesy, began to speak at the dinner table, I would have fetched her ruddy horse from Beckfoot. I don't know what she took me for.'

'You're making this up,' I tell him. 'I can remember that time, everything Corrie told me. It's crystal. Her friend, Mary, confirmed what you'd done. Mary in the stables, lived where you're living now. She worked for you in those days, she knew you'd killed the horse. Had it killed.' The bitter old farmer is eyeing me, waiting for me to finish. I know he's an out and out liar—a buggering bastard—I'm on a roll. 'Cat food.' I let him see that I know all the details. 'Slaughtered the horse Corrie loved, had it made into cat food.'

'I was never stupid...' Dalton stretches out his ageing neck, turns his profile to the grander houses of this leafy suburban avenue. He is drawing pride from this appalling story. '...couldn't trust the Donnellys with the truth—Mary Donnelly, or her husband neither—they liked my youngest more than they did me.' He gives a short laugh after he says this. 'Not to be trusted for one blink that pair. I span a yarn, said that the old nag had been put down. Probably like you say. Let Vincent and the rest of them think the same. I wasn't going to climb down before my littlest daughter did. You won't like thinking on it today but you must have had to face down your young lad once or twice, it's what father's do. Do you know, young man, you and she came to Low Fell one Christmas, years and years later. That horse, Ghost as you say it were called, was with Collins by this time. He paid me a few guineas for it when it was plain to see Corrie would never be living back. She'd given up piano and the country ways; I felt sorry for her, having to live in Stockport, it was her choice, not mine. Her funeral. That Christmas you came to stay, I was to borrow the nag. Collins was a good friend, all for the lending. If Cordelia had just come out to hunt like a proper Dalton, she would have seen her horse again. Seen it on that Boxing Day. A resurrection, you might say.' The stupid man giggles as he says it. What kind of religion he practices stumps me. 'I asked her the evening before, on Christmas night, "You'll hunt with us this year won't you, Cordelia?" I think you and she had been at the Christmas drinks more than you could handle. Well, Cordelia had, most certainly. I'll not say how she replied but I remember it to this day. Remember it began with the letter F, young man. And David Collins was lined up and ready to fetch her beloved horse early next morning. Had my horsebox

Our Stairs at Night

waiting on his drive. That Christmas night I phoned him and said there was no need. If she was a little more civil, a little more respectful of the man who paid for her piano lessons, she would have seen her Ghost again. Could have ridden it on the fox chase. Ridden it wherever she wanted to go, like she used to do. I don't like swearing, young Simon. I've never liked it at all. She was downright rude to me all through that Christmas visit, and no longer a child at that point. No excuses, to my thinking. I might be soft in my heart but I'm not soft in my head.'

This man staggers me. I think he might be telling the truth and it changes nothing. 'Killian's wedding: was it in the stables then? Did you have Ghost in the stables on the off chance?'

'She ruined that wedding; made an exhibition of herself. I'll give Vincent his due, he can hold his drink and his sister canna. Her laughing and cavorting, all through that day, ruined it. I've got better behaved cattle. I don't believe in curses, superstition, but Killian and Sarah are having a rough patch now. Cordelia could have given them a better start than she chose to. Carrying on at their wedding like she was the one a-marrying. And not like she was happy with the prospect, neither.'

'She was fine. Life and soul of the party.'

'She was never quite right with that couple. Not with our Killian or his girl, his Sarah.'

'Was the horse there?'

'Dead. Nothing lasts forever, Simon.'

I turn away from him. I have a tear in my eye, not for Ghost, a horse forever unseen by me. Possibly for Corrie, another story which will upset her. Probably because I've spent fifteen minutes not thinking about Morty properly. Not as I feel I am pledged to do.

'I'm not listening to any more of this crap,' I tell him. 'You're not welcome in our house. Not ever.' I don't look around. I walk to number eleven Palmerston Crescent with my back to him. I don't know where his car is. Don't care if he leaves his seatbelt unbuckled. It saddens me immensely that I have spoken with that man more recently than I have my youngest son. That this will always be the order of things. Everything has been turned upside down. Trashed.

* * *

When I re-enter the house, it is unchanged. Music blaring, four youngsters sitting on the stairs, others standing. Sausage rolls and chicken sandwiches, empty crisp packets on every side.

Leo comes towards me. 'Mum wanted you.' His face is an intelligent one, hair long but he always keeps it tidy enough. Leo has coped better than Corrie or I, and still this dreadful visitation upon Mortimer has managed to foul up his first year of university. He says he'll sit the exams; I know he doesn't sleep, hardly sleeps. This is not the snoring house we once enjoyed.

I go through into the lounge, to Corrie. 'You wanted me?'

'I think you've got more ginger beer in the garage. We're running pretty low.'

'I'll fetch it.'

Practical chores are a good thing. I have work to do this week with the car rental. I could sell it to one of the big boys. That was in the plan before all this. It is no longer the money which inspires. And if I don't run a car rental company, I am not sure what I would get out of bed for. I have always been a lover of life, of Corrie, Leo and Morty, I didn't know it was a house of cards. I can carry ginger beer, wash pots at a pinch. It is my plans for the future which have fallen apart, found their way to the shredder.

2.

I'm thinking back to one hot and sticky night, Corrie lay beside me as she does now. Couldn't sleep. It was only I who was still awake on the night I am thinking about, or so I thought. This was years ago. Tonight, Corrie is as restless as me. The exceptional warmth was the difficulty back then. The heat of summer. Leo was staying over at Max's house, arranged by telephone at nine-thirty. Four hours earlier. It felt as if my son had engineered it and I would rather he'd simply asked me if he could stay, done so before we dropped him there at lunchtime. We have always let him have what he wants. Pretty much. Still, he probably notched it up as a victory: went for tea, stayed all night. Max's family are a nice crew. We had no problem with him being there. Sleepovers are fun for kids.

Corrie looked to be sleeping serenely that night; landing light, open door, her face was tanned beautifully, a gentle breath when I put a hand afore those lips I love to kiss. On her back, stock still, and she can often be one for tossing and turning. I remember her enjoying the fine weather of that summer, spent more time outdoors than was her habit.

Earlier in the day we had been sitting together in the garden, Leo already at his friend's house. Still expected home by eight. Morty was on a garden chair, feet in the paddling pool. Our boys laughed long and loud at the inflatable toddler toy which we still blew up on summer afternoons, and they enjoyed splashing in it when the weather was as hot as that August day. Note, strictly no splashing took place on the afternoon in question. My younger son's arm was in a cast. He had fallen from his bike the Monday before, landed awkwardly. I was working at the car lot when it happened; Corrie had to spend an age in casualty. That's the way of it at hospital, queuing to be seen and then again to be plastered. She had to cancel a piano lesson, phone the student's mother before she took Mortimer down to the infirmary. Corrie was only teaching the keen ones by this time, those who take lessons in the holidays, practise seven days a week. She said Morty was in tears when she was driving him down to Stockport, to the hospital, laughing all through the journey home. Best son a bloke could have, clumsy on a bike.

I think the accident botched up Morty's plans for the month. We were yet to figure quite how to keep the following week's camping holiday on track. Did it in the end, North Yorkshire,

373

a couple of miles from Whitby. Called in at Rosie's on the way home, a couple of hours at Penton, too. The family farm had still to peter out although Dad—my dad—was struggling to milk a cow or knock in a fencing post by this time.

'At least I can still read,' said Morty from our modest poolside, a kid's comic novel in his hand. I loved his sunny stoicism. We were never so very different, Morty and I.

Corrie sunbathed. Earlier in our marriage she was self-conscious about that stuff. Wearing a swimsuit in the garden. Neighbours at back and side can see our lawn from their upstairs windows; we look across at theirs. She never had a thing to worry about. Her costume kept her decent, her figure always beautiful. More tanned than before or since. In her youth she wore jeans as a nun wears a habit. Wore them well, I was in love with her figure before I ever saw beneath the denim. I was seventeen years old, maybe love and lust were confused in my mind. It is easily done. The same person has been the only recipient of mine on both counts. Corrie was always the best wife, the best mother. However biased I might sound, I was actually—back then in nineteen ninety-three—bringing to this judgement the objectivity, shrewdness of thought, which was behind Tripps recent award for Best Small Business, Stockport East category. No mean feat, that one. Picture of the team in the local rag, a half-page interview with yours truly. And it was always Corrie I was most proud of, the award something or nothing. My wife has always been more level-headed than me, applied consistent rules to her children's upbringing with a light and loving touch. A neighbour's daughter—sixth former—used to mind the boys if we went out, saw friends, a meal. We tried salsa dancing and I was so poor she had to lead. I enjoyed feeling her hands upon me, pushing me this way and that. In the bedroom I mostly lead but our marriage is not undemocratic. Not in any way.

Corrie has an exceptional musical ability and that has enabled her to teach piano to talented children. A far cry from my meagre skill set: doing the arithmetic to let out cars with a

Our Stairs at Night

degree of profit at the end of it; a cheesy smile for customers, they seem to like that sort of thing. It isn't really a talent, just a way of spending Mondays to Fridays. I'd find dossing about obscene: that's a farm upbringing for you. All Corrie's custom came from the recommendations of other teachers, that was how it had been for three or four years by this time. When they spotted a child destined to play better than they did, they picked up the phone. Passed across the prodigies. She is as skilled didactically as she is at tapping the ivories herself. She used to entertain us frequently, me and the boys, our friends too. Tommie and John Stapley when they visited. We had long had a Bechstein by then, best upright they do. I would ask her to play Absalom, My Brother and, for laughs, she'd subvert my request, do Crazy Maisie instead. Sang it better than Johnson Ronson which is going some. She called all pop songs piffle. Still does, I think. It's a funny word. Beethoven, Debussy, that's the stuff she goes for. Plays it bloody brilliantly although I don't quite get it.

For all her many skills I have thought her a troubled soul. She couldn't have treated me better, yet I knew by then that she had accidentally married a philistine. A different life awaited her and I persuaded her to jump on a train away from all that. Ulverston to Lancaster, change for Manchester Victoria. We chose not to stay in the city centre, thought it an intimidating place. Unsuitable for a couple of bumpkins. Which is exactly what we were back in nineteen seventy-six. We neither said so at the time. Corrie was always going to rise above it. I understood that—it was obvious that she would— never guessed that I might inhibit her. Limit how far above the humdrum she would rise. And she is above it. With Jeremy Dalton's money and her talent, artistic sensibility, work ethic, she would have been at the conservatoire aged eighteen, not playing pub piano like she ended up. Corrie could have been a concert pianist and instead she found herself chasing youngsters up the ladder she'd missed out on. There is no altering how it's gone. She exchanged a moneyed and self-important family with a bedlamite at its helm, for a simpler, more loving one. Never once expressed regret. Not to me.

Just that morning, before Leo had even gone to Max's house, An American in Paris was playing on the CD player—Gershwin; I've become familiar with the music she listens to—while she was tidying away the breakfast things. From the hallway I caught sight of her, frozen in space, beakers in hand. Hovering in front of the washing up bowl for thirty seconds. She was lost in the music, in the place she once wanted to live.

And in the afternoon, I spent well over thirty seconds—thirty minutes, more like—looking at her on the sun-lounger, drinking in her still-slim figure, the little more on her hips being a welcome addition. A sign that we live well, eat and drink as we choose. I was exactly where I wished to be. I've no musical talent and farming is a mug's game.

When Mortimer began to feel sorry for himself, missing out on cycling, on the park, all the usual horseplay of the summer holidays, she called him to her. The small child, thin, moppish brown hair—a smile of contentment in response to her offer—snuggled up to his loving mother. She was ever so careful of the metallic edges of the garden lounger, put her fingers round his bare leg. I watched them from behind the book I held. I was not jealous of my son's proximity to her flesh. Momentary envy, perhaps, but she is generous with me.

Much later that day—it was close to midnight when we went up—she and I partook of the pleasures that husbands and wives must on summer's evenings across the country. I hope they do. That night she was determined in her love-making. Pushed me, rolled me, then lay back for me: the works. I think it was that delve into fleshy pleasure which gave her easy sleep. Sent away her troubles for a few silent hours. Meanwhile, the heat rendered me an insomniac. I was happy to be awake in the bosom of my family, Sunday to follow and no real need of shuteye to get through those.

I opened the bedroom door very slowly. A drink of water in the kitchen needed, my mouth was dry in the summer heat. I

Our Stairs at Night

had thrown Corrie's dressing gown around my naked person. My own being a thick winter affair. The one I wore was silky. The shoulders were far too narrow; I feared pulling the stitching out. The door clicked behind me; I'd not been careful enough. I listened from the landing—didn't think I'd woken her—hoped not. Corrie hates to bubble back into consciousness alone. We've been sleeping in each other's arms since Hillgate. Every night except for those hospital stays of hers. Just the two: dropping babies.

On the landing my heart missed a beat. A figure sat hunched up, three stairs from the top.

'Morty,' I whispered.

He turned and smiled, indicated his injured arm. 'Itching,' is all he said.

'Let's go downstairs,' I whispered.

'I like it here.'

I said that I was going to fetch a glass of water, offered to bring him one.

He said no, he was for stair-sitting, had no thirst.

When I came back, sat beside him on the stair, he was giggling, said I looked like Mummy in her cream housecoat with its flowered border.

'I do not. This is Mummy's manliest dressing gown. All the famous boxers wear silk gowns. Sugar Ray Leonard has one.' I feigned insult at his giggling.

'Sugar,' he said. 'Sugar-Sugar, the lady boxer.'

'Yes, I look like her. She's manly.'

'You look like Mummy. She beats you at boxing.'

This was playful night-time insolence; nothing to how Leo used to talk to me, and I always laughed at that. Morty was generally less inclined to rib; he laughed at all sorts without it ever getting personal.

'Is this your special stair?'

'It's all I've got,' he said.

I laughed out loud. His phrase was a punchline from a comedy show we used to watch, one Leo was always repeating, imitating. I thought the show went over Morty's head but he must have got something from it. Timed it like a pro.

'Well now you've got to share it with me. Do you catch the goblins coming up the stairs now it's after midnight?'

My son eyed me like I was the village idiot. 'There are no goblins.' he said with disdain. 'I catch the lady boxers. Stop them from whacking you and Mummy.'

'Oh, no need for that...' As I was replying, voice louder than it really needed to be, I must have failed to hear the door opening or the light footsteps behind me.

'Lady boxer coming,' said Mortimer.

His acting was good, funny. I jumped slightly when an ungloved hand ran itself through my hair. Reoriented myself quite quickly.

'Is it a boys' party,' said Corrie, 'or may I join?'

My wife kissed me on the cheek, perhaps she sensed my surprise.

'Did we wake you?'

'I thought I heard the Mortimer owl. It usually hoots all day and snores all night but August is his upside-down month.'

Morty turned himself around, started to swivel his bottom on his favourite stair. His unsheathed arm swung across his body and he grasped a hold of the banister, clung to it tightly as he leant back. His legs pointed up the stairs and his back angling down them. His overlong hair falling a stair further below.

'Whoa, careful,' I implored him.

'It's my upside-down month.'

Corrie laughed at her boy. 'Don't make it your two-broken-arms month, Dafty.'

I nipped down a couple of stairs, took a hold of him. 'I want you back on dry land,' I said. Gently, I cradled my son back to the seated posture in which he began.

Corrie wore only a summer nightie, her robe upon me. It rode up her thighs and she tugged it back down as best she could. We were never parents who paraded naked in front of our sons.

'This is the look-out station,' I told her. 'Mortimer keeps all the objectionable types at bay. Keeps you and I safe.'

'Do you not let anyone pass?' asked Corrie.

'Leo,' he answered.

'He can come up, or not?'

'Up. Why isn't he here tonight?'

'He's playing at Max's.'

'He can't play now. He's got to sleep,' said Morty.

'He's sleeping over in Max's bedroom. A sleepover party.'

'It's better when he's here, when we're all in the right place,' said Mortimer.

'Is that why you can't sleep, sweetie?'

Morty nodded, snuggled into his mummy's thin negligee. Once more I might have felt a smidgen of envy for his comfort. His blending into the flesh that I too had taken as refuge from personal singularity earlier on that hot night.

If she and I could sit on a stair with him this night, I would happily never sleep again. If we could keep vigil with beautiful Mortimer just once more, it would surely dispel the gloom which besets us.

3.

Tonight, it is not hot at all, it is the cremation of our son's cancer-riddled body which prevents us from sleeping. The finality of it. Corrie and I toss and turn. She slides from the side of the duvet.

'Tea?' she asks.

'Uh-huh.' This is a less effusive yes than I am known for. If I am still me.

I hear her pad down the stairs, heavier steps than her true self. The burden of loss is in the thump of her walk. I think gravity has attached itself more resolutely to the Tripp family. We are each weighed down by a soul we can no longer speak to. Nor even share a stair with.

As I ponder my wife, the changes these short months have ravaged upon her, it is not the whitening of hair or the loss of her ready smile I mourn. She has lived a life of triumph over adversity. It has destabilised her now and then, so frequently is she fighting fate. This time there was no contest: trains and pianos and barking an angry rebuke at the unfairness of life— even working hard—these old staples could not save Morty. It comes to me that this one could break us. Whatever Cordelia Dalton saw in Simon Tripp all those years ago, this was not it. I think Mortimer favoured me, not in his voluntary choices, but in his appearance. Not eye colour—like Leo's, that came distinctly from his brown-eyed mother—but the set of his face. His and mine are alike. I am still here despite my certain belief that a father should not outlive his son. Cordelia must see this as I do, feel affronted by my presence.

I hear the whistle of the kettle. It is not shrill, not even the intention of the manufacturers. A piece of metal has fractured away from the element, we think, become detached and lodged itself in the spout. On boiling it makes a vibration. We only call it a whistle in homage to the old-fashioned kettles, as we used to own on Charles Street, Hillgate. Still had one when we first moved into this house almost sixteen years ago. Corrie says it hums T-sharp, although even I know that such a note is not to be found upon a piano.

I look at the clock—one-thirty—I could play at car hire tomorrow, satisfy myself that my employees are not swinging the lead. I fear my lethargy has infected them. It may have felt disrespectful—even to them—to work hard on what is unimportant. The entire firm, my five employees, were in the church earlier today. Yesterday in fact, time still rinsing forward, as it does. Two brought their partners. I can't say it helped me; I might feel differently in years to come. I do expect to dwell upon it for years and years. It is the forgetting that I fear.

Only as she arrives back in the room—tray of tea, digestive biscuits—do I see the old silk dressing gown Corrie wears. She hasn't worn it in months. Years. Two Christmas's past I bought her a new one. Nicer in my view, richer colours than this plain cream with its pastel-pink flowered border. I should ask where the better one is. Corrie may have put it to wash and I am not minded to talk of such trivia. She wore this one to keep herself warm in our night-time kitchen, it will have supported that aim adequately.

'He came to the house, didn't he?' says Corrie upon sliding once more under the covers.

'I didn't let him in.'

Corrie leans over to the bedside table, picks up her tea, cupping the mug with both hands as if its warmth is a needed thing. 'Mm-mm.'

'Did I do right?'

'I think so, Simon. What did he want?'

'Paying respects, he said.' I feel conflicted. The story of the horse—Ghost—learning that it lived a full term, might hearten her. It is equally a frustrating story. I find myself despising the nasty old bastard more for his deceit than I probably did for the presumed slaughter. It was for the inconsolable upset he caused within Corrie that I made my decision to hate him. I have never been sentimental about animals. I understood Jeremy Dalton to be a red-faced, short-fused and unimaginative swine. He has the power which owning a substantial tract of south Cumbrian farmland bestows upon a man. The mist which shrouds the fells is also within his head, gives him no horizon. That he could withhold the truth about her horse from his own daughter, let her believe the poor creature dead for a period longer than she ever lived in his cherished Low Fell is beyond my comprehension. The mists lift with the wind, with the seasons, and the self-aggrandising fool sees only the cleverness in his trick, not its abject cruelty.

'You walked with him.'

'He wished me to. I didn't want a scene among the boys, the guests. I wouldn't let him see you. That seemed like the right thing.'

'He never knew Mortimer. Knew about him, I'm sure. Tommie and John, Vinny too, will have told him many nice things. Not just now but over the years. My father never made a connection with him...' I feel tears touching the backs of my eyes. Corrie talks dispassionately about this, and I've always wondered if Leo or Morty might one day seek to know the family we have denied them. My youngest never shall. '...wouldn't have understood so carefree a child even if he'd had the chance. Daddy hasn't a clue about what I'm feeling.'

I hear anger in the deepening of her voice. I fear she is taking my short time in her father's company as a betrayal. 'We argued,' I tell her. She turns upon the mattress, looks around, directly into my face. 'I don't want to talk about it. Not tonight.'

Corrie puts a hand to my cheek, leans in, kisses it lightly. Then returns her second hand to the mug of tea, holds it close. I pick mine off the dresser on my side of the bed, mirror her posture. Knees up, tea held within two hands, supping noisily, the drink still very hot.

'Was he up to his old tricks?' she asks after a lengthy silence.
'Worse.'
'Tell me.'
'Oh, Corrie. It's got nothing to do with Morty. It's all those years ago. He said...' I find myself choking on the tea. This is not the conversation I want at this time, nor do I ever hide anything from my wife. The world has become too dissonant to inhabit. Even my own bed—within which I sit with the woman I love—has become a discomfort. '...do you want to hear it? It could wait?'

'Tell me, sweetie.'

'The horse. He said that you've stayed angry with him all these years because he had Ghost killed, made into cat food. It never really happened. He was waiting...' I have turned towards her. Corrie has a look of expectancy on her face, or of doing a crossword puzzle. The answer close to her grasp. '...he said you would have seen Ghost in the stables that Christmas we visited. When Leo was a baby. Someone called Collins was looking after it. He farmed nearby. Ghost never got turned into cat food at all.'

'I know all this, Si. That he hid it.' She says it very, very calmly.

I feel completely flustered. It comes to me that it is something she learnt from one of the crazy clairvoyants. My brain overrules this improbability: I was there, to my certain knowledge I sat at every Ouija board she did. I'm sure that she has had no contact with Jeremy in years and years. None at all. I phoned Low Fell and the cottage to tell them the funeral arrangements, did it with her agreement but she was unenthusiastic. We weren't certain they would come.

'Was there anything new?'

'It was all new to me, Corrie. He's never had this conversation with you…'

'I remember now,' she interrupts. 'Mummy, at the hospital. She told me. I've known for fifteen years, Simon.'

'Well, I haven't known.'

'It's all too late, isn't it?'

'I never knew,' I say again, voice raised, a feeling of anger welling inside me. I keep nothing from my wife and she has kept this as her own private knowledge for the entire duration of my younger son's life. She learnt it at the hospital, when her mother visited, Morty born but yet to venture beyond the walls of Stepping Hill. 'You've never said it to me. Not a word, Corrie.' I've lost control of the volume knob. It's going up, up, up.

'No, sorry. It wasn't your horse…' She couldn't be more matter of fact.

'Of course not, but you're my wife, Corrie! We tell each other what we know, don't we?' I'm shouting now. It isn't how I want to behave but it is happening.

'Look, Simon…' Corrie has put her tea on the bedside table, a little colour has risen into her face. She speaks quietly, '…I didn't think about it for a long time. Mummy came to see us and then died with so much left unsaid. Telling me that, about

Ghost, it seemed like a small thing in the bigger…'

'We've hated him for it all our lives, Corrie. Now I don't quite get why. It's like you didn't want me to know.'

'I didn't want our marriage to be about Daddy, that's true, Simon. You got me away from the mad fucker, I didn't want us to live with him always half a step behind.'

'Well, that worked out!' I shout.

'Simon…' Corrie seems to have collected herself now, as I have not. '…I never actually learnt if my mother had agreed with him that she would tell me. Do you remember when she came, when Morty was born…'

I let my voice get senselessly loud. 'Of course, I remember, Corrie!' And then the catch that was in her throat penetrates my consciousness. As she said 'when Morty was born,' it is as though the hope and the joy of that occasion have rounded on us, found us arguing on the night of the poor boy's funeral. I feel ashamed. Take a hold of my wife's hand. 'Tell me?'

'No,' she replies. 'It's for another time.'

Tears are falling down her cheeks as she says this. Maybe tears I have caused, brought about because I have argued fiercely with her. We hardly ever. Tiny disagreements about stuff but I've loved her like a mantra and she has not been demanding of me. Knows I am loyal and true. Now, in this not-so-warm bed, I try to tally in my head, not really counting just remembering: Corrie has cried a bit since our son died, quietly before he died too, but really nothing like as much as she did back in the seventies, crying over the living Ghost. The horse that never died. Not before its time. I feel like she has been toying with me for a married life. 'What the hell did Honoria actually tell you?' I demand. I care less for her upset than I have ever done. I did not know that I was alone in this marriage until now.

Corrie grimaces. 'It's not really about you,' she says, finally matching my volume. Picking up the combat of the conversation; reason no longer required. Poor Morty, ashes not yet back in the house and we are shouting about a dead horse.

Our Stairs at Night

She and I. Corrie was always surprised if I got emotional about her family. It is as if she does not want me feeling anything for her, for what she's been through. 'It was virtually the last thing she said to me, Si. The last thing before she left. Before she died. I didn't think about it for a long time after…'

'Fifteen years. You could have mentioned it in fifteen years, Cordelia.' I do not know why I've used her christened name. I never do that. She bristles with the formality of it.

'We don't talk about Ghost or the bastard's stick. We talk about piano in the pub, the break that Pete gave you at the garage. Happy days on Hillgate. That's been us. Why go on about the fucking horse, Simon.'

I like hearing her shouting. Must admit, she is making more sense than me; what she says is true. I am proud of that time, when we first came down to Stockport, I was a poor farm kid, she a rich but mistreated one. We turned it around, became other people. Found out that birthright is all bullshit. I did; I still think she has regretted more than me, that might be at the bottom of this. 'Your father brought it up, filled me in. You've always known. And it was the reason you fled Low Fell. I wanted you away from him. You said you were never worried about that, the beatings. You said not. I was cut up about all that, the way he hit you, sticks and everything. That was why I persuaded you to get out of there, Corrie. They lock people up for treating dogs that way nowadays. I would have killed to stop it. Should have, probably. The horse didn't matter to me but it was the only reason you would accept for getting away…'

'I know you thought Ghost was a silly reason,' she says. With her left arm, her nearest, she is raining tiny rabbit punches on me. Not to hurt me, just to let me know she might like to.

'It's not the fucking horse…' I start to say just as she puts a hand on my mouth, arrests my speech.

'I thought I'd talk about it with Mummy again…'

We both look up, stare at Leo who is filling the doorway. He looks as tearful as Corrie; his cheeks are stained.

'Stop shouting. I hear you. Shouting to wake the dead. Please don't. Shouting about a horse…'

We both murmur sorry to our son, the feeling within my stomach still whirls.

'…you said ghost something or other, Mum. Don't do it. Please don't do it. I loved him whether you knew it or not. Please leave him be. No stupid mediums, not now, not ever. I couldn't stand it, Mum.'

'Leo…' Corrie has slipped out from the covers. She is still in her old dressing gown, wearing it over winter pyjamas. She stretches an arm across our son's shoulders. '…of course you love him. We all love him.'

'I teased and tormented him.'

'It was never torment. He loved you, Leo.'

'He did. He was better than me.'

'Don't say that,' she whispers. 'Don't ever say that.'

Leo's face looks ashen. 'I didn't treat him right. I'll always have to live with it. How much I wound him up.'

My wife embraces our son firmly, warmly. 'Morty loved you and me and Daddy. Loved us the way we are, Leo. Didn't want us to be different. You were the brother he wanted; you are the brother he wants.'

'And you're not going to mediums again?'

'Leo! I'm not crackers, you know?'

He laughs in an odd way; he's had the most upsetting day.

I don't know what's got into my head. The news about the horse is of no consequence, just mad-fucker Dalton trying to give his final confession, tell the sins of which he remains proud to a bereaved father. He's not right in the head; people like that disturb others. And Corrie is right. Ghost was nothing to me, I didn't see him, not once. To me, it's a horse that never was.

* * *

In the morning we are civil with each other. We understand that grief has thrown us down a mineshaft from which we must find the strength to clamber out. The air is heavier down here, and I am still prevaricating about whether to work for the distraction it will bring me, or mourn which I can neither enjoy doing nor neglecting. I've told Corrie I'm going in and that I'm staying home about three times each. She doesn't seem bothered which I do. I fear she hasn't the bolthole I have.

'Dad,' asks Leo, 'would you run me up to Uni tomorrow?'

There is no question that I will do it, then find myself taking too long to answer. I was thinking about Corrie and I being childless in the house. Not since eighty-one has it been so. Not for a single night in this one. On Palmerstone Crescent.

'I don't fancy the train, Dad. Everyone will stare at me if I cry.'

I put an arm across his shoulder. 'I'll take you, mate. Morning, evening, whenever suits. I should ask Mum if she wants to come along.'

'No, Dad, just a drop off. I can't face a re-enactment of the first-day drama.' Leo quickly looks into my face. 'Please?' he says, his brown eyes pleading with me. And then he's up the stairs to his room.

I go to find Corrie and tell her what's going on, our son's mixed-up state. She is in the lounge, sitting on the piano stool. The lid is down, a musical score in her hands, eyes facing it. I cannot tell if she is studying it, or simply sitting without taking in the content of that which she holds.

'He wants to go back tomorrow.'

Corrie nods, doesn't seem surprised. We'll miss him but we were delighted when he got the place only last summer. Learning, studying, will surely be the way for Leo to get back on track. 'Don't let my shitty father come between us, Si.'

I put a hand on the small of her back. We stay close for a moment. I think we are a full family and it is this hollowed out feeling that doesn't belong, that must leave me when I've found my centre again. Morty will stay in our hearts for these three lifetimes, I am sure. That my wife harboured the secret about her horse, never thought to tell me that her father played a trick—the act of sadism purely on her, not upon the beast—bothers me more than it should. It is not because I cannot trust her. The timing of it all came to me later in the night, came as sleep did not. We've never talked about the horse since Honoria's accident. Incredible. It was a too-frequent topic in our Hillgate days, and they are long, long ago. It was a truly awful time when her mother died. A new baby which we loved infinitely, a funeral we could not attend. Corrie and I sat in the lounge of this house for the hour that the service of remembrance was taking place far to the north. Our Lady of the Rosary, Coniston, with its shadows and memories. Harriet Jackson—a friend of Corrie's and the most understanding of women—minded both our children in an upstairs room here while we held our imitation service. Corrie prayed. Prayed and cried. Held my hand for a short time. I did nothing, even the hand-holding felt superfluous to me. I sympathised with Corrie's grief while feeling none of it. I would have minded the children had it not seemed insensitive to suggest it. Nothing against Honoria, I simply never knew her.

Just last year, one of the mediums sprouted something about it. Spelled out H-O-R-S-E on a Ouija board, I think. We said, 'How did she know that?' Something of that nature. Never clarified that we each knew different endings to the story: into tins of cat food or a pasture overlooking Wast Water. It was the buggering bastard who deprived her of the horse, no matter of the details or the mechanics. I hate him in both versions.

Jeremy Dalton has loomed in the background of Corrie's life, not in mine save for my constant calculation of how much he has weighed hers down. He is a haunting from her troubled past and yet the knowledge of it—the unbearable episodes he has inflicted upon her—cast a shadow upon my life too. That is a fact I try to hide from Corrie. I try not to talk that way even when she feels a need to bring up the days of her childhood. It would make me look as if I want pity for her hurt and I do not. I think there were many more moments of sadism by that repugnant man towards Corrie and Vinny—every member of the family, is my best guess—than they can readily bring to mind. I think a little less of Jeremy Dalton every time I spare him a thought. I was ostracised before we met and have subsequently found it a fortunate state.

I do wonder what Honoria said to Corrie those fifteen years ago. How she explained it, her own eight-year silence. The horse truly dead by the time she confessed. She wasn't wearing a seatbelt. A coincidence, or is God more twisted than even a cynic like me could credit?

I kiss my wife goodbye. There is something missing in the feeling I put into it but it is the right ritual to follow. I am going into the office this morning—my thinking space—only a mile and a half down the road. She will call me when Bertram's, the undertakers, have phoned. I will be back here when Mortimer returns in a small urn. We shall bury that at a later date, just the three of us in attendance. We haven't planned where or how, or rather we've changed the plan on a daily basis. We can't let him go although we all know he's gone.

4.

I have concluded the sale of my car rental business. It is the right time: the money will make us more secure than we've ever been in our lives. John Stapley is going to invest it on my behalf, understands that malarkey way better than I ever will.

Corrie thinks I'm a bit daft, that I'll be at one loose end after another. It's not true at all: I've agreed to manage the place on behalf of Super Rentals, the new owners. I see that as twelve months on a decent salary without having to bust a gut. I'm unsackable until July two thousand and one. When my stint as branch manager—the contractual obligation—comes to an end, I might do some milking for a farmer friend up in Mellor. Might and might not. She says that I'm off my rocker even imagining it. Farming was never in Corrie's veins, she's the musician.

I'm in the kitchen, hovering really, listening. The door to the lounge-diner is open. She has Stella Pope on the piano stool, a girl in the same year as Morty. He was not in her form and nor were they friends. I recall that Stella came to the house after the funeral; I think she was paying respects to her bereaved piano teacher, not grieving for our son. That's just how it was, no one knows everybody. Corrie says that Stella is the most promising student in Marple. Real potential. I hear them talking together—the piano keys untouched for an age—speaking very animatedly about how to take on a challenging piece. I can't say I understand the content, then again, Corrie doesn't change oil. She is telling Stella that feeling in music is not simply whatever you are feeling. One must know the piece inside out, see what it expresses intrinsically, use that to inform the manner in which it is played. She is a genius but I still liked her playing Absalom, My Brother best of all. I understood the feeling she put into that. The classical pieces are too abstract, too obscure for me. Good in small doses but after a time I just start thinking about football.

Through the doorway I see that she has a flat palm on the small of Stella's back. It is a supportive gesture, not intimidating. She brings out their skill. Corrie has never berated a student in her life. She says that's for the grade teachers. She sets no goals. 'Artistry will out,' is her catchphrase. Said it so many times it has set in my mind; Corrie can explain it better than me. In fact, I can't.

She has sat both our sons on that piano stool for a time. Only when they wished, never pushed. Leo took it quite seriously. Methodically learnt a few pieces. He was frustrated that it did not come easily to him. He said that although music is mathematical, it is not logical. He doesn't just want to hear patterns; he expects one piece to be better than others based on definable criteria. Feeling isn't proof.

Morty had a different approach. He would give it a go for twenty minutes, half an hour, neither prodigy nor entirely useless. Then when the mini-lesson was over and he and Corrie had left the room, the little imp would sneak back in, bash out chopsticks as loud as possible, foot down hard on the sustaining pedal. He knew that his mother would rush back in, shout at

Our Stairs at Night

him not to play such rubbish. Hug him too, it was a big joke. She has never confused her love of music and her love of family.

This young girl, Stella, will go far, she has already played recitals. Not just at Marple Wood, done so in several other Greater Manchester schools—won competitions—Corrie attends if she can.

Only Morty ever got a hug for playing chopsticks.

* * *

In the evening the telephone rings. I dash to it, think it might be Leo. Four or five weeks ago, third day back at university, he called in a state. Missing us as we were missing him. I think it was just a wobble, he's a sensible lad. Scientists always figure stuff out in the end—he was temporarily lost in the data, needed time—we all do.

'Cordelia please, young man,' says the too-familiar voice.

'Wait,' I say abruptly. I put my hand over the mouthpiece, wrap it around like I am throttling the damned thing. 'Corrie,' I call. It is with a shouted whisper that I have beckoned her. She emerges from the lounge with a questioning look upon her face. 'Your father,' I whisper to her. 'Do you want to talk to him?'

She shakes her head, steps closer, leans into me, 'You see what he wants, Si.'

'She can't come to the phone right now,' I tell the old sod.

'I'll take that for won't,' he says. 'Will you hear what I've to say, Simon-lad?'

'Try me.'

'I've a proposition for you. For you and my Cordelia. Something to do together.'

Corrie has her ear to the outside of the telephone earpiece, listening into the conversation she does not wish to actively join.

'We call our own tune,' I say. 'You know that.'

'Aye, but I'm maybe for changing my will. What do you think about that, young man?'

'I think it's for you to do as you please. Nothing to do with

Corrie and I.'

My wife nudges me, gives me a thumbs up. She likes how I am handling him. Keeping the odious crab at a distance.

'You don't know as I'm back farming, I expect?'

I did not know this. He's too old by a distance, gave it all to Killian five years back. We understood that the son was doing the bulk of the work long before then. 'News to me,' I confirm.

'And you could be back farming. I can let you have the place if you're minded to live back.'

'What?'

'I am going to will Low Fell to Cordelia and yourself, provided you farm it, not sell it out of the family. I don't know if your son might have what it takes down the line. That's not my concern. It will be for you to decide who has it next. Family, I hope, but if I will it to you, then it's final. I'll be long under the sod before you retire. You've more than thirty year on me…'

'Mr Dalton. I don't understand…'

'You want the sorry details, I expect?'

'Killian is farming Low Fell. He will inherit…'

'Killian is doing nothing at all on this farm. Certainly not, not any longer,' says Jeremy in a quiet monotone packing the venom I recall from the doorstep of his austere farmhouse all those years ago. And the dismissal of Killian is an unthinkable development in my mind. I've always thought of him as a mini-Jeremy, thank the God I don't believe in that he's sired no children. Holding the phone slightly to the side, I turn so that I can see Corrie's face. She is shaking her head in disbelief. We neither have the first idea what has prompted this man's abandonment of his eldest son. Called time on Killian's favoured status. 'Sarah left the farm two months back,' he continues. 'You didn't know that?'

'No. It's the first…we don't really speak…'

'Around the time you lost your boy. I was upset but I expect you got the worst of it.'

'I'm sorry?' I say not in apology, seeking clarification. 'Has

Our Stairs at Night

Sarah left Killian?'

'I should think so. That's the size of it. The devious ruddy no-good made out it was something and nothing, that she might be back. Said as much when we were driving down to Stockport, young Mortimer's funeral, God rest his soul. Then I learnt he had a man living in the house, a young man if you'll follow what I'm saying. I won't spell it out but there was a bit of this when he was much younger. He long ago led me to believe he'd grown out of it, but no, back to ways that we don't countenance in the church. That don't belong on my farm. And there is far too much of it now, they're always making out it's normal. Pop singers are at it, lots of them. Well, I'm sure you're as sick of it as I am. I can tell you, Simon, there is no chance in this world that Killian will ever live in Low Fell with a man sleeping where his wife ought. You wouldn't let him if you were in my shoes, would you, young man? God knows where the two of them are now. I've no interest to find out quite frankly. And if you're in the know, don't tell me…'

I start to tell him that I don't know where Killian is, before I've said much at all, Corrie snatches the phone from me.

'You old hater!' she yells down the mouthpiece. Then in her softer voice she says, 'Poor Sarah—I'll call her—who knows what she's going through. Some father you ever were. You knew how he was all your grown life and cared only what the fucking priests thought. And half of them are the same as Killie, you know. Let him farm with his boyfriend. Why don't you, you mealy-mouthed sod? We don't want Low Fell, now or ever. We're a million times better off out of it.'

She slams the receiver down. Hard. I think she might have broken it, not that I give a fig about that. I hug her immediately, my wife who always sees to the heart of the matter.

'Well done,' I say, but the words are not enough and I wrap her in the closest hug. Hold my cheek against hers as we've been doing since we were younger than Leo is now. Corrie could never be happy up in that place. She was more than done with it at sixteen. I'll milk cows for Farmer Styles in Mellor.

Cumbria is not our county—never again—Stockport's nothing special but we love it. 'Why doesn't he give it to Vincent? He still farms all day every day.'

'Still drinks too. I think Daddy is not through with tormenting poor Vinny. I'm sure that was part of the plan. Shame Vincent by moving us back in to Low Fell. Two sons and still a daughter gets it.'

I want to laugh at that. Back at the Young Farmers meetings in Broughton-in-Furness, I'd been the one who put looks over inheritance in choosing which girl to chase. Not just looks, she's a hell of a character. Fourth child: I was strictly not after the farm; it was the girl who got inside me. Heart, mind, blood. Now that she's passed up the chance of it—inheriting a big splotch of Cumbria—I think I love her more. She's a girl who knows what she doesn't want.

'Where's Killian, do you think?'

Corrie shrugs. 'I could see if Tommie knows,' she says eyeing the cracked telephone handset.

'And do we care?'

She puts an arm around my waist. 'Quite right, Simon. Any one of them can have the farm. If Vinny gets it, he can still come here. I won't be going there again. Not so long as that hateful old bigot lives in the tied cottage.'

She walks, guides me with her arm, over to the mantlepiece. A simple grey urn, fired clay, the white stencil of a few flowers upon it, which we expected to have buried by now, has a prominent place in the centre. She puts her left hand upon it.

'Here we stay,' she says, as I put my head against hers.

Grief has not separated us, however alone we feel at our lowest. I think we will always live with Morty, even as we learn to live without him. Horses, farms, these we can easily discard. Whatever emotions they once stirred, they are no longer a part of our lives. I hope we never leave this house, the house in which Morty lived out his too-short time. Corrie, Leo and I with him, sharing each day of his precious life. That must be why her words, here we stay, have nestled so snugly in my

Our Stairs at Night

mind. I love the rich feelings which her remarkable piano playing can stir within but seldom can I hold on to them. A simple farm boy, of course. Here we stay: it's a lyric I can relate to, makes everything fit into place. Corrie and I are staying put. I'd like Leo here, to explain to him what it is she has said, done. The beauty of forfeiting that stupid farm. It is complicated and may burden him, the sense that this little house is the only place where we can remain true to ourselves. And yet I must let him know. Leo will go far and it will not be anywhere directed by the grandfather he has never known. And if my role was small, still I feel a certain pride. The devious old git always did his level best to ruin Corrie's life. Knocked on our door and I never let him in.

Printed in Dunstable, United Kingdom